Last Dance in London

ALSO BY **SYDNEY JANE BAILY**

The RAKES ON THE RUN Series
Last Dance in London
Pursued in Paris
Banished to Brighton
Gretna Green by Sunset

The DIAMONDS OF THE FIRST WATER Series
Clarity
Purity
Adam
Radiance
Brilliance

The RARE CONFECTIONERY Series
The Duchess of Chocolate
The Toffee Heiress
My Lady Marzipan

The DEFIANT HEARTS Series
An Improper Situation
An Irresistible Temptation
An Inescapable Attraction
An Inconceivable Deception
An Intriguing Proposition
An Impassioned Redemption

The BEASTLY LORDS Series
Lord Despair
Lord Anguish
Lord Vile
Lord Darkness
Lord Misery
Lord Wrath
Lord Corsair
Eleanor

Last Dance in London

RAKES ON THE RUN

SYDNEY JANE BAILY

cat whisker press
Massachusetts

DEDICATION

To my sweet and spirited Perry

Your life was a tremendous story of adventure
and adversity, laughter and loyalty.
And above all, love!
I love you beyond words and feel blessed
to have been loved by you.

ACKNOWLEDGMENTS

Thanks to Philip Ré, an excellent sounding board and idea-sparker, and to Toni Young, who will read anything I give her and make it better. And, as always, thanks to my mom, Beryl Baily, for loving me and for loads of other stuff, too.

PROLOGUE

1814, London

J asper Ashton, the Earl of Marshfield, surveyed the crowded upstairs room at White's. He didn't gamble at cards, although he was game to wager upon a good racehorse. So why, when pressed by the man seated opposite him, did he agree to a silly wager about his marital status?

"I tell you I shall not marry," he said, a little loudly because it was late and he'd had his share of brandy, and perhaps someone else's share, too. "Despite how I've been pursued recently." Over the past months, the papers had practically posted the banns for him over one or two young ladies who spoke out of turn about his devotion.

He was only devoted to how much he could get away with, which due to his looks and title was usually quite a lot.

"For how long?" a fellow club member cried out, and the rest of the men started to slap the tables, knowing a wager was instantly brewing.

"What are the stakes?" someone else called out.

Jasper sighed, but he was assured of winning. "All right, gentlemen. I vow I shall not marry, even if I'm presented with the Queen of Sheba, herself."

"Or Cleopatra," a voice interrupted.

"Or Prinny's mistress," said another.

Jasper ignored them. "Eventually, of course, I must carry on my family name. But not this year." *How long could he continue to enjoy his bachelorhood and his status as London's premiere rake?* Or so he prided himself he was.

"I shall be a bachelor until we see the last day of our Lord 1815, or I shall forfeit a goodly sum."

"How much?" came instantly from more than one, amidst laughter.

"One hundred pounds," he said.

"So, you doubt yourself, eh, Marshfield?" More laughter erupted.

"Five hundred pounds, then." He nearly made it a thousand, but there was no need to tempt the devil.

CHAPTER ONE

"Lord M__ threw a dinner party in which he seemed to
ignore his latest lady-love, Miss T__, in favor of an
unknown country miss. Nothing surprising from this
rakish earl."

—The Morning Post

"What are you doing in here?"

Julia startled at the smooth male voice behind
her, but she didn't turn, not at first. Instead, she took a
steadying breath and calmed her racing heart. She had
counted on being the only dinner guest who'd ventured
away from the party, the only guest upstairs in the Earl of
Marshfield's private rooms on the third floor of the four-
story house on Grosvenor Square.

What a nuisance!

"The question is," she began, hoping to put the
inquisitor on the defensive, "what are *you* doing here?"

Turning slowly and with dignity, as if she were not at all
out of place, Julia encountered the well-heeled, impressive
figure of the evening's host, Lord Marshfield himself.

Blast it all!

At her question, his dark eyebrows rose above his coffee-colored eyes, practically to his hairline of thick, brown hair. Then he grinned, and she recalled his reputation. Certainly, his smile caused a flutter inside her, and she could imagine many a female had been won over by the same.

"I beg your pardon," he said, with no outrage to his words but only amusement. Appearing entirely at ease with her presence in his bedchamber, he leaned against the door casing, arms folded, and appraised her from head to toe.

And back again!

"If you would truly like to know what I usually do in this particular room," the earl said, "we can partake in a demonstration. By necessity, with a drawing room full of guests, it would have to be done in haste. A quick *mixing of the giblets* before anyone realizes we've stolen away."

Julia ought to be shocked, or perhaps even frightened, but the reputation of Lord Marshfield was well-known even to her, who had been in London for barely a year. He liked female flesh and had a great many public associations—and probably many more private ones with ladies of the *bon ton*.

However, he had never been reputed to have forced a woman. He simply lavished a certain brand of charm that made them willingly lift their skirts for him.

Thus, with her singular purpose having nothing to do with romance, she didn't feel the least qualms about being alone in a room with him. Even *this* room of rich brocades and silken bed covers, with a thick, colorful carpet she knew must be from Turkey or Persia, which would feel unimaginably soft under her bare toes.

He clearly had good taste in burnished mahogany furniture, including a tall armoire in which she'd already had more than a passing glance. She'd quickly discovered it was where he kept his valuables.

"My lord," she said, remaining unruffled, a good trait to have when up to mischief. "My apologies. I thought you were an intruder, a rum dubber."

"Me, a thief?" He lowered his arms.

"Obviously, I was mistaken, sir. Now that I know it is you, I shall return downstairs. The *hors-d'oeuvres* were excellent, by the way."

Thinking to escape, Julia headed straight for him. He would have to step aside and let her pass or rudely cause a collision.

In a moment, she bumped against his tall, unyielding form and felt his hands grasp her upper arms while she looked steadily at his black silk cravat. Then she raised her eyes higher.

Zeus's thighs but he was a handsome devil!

"Why are you in my room?" he asked her once again.

Julia sighed. "You've caught me, sir. I sought a token, such as a handkerchief with your monogram upon it to prove to my friends I was really at this esteemed dinner party."

He frowned. "A husband hunter, trying to trap me?"

A frisson of disgust shivered down her spine. She nearly protested her innocence in that regard. It was, after all, a deplorable practice, designed to gain a fortune or a title while leaving the couple in heinous, hateful wedlock until death did them part.

On the other hand, if she allowed him to believe such, he would usher her from the room swiftly and surely, wanting nothing more to do with her.

"Perhaps," she said softly. "You are, after all, a coveted morsel of a man."

"Morsel of a . . . ?" he trailed off. Then, to her surprise, he laughed.

"You are a bold chick-a-biddy, but not the first cunning baggage to try that particular sport."

"Sport, sir?" She was well-aware he still had a firm grip upon her. In fact, his brown eyes were blazing a trail down her throat to the fashionably low décolletage of her borrowed gown. His gaze lingered on the upper swell of her breasts, before flicking back to her face.

"Husband hunting," he said succinctly, "and with no weapon needed except your beauty."

Her beauty? She felt a surge of warmth toward him for paying her the compliment, and found herself not the least put out by his low opinion of her as a fortune hunter.

She shrugged, which caused him to release her. Strangely, the smallest pinprick of disappointment lanced her when he did.

"You ought to take care, Miss . . . ?"

Should she tell him her name? She might as well. After all, she'd come as the guest of another man, so the earl could easily discover her identity.

"Miss Sudbury," she disclosed. "Lately of London, formerly of Chislehurst."

"A pleasure to make your acquaintance," he said, his gaze now firmly locked on hers, notwithstanding how her feminine curves still tingled where he'd scrutinized them.

"And yet?" she prompted, looking at his mouth. She thought it an attractive one. Lips neither too large, nor too thin. And the way he said the word *pleasure* actually made her toes curl.

"And yet what, Miss Sudbury?"

Now his gaze was upon her lips, causing her insides to flutter. He smelled good, looked better, and seemed interested in her. These London nobs could make a girl's head spin.

"You said I ought to take care. Thus, despite any pleasure you may proclaim at meeting me, I fear you are about to issue a caveat or dire warning of some kind. Is that not correct, sir?"

"Yes, I suppose it is. You ought to take care which man's bedroom you sneak into and certainly at which man you set your cap."

He stepped closer, lowered his mouth to hers, and claimed a kiss.

She gasped at the unexpected contact and the resulting flush of heat that instantly coursed through her. By opening her mouth, she'd given him access to deepen the kiss, and for a shocking moment, his tongue swept between her lips.

Julia couldn't deny she enjoyed the brazen, clandestine nature of what they were doing. A tremor of desire wracked her body, even though no other part of him touched her.

When he abandoned her mouth, she opened her eyes and stared into his, feeling out of kilter. The searing kiss had been remarkable for its intensity.

"Yes, as I said, a pleasure," he quipped, "but also as I warned, you never know when you'll meet a rake."

There wasn't much she could say to that, so she didn't. He stepped aside, and Julia made her way downstairs on slightly wobbly legs. Her escort for the evening, a viscount's stodgy son, Mr. Furley, was sipping wine in the drawing room oblivious to her disappearance. Next to him was *his* choice of chaperone, his dear mummy, Lady Pomony. Obviously, the viscountess was there solely for the benefit of protecting her precious heir, should Julia be the fortune hunter the Earl of Marshfield had supposed her to be.

Regardless, her unappealing escort mattered not a whit. Mr. Furley, with an invitation in hand, had been purely a means to an end—the end being easy entrance to the earl's house and bedroom. She might have been rudely interrupted, but she hadn't come away empty-handed.

Giving her wrist a little shake, Julia's delicate silk beaded bag of the palest dove gray swung to and fro. Inside was the earl's stunning gold and sapphire cravat pin.

Accepting a glass of wine offered by a passing servant, Julia took her place beside Mr. Furley and his mother, ready to partake of an evening filled with good food and a musical concert before she would be dropped home with her new dazzler.

JASPER GEORGE ASHTON, THE Earl of Marshfield, couldn't keep his eyes off the young blonde woman with the bewitching blue eyes. He'd been ready to give her the handkerchief she sought, as well as a quick tupping if she'd been willing. However, Miss Sudbury had vacated his room so swiftly he'd almost imagined she'd never been there. Except he could still make out the delicate floral fragrance he'd inhaled when kissing her, which lingered like a whisper in his chamber.

When he'd descended to his drawing room a few minutes later, he'd discovered with a modicum of surprise she was partnered with the impossibly bland Furley, a good chap if a bit of a mutton-head. Indeed, the viscount's son was only on the earl's guest list because their mothers were friends and his own had requested the kindness.

Miss Sudbury seemed far too spirited for the man. Moreover, Jasper had only to look at the man's overbearing mother to know there would be no feather bed jig for Furley and the intriguing young woman, nor even a hurried flyer against the wall.

That thought pleased him, and he wasn't sure why. It wasn't as if he, himself, was going to pursue her. *Was he?*

Perhaps he would. To better make up his mind, Jasper went as the crow flies directly across the room to where she stood. Her aplomb as she looked up at him gave him pause.

Was she an interesting tidbit or was she something more dangerous?

"Good evening, Lady Pomony," Jasper greeted the viscountess first. "Furley," he added, nodding to the man who was only a couple years younger than he was, but seemed like a university boy. Then he turned his attention to the female who'd called him a *morsel.* "And who is this delightful creature?"

Furley coughed, maybe at Jasper's flowery language. "You met her when we arrived, my lord."

Jasper tilted his head and looked at her. He'd met her even better in his bedroom, but he didn't want Furley to think he recalled the chit at all.

"This is Miss Sudbury, sir," Furley continued. "Her sister is the widow, Lady Worthington."

This news made him look at the female again with fresh eyes. That explained why he'd never seen her before. The old Earl of Worthington had gone to a country parish and grabbed himself a young wife about two years prior. Then he'd unluckily up and died a couple weeks after the nuptials. The new wife had been left to fend for herself in London society, undoubtedly spending most of the time in mourning.

That also clarified this particular young woman's intrepid nature. Her sister had done well for herself. *Why not her?*

Taking her hand, he bowed over it. There was that delicate perfume. As if he were a randy youth, it made his loins tighten.

"My apologies for not recalling our meeting in my receiving line," he intoned.

She fixed him with a sardonic gaze. "That's quite all right, Lord Marshfield. With so many guests, how could you possibly remember any one person new to you? One would almost have to do something outrageous to stand out."

She gave a pretty smile. He returned it with a grin.

"What a thing to say!" Lady Pomony exclaimed, looking nervously from Jasper to her son, as if Furley might be tainted by something Miss Sudbury said or did.

The man should be so lucky, Jasper thought, *as to be intimately connected with this minx.*

During the dinner, Jasper changed his mind half a dozen times as to pursuing his interest in Miss Sudbury, watching her sip his wine, eat his food, chat with the insipid Furley on one side of her and another young buck on the other. All the other ladies, including his own current flame, Miss Louisa Tufton, seemed to pale in comparison.

Besides, Louisa was more of a flicker than a flame—a baron's daughter whom he was stringing along while deciding whether it was worth the headache to bed her before cleanly extricating himself from any long-lasting association.

Louisa was seated on his right, not at the other end of the table, as he wouldn't bestow such an honor on any miss in case it gave her a swelled head and too much certainty in her future. Yet he'd hardly looked at Louisa after beginning his study of Miss Sudbury, noticing everything about her from her sparkling eyes and her sweet mouth to her luscious curves. He even saw she wore a sparkling ruby on her right hand.

He sighed.

"Is everything all right, my lord?" Louisa asked, always hanging on his every word.

He nodded and sent her a reassuring smile. At the same time, he made two decisions. One, it was time to set her free. She needed an honorable young man who wouldn't ruin her for no reason other than a pleasant hour's diversion—someone like Furley, perhaps.

And two, he would very much like to spend such a wicked hour ruining Miss Sudbury instead. She stirred him as no female had done that year, and it was already July!

To that end, after dinner, Jasper did his duty escorting Louisa Tufton to a chair in his salon, large enough for small dances but which was now set up for an intimate concert. She looked up expectantly, ready for him to sit beside her. But he merely bowed and walked away. He was a rascal, and he knew it.

Furley and Miss Sudbury entered the room, and they seemed to be chatting like old friends. That soured Jasper's stomach slightly.

How could he get her away from the viscount's son without giving offense? The answer was he couldn't, so he would be forced to offend. After all, they were in his home, his title outranked Furley's father, and Jasper was already considered a rogue of the first order. So be it.

"I say, Furley, did you enjoy eating from my lavish spread?"

The young man's eyes darted a little nervously toward Miss Sudbury. He didn't want to be embarrassed in front of her, and Jasper's words sounded almost like a challenge.

"To be sure, wot-wot," Furley said. "Exceptional course after course."

"Good," Jasper said. "How about you let me have the rest of the evening in the company of the charming Miss Sudbury?"

Furley froze. His mother standing close behind the couple audibly gasped. However, the tidbit in question simply gazed at Jasper with open interest.

"Why, my lord," Furley began, "I'm not sure that's—"

"Merely to show your gratitude," Jasper pressed, "for your presence in my home. And you may go sit with Miss Tufton up front? Won't that be a treat?"

"That is not done nicely, sir," the Viscountess Pomony said, pushing between the couple, stepping to the forefront to defend her son.

"Isn't it?" Jasper had a smile on his face which he couldn't wipe away because the woman with her pursed lips and flaring nostrils was as comical as Punchinello. "But it's an honor, isn't it, to move to the front? Otherwise, you'll be seated back here, hardly able to see past the other guests, barely able to hear the musicians."

Lady Pomony and her son glanced at one another, trying to discern if this was an honor or not. While they worked it out, Jasper eyed Miss Sudbury to see if she were bothered by the interruption to her evening or having her escort booted away. By the saucy way she raised an eyebrow, he guessed she was not in the least troubled.

"Hurry up, Furley, the concert is about to start," Jasper urged. "Let me introduce you to a splendid girl. A baron's daughter. Her father's wealthier than Midas, I hear."

Without waiting to see if they followed, knowing they would, Jasper turned on his heel and strode back up the makeshift aisle between the chairs.

"Miss Tufton, may I introduce to you Mr. Furley and his illustrious mother, the Viscountess Pomony."

Louisa Tufton raised her puzzled gaze.

"As a special favor to me," Jasper added, "I would appreciate if you would make them feel welcome here beside you."

There! Jasper congratulated himself on how he'd honored her, too, by allowing her to act as his hostess. And she believed it, if her gracious nod and proud tilt of her chin were any indication.

He waited only long enough to see them move into the row before pushing his way back through his guests to find Miss Sudbury. He had a plan. The farther they sat from the musicians, the less anyone would notice them. In fact, he had a particular window seat in mind for the next forty minutes.

However, when Jasper got to where he'd left her, the woman had vanished.

"Devil take her!" he exclaimed, glancing around. Nearly everyone had taken a seat now, and plainly, she was nowhere to be seen. His quarry had escaped.

Why on earth would she do that when she was about to have the pleasure of his undivided attention?

With a shake of his head, Jasper took the nearest chair. He had the gilflirt's name, and if she was staying with her widowed sister, then he knew her residence, too. Old Worthington had lived at Hanover Square practically since it was built.

Miss Sudbury wouldn't escape him for long.

CHAPTER TWO

"A certain heretofore unknown Miss S__ has caught the wickedly wandering eye of Lord M__, much to her peril, we fear."

—The Gazette

Julia awakened to a knocking at her bedroom door, but before she could speak, her sister, Sarah, swept in looking every bit the countess she'd become two years earlier when she'd married the old earl. Conveniently, he'd passed away within a fortnight of their wedding.

It wasn't as if her sister had planned such a happy occurrence. In fact, the marriage had been entirely arranged by their father, the Vicar of Chislehurst and the Earl of Worthington, who'd taken a liking to the eldest Sudbury daughter. *And why wouldn't he?*

Sarah was pretty and sweet. Moreover, she'd given in to their father since the elderly earl was promising not only would she be taken care of, but so would the entire parish of Chislehurst.

Julia remembered crying with her sister the night before the dreaded wedding, but Sarah had been dutiful and determined.

Then she'd been blissfully widowed and had even brought Julia to London to stay with her during her mourning and beyond. It hadn't taken long for Julia to see for herself the excess and frivolous nature of most members of the *beau monde*. Especially when compared to the stark poverty outside the small privileged area of Mayfair.

While inspired by the good works of her own father through his vicarage, Julia realized there was little difference she could make to the lives of the poor who lived in such dreadful areas as the Mint, Devil's Acre, or the Rookery.

And then, one evening, inspiration struck—or rather, fell to the floor. Naturally, because of Sarah's new title, Julia had entry into the best houses, rubbing elbows with the wealthiest people, dripping with jewels. When a lady's earring fell off during a ball in Bloomsbury, right at Julia's feet, they made eye contact. The jaded female didn't deign to stoop to pick it up, merely shrugging before continuing to dance. Undoubtedly, a wealthy parent or paramour would provide her with another.

Julia hadn't minded stooping, and did so quickly before the earring disappeared midst the many slippered and booted feet. Examining her prize, she walked slowly back to the edge of the room. Sarah, wearing black crape near the end of her year of mourning, had agreed to chaperone.

Julia realized she held in her hand a diamond and an emerald in a silver setting. *Amazing!*

"What have you there?" Sarah had asked.

"An earring." Julia held out her palm to show her.

"Oh dear. I wonder if we can find the owner."

"I know who the owner is, and she doesn't want it."

"Whatever do you mean?" Her sister had frowned.

After all, who in their right mind could imagine such foolishness?

"I mean exactly that—the spoiled lady turned her nose up at claiming her eardrop because it was on the floor. Can you imagine such an indulgent creature?"

"I cannot," her sister confessed.

And then an idea had come into Julia's head. There was probably an abundance of baubles and dazzlers the wealthy neither cared about, nor needed. And if Julia could only skim a few of those and find someone to buy them from her, then she could help the poor after all. While she couldn't provide jobs or housing, she might be able to give them the means to eat for a week and pay rent for a month.

Taking a page from John Major's *History of Greater Britain*, she'd decided to become a female Robin Hood. Locating a shop in Manchester Square with the traditional sign of three gold balls, signifying the business of the pawnbroker, she'd entered to find an air of desperation. It was a place where some went as a last effort when all other means to secure loans or coin had failed.

Stepping forward between the useful privacy screens dividing customers at the counter, she sold the single earring easily for a modest sum. She would have received more for a pair, but still, the broker would take the stones out of the setting and sell them separately, and sell the silver to a smith to be reworked.

It was so easy, Julia wondered why many seemed to end up in Newgate jail. That small beginning had been two months earlier, and so far, she'd done well at this lark.

"Still abed?" her sister asked her, looking good-humored that morning, as she picked up a ribbon-tied posy from the chest of drawers.

Sarah was developing a *tendre* for a certain viscount, and Julia was happy for her. She would be even happier if her sister wasn't always insisting that she, herself, find a dashing man of her own. The single men at the balls and parties were all eager enough to meet the sister of a countess, and just as eager to run the other way when they learned she was but a vicar's daughter with no dowry to speak of.

Nevertheless, Julia was out in society. And society had a lot of jewelry!

"It was an exciting evening with Mr. Furley and his mother," she said, sitting up and stretching. The curtains were open, and a watery sunlight was playing across her rose-colored counterpane.

"*Hm.* Exciting was it?" Sarah asked. "Yet Mr. Dawson said you came home in a hackney."

Why did the blasted butler have to say anything at all? Julia wondered.

"Yes, so what of it?"

Sarah rolled her eyes. "You know very well the rules. You cannot abandon your escort and chaperone and run around as you please. This is *not* Chislehurst."

"I know. But that viscountess! She kept looking at me as if I had designs on her precious son. He should be so fortunate!"

Sarah laughed. "True. He would be a fortunate man if you bestowed your affection upon him. I take it that was not the case. A wasted evening, was it?"

Julia thought of her encounter in Marshfield's bedroom and smiled.

"What is that devilish look for?" her sister asked. "What happened?"

Swinging her feet over the side of her bed, she yawned.

"Nothing really. But the Earl of Marshfield is quite a rum duke. You didn't warn me."

Sarah's mouth dropped open slightly.

"Do not even think about that man. At least not in such a favorable manner."

At this, Julia snatched for her dressing gown and stood before draping it around her.

"Yes, tea *would* be lovely, thank you," she said, tartly. "Is the dining room set for breakfast, or did I miss it?"

"He is *not* a handsome fellow," Sarah persisted.

Julia lifted an eyebrow at her sister's blatantly false statement.

"Yes, all right, he is," Sarah continued, dropping the little bouquet onto the pile of posies Julia had on her dresser, "but he's also reputed to be a rake, a libertine, a buck of the first head. Far more of a licentious earl than a rum duke, as you put it."

"Fascinating," Julia said, sliding her feet into some comfortable slippers.

"No, he's not. You were supposed to be safe with that overbearing viscountess and her milksop son, or I would never have let you go anywhere near Marshfield's party."

"I *was* safe. I even left early, so no harm was done."

"I think we must find you a dedicated chaperone for the rest of the Season," Sarah decided.

"What about you? Don't you want to come with me?"

"I'll go out sometimes," Sarah said vaguely, "but I don't want to get in your way."

"You mean now that you've met that viscount, you don't want to waste your time."

Sarah blushed. "I was partnered with him at a single dinner. Don't exaggerate. Anyway, I've had one marriage already and am in no hurry for another. Let's get a fiancé for you, instead. But *not* Marshfield," she added with a shudder. "And you didn't do anything else last night, nothing disagreeable, did you?"

Julia's thoughts flew to kissing Marshfield, despite knowing her sister was not referring to any such behavior. She had made the mistake of telling Sarah how easy it would be to relieve an aristocrat of a piece of jewelry, and how much good use could be made of it.

Sarah hadn't seen the rightness of it. Indeed, she'd been aghast. Thus, she had no idea Julia had become adept at stealing, pawning, and giving large charitable donations.

"Don't get in the suds, dear sister," Sarah said. "Nothing that will end up in a trial with your getting put in the pillory, if you please." She laughed at her own words, never suspecting Julia had the Earl of Marshfield's cravat pin that very moment in the bottom drawer of her chiffonier.

"No, dear sister. I won't."

"And stop buying so many posies," Sarah added, but with no vehemence to her words. They both knew it was one of Julia's ways of supporting the poor, by buying from the youngest flower girls who stood on London's street corners. "No, don't stop," she amended, crossing the room to give Julia a kiss on the cheek. "I'll see you at breakfast."

"THE DEUCE!" JASPER SWORE. "It can't have simply vanished, Blumsey. It is vexing, to be sure."

His valet blinked. "Yes, my lord. Vexing."

"You know I have a particular fondness for that pin." His father had given it to him. And now, when he thought of it, the stunning sapphire reminded him of Miss Julia Sudbury's equally stunning eyes. If only he could find the damnable thing.

"I know, sir." Blumsey was so particular, too, always putting everything in its place. And entirely trustworthy, to boot.

Moreover, Jasper had brought on no new staff for over a year, no one he might doubt as being light-fingered. There'd been an incident with a frisky maid two months earlier, trying to tempt him in some scheme she'd cooked up. He'd been too smart to fall into that muddy puddle of trouble. And no one else had been in his bedroom since last autumn when he'd allowed a willing widow to come home with him, usually preferring to do the deed at the lady's home so he could leave when ready.

Tonight, he wanted that particular pin, front and center on his perfectly tied cravat when he met up with—

"Miss Sudbury!"

"I beg your pardon, sir?" Blumsey asked.

"A young woman was in my bedroom. And I was *not* wearing the pin that night. Remember last week for the concert?"

"Yes, sir. You had on a black cravat and your diamond pin with the gray pearl."

His valet had a good memory, which was crucial if one didn't want to show up at every ball or party looking precisely the same. Moreover, the man had enough discretion he neither raised an eyebrow at the notion of a woman in his master's room, nor would ever mention it outside the four walls.

"Just so, Blumsey. Is it possible she came in here to steal from me?"

His valet remained silent and expressionless.

Then Jasper shook his head. "Why, yes, it is! She all but admitted she had. She said she was here for a token, a handkerchief! I bet she took something more valuable."

"Indeed, sir."

Such a response was intense for his unflappable valet.

"I shall see the very same female tonight at Pritchard's ball, and I intend to confront her. Hurry, Blumsey." Jasper held his hands out for his jacket. "I was going to show up fashionably late, but now I don't want to chance missing her."

JULIA KNEW HER QUARRY for the evening, and it was an easy one. Lady Pritchard was renowned for wearing a different set of earrings every day of the year. The sheer quantity of her jewelry collection was astounding, and Julia intended to relieve her of a negligible, hopefully unnoticeable amount. With a little luck, the viscountess wouldn't realize anything was missing until the following year.

After her mantle was stowed in the cloakroom of Lady Pritchard's mansion on St James's Square, Julia ascended the stairs to the public rooms. By her side was a married acquaintance of Sarah's, Mrs. Zebodar. The matron had been eager to accompany her as a chaperone, disclosing in the carriage how bored she was at home. Her husband, an officer, had spent most of the past decade fighting Bonaparte's army. Now home in jolly old England, Mr. Zebodar wanted to stay in his own parlor with his feet up and a glass of French brandy in hand to remind him of his victories.

"So glad your sister asked me," Mrs. Zebodar said for the umpteenth time as they wandered into the dazzling ballroom.

Julia sent a discerning gaze over the evening's setting. The parquet floor shone like a mirror, and the flame of oil lamps danced merrily all around the great room, augmenting the chandeliers. The musicians were warming up, and with the early guests who'd already arrived, one could smell the familiar fragrances of citrus, rose, lavender, and the pervasive bay scent.

The distraction of a crowded ball would be perfect. Julia could accomplish her task before the midnight meal and then relax and potentially enjoy herself.

"You look lovely," Mrs. Zebodar added, gesturing to Julia's blue satin dress. "I shall begin at once my task of securing you a husband."

"Oh," Julia said, stopping in her tracks. "I thought you would simply keep me company and make sure I didn't wander out into the garden with some ne'er-do-well."

The matron nodded. "Those are my tasks, too. But any good chaperone must help secure an appropriate beau for her charge. Matchmaking is definitely under my purview, and I relish the notion."

"Really?" Julia would have to take this up with Sarah when she got home. She didn't want to be Mrs. Zebodar's *charge*, nor was she interested in the woman's matchmaking abilities. If she wanted a man, why, she could simply turn around and smile at the first one she laid eyes on.

Testing out her theory, Julia turned and spotted the Earl of Marshfield bearing down upon her, looking purposeful despite a pleasant expression. A delicious frisson of excitement sizzled down her spine.

"Miss Sudbury, how delightful to see you again," he said, his dark gaze locking with hers, as he took her gloved hand in his and bowed over it.

"Lord Marshfield, we meet again."

"Tut, tut," Mrs. Zebodar said. "This is highly inappropriate."

"No, it's quite all right," Julia explained. "I was at the earl's home for dinner recently, so we've already been introduced, and nothing could be more appropriate."

"My lord, you should have spoken to me first," Mrs. Zebodar insisted, bristling and staring the earl down. "Nor should you have so freely taken the young lady's hand."

At this, Julia pulled her hand free from his warm grasp.

"Truly," the earl said with a frown. "But I am already acquainted with Miss Sudbury, while you and I have not yet been introduced. For all I know, you are in your first Season and she is *your* chaperone. You cannot be more than sixteen, surely."

Julia nearly groaned at the bold flattery. However, the matron put a hand to her chest and blatantly blushed, her mouth forming a pout and her eyelashes fluttering.

"Very well, sir. I suppose mistakes can be made and forgiven. I am the young lady's chaperone, Mrs. Zebodar."

He took the woman's hand and bowed over it.

Julia stared at the woman. As a chaperone, Mrs. Zebodar was probably useless, easily won over by a notorious rake or undoubtedly any man with a smooth tongue. And that was a good thing, for while she wanted the protection of keeping a good reputation, which Sarah's' married friend could provide, she didn't want to be under anyone's thumb.

"Are you here to ask for a dance with my charge?" Mrs. Zebodar was quick to begin her matchmaking duties.

Julia cringed at the word, as if she were a two-year-old on leading strings. Moreover, back in Chislehurst, a dance in someone's country home was a great deal less formal.

"Yes, in fact, I am." His glance looked amused as if he knew she didn't like all this fuss.

After all, she'd already told him she wasn't born to this world. In truth, Julia hadn't given much thought to dancing, far more interested in escaping to the private apartments of their hostess on the next floor up. However, she was interested enough in Lord Marshfield, especially after her sister had warned her away from the man, that she nodded in agreement.

"Do you have a pencil, sir?" Mrs. Zebodar asked, fishing in her own reticule. "For I shall keep track of Miss Sudbury's partners in my little keepsake book."

"Alas, my valet does not usually provide me one," he confessed. However, reaching into his pocket to confirm his words, he opened his palm to reveal an ivory toothpick-case and a few stray anise comfits.

The tools of a rake who did a lot of kissing, Julia supposed. Lifting her glance to his, she was certain his cheeks flushed slightly, as if he knew she assumed he had a pocket full of things to keep his teeth clean and breath fresh for the sole purpose of kissing.

"Never mind, I have found one," her chaperone commented into the silence.

The earl dropped the items back into his coat pocket.

"And since we are known to one another, I suppose it would be entirely appropriate," he added, turning his gaze to the matron once more, "if I requested a second dance with Miss Sudbury later in the evening."

"Yes, I will allow it," Mrs. Zebodar said.

Julia couldn't help rolling her eyes. The woman was taking her role entirely too seriously. If they were to continue for the remainder of the Season in this arrangement, then Sarah would have to have a talk with her friend.

"Very well," the earl said, with a nod of his head to each of them. Then he looked squarely at Julia. "I will claim you soon," he promised.

Gracious! That made her female parts do a little dance of their own.

"I look forward to it, my lord," she said, hoping to sound as worldly as he did.

One of his eyebrows lifted before he walked away.

"Mm-mm," said Mrs. Zebodar. "I'd heard he was quite an out and outer, but he seems perfectly polite to me. Not to mention a rum duke."

Julia smiled at hearing her own words repeated by a woman who was at least a decade older. And more than merely handsome, the earl had something dangerously wicked about him that Mrs. Zebodar hadn't picked up on. Maybe that was because Marshfield hadn't directed an ounce of his wickedness toward the chaperone.

But Julia had felt it, down to her toes.

Claimed by him indeed!

CHAPTER THREE

"At Lady Pritchard's ball, Lord M__ was seen dancing
with the aforementioned country miss, now known to be
the penniless sister of Lady W__."

—The Morning Post

It wasn't too long before the ballroom filled up, just like
a dozen balls Jasper attended before. *Or was it hundreds?*
He'd lost count.

Sighing, he helped himself to a glass of champagne. As
he wandered the parquet floor, he spied a few women he
knew, and to these he sent a polite nod. He also saw a few
whom he'd bedded, and to these he swiftly turned his back
and ducked in the other direction. Sometimes, the speed
with which he broke off an association after swiving caused
hurt feelings.

And if the girl's mother had found out, more the worse
for everyone! He'd been the source of one or two nasty
scenes and wished to avoid another that night.

Besides, he didn't want to ask anyone else to dance,
regardless of what a terrible guest that made him. Lady
Pritchard would certainly take him to task if she noticed him

standing about while single ladies lacked partners, but that wasn't his problem.

Jasper wanted to keep his eyes upon a certain mysterious blonde female. Moreover, he couldn't deny he wanted to put his hands and lips on her, too, if she was willing. He couldn't tell yet if she were a chaste and cool princum prancum or a loose blowsabella, who would give him a good roll and then smile at the end of it.

By God, he hoped she was the latter! Approaching her a mere minute before their dance so there was no time for more prattle with the dreaded chaperone—the bane of most single men's existence—he nodded to the older woman and took his prey's arm in his.

"Are you enjoying the evening so far, Miss Sudbury?"

"The night is young, yet, my lord."

"True, but I can confirm the champagne is cold, and that's a better start than at many balls."

He turned her toward the room's center and away from the matron's hearing. "Although the dragon protecting you might allow you *only* lemonade."

She laughed, and his rod twitched against the inside of his breeches. *What a delightful sound!* Moreover, she didn't hide it behind her gloved hand.

The first dance, a cotillion, had just ended and had been performed in the elegant, slow French style. He'd noticed Miss Sudbury hadn't danced but had watched intently. Their dance was to be a waltz, considered somewhat scandalous by some of the stiff-rumped hosts. He'd been pleased to learn Lady Pritchard would allow it. Moreover, he was determined to keep Miss Sudbury tight against him while he had her undivided attention.

"You have not lived long in London, I understand," the earl remarked, "and this is your first Season."

"You are wrong on both counts, sir," she said, and nothing more.

The deuce! What a bewattling ewe!

"Why don't you enlighten me?" he prompted before spinning her past the marble fireplace over which hung a wide mirror, bouncing light in every direction.

Jasper had danced there before. When he looked up at just the right angle, he could see down her décolletage to the pale swell of her ample bosom. *Beautiful!* And then they had waltzed past it, and he focused on her face again.

"I have been in London for nearly two years," she said. "While I haven't had anything like a formal Season, I accompanied my sister to a number of social events once she was out of mourning this year."

"Ah, yes, Lady Worthington."

Miss Sudbury tilted her head, never missing a step.

"You say that as if you are acquainted with my sister, yet I do not believe you are." She paused, looking at him from under her lovely brown lashes, darker than her fair hair and perfectly framing her periwinkle blue eyes.

"Although she seems well aware of *you*, my lord."

The smile died upon his face. Despite her pleasant expression, he knew by her tone Miss Sudbury was referring to the very worst of his behavior, the lascivious deeds, often exaggerated, tattled in the gossip rags. This was the shady conduct that made the mothers terrified and their daughters curious.

He sighed, pressing his hand more tightly against her waist as if she might flee from him and his monstrous nature.

"Your sister may have read about me, but you are correct. We are not personally acquainted, nor does a pot of muddy gossip-water make for clarity or truth."

"Really?" She blinked at him. "In polite society, we cannot discuss what you may or may not have done lest my chaperone's ears turn a brilliant shade of red. But honestly, Lord Marshfield, are you saying there is no truth behind the rumors of your devilish deeds that left more than one female regretting the day she met you?"

He had opened his mouth to form a rebuttal but snapped it closed. Staring into her eyes, so pure and clear like a late-August sky, he couldn't simply brush away her words, nor lie to her.

"Well?" she asked. She almost seemed to want him to deny being a rake.

Hm. Maybe she hoped the gossips were lying. Perhaps she wanted to form an attachment if he were not as bad as the papers said. On the other hand, she might be titillated by his reputation and thus hoped it were true.

"You are correct, Miss Sudbury. We cannot really discuss this matter." And he went silent for a few twirls around the floor before recalling she was the one who'd committed the grave infraction and entered *his* bedroom. And if his hunch was correct, she'd stolen from him.

"I must bring up the other night at my home, specifically where I encountered you."

She stiffened in his arms.

"Must you?" she asked. "For having since learned of your character, I now feel foolish in having hoped to take a handkerchief. In fact, a token from you is the last thing any young woman of genteel breeding who cares about her reputation would wish to have in her possession."

She had insulted him. *He was an earl, by God!* Yet she considered him no longer worth trapping into marriage, not that he would let himself be trapped, but still!

"Imagine if I had shown someone such a thing as a pocket square with *your* monogram," she continued. "I would be ruined. Why, I'm glad this dance is nearly at an end. My good name is undoubtedly at risk for allowing myself to waltz even once with you."

She was an evil shrew, Jasper decided. She would be lucky if he deigned to ruin her blasted reputation! Good name, indeed! *Who had ever heard of her?*

They lapsed into silence for the duration of the dance, which he couldn't help noticing she accomplished impeccably. Moreover, her sweet orange blossom and jasmine scent, floating around them as they danced, had become most intoxicating.

When he led her from the floor, back toward her watchful chaperone, he had to ask, "If you were not born and bred for a London Season, how is it you dance so well?"

She gave a charming dip of her shoulder in response. "We are not all farmers in the country, sir."

True enough! Apparently, there were women out there in the wilds beyond the city who could catch the eye of an earl, or like this one, who had his complete attention. Although from some of her remarks, her nature might be waspish, in which case he would want nothing more to do with her.

"What does your family do?" he asked, thinking it a safe enough topic.

"What does my family *do*?" she repeated, as if not understanding his import. "That's a strange question considering most of the people in this room do absolutely nothing, nor do their families. Mere boils on the face of life, as it were."

Again, she had rendered him speechless. She'd also paused halfway between her chaperone and the guests who were taking up partners ready for the next dance.

"I mean, look around you, sir. Or even in the mirror. What does the nobility do besides collect rents to keep them in silks and sparkling baubles?"

She glanced at his cravat, upon which was affixed a ruby pin. He felt soiled somehow, as if wearing even the smallest jewel made him complicit in some extraordinary scheme of laziness and deceit. *Beyond waspish, she was intolerably venomous!*

Clearing his throat, he decided he'd best put her in her place.

"I assure you, many of the people in this room do a great deal." He glanced around him, seeing the youngest and most frivolous among them. "Well, maybe not *these* particular people, but in many of the rooms in Mayfair and in London proper, there are industrious folk, I assure you. For the nobility are also statesmen and lawmakers and . . . and—"

"Men of business?" she offered helpfully, although they both knew a titled gentleman would rather eat his own arm than say he was in the business class.

"Stewards of the land," he finished.

"But not farmers," she said. "As I said rent collectors. As for statesmen, I say *pish!*"

"*Pish?*" This was the strangest conversation he'd ever had in a ballroom.

"Yes. Sitting around in the Palace of Westminster, holding your precious parliamentary sessions, deciding how the rest of us must conduct ourselves and how much tax we must pay to the crown's coffers."

He frowned. She had a very low opinion of nobility to be sure.

"What about the wars?" he asked, and his tone had become a little gruff. After all, he'd lost a few friends whom he'd met in his school days at Harrow and at All Souls College at Oxford. He'd been one of the lucky ones to escape the wars with all his limbs and his senses intact.

"I will give the noblemen their due in that regard," Miss Sudbury said. "I'm certain the wealthy officers make as good a target in their scarlet coats as any foot soldier, and being high upon a horse, perhaps even more so."

Was she mocking him and his comrades-in-arms?

"Lord Marshfield," she added, her features softening, "there is not a loyal subject of Britain who doesn't appreciate what our soldiers have done in Europe. Did *you* go to war?"

"I did." He tried not to be a stiff priss, but it was becoming increasingly difficult to carry on a civil conversation when she seemed intent on shooting arrows his way.

She nodded. "Then I thank you, sir. How nice you could return to *this* world." She gestured around them, and at that moment, a servant approached with glasses of champagne. She took one.

"However, many of the regulars who fought just as loyally are seen begging in the streets, their once proud uniforms in tatters. Next time you and your friends are taking on your *heavy* mantle of statesmanship, you might want to consider ways in which Parliament can help out those who served under you. And I don't mean your horse."

She tipped her glass to him in salute before walking away. He'd been roundly dismissed.

Left staring after her, Jasper finally sauntered to an empty table, head held high.

Now what? That hadn't gone as planned, nor had he even questioned Miss Sudbury about his blasted sapphire cravat pin. He almost felt embarrassed to bring up the subject of jewelry. Moreover, she no longer seemed the type to indulge in thievery, so righteous over the injustices of society.

JULIA WISHED SHE HADN'T been quite so tart-tongued with the earl. After all, he needn't have put himself in harm's way in France at all. Many of the nobility hadn't. Yet his arguments for the usefulness of aristocrats in London were laughable, especially in a room filled with vapid young snout-faces, all hoping to make a match based on family connections, titles, and wealth.

Regardless, she hoped she hadn't made an enemy because he was two things—powerful, thus potentially dangerous if he ever discovered her illicit actions, and he was incredibly attractive.

Of course, that was neither here nor there, but Julia couldn't ignore it. He made her heart beat quickly and her body pulse along with it. How amusing it would be to relax into some sort of easy banter with the man and, even better, enjoy her first full-fledged tryst. She sighed, knowing she had probably scared him off.

It didn't matter at that moment. She had her own important task to perform.

"I'm going to the ladies' retiring room," she announced to Mrs. Zebodar. Unfortunately, her chaperone nodded and rose to her feet.

"Oh, are you coming, too?"

"Indubitably," the woman replied.

Julia grimaced. Her normally easy mission, although occasionally heart-thumping, was no longer going to occur on her own schedule if she had to worry about dodging Mrs. Zebodar every time she wasn't with a dance partner.

"Surely you don't think I'll come to any harm in Lady Pritchard's retiring room?"

Her chaperone pursed her lips. "You cannot wander on your own. You might be assaulted in a hallway or dragged outside or abducted into a carriage. What if someone tries to kiss you?"

Julia nearly laughed. Mrs. Zebodar was equating a kiss with some other truly dreadful actions. And she, for one, wouldn't have missed the thrilling kiss with the Earl of Marshfield for all the world. Although not her first, it was undoubtedly the best she'd ever experienced.

Glancing around, she noticed the very man himself was staring at her as she crossed the room. At his piercing gaze and dour expression, she nearly smiled and waved just to be cheeky, but decided such behavior was a tad vulgar.

Instead, Julia turned her thoughts to the hound of a chaperone by her side. *How would she ever manage to get away from the woman?*

Then a thought struck her. "I think before we go to the retiring room, we ought to secure a few more partners. There will be four more dances altogether, I believe, and I have one secured by the Earl of Marshfield." *If he still showed up after her impertinence.* "I don't want to incur the reputation for being a wallflower, do I?"

"Heavens, no!" Mrs. Zebodar looked alarmed. "That would reflect badly on me, indeed. And you are such a lovely girl. There is no reason you shouldn't enjoy every dance until the wee hours."

What a horrifying notion! Dancing with strangers all night didn't sound appealing at all. If only the country dances, as the people in Town called them despite doing them in the London ballrooms, weren't so very long.

Although the waltz with Lord Marshfield hadn't seemed long at all.

"I know that young man," Mrs. Zebodar exclaimed, nodding her head toward a gangly buck, leaning against the wall, talking with a few others. "He's a baron's son. His mother is an acquaintance of mine. Let's see if he has yet to promise for all the dances."

Exactly so! Julia wouldn't give a fig if she stood him up, leaving him on the edge of the dance floor, which was what she needed to do to slip away upstairs.

After meeting the unfortunately named baron's eldest, Mr. Boreman, and letting him claim a quadrille, as well as two more partners whom Mrs. Zebodar sniffed out, at last, they went to the retiring room to freshen up.

An hour later, Julia's plan worked like a charm. When her partner claimed her from her chaperone, on the way to the dance floor, suddenly she begged off with a cry of dismay.

"I've torn my hem. So clumsy of me. I'll go to the cloakroom where they'll be able to assist me with a quick stitch. I'll meet you by the fireplace," she assured him. "While we can't dive interrupt the flow of this dance, I believe my next one is free."

Before her partner could offer to go with her, Julia disappeared amongst the tide of people crowding toward the dance floor.

In a very few minutes, she was on the level above and prowling the deserted hallway, hoping to find her hostess's bedroom.

CHAPTER FOUR

"There was a battle of the petticoat and the cravat at Lady
Pritchard's ball, when Miss T__ in quite a pelt gave Lord
M__ a sound tongue-lashing near the ladies' retiring room.
Although no good can come of eavesdropping, a nearby
female heard the earl offer to . . . Alas, dear reader, we
cannot print his words lest we lose our license."

—The Gazette

Jasper watched Miss Sudbury give her hapless partner the
slip and leave the room. *Hm. Where was the hoyden off to?* So
much for a chaperone.

Frowning, he searched for the Zebodar woman, only to
find her sipping champagne and chatting with someone at
the next table.

Not really sure why he was still interested or what he was
going to do, he followed Miss Sudbury. By the time he
pushed his way through the throng in the ever-hotter
ballroom and strode into the hallway, there was no sign of
her.

In all probability, she was in the ladies' retiring room,
and he didn't want to be discovered lurking outside that

particular door. Still, he could stroll the passageway until she returned.

While their next dance wasn't until after dinner, if he ran into her, he could escort her back into the ballroom, and perhaps even ask her in a very roundabout way whether she had somehow—by mistake and completely innocently—opened his jewelry box inside his armoire and helped herself to his father's sapphire cravat pin.

He realized all her antagonistic words had occurred as soon as he'd broached the topic previously. She'd created a good distraction, and he'd fallen for it.

Yet if her pretty cheeks turned pink and her sparkling blue eyes darted back and forth when he asked her, he would know the truth.

Thus, he began to pace, going to the end of the hall where long curtains were pulled across the window overlooking the street. And then he strolled back again, trying to keep his eyes averted as ladies came and went.

After a few minutes, he considered the staircase. *Was it possible she'd gone back downstairs, maybe to the cloakroom?* There was usually a seamstress there. However, it seemed unthinkable the girl would leave the floor without her chaperone.

He eyed the staircase again. She could have no reason to go upstairs. Yet he took a few steps toward it, unsure whether he would go down or ascend. Then he halted. This was madness.

At that moment, however, movement on the stairs caused his head to whip around, fully expecting Miss Sudbury to come into view.

A young man, his coat buttoned crookedly, and a disheveled young lady with very red lips and flushed cheeks descended. Relief flooded him that it wasn't Miss Sudbury. Until that moment, it hadn't occurred to him she might have taken off to enjoy a dalliance with some mutton monger.

On the other hand, these two were in for trouble if they returned to the ballroom in such a state.

Intercepting the wayward pair, Jasper ignored how the young man swallowed nervously and the pretty miss couldn't meet his eyes. His glance took them both in and then looked decidedly past them.

"May I suggest you each go to your respective retiring room and rectify any issues with your appearance?"

The couple glanced at one another before the man nodded curtly, and they separated. Sighing at their carelessness, Jasper wondered how anyone had an assignation these days without getting caught and forced into marriage at the first kiss.

Which brought his thoughts back to Miss Sudbury. They'd shared an excellent first kiss, one he wished to repeat despite her having an acerbic saucebox. Again, he glanced up the stairs. If she were to dally with anyone that night, he hoped it would be him.

"There you are," came a voice at his elbow.

Turning, he faced Louisa Tufton, looking to be in extremely high dander!

IT HAD TAKEN JULIA a little longer than she would have liked, but she found herself in Lady Pritchard's dressing room after only one wrong turn. Naturally, there'd been nothing in the woman's bedchamber. This lady had to house not only her clothing but her extensive jewelry collection in its own separate room.

Julia considered her options as quickly as possible. It was tempting to take more than she usually did because it seemed impossible her ladyship could miss even half of what she'd carelessly tossed in small velvet boxes and larger satin boxes and silver boxes and even bejeweled wooden boxes, all of which held baubles and dazzlers.

Feeling a little ill at the wealth before her while others shared a loaf of bread over an entire week, Julia nevertheless moved swiftly, picking over the choices. She'd learned her lesson about taking only one of a set. While it made the owner less likely to think the mate had been stolen, it also lessened the value considerably at the pawnbroker.

Thus, after slipping three pairs of earrings into her reticule, she turned to leave. One more set wouldn't hurt and would do so much good in London's poor neighborhoods. In the space of a heartbeat, she snatched another pair that looked to be black pearls surrounded by diamonds. And then, she slipped from the room as silently as she'd entered.

Taking the servants' stairs, she met no one. When she returned to the ballroom, the dance had ended, a quadrille was about to begin, and her partner was doing his diligence by the fireplace.

"Jolly good," Mr. Boreman said. "We won't miss even a step if we start the next one. You did say you have it free."

And before she knew it, she was whirling around the parquet.

"I suggest you leave your reticule with your chaperone next time," the young man said, as her bag swung around and clobbered him repeatedly.

Since most women carried only a handkerchief and some visiting cards, of which she had none since there was no one who could possibly expect or want a visit from her, she supposed he found her weighted bag to be irksome.

Nevertheless, she wouldn't risk leaving her bag where someone might discover its contents. Since he smelled good, though, and was affable, she smiled up at him.

"It was remiss of me, but I didn't want to go back to the table and miss the chance to dance with you."

That made him stand up even straighter and thrust out his chest. Apparently, he believed he'd made a conquest.

"Would you care to take a walk in the garden to cool off afterward?" he asked quietly.

He definitely believed he'd made a conquest. She tried to keep a serious expression when she wanted to smile.

"My chaperone would not allow such a breach, I'm sorry to say." She wasn't sorry at all, but the man looked instantly crestfallen.

"Perhaps we could dine together," she offered, thinking he wouldn't be the worst dining partner with whom she could be saddled.

"Sadly, I am dancing with another before the break."

She nodded. It was understood one escorted to dinner the partner with whom one was dancing directly prior. If Julia didn't have a partner for that dance, she would be assigned an escort.

For a moment, she had a delectable hope the Earl of Marshfield would be her dinner partner. But then thought better of it. She ought to stay away from him when there was the chance for a prolonged conversation in case he brought up his bedroom again.

"THIS IS UNACCEPTABLE," LOUISA Tufton stated, emphasizing her words with a wallop of her fan against her skirts. "You cannot just decide to end it."

"End what precisely?" Jasper asked her.

She paled. "How can you be so cruel?"

He expelled a breath of exasperation. "You are not thinking clearly. Breaking off our brief association is not cruel. It is the height of kindness. The best I can do for you, in fact."

She raised watery eyes to him, and he swore under his breath.

"Seriously, Miss Tufton, your tears are entirely misplaced unless you were under the incorrect notion that I was ever going to offer for you."

"But you invited me to your home for dinner," she said.

"I invite many people to my home for dinner," Jasper explained. "But I did not, you'll recall, invite you to my bedroom."

She blanched again. "Of course not, nor would I have gone."

"And now we're getting to the heart of the matter. Sooner rather than later, I would have attempted to seduce you. I would have succeeded. Moreover, after said seduction, which I believe you would have enjoyed as other females have—"

He paused momentarily when she gasped. He had truly chosen badly this time. She was behaving like a child. If he'd ever kissed Miss Tufton in his bedroom the way he'd done with Miss Sudbury, he had a feeling she would have fainted or gone shrieking out of his house.

"After seducing you, I would have broken off with you at any rate, and you would have been in a far worse situation if you'd imagined your heart—or worse, mine—was in any way involved. I assure you, mine is not. Therefore, I contend breaking our association now is a kindness."

He cocked his head and considered her, from head to toe.

"However, if you insist on lingering, we can probably find an empty room with a sofa, and play this out to the enjoyable end. The outcome will be the same, but we will have had a bit of fun. The choice is yours."

He crossed his arms and waited. If she was the tiniest bit curious about love-making, he would indulge her, since he'd been feeling randy ever since kissing Miss Sudbury. He would rather be standing there with the blue-eyed minx, but perhaps Miss Tufton was only annoyed she wasn't going to have a good tupping.

If that was the case, he could certainly satisfy.

Her palm met his cheek with a resounding smack. It was unexpected and showed she had a little gumption at least. It smarted, too, stinging while his soft assailant turned and walked away.

Louisa Tufton was elevated a little in his esteem at that moment. And finally, he was free to look for Miss Sudbury once more. To that end, he returned to the ballroom. Naturally, she was dancing, where any respectable miss ought to be. He'd been foolishly loitering in the hallway, when all she'd done was freshen up and return to the ball. He wished he'd claimed the dance directly before dinner, and then thought perhaps it wasn't too late.

While she was still partnered elsewhere, he went directly as the crow flies toward Mrs. Zebodar.

"Please excuse my intrusion," he said, interrupting her conversation with a lady at the next table. "I am wondering whether Miss Sudbury is available for the next dance after this."

"You wish to escort her to the dinner break?" the matron asked getting right to the point.

He could lie and pretend he didn't realize that dance was the important one, but decided against equivocation with this woman.

"Indeed, I wish to converse with her in an easier fashion than can occur while dancing."

"I shall have to sit upon your other side," she reminded him.

"Naturally," he agreed. Because nothing would be out of place, neither by number nor by sex in Lady Pritchard's two vast dining rooms.

"Very well. Miss Sudbury is free for that dance and for dinner."

He nodded. "Thank you. I shall return anon."

Walking away, he knew Mrs. Zebodar's eyes were boring into his back. He also knew if she'd an inkling he'd recently been in the hallway offering to make love to another woman, he wouldn't be dining with her charge.

Jasper couldn't help looking forward to claiming Miss Sudbury again. Her expression was priceless when he next appeared.

"I'm sorry," she said. "I believe our next dance isn't until later."

To his delight, she actually sounded sorry. Despite her earlier attempt to set him down a peg with her talk of do-nothing noblemen, he had a blossoming hope she was interested in him in return.

"Your chaperone has given her permission for us to dance and to take our dinner together. Isn't that so, Mrs. Zebodar?"

"Indeed," the woman said, then turned to Miss Sudbury. "He is an earl, after all," she added in a whisper that even the next table could hear.

Rather ill-mannered some might say, but that was the way of it. If Jasper hadn't a title and had already claimed two dances, the chaperone might have refused him a third as well as a dining companion. Yet because he was who he was, nearly all paths were cleared for him.

Glancing again at Miss Sudbury, he was rewarded with a placid expression, a hint of smile, and a devilish twinkle in her eyes.

"I understand Lady Pritchard is serving quite a feast in *both* dining rooms," she said. "We can all be thankful no one will go hungry tonight, and least not within these gilded walls, can't we?"

He narrowed his eyes. She was being sharp again, but he chose to ignore it.

"All this dancing and carrying our heads so extremely high does work up an appetite," he agreed, wryly, taking her hand in his. "Shall we?"

To his delight, she relaxed under his touch and even laughed again, the same delightful sound as before. He would swear lust had replaced blood in his veins and was coursing to all points south.

Randy was far too tepid a word. Despite how Miss Sudbury had stolen from him in all likelihood and had given him a good dressing down with her harsh tongue, he still wanted to suck that very tongue and use his own to give her a different kind of lashing altogether.

It was a relief to put his hands on her, even if it was merely palm to palm for a country dance and not a waltz. And when her citrus and floral aroma reached him again, he wanted to sniff it directly from her bare skin.

Madness!

They didn't speak, which probably enhanced her desirability. Jasper wasn't interested in being insulted by her anymore. He would far rather feel her thighs around his hips while they enjoyed one another. Words would be unnecessary, unless she was crying out his name.

"My lord, you look flushed," she said.

He did, in fact, feel hot under the collar. If he didn't have a woman soon, he would embarrass himself.

"Perhaps you merely need to slake your hunger," she added, her sparkling gaze mocking him.

She knew, dammit! The chick-a-biddy knew he wanted her and it only increased the sport!

CHAPTER FIVE

If she wasn't careful, Julia would find herself in love with
a rake. The following day, she took herself to task as she
mused upon Lord Marshfield's fine figure and his
handsome face. He had been attentive and charming during
Lady Pritchard's sumptuous dinner, telling her amusing
story after story. And he'd asked her many questions about
herself, astonished to learn she was a vicar's daughter.

Moreover, she had the distinct impression he suspected
she'd stolen from him. Once again, he'd started to reference
finding her in his bedroom, but she'd managed to divert
him. Still, she couldn't help feeling an uncomfortable
emotion she hadn't previously had, not even once since
beginning to take from the ridiculously wealthy and give to
the unbearably poor.

She'd experienced a pang of guilt.

After dinner ended, they still had another dance to go,
and when her reticule walloped him in the shoulder, he'd
offered to put it in his pocket for the duration.

"No," she'd practically shrieked when he'd reached for it, losing her calm demeanor for the first time.

He'd given her such a curious look, she feared he knew what was in her small satin bag.

"My apologies," she muttered quickly. "One is taught when in London to be wary with one's purse at all times."

He'd smiled wryly. "I don't think that applies to earls."

Nevertheless, he'd let her reticule alone. And she'd been sorry to part with him when Mrs. Zebodar deemed it time to leave. It was the first event in London in which Julia had enjoyed the company more than anything else. Usually, the success of snagging a few baubles was the reward of the night, knowing within two days, she would be able to turn over a sizable sum to an orphanage or workhouse.

That night, however, she'd gone to bed feeling something else entirely—the thrill of being interested in a man who seemed to be interested in return.

Moreover, Julia started thinking about when Sarah might marry again. If this Denbigh fellow her sister had enjoyed meeting a few weeks earlier turned out to be a love interest, that would be splendid. Not that Julia wished to be rid of her, but Sarah had promised her the Worthington house if ever she remarried. And the previous night, it had occurred to her a single woman with a modest allowance, as she received from her sister, could fairly well do as she pleased if she had a home of her own.

Julia could, in fact, invite a certain earl over for a late supper with no one the wiser. And Marshfield seemed exactly the type of man who would accept.

Which was precisely why she shouldn't be dreaming of spending time with him, particularly not time alone. His reputation was well-earned, and she would be nothing but a passing fancy of his. In the interim, before his fancy passed, she could—and probably would—get into all sorts of trouble.

Sighing and finishing her breakfast, she turned her thoughts to a higher calling than dallying with the earl and kissing him and feeling his hands on her, not just while dancing but while doing other wicked things.

Instead, she would sell the valuables and seek out St. James's Workhouse, one of the most well-respected of London's residences for the poor, of which she believed there to be about seventy others. Months ago, she'd sent her father a letter, asking his advice on what he would do were he in London, surrounded by such poverty. He'd suggested she ask if they needed spiritual guidance. It was far more likely they needed new linens, meat, vegetables and ale.

To that end, at eleven o'clock, wearing a day dress of pale primrose with cream trim, she set out for a new place to pawn, having decided her regular shop didn't have the funds necessary to pay her a fair price, not for everything she had with her that day.

Leaving Sarah's maid in the carriage, Julia entered through the attractive four-columned storefront of the jeweler Rundell, Bridge, and Rundell, in the shadow of St. Paul's Cathedral. She not only had Lady Pritchard's earrings, but also Lord Marshfield's cravat pin. If he hadn't been wearing another fine one at the ball, she might have relented and slipped his pin into his pocket at some future occasion.

The store's interior was plainer than she'd expected for such a well-known establishment, but all around her were sumptuous wares, indicating they dealt in high-cost items.

As if to assure himself of not being culpable in any crime, the jeweler with whom she spoke, Mr. Bridge, asked her in a rather bored tone if the goods she wanted to sell had come into her possession from a thief to the best of her knowledge. Since no thief had given them to her, she answered truthfully.

"No, sir."

After Mr. Bridge inspected the jewelry, particularly the large sapphire in the earl's pin, he gave her a long stare. She held his gaze without blinking, until, finally, he broke away first and pronounced a grand sum.

When they'd concluded their business, Julia headed off to St. James's Workhouse, a large brick building on Poland Street. This time bringing the maid, she entered to find plain walls but also enormous windows letting in the light. While colonnades of posts held up the high ceiling, sadly, much of that ceiling's plaster had already come down.

As usual, more women and children, along with many elderly people, made up the residents despite the workhouse being designed to house the able-bodied poor. Some had crutches or were seated in invalid chairs on the wooden floor, which while appearing swept clean appeared prone to damaged planks and rather large gaps.

In the main room, women were gathered in groups, some seated on benches, some standing by tables. Those who could see well enough were sewing various items, all hunched in a position that seemed permanent.

Julia straightened, feeling her back twinge in sympathy, and glanced at Sarah's maid, whose eyes were round, taking it all in. Undoubtedly, she was thinking how but for the grace of God—and a good servant's job in Mayfair—this could easily have been her fate, too. Although wearing a haunted look whenever she accompanied Julia, the maid was sworn to secrecy by way of a few coins for her and a couple more for the driver.

Julia ventured farther inside. A tall porter, the only hale man in the large room, intercepted her at once.

"What's your business, miss?" he demanded.

"I wish to speak with the master or matron," she told him, "to make a donation."

At that last word, the man's eyes lit up a little, and he nodded.

"Actually, you'll be wanting the clerk, miss. Go through that doorway, past the women's ward and the infirmary, and you'll see a door with a brass knob. That's the clerk. He handles all the money."

"Thank you." Julia made her way out of the room and along the passage. More signs of dilapidated, half-hearted repairs were everywhere. Wishing it were more pleasant for its inhabitants, she knocked on the clerk's office door.

"Enter."

A craggy man with spectacles arose from his chair upon her entrance.

"Good day. I was told you handle the donations," she said directly.

"Yes, miss." He frowned, probably not receiving many single females with such a stated purpose. "Or is it 'my lady'?"

Julia ignored his question. Glancing once at the silent maid beside her, she asked, "Why does the facility appear in such disrepair? Aren't you supported by this parish?"

"Too many poor," he said. "Too little funding." Then the man sighed. "You mentioned a donation? You may want to save your pennies. It would take quite a bit to make any difference."

"Is there one thing in particular that St. James's needs?" Julia asked.

"The poor get three meals a day, and plum pudding on Saturday," he told her, as if she suspected him of starving the residents.

"That's fifteen pounds of suet, eighteen quarts of milk, and fifteen quarts of raisins for one day alone," he continued, and stared past her shoulder as if imagining all those raisins.

"That's all very well, but what about the building's structure? There seems to be some need for repairs. The floor in the common room, for instance."

He focused on her again. "Do you wish to pay for a floor, miss?" His tone suggested she had no idea what she was saying.

"Yes, I believe I do. It looked downright dangerous. Are the floors in the wards in the same state? What about the children's room?"

His eyes narrowed and his mouth twisted. Clearly, he was starting to feel as if she were criticizing the workhouse, and maybe its staff. To allay any of his defenses, she withdrew the bag she carried tucked under her arm and attached to her wrist by strong silken cords. Bigger and sturdier than her normal coin purse or reticule, it gave her a feeling of security when she had to carry a donation.

Without fanfare, she dumped the contents onto the man's orderly desk.

Silently, he stared at the pile of silver and gold coins. There were even two London banknotes of substantial amounts.

"Good God!" he finally exclaimed, sitting down before jumping to his feet again since Julia remained standing. Then he raised his gaze to her face again. "My lady, this is a tremendous donation."

"Enough for a floor?" she asked.

"Yes, certainly," he agreed. "More than one."

"I shall come back to ascertain the progress. I would be very disappointed if the money wasn't used as promised, sir."

Julia often made the idle threat with no idea how she would follow up on any type of retribution should the man simply take the money and go to Scotland or Spain.

"I understand, miss. If you can wait, I shall write up a donation receipt of funds and you can sign—"

"There is no need. I intend to remain anonymous. If all goes well, you may receive more. If you fail to put it to good use," she trailed off, considering whether to mention contacting the authorities if she even knew whom they might be.

The clerk nodded. "Very well. I shall still count it and write up a receipt and sign it myself. I like to keep things all above board."

"I appreciate that. Good day, sir." And as easily as that, she'd done some good in the world and could count it a day worth living.

JASPER CONSIDERED HAVING HIS trusted footman, Rigley, leave his calling card at the Countess of Worthington's house, but it smacked of eagerness. He wanted to see Miss Sudbury again, but he didn't want to appear like a hell-born babe.

That, in itself, was an oddity. He usually didn't care a fig for how his reputation preceded him or if he appeared to be precisely what he was, a scapegrace, a man of the Town. As far as he was concerned, it was often better for a female to see him coming a mile away and know what she was getting in to. Yet he'd made a judgment error by choosing Louisa Tufton, and he didn't want a repeat of that unpleasantness.

However, Miss Sudbury had a pragmatic air about her when she was in the company of the nobility, a class she deemed less than honorable, and he wanted to surpass her expectations. Of course, he still wanted to bed her, and he was certain he'd detected enough interest from her in his own person that he should count on said occurrence.

Another ball or dinner party wasn't going to get him any closer to his goal. *Unless it was a party of two!*

To that end, Jasper sat in his study and wrote a brief invitation, barely couching the intimate nature of it in terms that could be taken another way. If she arrived and was surprised by there being only two of them, then he could claim her misunderstanding, but Miss Sudbury would have to be a dimwit, indeed, not to understand his meaning.

Signed, sealed, and stamped with his ring, the letter went off with Rigley for immediate delivery. He almost instructed his footman to wait for a reply, but again, that gave the appearance of being too enthusiastic, which in his experience was the wrong way to gain a female's attention. Instead, Jasper needed to keep himself busy.

Naturally, he went to White's and met with two old pals from Oxford. After a game of billiards and a discussion of the news of the day, he detoured to Watier's, owned by the Prince Regent's favorite chef. The food, as expected, was divine. By the time Jasper returned home, he was hoping against hope Miss Sudbury had seen her way clear to respond.

She had!

Dear Lord Marshfield,

First, I must thank you for your invitation, so unexpected. Some, I suppose, might consider it an honor.

However, if I am reading it correctly, then I must decline with one line of explanation: Let me remind you, sir, I am a vicar's daughter.

Yours truly,

J. Sudbury

The deuce! She'd understood his bold invitation for what it was, an attempt to get her alone for a possible after-dinner seduction. *If not during dinner!* For he could easily imagine sending a few plates flying to the floor in order to press her down upon the tablecloth and feast upon her.

While he had an excellent cook, he could be certain Miss Sudbury would enjoy that particular course most of all. He definitely would!

Vicar's daughter, indeed! She was as worldly as any Drury Lane strumpet, or he would eat his hat. At least, she gave off a knowing confidence. He would believe her words, but her kiss gave them the lie. She kissed like a woman who knew what she was doing.

Regardless, she had turned him down and insulted him with her words about it being a *supposed* honor. He grinned. She could pack more meaning into a line than most into a book.

Yet she hadn't told him to leave her at peace. He would try again with a better invitation after a few day's cooling off.

With that plan in mind, he was surprised to receive a missive from the brazen baggage the very next day.

Dear Lord Marshfield,

My sister, the Countess of Worthington, and the Viscount Denbigh, are having a small get-together tomorrow night. If you would care to come to our home on Hanover Square, I would be most pleased to have you as my dining partner.

Yours truly,

J. Sudbury

Jasper grinned to himself. *Well. Well. Well.*

CHAPTER SIX

"Lord M__'s carriage was seen depositing the earl at the Hanover Square home of Lady W__ this week, long past polite afternoon visiting hours. Perhaps he attended a dinner party, dear reader. Yet no other guests were noticed!"

—The Morning Post

Julia had to restrain herself from pushing Sarah out the front door and into her carriage. She hadn't told her she was having company over for the precise reason that her sister would look at her with her great big blue eyes and then say no.

Yet tired of being a saint and doing nothing but her good works, Julia wanted companionship and fun. Moreover, she'd decided she wanted both with the Earl of Marshfield since he was the most dash-fire man she'd met in London. Despite his rakish air, something about him reached inside her and gave her the most delightful tickle.

"Are you sure you won't come?" Sarah asked for the umpteenth time, yet positively without enthusiasm. "The viscount won't mind, I'm sure."

Julia shook her head. "Go enjoy spending time with that handsome man, for goodness' sake! I saw the white silk chemise your maid laid out and the rosy silk stockings." She couldn't help teasing her sister, making Sarah's cheeks turn pink. There was no reason in the world two adults who were madly attracted to each other shouldn't enjoy intimate relations.

No reason at all. Julia shivered.

That type of constraint was all very well for the upper-class women who couldn't be trusted not to pass the wrong babe off as an heir to a title, but what had it to do with Julia or even the widowed Sarah or all the ordinary women of Britain? They shouldn't have to wait interminably, with legs firmly crossed, for a husband when so many marriageable men had been killed during the wars with France. That meant perhaps never experiencing bliss in a man's arms.

At least *not* if one waited for matrimonial bliss.

Besides, Julia's prospects in that regard were sorely curtailed by the current company she kept—the English quality set. She couldn't imagine a more insular, narrow-minded group of people when it came to marriage.

"Very well. I hope you enjoy your evening. I probably won't see you until morning," Sarah added, and then, realizing how brazen that sounded, her cheeks grew even redder as she yanked on her gloves.

Trying to urge her out, Julia picked up a posy from the glove stand in the hall and placed it into her sister's hand.

"For the viscount," she said, and then gave Sarah a firm little press to her back to send her on her way.

Finally, Julia was alone. Dashing back to the kitchen, she burst in, frightening the kitchen maid and making the cook exclaim loudly, "My word!"

"My apologies," Julia said. "I simply wanted to make certain everything was going well."

Both pairs of eyes stared at her, and she realized her *faux pas* in doubting the expertly run kitchen of the Worthington home. She should have known better. After all the cook's reputation was on the line.

As was Julia's. She was playing with fire, and she knew it, prepared to be burnt if necessary. In fact, she was counting on it.

"Very good, then," she said into the continued silence of the insulted kitchen staff. "I had best prepare myself and leave you to it." She turned away, then looked back. "Thank you."

The cook rolled her eyes, and Julia hoped the woman wouldn't poison her meal.

Having learned her lesson, she wasn't going to ask the butler if he had lit the exterior oil lamps, nor the footman if he'd swept the stoop, nor the housemaid if she'd lit a fire in the drawing and dining rooms. They all knew their jobs, and it was up to her merely to play the refined hostess and for the earl to show up.

Upstairs, she accepted the help of another of her sister's maids to dress. She usually wore blue if she wanted to look her best but decided to change her appearance, since Marshfield had already seen her in blue.

Torn between a burgundy satin and a silver silk, she went with the warmer color until she looked at herself in the mirror and decided it was too gaudy.

"It's not vulgar, miss, I promise you," the maid insisted.

"Still, I think the silver is a better choice." Julia would look less as though she was offering herself up as a tasty morsel of meat or a delicious glass of Spanish wine.

"Yes, miss." With the maid's help, she changed into a fine muslin petticoat, worn under the silver silk gown, which was embroidered with darker silver and topped with a small, snug plum-colored bodice.

Julia took another look at herself. The short full sleeves and the tight bosom trimmed with a thick silver border of ribbon were most becoming. She turned and twisted in front of the mirror, trying to see her back, and then gestured for the hand mirror so she could see it properly. Fluted lace over her rear kept the dress from being too plain and a silver fringe at her waist added an unusual touch.

"I think it's suits, don't you?"

"Yes, miss," said the maid, who looked as if she wanted to move on to her next chore.

"I thank you," Julia assured her. "I particularly like the way you've styled my hair. The curls are loose and not rigid and regular. Quite natural looking, and the pearl bandeau is perfect."

Julia was babbling nervously, not sure why this one dinner mattered when the earl had already seen her in evening dress twice before.

Feeling a little like a hypocrite, she picked out a few pieces of her sister's jewelry to complement the gown, a pearl necklace and pearl eardrops with silver bracelets on her left arm. And then immediately took them all off and made do with her single ruby ring that had belonged to her mother and which she never removed.

"Now I wait," she muttered. "I'll go into the drawing room," she said to no one, realizing the maid had already dismissed herself.

Hoping it was all right to begin with a glass of Sarah's claret before her guest arrived, she asked Mr. Dawson, the butler, to bring it in, then took a seat by the fire. The staff already considered her peculiar, what with paying off two of them to secrecy, which meant all the household staff knew of her weekly trips. Moreover, Julia had always been perfectly happy borrowing her sister's dresses, not indulging in the purchasing of her own. This worked fine except it kept the maid running back and forth between bedchambers looking for gowns. Then she'd gone into the cook's domain like a ninny, as if she was going to start peeling potatoes the way she had when a child in Chislehurst.

A sip or two calmed her nerves, and soon, she was not the least bit anxious.

Until she heard the rapping at the front door. She stood, then sat, then stood. *Gracious!*

Finally, she remembered to set her glass down just as Mr. Dawson admitted the earl to the room.

"Lord Marshfield, miss," he announced.

If possible, the earl looked even more handsome than she recalled. Rather magnificent in a gray evening coat and black breeches and boots.

If only it were polite to openly stare at him.

With nerves fluttering in her belly, she smiled.

For his part, the earl had taken two steps into the room, looked at her, glanced around in puzzlement at the lack of other guests, then jumped slightly when the butler closed the door behind him.

All at once, she realized it was her place to greet him first.

"My Lord Marshfield, so good of you to come." She sounded like a stuffy matron, but it was the best she could do with her heart racing and her mouth gone suddenly bone dry. Julia offered him the curtsy due his station and waited.

As a gentleman, he stripped off his gloves, approached close enough to take her hand, and while keeping his coffee-brown eyes locked on hers, bowed over her bare fingers. Without gloves, it felt extremely intimate, and she nearly sighed.

Still holding her hand, standing a bit too close, he frowned slightly.

"Am I early?"

"No, sir," she said. "Exactly on time." If he'd kept her waiting any longer, she might have jumped out of her own skin.

"Then I assume your sister is still dressing, and Denbigh is fashionably late."

"Why, no. My sister is never so long at her toilette that she would let a guest arrive while she was still above stairs. She may not have been born a titled lady, sir, but she has impeccable manners. I believe she and Lord Denbigh are already happily dining together, or at least seated close and sharing a glass of wine."

He blinked. "Are they in the dining room? Without us?"

"I could not say whether they are in *a* dining room, but most assuredly without us," she confessed at last. "For you see, neither one is here."

He released her hand and took a step back. "Was I not invited over for dinner tonight?"

"Yes, of course."

"Did you not write to me they were having a small get-together and ask me to be your—?" he broke off. His mouth hung open a second. Then the earl shook his head.

"You are a sneaky wench, just as I suspected all along."

"Wench?" She ought to be offended, but it sounded rather flattering, the way he said it with admiration in his eyes.

"Absolutely. A saucy one at that." He sat down and started to laugh. The sound, richly sonorous, did funny things to her, relaxing and titillating at the same time. "You tricked me."

"I suppose I did," she agreed, taking a seat on the same couch before he could recall his manners and jump to his feet again. For the sake of respectability, however, she left two feet between them.

"And it's so bloody outrageous," the earl added. "May I have some of that wine?"

Reaching to the table in front of them, she poured a glass and held it out, knowing their fingers would touch, relishing the frisson that sizzled through her when they did.

Picking up her own glass, she leaned back.

"Would you have come if I had worded it differently? If you'd known you might be entering a parson's mousetrap?"

"Or a vicar's daughter's trap in this case," he quipped.

"Just so."

"I probably would have come anyway out of sheer curiosity as to how a well-connected, politely raised young woman could think this to be a good idea."

She lifted a shoulder in a shrug, watching his eyes flicker to the décolletage of her bodice.

"You sent me a bold invitation," she reminded him, recalling how she'd felt upon reading his missive. "It was entirely inappropriate. An offer that I could not possibly agree to. Basically, you invited me to your home for a romp."

He spluttered wine through his teeth and, leaning forward, began to cough. After a couple seconds, Julia moved closer and pounded his back until he held up his hand. Then he reached into his pocket and withdrew a handkerchief with which he wiped his mouth and the end of his nose. Lastly, he glanced down at his charcoal gray breeches and dabbed at them, although she couldn't see any spots of claret.

"Am I wrong?" she demanded when he finally looked at her after setting his glass upon the low table.

After a moment's hesitation, he said, "No," with the grace to look sheepish.

"I thought not. I decided to show you how such an invitation could be handled more elegantly, and if my missive had been read by anyone else, he or she would never guess we were to dine alone. Just as you didn't."

"Indeed, you have shown me how it can be done," he agreed. "And now we are alone in your sister's drawing room. What next?"

She sipped her wine, feeling more adventurous than she ever had in her entire life, and she'd had more than her own fair share of escapades recently.

"I suppose we have a civilized chat and then dine together on what will be absolutely delicious fare if I know my sister's cook. And then . . . ," she trailed off.

"And then?" He reached out and took her nearly empty glass from her. Outrageously, he tilted his head back and drank the last few drops before setting the glass down.

When he put a gentle hand on her forearm, the warmth of his fingers made her stomach do a thrilled little jig.

Julia couldn't speak. She could only watch as he drew her steadily closer, and then close her eyes when he lowered his mouth to hers. Ever so slowly. Nothing quick, nothing to jar or scare her. Simply his familiar lips firmly touching her own, tasting of wine. His other hand came to rest on her shoulder, turning her to face him more squarely.

With sensation winging from one part of her body to the next, Julia placed her hands on his chest, feeling the fine wool of his suit followed by the slippery silk of his cravat between her fingers as she explored.

Cocking his head, the earl slanted his mouth expertly across hers, and their connection was complete.

"*Mm,*" she sighed before feeling the tip of his tongue touch the seam of her lips. She didn't feign surprise. She knew about this open-mouthed kissing, and fearlessly parted to admit him.

The first touch of his tongue against her own did, in fact, shock her. It was hot and arousing and hinted of other intimacies to come. Exploring her mouth, ever so slightly he sucked her tongue, and she shivered. His hands tightened upon her.

When he drew back, she leaned toward him as if she would follow his kiss to the ends of the earth. Opening her eyes and looking into his, Julia recalled her surroundings. The dark passion swirling in the rich umber of the earl's gaze was a little frightening. He had gone places she most certainly had not.

But now she longed to do so—with him!

"You are very good at kissing," she said.

His eyes widened for the briefest moment, and then he leaned back, away from her, making her do the same if she wasn't to feel an eager fool.

"I am, aren't I?" he agreed, sounding smug.

At the same time, Julia was relieved not to detect a smirk upon his face.

Then he cocked his head. "But how can you judge my kiss unless you've had a few yourself?"

"That does not signify, sir. Even if I'd never had a hunk of freshly baked bread, warm from the oven and buttered within an inch of its life, that would hardly mean I couldn't pass judgement on the deliciousness of a loaf, nor take in all that made it good—its aroma, its softness, and its taste.

He stared at her. "Miss Sudbury, you are unique."

She hoped it was a nice uniqueness and not an off-putting one.

"Thank you." And for want of anything else to do, she poured them each another glass of wine and wondered why he'd kissed her at that moment and whether he would do it again.

"Why did you—?" Before she could ask either question as she intended to do since they seemed to have moved into the realm of intimate familiarity, the drawing room door opened.

"Dinner, miss," announced Mr. Dawson.

THANK GOD FOR THE *interruption!* Jasper had the distinct feeling the bold female before him had been about to ask him something inappropriate. She was already too adorable by half, and he couldn't help wondering why she was allowing him anywhere near her.

Obviously clever and in possession of all her faculties, why would she dine with an infamous libertine?

As he rose to his feet and took her arm, he couldn't help feeling blessed by the entire evening. Never to his knowledge had a woman arranged, and so expertly, to be alone with him. And he knew down to his bones she had not told her sister. No family member would allow such an impropriety.

Yet there he was, escorting the lovely Miss Sudbury, who was shimmering in the candlelight in her exquisite silvery gown, looking like a precious jewel.

He wanted simply to stare at her. At the same time, he wanted to remove every stitch of her clothing and worship her with his hands, mouth, and body. Drawing out her chair in the pale puce and cream dining room, he had the distinct notion such a delightful event was in store for them later. And while he'd felt a heavy ache in his loins from the moment he'd discovered her by herself in the drawing room, now, it turned into a persistent throb. Assuredly, the ultimate reward was worth every pain of anticipation.

Seated at one end of the table, across from one another, they were as intimate as one could be in a formal dining room.

"Have you been here before, when Lord Worthington still lived?" she asked as the footman began to serve.

"Never. He wasn't among my set, nor even my father's. Perhaps my grandfather's," he added with a wry smile.

"He wasn't that old," she protested. Then blushed. "Yes, I suppose he was. Regardless, although my sister wasn't thrilled at the prospect, her marriage turned out well."

"Because Worthington had a meeting with old Mr. Grim and was put in his eternity box within a fortnight of the vows, if I recall."

Jasper watched her take a turn at spluttering, as she blew the pottage off her spoon and onto the tablecloth. His words had made her laugh. However, since she recovered quickly and wasn't choking, he didn't jump up and attack her back as she had his.

"My sister could hardly have planned on that, sir. I, for one, will be thrilled if she finds her heart's desire in Lord Denbigh, although I have yet to meet him. I don't suppose you know any reasons as to why he wouldn't make her a good match."

Jasper considered. This was a little too close to tongue-wagging for his liking, but after recovering from the silly notion of one's *heart's desire*, he thought for a moment.

"I know the viscount went to France for a period on behalf of the Prince Regent, and has just returned from

Ghent regarding a treaty with America. Other than that and a rumor he occasionally works as a hound for Bow Street, I know very little."

Was he imagining it or had the girl paled over the information? He didn't think there was anything in what he'd said that would disqualify Denbigh from being husband material.

In any case, Jasper didn't want to discuss him any further. While the man had a reputation for being a bit of a buck, it was minor in comparison to his own escapades, as most men's were. Besides, it was the widow's worry if the man wasn't worthy of her.

"And what about you, Miss Sudbury? Any aspirations regarding making a match? After all, you've been to a number of soirées, danced with the eligible men of London and probably some not so eligible. Any designs on them?"

"You sound like an old woman with a pot of gossip-water, my lord."

What! If he did, it was her fault for asking him questions.

Yet in truth, he didn't know why he'd asked her anything so personal. If she did have designs on some churl, what was it to him?

"You needn't tell me. After all, I am the one dining with you this evening, so any other man is already the loser."

She beamed. "That's very kind of you to say, sir. In any case, I would be more likely to give my heart to a genuine, country Harry than the pack of dandy prats I've encountered in Mayfair."

He set down his spoon with a thump.

"You? Matched with some hobnail, some chaw bacon sporting dirty fingers and patches?" Jasper couldn't help laughing, given her fine surroundings. "I don't know your former situation in the country, but I doubt you could wear that gorgeous, glittering gown as the wife of a Johnny-raw. And that, in my opinion, would be a terrible shame and waste of beautiful female flesh."

Her cheeks pinkened, and he thought she was pleased until she spoke.

"Female flesh, indeed!" Her tone was scathing. "Like a cow or pig at the market, I suppose!"

Where had he gone so wrong?

CHAPTER SEVEN

"Lord and Lady Chandron hosted a veritable galaxy of the
quality folk at their ball. Naturally, Lord M__ was there.
How many ladies' hearts did he break?"

"Miss Sudbury," he implored, fearing the coveted
prize of a place between her smooth thighs had
just been snatched from him, and by his own
thoughtlessness. "The term was meant as an accolade, not a
denigration. Yet I offer my sincere apology for insulting
you."

She pursed her lips, then nodded, instantly easing the
band of apprehension that had tightened around his chest.

"Your apology is accepted. And I must give one in
return. I jumped into a great tweague, but it isn't truly your
fault." She eyed him over the next course, a delicate filet of
sole.

"I know you wish to indulge in a gay evening," she
continued, "so I shall not overwhelm you with stories of the
country folk. Yet I can only assume you are unaware how a
poor man may be forced to sell even his wife and do so at a
common marketplace, exactly like a cow or pig."

Jasper drew back. *What nonsense was she sputtering?*

"Sell one's wife? That's absurd. A lie. This is England in 1814, not 1418!"

"Nevertheless, it's true," she insisted. "For one thing, in most cases, living separately or seeking a divorce is beyond the reach for those outside your class. Instead, by agreement, a woman can ask to be sold in some cases to a man to whom she would rather be married, taking her children with her, too."

Jasper tried to imagine letting one's children be sold and raised by someone else.

"I'm not sure I want to hear any more of this barbaric behavior." He sipped his wine. "However, you did say it was done by agreement."

"Sometimes, yes. A wife might initiate the sale if her husband has gone missing, say during the war. I warrant some of those men fighting under your command came home to find their wives had been bought by another. However, in other cases," she continued, "it is against both parties' wishes. To keep more people from becoming a burden on a given parish, like my own dear Chislehurst where I grew up, the Poor Law of our great nation allows local authorities to force a husband to sell his wife to keep her out of their parish workhouse. And as surely as I've seen an amusing caricature of dear John Bull holding Bonaparte's head on a pitchfork, I've seen a man forced to send his wife to market to be sold in a different parish."

"That's horrendous." A morsel of food stuck in his throat, and he swallowed twice to get it down.

Miss Sudbury gave her customary delicate shrug of one shoulder.

"I have heard that a woman and her new husband may at least be bought a meal by the parish authorities who forced the sale." Sarcasm dripped from her tone.

"How kind of them," Jasper put forth with equal irony, before downing the dregs of his wine and gesturing for the footman to refill it. "And what of the old husband?"

"He does not get a meal," she said coolly.

They blinked at one another over the next course of the best British beef. He was starting to feel guilty just having a good dinner.

"But he does get to stay in the parish poorhouse as a single man," she added, "and that keeps him from being a beggar on the street."

She sighed, her bosom rising and falling under his gaze, and it was a beautiful thing to watch.

"Wealth is the key to freedom in Britain." Miss Sudbury said the words half to herself, half to him.

"Indeed." To that, he agreed. He was not unaware of the benefits he enjoyed by having been born on the right side of the blanket in his particular household.

However, it was time to turn their conversation back to the path of more pleasant niceties. For selling one's wife for cheap, along with one's child, hardly made for an aphrodisiac to love-making.

To that end, he told her of the last horse race he'd attended, correctly choosing the winner, of a ballet he'd seen in which two dancers collided on stage, and lastly, of a play in which the main actor forgot nearly all his lines, then drew out a flask, downed it, swore excoriatingly, and stomped off stage.

They were both laughing when he was done, and he felt vindicated as a good dinner guest who'd earned his place at the table, especially after his earlier *faux pas*.

"The meal was superb," he told her, wiping his lips and setting his napkin beside his plate after a dessert that had been meant to dazzle and had succeeded.

A platter of sugar biscuits and meringues artfully arranged around a tooth-cracking pastillage sculpture of a massive pineapple had been only the beginning. It was followed by small cups of the richest custard and then, lastly, ratafia cakes which melted in his mouth so easily, Jasper had eaten three.

"Thank you," said Miss Sudbury.

Despite the many courses, she'd done her fair share of enjoying the desserts, and he admired a woman with a hearty appetite in all senses of the word.

"Although, as I had nothing to do with it," she continued, "I shall send your approval back to my sister's cook." Then quietly, she added, "However, I *can* cook, in case you were wondering."

Her soft words surprised him. He hadn't been wondering anything of the sort. It never occurred to him she could do so, nor that she would need to. Yet she seemed to be trying to impress him with her domestic abilities. *How strange!* He couldn't imagine any other lady of his acquaintance ever uttering such a low phrase or letting him picture her for one moment in the harsh environment of a kitchen.

However, the image of Miss Sudbury, chopping vegetables or stirring stew, her soft curls sticking to the damp skin of her forehead and neck, appealed to him in an entirely visceral way—especially when he imagined her in nothing but an apron barely covering her full breasts and only the apron strings across her bare back, tied in a bow at her waist with the long ends draping down over her lush buttocks.

Swallowing the lump of desire in his throat, he rose to his feet. Moving swiftly around the end of the table, he drew out her chair, taking a moment to glance down her décolletage. Naturally! *Wasn't that why women wore the fashion they did?*

With her amethyst-colored bodice stretched tightly across her breasts, it left a dark and dangerous valley he longed to explore.

"I think that's a fine skill," he said, his tone suddenly husky.

Drawing her to her feet, he thought her the most alluring female he'd ever known.

"Perhaps some time, you can show me what you can cook."

Her lips parted questioningly, as her gaze sought his, trying to determine his shifting mood perhaps.

With a groan, he slid his fingers into her perfectly coiffed hair and held her lovely face still. Lowering his mouth to Miss Sudbury's, he claimed her luscious lips, trying to remain gentle, but feeling voracious, wanting to taste her—*all of her!*—at once.

She didn't protest. If she'd so much as gasped, he would have withdrawn immediately. But she touched his tongue with her own before leaning into him.

Releasing her sweet cheeks, Jasper swept his hands down her back and took hold of her other ones, her soft, rounded nether globes. With his palms, he tilted her hips against his strained breeches so she could feel his arousal.

Her frank innocence, which she yielded willingly to him, was his undoing. She would probably let him take her on the damn table exactly as he'd fantasized. Sucking her lower lip between his teeth, he heard her make the softest mewling sound and wanted to fall at her feet.

The feet of a vicar's daughter.

Damn him for a shameless satyr, a hell-hound of the first order!

He lurched back as if she were the hottest flame.

"I apologize. That was not well done of me." He ran a hand through his hair, trying to figure out which way his thoughts and his body were going next. He'd never felt so torn in his adult life. If she were any other woman, he would not have stopped. Moreover, he wasn't at all sure why he had.

All he knew was he felt, perhaps for the first time, like a scoundrel. And he didn't like it one bit. Worse, she seemed utterly willing to let herself be ruined by him. Her lack of self-preservation simply didn't sit well. That was probably the true reason why he'd felt the need to stop.

If she'd been the least simpering or coy, he would have known her for a flirt. Then, the game would have been afoot for sure. Instead, she seemed like a lamb wobbling unknowingly to the slaughter.

"I must be on my way," he said, surprising himself.

By the look upon her face, he'd baffled her, too.

"I intended to serve port in the drawing room, my lord, unless you're in a hurry."

If he stayed, he would continue to make further, bolder advances upon her, and apparently, she would let him.

What if Lady Worthington returned in the middle of it? Even if she was staying the night elsewhere, the notion of simply indulging himself by taking to Miss Sudbury's bed until dawn, much as he would relish it, seemed beyond the pale even for him. She was not the caliber of his usual conquests.

No, she was far above it! She had the aura of decency clinging to her. *Dammit!*

"It has been a most enjoyable evening, but I really should be getting home. Parliamentary session starts early in the morning."

Looking as if she could see right through his paltry excuse, the chit smiled at him.

"I know you take your duties seriously, so I will detain you no longer. You must need a good night's rest in order to sit in the House of Lords and listen to men drone on."

She turned from him, and he hoped she wasn't offended after all. Surely, she must know how much he wanted her.

"I'll get Mr. Dawson to retrieve your things."

He nearly stopped her but didn't. *What kind of rake turned down a woman's offer for port by the fireplace in the drawing room?*

A bloody stupid one!

JULIA SAT ON THE end of her bed, in her nightgown and slippers, contemplating the evening and Marshfield's strange behavior. He probably considered her own to be equally strange. Mayhap that had caused his hurried departure.

She rather believed it was because he had qualms about seducing her, which meant he had a conscience and might not be the dreadful dog everyone, including Sarah, believed him to be.

Lying back on the counterpane, she stared at the rose-colored canopy above her.

Drat! Having been more than ready to leave the last vestiges of youthful innocence behind her—and at the hands of an experienced lover—it was a let-down to be still entirely intact. At least she could be assured of his desire for her. That had been evident in his kiss and in his breeches.

All in all, it was probably for the better. This way, they could continue on an even footing—dancing, flirting, kissing. She imagined once the wicked deed was done, their association would necessarily change. Either he would be satiated and end any blossoming friendship for fear she might grow attached to him, or they would in fact grow closer and, indeed, her heart would become involved. Most likely it would get bruised by him, too.

That didn't mean she intended to stop. A bruised heart seemed worth it when a man kissed the way he did. Moreover, his hands had roamed her body and grabbed her bottom.

She threw her arm over her face at the memory. The earl had wrapped his fingers around her arse and held it. What's more, he'd pressed her against him, and she'd felt his hardened manhood. *What if they'd actually tupped, either upon her sister's sofa or in her bedroom?*

Julia couldn't help grinning as her whole body tingled at the thought.

She couldn't deny she still hoped such an experience was not too far in the future.

ANOTHER LAVISH DANCE, AND while Julia was prepared to venture upstairs and relieve the host and hostess of a few dazzlers, she was lagging in the ballroom with Mrs. Zebodar, hoping to see Lord Marshfield. It had been nearly a week since their intimate dinner, and she'd given up waiting for a note from him with a cordial invitation for some outing. After all, they didn't have an arrangement.

Still, Julia had hoped she was somehow special and had to take herself to task for such a silly notion. Every woman must think that exact same way, which meant none of them were special at all. *Ninny-pated fool!*

His last association in the papers had been with the young lady she'd encountered briefly at the earl's dinner party. And according to the gossip rags, they'd been seen having heated words at Lady Pritchard's ball.

When Julia crossed paths again with the earl, no doubt he would welcome her with his attractive smile and ask her for a dance. In the meanwhile, she tamped down her disappointment.

Eventually, she let a partner lead her to the polished floor, then begged off with a torn hem and disappeared from the ballroom, just as before. It worked as easily as the many times prior, and she found herself passing through the Viscountess Chandron's bedroom to her dressing room.

A beautiful woman, it was reputed she cuckolded her husband regularly, and many of the more debauched aristocrats had been reported to take a good slice of her. Of course, as Sarah pointed out, the accounts in the meanest pages of the papers, slyly or openly cutting down those considered to be members of the *bon ton,* were all brutally embellished and exaggerated.

For all Julia knew, the lady might live the life of a nun. Yet she glanced at the large bed as she passed it by, and the stark image of Lord Marshfield entangled in the sheets with Lady Chandron brought forth a sting of jealousy.

A nasty, unfamiliar emotion!

Frowning, Julia made her way through the open door to the dressing room and immediately spied a jewelry box. Making quick work of it, she took an emerald brooch, only because there were two of them, and then reached for a sapphire bracelet that made her think of Lord Marshfield's cravat pin.

Hesitating for the briefest moment, she slid this into her reticule as well. Deciding two such pieces were enough for one night's work, she left the chamber, passed through the bedroom, trying not to think of a particular man grabbing a woman's buttocks that weren't hers, and popped into the hallway.

"Here now, what are you doing?"

Julia froze. While her thoughts had been consumed with the earl, she hadn't even peeked out and looked in either direction. And she'd stepped directly into someone's path.

Turning toward the voice, she saw it was the Viscount Chandron himself.

Even worse!

All at once the weight of the two pieces of his wife's jewelry dragged her reticule down from her wrist, and she was certain it looked suspicious.

With her heart beating a fast tattoo, she fixed on a friendly smile as the man closed the space between them. When he stopped in front of her, she gave a respectful curtsy. When she rose, his gaze was firmly locked upon her cleavage.

"You have a lovely home, my lord," she said, getting his attention. "Unfortunately, it is larger than what I am used to. I became quite turned around and lost."

His face was a stone façade. In comparison to his stunning wife, he was plain at best. Some might even go so far as to say he gave the impression of a toad.

Unfortunate. While a lack of good looks was no reason for adultery, and she considered marriage vows to be sacred, Julia could sympathize a little with the man's wife.

"Lost, are you?" he said with a sneer. "Let me see if I can help you. That's a bedroom." He indicated the door beside them. "*Not* a ballroom, which is one floor down."

"Of course." She didn't care for his disparaging tone. "You see, I had a tear in the hem of my gown and went down to the ground floor seeking assistance. When I climbed the stairs, naturally, I was looking at your magnificent art collection. I went up too far without even noticing. I won't bother you another minute."

Dropping again into a curtsy, Julia rose and turned at the same time.

Quick as a whip, his hand reached out and grabbed her arm, brushing the side of her breast as he did.

"Are you sure you weren't meeting someone here for a tryst?"

Frowning back at him, she shook her head. "No, sir."

"My wife," he said the word as if it were an unpleasantly bitter brew, "often enjoys the company of both men *and* women in her bed."

Julia swallowed. It wasn't her business, nor did she care, but the viscount seemed put out. Perhaps if he'd been invited to be one of the participants, he would be more tolerant.

"I assure you, sir, I wasn't here to meet your wife."

"Are you titled?" he demanded.

"No, my lord. But my—"

"Are you the daughter of a member of the nobility?" he persisted.

"No, sir. I am—"

"Good. It's tedious when one gets into hot water with someone who has a whit of power." In a flash, he'd opened his wife's bedroom door and shoved Julia inside, slamming it closed behind them.

"How dare you!" she raged. At the same time, a snake of fear slithered through her, and being caught stealing jewels had become the least of her problems.

CHAPTER EIGHT

"Lord M__ was seen coming down the stairs from the
private rooms of Lady Chandron during the ball.
Speculation rippled through the other guests. And where
was Lord Chandron during this time?"

—The Gazette

The traffic in London was becoming more of a
nightmare every year. The population had doubled
since Jasper's birth, or so his mother was always
complaining, and it was reputed to be the largest city in the
world. At that moment, he believed it, and every infernal
citizen was out in his carriage clogging Mayfair and
preventing him from getting to the ball.

He rapped on the roof with his cane. The carriage was
stopped anyway, so Rigley jumped down and came to the
window.

"Yes, my lord?"

"Where are we?"

"New Bond Street, sir. Probably another half an hour by
the look of it."

"Thirty more minutes! That's outrageous. Step aside."
As soon as his footman was clear, Jasper shoved the carriage

door open with annoyance and jumped to the street. "I'll be there in seven."

Striding along toward Piccadilly in the evening fog and chill, he felt good passing the rest of London's elite, as they sat thwarted in their attempt to get anywhere. Glancing at the doorway of Gentleman Jackson's Boxing Academy of which he was a long-standing member, Jasper strolled past and, as he'd expected, was mounting the steps to the Chandrons' house in less than ten minutes.

Leaving his coat and hat with the greeter, he went up a flight of stairs, keeping his eyes open for his blonde, blue-eyed favorite female. Normally, he wouldn't attend a party at this particular residence, having had a brief affair with the viscountess two years prior, which ended abruptly when she announced she wished to leave her husband for Jasper.

With any luck, he wouldn't even see his hosts. And after a week of dry discussions with other members of Parliament forming alliances before its November opening, he was nearly giddy at the notion of seeing Miss Sudbury again.

Within a very few minutes, however, he was dismayed by his inability to find her. There was probably another party going on in Town, but the Chandrons' was the foremost one for the week. The choice of events was becoming fewer as many had left London already for their country estates, some staying away until springtime.

Just when he feared Miss Sudbury was across town eating roasted pheasant at a small dinner gathering, he suddenly spied Mrs. Zebodar, and his spirits soared. If the dragon was there, so was her charge.

Knowing better than to alert her chaperone that he was on the hunt, he went to the terrace and did a quick surveil. She wasn't outside, snd the garden was too small and brightly lit by flaming torches to conceal lovers.

Thank God! The notion, of her enjoying a kiss with some fop who didn't deserve her gnawed at his gut.

Back indoors, Jasper crossed the parquet, his jacket flying out behind him, and then he did what he wouldn't do previously. He made a conspicuous ass of himself in front of the retiring room set up for the ladies.

"Is there a fair-haired woman in there?" he asked the first female who came out.

"No, my lord."

"Are you certain?"

"Yes. I promise you. Only two with hair as brown as mine and one of red." She left him standing there.

He couldn't very well call out her name, but he could confirm the information.

"Is a blonde woman therein?"

He heard giggling but no response. Sighing, he supposed he ought to return to the ballroom and wait.

"GET ON THE BED," Lord Chandron said, his voice neutral, sounding almost bored. "And draw up your skirts."

"I beg your pardon." Julia had been wondering how she would get around him, but his quiet tone scared her more than if he'd been shouting loudly. He was entirely too sure of himself.

"You are a common mopsey, and while I'm used to better, I am in need of relief. Do as I say, or I shall tear off your gown, and then you will have to go downstairs in disgrace."

Curtsying to this monster had clearly been a mistake, she thought.

"If I go downstairs with my dress torn, everyone will know you are a beast for I shall scream it at the top of my lungs."

He shrugged. "I've weathered worse. Easy enough to vow you came up here and lured me with your wiles, probably in order to blackmail me. After all, we both know you were up to no good, although I'm not sure what."

She remained motionless. The viscount couldn't seriously imagine she was going to acquiesce and let him have sexual relations with her, merely because he was a member of the nobility and a bully.

He took a step toward her. "Hurry up, or I shall lose my patience. After all, if you aren't titled, you shouldn't even be at my party. Therefore, you must pay for the champagne you've had at my expense. And I intend to exact compensation."

She considered locking herself in the dressing room until he grew tired of tormenting her. To that end, she took a couple steps in the direction of the only other door in the room. Unfortunately, it took her closer to the bed.

"Good girl." With those words, he released the fall front of his breeches, and his shaft sprung free.

She screamed before she even realized she was doing so, unable to take her eyes from her first live view of the male organ.

"No one else is on this floor," he warned, "except servants, and they won't help you."

Suddenly, with wings for feet, she rushed to the dressing room door, nearly managing to open it before he crashed into her from behind. Feeling herself flung in an arc, she landed on her back on the edge of the viscountess's bed. In the next instant, Lord Chandron had lifted her skirts and was between her legs so she couldn't close them.

"My sister is a countess," Julia hissed.

He hesitated for the briefest of moments, then his fingers were at the juncture where the legs of her winter drawers met. Wearing them was a practice considered coarse by some, but they kept her warm. Moreover, she was glad of even their scant protection as he sought to find her intimate channel.

"Probably a lie, and no matter really. Any type of person," he paused as he pressed his erection to her most sensitive, private area, "seems to marry into the nobility these days. Whores, even."

Bucking and pushing at him, Julia screamed again.

"Hold still!" he ordered as if he were commanding a servant to do his bidding.

Writhing, she screamed again. To her amazement, the door burst open, although she couldn't see past the brute. It didn't matter. Regardless of who had found her, her reputation would be ruined but her virtue saved!

"Get out!" the viscount called over his shoulder, and since he was master of the house, she assumed the person would do as he ordered.

"Help!" she yelled, in any case, hoping even a servant might take pity and come to her aid.

She heard a roar of outrage before, quite abruptly, the viscount was jerked away, seeming to fly off her as if he weighed nothing at all. Frantically, she lowered her skirts and looked up to see the furious face of the Earl of Marshfield.

She'd heard the term "eyes flashing in anger" yet had never seen such a thing until that moment.

"Get up," he growled, as if she were resting there on a lazy Sunday.

Julia scrambled to her feet. The most important thing at that instant was to get out of the room where she'd been alone with a man and back where others could see her.

"Marshfield!" exclaimed the viscount, when Julia had already reached the door. Staggering to his feet, the man was doing up the buttons of his breeches. "That was a monstrous pitch and quite out of place, too!"

Glancing at her savior, the earl's jaw was tight as an archer's bow and both his hands were clenched.

"If you wanted the bitch," Lord Chandron continued, "you ought to have had the decency to wait your turn. Host's privilege and all—"

Before he could finish, Marshfield had grabbed him by the cravat and landed a hard blow to his toady face. The viscount's head flopped back, but his limp body remained suspended by his cravat.

"You are a disgrace," the earl ground out before allowing the man to slip to the floor. Then he nodded curtly to her to precede him from the room.

Needing no further entreaty, Julia wrenched open the door. However, having learned her lesson earlier, she peeked out, searching the hall in both directions. It was empty. Slipping out, she ran for the stairs.

"Wait," Marshfield ordered, and although she desperately wanted to get as far away from Lord Chandron as possible, she halted at his command, realizing she was shaking.

"You can't walk into the ballroom like that," he said from behind her. "Your dress isn't too terrible, but your hair looks like you've been doing exactly what you were, rolling around on your back."

Nerves taut, Julia turned around and slapped his cheek. Then she gasped.

"I'm sorry," she whispered even though he said nothing, nor even looked as if he'd felt it. "It's just . . . ," she trailed off. "I want to go home."

"I cannot accompany you down the stairs. If someone were to see us, your reputation would be ruined as surely as if you were discovered on that bed. I'll go first and if anyone's loitering about, I'll send them away. You're adept at sneaking around," he added, and she felt like crying at having lost his good opinion of her.

"Slip into the ladies' retiring room and get the maid there to assist with your hair. They do that sort of thing, don't they?"

"Yes." Her voice had lost all its strength, so she nodded, too.

"Would you like me to alert your chaperone and bring her to you? She must be frantic with worry." His tone was unfriendly, and she'd never seen his mouth tight with anger.

All because of her. This was no game, and she'd nearly been the victim of something truly awful. And Mrs. Zebodar would never have forgiven herself, neither would Sarah.

"No." She straightened and took a deep breath. "If you see her looking for me, please tell her I'll be in the ballroom shortly."

He didn't acknowledge her words. "Wait a few seconds for me to make sure it's clear." He glanced back at the viscountess's bedroom door. "Unless that door opens, in which case, run downstairs as if the devil himself is chasing you."

With that, he descended quickly. She shivered, and the skin at the back of her neck was prickling. Julia started after him, probably too soon, but she was terrified of staying where she was in case the viscount did emerge.

Luckily, there was only Marshfield's broad rigid back at one end of the hall, and between them, the ladies' retiring room. He barely glanced her way but seemed to be waiting for her to get to safety before he returned to the ballroom.

Wishing he would send her a compassionate look while knowing he wouldn't, Julia entered the sanctuary to seek assistance.

When she returned to the ballroom, she had gathered her emotions and her wits and hoped she looked wholly respectable. Crossing to where her chaperone awaited, she couldn't help searching for the earl.

"You took so long getting your hem fixed, or was it your hair?" Mrs. Zebodar asked, frowning as she scrutinized the slightly different coiffure done by the viscountess's maid. Then the woman shook her head. "As I said, you took so long, two partners have been over here grumbling at your absence.

Pasting on a smile, Julia said, "One cannot dance with a loose hem. By any chance, did the Earl of Marshfield speak with you?"

"Yes, looking quite grim tonight. When I expressed concern at your absence, he said he'd noticed you entering the retiring room."

"That was kind of him to ease your mind. I would like to reward him with a dance."

"Impossible," Mrs. Zebodar said. "He left immediately after speaking with me. I saw him depart."

"I see." Obviously her voice had betrayed some emotion, for her chaperone gave her a second look.

"Come, my girl. Don't set your cap at that one. The earl is the last person a nice young woman like yourself should sigh after. He may have just done you a kindness, but he is a rake through and through, and would as soon take advantage of you as not."

Julia knew that to be a lie but bit her tongue.

"I have a terrible megrim."

Her chaperone's eyes opened wide. "Truly?"

"Yes." In fact, her temples were starting to throb. "Luckily, I didn't speak with many gentlemen tonight so only one or two will be disappointed if we leave." She glanced down at her reticule—or where it should be. Her wrist was bare! And there was only one place the bag could be.

On the Viscountess of Chandron's bed!

CHAPTER NINE

"Lord M__ was seen entering the Hanover Square home
of Lady W__ AGAIN this week! Is it possible the two are
coming to some understanding? Or is our rakish earl
merely enjoying a widow's company without being caught
in a parson's mousetrap?"

—The Morning Post

Earlier than usual for polite society, at half past eleven in the morning, Jasper had his driver stop outside the Worthington house. His footman delivered his card with the message he was waiting outside. Although knowing it was rude to drop by uninvited and demand an audience—not to mention announce one's intent to wait in one's carriage—neither infraction of civility deterred him for a moment.

He knew, if home, Miss Sudbury would agree to see him.

Within minutes, he was standing in the deceased earl's drawing room. He was struck by how recently he'd been there, sharing a kiss with her. Yet, it also seemed as if it were long ago when he still thought her a delightful innocent.

He paced the room. Old Worthington's young widow wasn't wasting his money on redecorating, for it looked a little dated if not shabby unlike the homes of many of his peers, who were forever changing the décor in order to be utterly *pink of the mode.*

Yet it was comfortable and strangely full of little bunches of flowers. More posies in one place than he'd ever seen outside a flower stall littered the surfaces. He might have noticed a few scattered around when he'd been invited to dinner, yet his attention had been all on Miss Sudbury.

Glancing at the sofa, he recalled exactly how comfortable it had been when he'd had her in his arms.

And then the door opened, and she entered.

He let her curtsy, thinking it a little too deep at this stage. Moreover, her demure gown didn't afford him a view of her cleavage, not with some dreadful filmy thing lying across her décolletage. Ridiculous waste of a fine bosom, which, in his opinion, ought to always be on show for men to admire as much as decently possible. Elsewise, why be a beautiful woman with such splendid breasts?

Bowing shallowly in return, he nearly apologized for showing up unexpectedly but restrained himself. After all, the last time he'd barged in on her, her skirts were up and a man was trying to—

"Are you well?" he asked into the silence.

"Yes, thank you. And you?"

Jasper frowned. He'd been referring to her experience of the night before, not a general inquiry into her health. *Was she going to play coy?* It didn't suit her, nor would he allow it. Best to get right to the crux of the matter.

"Why were you upstairs last night, in the Chandrons' private space?"

She looked taken aback, as if not expecting him to question her behavior. In truth, he had no right. It wasn't his place, but he doubted she had told her sister of such a harrowing scrape. And with her useless chaperone, there was no guarantee it wasn't going to happen again if she were a careless rattle pate.

"I had a slight tear in the hem of my gown," she began.

"You nearly had a larger tear," he reminded her.

She paled at his crude meaning but continued, "Because of my hem, I went to find a maid. Often in the cloakroom or the retiring room, there is a maid to assist."

"Not upstairs in the private area of the host's home," Jasper pointed out.

"True, but I'd been climbing the stairs slowly, appreciating the artwork. I suppose I got distracted. Next thing I knew, I had gone up one floor too many."

She sounded like a simpleton. Moreover, she must think him to be one as well, to offer him such rubbish.

"And while distracted, you found yourself underneath Chandron on his wife's bed with his stiff member about to—"

"Stop," she commanded. "I know where I was and what he was about to do."

"Did you invite it?" He couldn't stop himself from asking, hoping he could tell if she was lying. After all, she might have enticed the man, hoping for a token the way she'd asked him in his bedroom, and then with Chandron, it had got out of her control.

"No!" she declared.

He believed her, maybe for his own sake because he didn't like to think he'd been wrong. Moreover, if she were such a loose cat, he would have been a fool for not taking what she'd seemed willing to give during their private dinner.

"Did you kiss him the way we did when I found you in my bedroom?"

Instead of more color draining away, her cheeks darkened immediately. Surely a blush was a good sign. She still had some sense of decency.

"No," she said again, more quietly. "He didn't try."

"If he had?" Again, Jasper was demanding answers to which he had no right to know.

"It would have been easier to fend him off, I imagine, and then I wouldn't have ended up in that predicament. Most women know a good thrust to a man's private area with her knee will unman him long enough so she can escape."

It was his turn to pale. He didn't know young ladies knew about such things, but it was good they did, he supposed.

"That knowledge did you no good once you were on your back."

"True." She stared at the carpet. "Once he stepped close . . . between my legs, I was trapped."

"That you were," he agreed, opening his mouth to ask again how she ended up in a bedroom with the lecherous Chandron.

Just as Jasper knew the viscountess was as easily had as Custom House goods—had experienced her first-hand—he and the rest of the *ton* knew the viscount was a boorish cad. Because of his behavior, he couldn't keep his female servants, nor a mistress.

"I ought to think about carrying a Queen Anne's pistol, don't you think?" Miss Sudbury said, coming a few steps closer before changing course to take a seat.

He gaped at the notion of her with a small weapon that might inadvertently discharge at any moment.

"No, I think you ought to stay with your chaperone or in your dining room chair or on the dance floor. If you hadn't been roaming the private floors, then you wouldn't have ended up in such a pucker."

"That's true," she agreed. And she said no more.

"Do you expect me to believe you found something so interesting amongst Chandron's paltry collection of tepid landscapes that you ended up in his wife's chamber?" he asked.

"Not at all. He pushed me in there and shut the door. Quite a churl, if I do say so."

He had the urge to punch the man in the face, and then remembered he'd already done so. If given the opportunity, Jasper would do it again, too.

"A *churl* seems rather mild. Thank God you screamed. I heard your shout and came running. Yet when I opened the door, at first, I thought it was an honest tupping with a willing woman."

She was silent for a moment.

"What were *you* doing upstairs?" she asked, at last, her eyes wide.

"Looking for you," he confessed before thinking better of it.

Her expression changed in a blink. She smiled, and his heart seemed to skip a beat. Then Miss Sudbury jumped up and rushed at him, causing him to clasp her in his arms before she knocked him over.

"Oh, sir! You were like a knight of yesteryear. I was in such a state last night, I am not sure if I even thanked you properly."

"Thanked him for what?" came an unfamiliar voice. "And, by the way, Marshfield, take your hands off my sister."

JULIA SIGHED AND STEPPED away from the earl, who looked entirely unruffled by being caught holding her. She supposed keeping his cool was a practiced talent.

Turning to Sarah, whose head had appeared around the door followed by the rest of her, Julia asked, "Are you properly acquainted with the Earl of Marshfield?"

"No, not personally," Sarah said, coming to stand shoulder to shoulder with Julia, staring up frankly at the earl.

Lord Marshfield, playing the perfect gentleman, took her sister's hand and bowed over it before releasing it promptly.

"Lady Worthington, you are looking well."

"Am I?" asked Sarah.

Julia wanted to elbow her for being even the slightest bit rude after how he'd saved her from ruin the night before. But she could never say that.

"By the way," the earl added, "in case any nasty rumors are about to start or I am to be badgered into marriage for being found alone with your sister, Miss Sudbury's hands were on me and not the other way around."

Julia couldn't help smiling at his defense.

"*Hm*," Sarah said. "From what I understand, being alone with a young woman and declaring yourself wholly innocent of any wrongdoing are nothing new for you."

Julia rolled her eyes at her sister's overprotectiveness. It was broad daylight and they had been standing in the middle of the drawing room. Not even on the sofa where mischief could certainly occur, as she was well aware.

Regardless, willingly, Julia backed him up. "It's true. The fault is mine. I was being overly enthusiastic."

"Yes, you were," Sarah said, a frown on her forehead. "Why? What *were* you thanking his lordship for?"

Julia caught her lip. The last thing she wanted to do was delve into the previous evening's misfortune. Sarah would guess instantly what she'd been doing on the upper floor as they'd discussed it at length before. Then her sister would know Julia was still attempting to be Robin Hood.

Into the hesitation, Lord Marshfield spoke. "We were at the same ball last night. Her chaperone was concerned about her, but since I had noticed Miss Sudbury going into the ladies' retiring room, I mentioned it to . . . Mrs. Zebodar, isn't it?"

"Yes," Sarah said, sounding doubtful.

"Otherwise," Julia chimed in, "she was ready to call out the Bow Street Runners. Besides, she would have been terribly cross at my disappearance and probably wouldn't want to accompany me to any more balls, not even to Almack's."

"You've never had an interest in Almack's," Sarah reminded her.

Julia realized she might have laid the marmalade on a bit thickly. Her sister was right, however. Since her present purpose was neither to dance nor to find a husband, and as there were no unattended jewels at the assembly hall on King Street, Almack's held absolutely no enticement for her. Not that she would qualify for a coveted ticket in any case.

"I shall take my leave," the earl said, obviously wanting to escape before any brewing tension became a messy argument.

It was Sarah's place as mistress of the house to urge him to stay. Naturally, she didn't. And Julia didn't either. She still hadn't answered him as to why she truly was on the Chandrons' private floor, and she had no intention of doing so. Besides, at any moment, Sarah would ask why the earl had dropped by.

Glancing at Lord Marshfield, she urged him to speed away.

Too late! Sarah was still questioning.

"Did you come all this distance in order to receive an earnest thank you from my sister? And what demonstration of gratitude might you be hoping for?"

"Sarah," Julia said sharply. Then tried to soften her tone. "His lordship has kindly invited me to . . . to . . . ," trailing off, she looked again at the earl for assistance.

"I came by to invite Miss Sudbury to Lord's Cricket Ground," came his swift reply.

"The what?" both girls asked in unison before Julia recalled she was supposed to already have been invited.

Recovering quickly, Julia nodded enthusiastically. "Yes," she declared. "Cricket! At Lord's in . . ."

"St. John's Wood," the earl supplied. "It recently opened. Perhaps you would like to join us, countess?"

"Maybe I will," Sarah said, although not sounding thrilled by the prospect.

"You would be welcome in my carriage," Lord Marshfield insisted with generosity.

Having mollified her, he bowed toward them each in turn and took his leave.

Sarah waited until they heard Mr. Dawson close the front door. Then she turned her bright blue eyes upon Julia.

"Well?" she demanded. "What was that really about?"

"I'm going to watch a cricket match, and apparently you are, too. Won't that be fun? Simply two sisters out with . . . ," Julia trailed off. "Well, I suppose it will be like when Father took us on an outing."

Sarah pursed her lips, looking concerned. "Marshfield is not anything like Father. And if you are of the opinion that man," she pointed toward the open door, "of whom I've read eye-blistering accounts of bad behavior is suddenly going to let you put a collar around his neck and lead him like a trained monkey, you are mistaken."

"It's just a cricket match, dear sister." And with that, Julia left Sarah mounted high upon her righteous horse and went upstairs. Quite possibly, tales of the earl's antics were greatly exaggerated in order to sell newspapers. At least, she hoped so.

Once in her room, she went back to fretting over the lost reticule. If Sarah hadn't barged in, Julia might have asked Lord Marshfield for his help, although what precisely he could do, she wasn't certain. When found and examined, as it had surely been by then, the reticule would have yielded damning evidence of thievery.

The latter fact had caused an ache in Julia's stomach all night. Every moment, she expected some sort of repercussion from her careless actions, although no one could know the bag was hers except the despicable viscount. *Would Lord Chandron say anything, considering his egregious attack?*

A knock on her door caused her to jump to her feet, yet it was merely the maid with a letter delivered a minute earlier by a footman.

Dear Miss Sudbury,

It seems we are going to a cricket match together. The weather promises to be good in two days, and I shall be at your Hanover Square home at one o'clock unless I hear back that such a time and day do not suit. Dress for the outdoors.

If your sister does not accompany us, please secure a suitable chaperone.

I look forward to seeing you again. I am, as ever, at your service.
Yours truly,
Marshfield

A smile spread over her face, and she clasped the note to her chest before she gave it a perfunctory sniff.

Her smile grew. The notepaper smelled like him, although she hadn't realized he even had a scent until his delightful cologne tickled her nose and reminded her of being in his arms. Predictably sandalwood, but with a more surprising aroma of juniper. Now, she would never forget it.

What's more, she now had something to show Sarah, transforming her fib into the truth. And the earl had impressed the need for a chaperone. All the better! It helped to distract her from the loss of the reticule.

Just before dinner, while Sarah and Julia were talking in the parlor, another footman arrived.

"Something more from the earl, do you think?" Sarah asked. "Maybe reneging on the invitation or wondering if he can bring his latest mistress."

Julia winced but looked with curiosity when the butler brought in a small bundle wrapped in coarse paper, as one would for a hunk of fish or meat. Despite its strange appearance, Mr. Dawson had put it on his usual silver tray upon which he brought in visiting cards and other missives.

"For you, my lady," he intoned, holding it out to Sarah, seated on the sofa, before disappearing as swiftly as a cat.

They both stared at the package on Sarah's lap, and then Julia set down her glass of claret and scooted closer.

"A gift maybe?" she guessed. "From *your* Lord Denbigh." She wiggled her eyebrows, teasing her.

Even if the man truly was a Bow Street hound as Lord Marshfield had indicated, if he made her sister happy, then Julia would simply figure out how to steer clear of him.

In any case, ever since Sarah's evening alone with Lord Denbigh, she'd been behaving strangely. Melancholy one moment, then devil-may-care the next.

Her sister merely shrugged, ignoring Julia's guess, as she undid the string and unwrapped the brown paper.

Julia gasped at the sight of her lost reticule, particularly when Sarah was suddenly holding it in her hands.

"I haven't used this purse in ages." Then her sister cocked her head. "Didn't I lend it to you last year?"

"Yes," Julia whispered, her heart pounding as Sarah began to open the drawstring.

CHAPTER TEN

"Today at the new Lord's Cricket Ground, Marylebone
Cricket Club played St. John's Wood Club. Quality folk
were rubbing elbows with the commoners. Lord M__
escorted two well-known females of his acquaintance, and
Lady Ch__ was there with friends of both sexes.
Marylebone handed St. John's a defeat!"

—The Times

"How strange." Sarah murmured, examining the
purse. "It's empty, except for this."
Julia held her breath, but the only thing her sister drew
out of the reticule was the handkerchief Julia had tucked
inside before attending the Chandrons' ball.
"No, not so strange," Julia said, as soon as she could
breathe again. "I left the bag by mistake in the ladies' retiring
room at the ball last night."
"You should be more careful," Sarah said, handing it to
her. "What if you'd had something valuable in there?"
Julia tried to laugh, but it sounded to her ears like
wheezing.
"What would I possibly take to a ball that was valuable?"
She glanced at the ruby ring on her right hand and shook it

before her sister's nose. "You know this is the only thing I own of any value, and I never take it off."

They both had a single piece of jewelry from their long-deceased mother. Even then, Sarah wore her ruby pendant on a silver chain around her neck.

"Nothing, I suppose. Maybe you might take an ivory comb."

"If someone needed to take a comb from my reticule," Julia stated, "he or she would be welcome to it."

"He?" Sarah said, and they giggled

Luckily, dinner was announced, and Sarah dropped the matter, saying nothing more about it that night and clearly suspecting nothing. It appeared as though a kind guest from the ball had returned the bag to its rightful owner.

However, Julia lay awake with a sense of unease. Who had found the bag, the lascivious viscount after he'd picked himself up off the floor or his wife when she'd retired for the evening?

Moreover, the finder had assumed the small purse belonged to the Countess of Worthington. At first, Julia couldn't imagine why. And then she remembered. While she had no visiting cards of her own, a couple of her sister's cards had been in the bag, and Julia had never had a reason to remove them.

"Dear God!" she whispered. *What if someone accused Sarah?*

JASPER HAD NO WAY of knowing whether he would be escorting only Julia or both sisters. It was all the same to him. He enjoyed watching cricket, and the weather, as promised, was fair without call for rain. Even if he did nothing more than sit amiably with two lovely ladies and drink a cup of lemonade, it would be a day well spent.

As it turned out, it *was* both sisters.

"I've decided to accept your kind invitation to join you," the countess told him as both females adjusted their hats and tucked parasols under their arms to ward off the sun. "After all, cricket is becoming the national pastime."

Tapping his hat, he gestured for the door. The capable butler whipped it open, and they were on their way.

"Are either of you familiar with cricket teams?" he asked as his carriage got rolling toward St. John's Wood. Their blank stares gave him his answer. "Today's match is between Marylebone Cricket Club and St. John's Wood Club."

"Does the latter always play there?" Julia asked.

"No, the former does," he said.

Both ladies frowned. "Why doesn't the Marylebone Cricket Club play in Marylebone?" Miss Sudbury asked.

"They used to. They've been around since . . . oh, the late 1780s, I believe," he told them, trying to tamp down his enthusiasm, but fearing he would start to bore them with his facts and figures. "They had a place previously, not far away in Dorset Fields in Marylebone, hence the name. But now they're at St John's."

The countess raised an eyebrow and looked at her sister. "And where does St. John's Wood Cricket Club call home? Paris?"

He offered a wry smile, but before he could answer, Miss Sudbury asked, "Is the arena called Lord's because it is the sport of noblemen?"

At this, he laughed loudly. "Not at all. Anyone can enjoy cricket. The grounds are named for Thomas Lord, the owner. This is his third site, actually. After Dorset Fields, he moved his cricket grounds just a few streets over to the north end of Lisson Grove, but the canal—"

"The Regent's Canal?" the countess interrupted. "I was most interested in its development."

"I think everyone with an interest in progress is watching its development," Jasper agreed. "A fine piece of engineering. It will be eight miles when completed. You can buy shares, you know. I highly recommend you do so. One stands to make a tidy profit. Another two years, I warrant, and the first part will be open to traffic. Imagine the speedy progress of goods and people across town by way of the canal. Most exciting."

"I imagine Mr. Lord was not quite so excited," Miss Sudbury guessed.

"Correct," Jasper said. "His Middle Grounds had barely opened when he had to close them by order of Parliament. I must hand it to the man. He's getting up there in years. Must be in his sixties, but he picked himself up and relocated his cricket grounds again."

Jasper was looking forward to showing them everything and to experience watching a game for the first time, something he couldn't recall, as his father had always brought him to matches, and he had no memory of his first.

When they arrived, there were already people on the few benches dotted around opposite the pavilion, and others stood in small groups. A few men on horseback were keeping their mounts still while affording themselves a grand view.

Jasper's footman unloaded three folding chairs and carried them to a preferable spot. He felt rather proud as the ladies exclaimed over them.

"All the soldiers used them in France. Very handy," he agreed. "I took the liberty of having my cook pack a picnic, although there are refreshment stalls." He pointed them out across the field. "I didn't know if the fare would be up to your standards. I hope the food I brought is acceptable."

To his bemusement, both Miss Sudbury and the countess began to laugh heartily. Finally, Miss Sudbury wiped her eyes.

"That is rich, sir."

"Is it?" he asked, studying her sweetly pink cheeks and sparkling eyes. "How so?"

The object of his interest looked at her sister, then back at him.

"I'm sure we were both thinking of the picnics we had as youngsters, consisting of a bread, cheese, and an apple. We used to pretend it was a feast just for fun."

"In that case, I am sure you will be delighted by my cook's idea of picnic food. Also, there are proper facilities in the pavilion, and if your parasols aren't protection enough for your fair skin, we can always go in there to get a break from the sun."

With the three of them settled down and drinking barley water, the match began. Almost at once, Jasper was kept busy answering their questions about the rules. He explained who the favored players were, identified old Mr. Lord at one end, watching as he always did, and soon had the women cheering at the correct moment of play.

The only blight was when he had to ask the men beside him to keep it down for becoming rowdy.

"There are ladies present," he said, sending them a quelling glare.

"There shouldn't be," one said, and Jasper handed his glass to Rigley who stood by his elbow before rising to his feet. In two steps, he was nose-to-nose with the lout.

"And why not? Don't you think I would rather keep company with their beauty than have to look at your homely visage?"

A younger man next to him started to laugh. "He's got you there, Will. You are a muffin-faced squab, you must admit!"

The squab in question turned red in his muffin-face, but then he glanced past Jasper to the ladies whom he knew were watching.

"Apologize for being loud," Jasper ordered him. "And tell them they are most welcome at Lord's."

The man hesitated, but then he sniffed and tugged his jacket.

"My apologies, ladies, for my rough language. And it's . . . it's nice to see you here."

His younger friend broke out into gales of laughter, but Jasper was satisfied and backed down.

They were treated to several guest players for the match, although this meant nothing to the Sudbury sisters, as he'd come to think of them under his protection. The rest of the afternoon was spent enjoyably. Everything in the picnic basket—the pigeon pie and cold lamb, bread and jam, and currant cakes—was perfectly acceptable. Declared a fine feast, indeed.

As he hoped, Marylebone Cricket Club beat St. John's by four wickets. When they packed up, about to head toward the carriage at the edge of the field, suddenly, another merry party crossed their path. To Jasper's dismay, by surprising coincidence, the Viscountess Chandron, overly dressed and most would say inappropriately so for the time of day, was at the center.

Even more surprising was her frank stare, both at him and at the Sudbury sisters. As befitting each of their ranks, Miss Sudbury, while not looking the least bit pleased to run into the wife of the man who had assaulted her, gave a curtsy first. However, when the viscountess should have returned a greeting to the Countess of Worthington and to himself, she instead gave a cunning smile.

"*Both* sisters, Marshfield?"

Stunned, not believing she could mean what her words implied, not in public, he said nothing.

Then she settled her narrowed glance on Miss Sudbury's sister. "I gather you enjoyed yourself at my home," she said.

However, the Countess of Worthington shook her head, plainly puzzled. Before she could say anything more than "I believe you are mistaken," Lady Chandron gave her the shoulder, letting her group of hangers-on surround her again as she walked away.

Everyone in his circle knew the viscountess was a piece of work, but she usually kept her vulgarity hidden within her boudoir.

Lady Worthington looked at her sister and then at him.

"What a strange woman? I've never met her before. I wonder why she thought I was ever in her home."

"The last ball I attended was at Lord and Lady Chandron's home," Miss Sudbury explained, "and I'm sure it was my relation to you that got me in the door. More than that, I cannot say, as I don't think I spoke a word to her."

Yet her glance darted toward him. Clearly, Miss Sudbury was unsettled. He wished he had some comforting words, but he knew she wouldn't want him to mention the viscount's attack in front of her sister. Nor was he certain why she seemed on edge regarding the viscountess, unless she was affronted by the improper innuendo behind the woman's words.

And then he thought no more about the Chandrons as he helped the ladies into his carriage.

"We are firm converts to the joys of cricket," the countess said. "The physicality of the sport, the speed of the runners, and how hard they could throw and hit the ball, it was all very exciting."

"It was," Miss Sudbury agreed. "Yet without your tutelage, sir, on where the trig was and who the colt bowler was," she added, trying out some terms he'd taught them, "it would not have been nearly so enjoyable."

He couldn't help smiling. "It was my pleasure to introduce you both to the game." ·

And the more time he spent in Miss Sudbury's company, the more he wanted to spend. An unusual circumstance and one which he'd never experienced before.

After he dropped them home, he tried to decipher if this dawning attachment to a woman, this one in particular, was a good idea or even a desirable thing to have happen.

"To White's," he ordered his driver. Male company, billiards, and good brandy would knock some sense back into him.

However, a few hours later, he didn't stop off at one of the most luxurious and costly *houses of civil reception* with his friends. No Cyprian, no courtesan, regardless of her sensual talents, currently interested him. Nor did memories of any of his previous mistresses entice him, either.

At present, no one attracted him save for Miss Sudbury, who had snagged him in her delicate web without even trying.

There was only one thing to do. Tup her and move on.

CHAPTER ELEVEN

"The weather was unseasonably warm last night, causing many guests to take the night air during Lord and Lady Wendelson's ball. Lord M__ was seen leaving the ballroom with Miss S__ yet returned from the garden alone."

—The Morning Post

Jasper was firmly of the belief that horses were an excellent distraction for any ailment, be it physical, mental, or even relating to the emotions. Miss Sudbury qualified as all three. She had his body aching for her, his mind constantly thinking of the blasted woman, and somehow sappy sentiment was involved, too, with an unfamiliar happy emotion when picturing her face.

He headed to Tattersall's. Being surrounded by top-rate horse flesh at the Hyde Park Corner repository and auctioneer would drive the notion of a certain female from his mind. At least, he hoped so. Bidding on a new mount he didn't really need was a weakness he allowed himself since he had few other costly vices. He paid his groom and coachman more than the rest of his household staff. Moreover, the feeding and care of the horses he kept in the private mews behind his house was probably more than some folks paid for their own yearly nourishment.

Afterward, he would see who was lounging around the Jockey Club. He enjoyed the gathering place for gentlemen interested in all horse matters, particularly racing, even more than he cared for the company at White's. Too many of those men let cards and drink go to their heads. Better to focus on . . .

Miss Sudbury! To his amazement, barely ten minutes after he was positioned under Tattersall's columned portico, starting to bid on a matching pair of Cleveland Bays, he saw her out of the corner of his eye.

Faltering in his bid, Jasper turned to make sure it was really her. It was, and watching her pass by, his heartbeat sped up with excitement.

"Go on, Marshfield, outbid us all as usual," a fellow member of the Jockey Club said half in jest, although it was the truth. Of the dozen others surrounding them, some laughed ruefully, as they nearly always lost to him if he had his heart set on winning.

Jasper couldn't even recall the last amount he'd offered. Sighing, he decided to chase after the object of his desire, and it wasn't the pair of carriage horses.

"Too rich for my blood," he joked back. "I shall have to beg off." With that, he darted out of the courtyard of Tattersall's, and in a few steps, he'd caught up with her.

"Good day, Miss Sudbury," he said, watching her startle and then stop dead on the sidewalk. "Where are you off to in such a hurry?"

She smiled at him, and he felt a twinge of gladness right down to his toes. *What the devil!* Since when could a female fell him with a glance?

"I'm hurrying, my lord, because the smell here is one of the worst in all London, save for Smithfield market."

He chuckled. "I have never minded the smell of manure, but that's the price you pay for living in London. It seems we have nearly as many horses as people."

She nodded. "Truly," she agreed. "I'm on my way to St. James's Park."

"This is a little out of your way, isn't it? From Hanover Square, I mean."

"I came through Hyde Park. I confess I prefer most of London's green spaces to the streets."

He must have given her a curious look, for her cheeks pinkened. She was all but confessing herself a country maid, a female hobnail. It didn't detract from her appeal at all. He imagined laying her down in the fresh green grass near his ancestral home in Marshfield, seeing wildflowers in her hair, looking up at the blue sky together after swiving to mutual satisfaction.

"For the milk," she said, and Jasper realized she had continued speaking while he'd gawked at her.

"I beg your pardon, Miss Sudbury, did you say something about milk?"

"My sister and I prefer the milk from the cows at St. James's to what we can get from the cow keeper's shop close to home. They water it down."

"Water it down?" Jasper was trying to follow her speech, but in truth, he'd never given an ounce of thought to the milk in his home. He assumed his kitchen staff purchased good quality.

"Yes, sir. The cow keepers' shops don't let the cows graze outside, and they use any matter of foul water to thin the milk. Of course, they skim the cream, too."

"Skim the cream," he muttered. He was almost afraid to ask. "Do you milk the cow at St. James's Park yourself?"

She had started walking again with him beside her, but this made her halt once more and start to laugh. Eventually, she shook her head.

"Do I seem such a bumpkin? The cows' owners do the milking and will even deliver, which is what I shall pay a lad to do." She patted her reticule dangling from one wrist. "As you can see, I didn't bring my pail nor stool." She started to laugh again.

"*Ha ha*, Miss Sudbury. You have made your point." Jasper liked how she fell into good humor so readily, seeming to be not the least self-conscious. "So, you are out for milk? May I accompany you?"

"If your company won't get my name into the gossip column, I suppose you may."

Suddenly, he realized what seemed so singular about her compared to the females with whom he might normally have a brief word on the street.

"Where on earth is your lady's maid?"

"You are going to make me laugh until I cry today, aren't you, sir? I have no lady's maid because I am *not* a lady."

It was his turn to feel his cheeks heat. "You have no title, to be sure, but you're not a shop girl either, nor a flower girl, for pity's sake. Your sister is a countess! Surely, you don't traipse about London unaccompanied."

Even the nearly useless Mrs. Zebodar would be better than no one.

"Indeed, I quite often do exactly that," Miss Sudbury said cheekily.

"Zounds," he swore under his breath. *What was this world coming to?* She could fall into the hands of . . . well, of someone like himself. Or worse, some sly-boots or Jack nasty-face who might try to lure her into a brothel if she didn't know better.

In truth, he oughtn't to walk with her to St. James's Park, as if they were a couple, but knowing she had no protection, he would do precisely that. If someone with tongue enough for two sets of teeth happened to see them and report it to the papers, so be it.

They fell into step.

"Tell me about something interesting," she demanded in a familiar and endearing way, and he endeavored to do so for the fifteen-minute walk. Naturally, they took Constitution Hill through Green Park, coming up alongside Buckingham House at one end of St. James's long, oddly shaped green.

True enough, there were the cows, the milkmaids, the delivery lads, and quite a crowd purchasing fresh milk. He'd been shown something new by this woman in his own backyard.

"Thank you, sir, for the company. Please, go about your business now."

The vicar's daughter was dismissing him.

"I think it best if I accompany you home," Jasper proposed.

With great exaggeration, she rolled her pretty blue eyes.

"I am not helpless, nor in any danger. I promise you."

"Given the last time I rescued you and from whom," Jasper reminded her, "I am not sure your judgment on the matter of what is dangerous is entirely sound. Regardless, I intend to accompany you home, and we shall go the direct route, up St. James's Street to the delightful Bond Street. We can look in the shop windows. Isn't that what women like to do?"

Whatever protest she offered, he wasn't going to miss out on a minute of her company in the casual environment away from the ballroom. He found it great fun.

When the milk was purchased and the address given, with a generous tip for speedy delivery, they strolled northward.

"Just to be clear," Miss Sudbury told him, after they dodged carriages crossing Piccadilly and stepped onto Old Bond Street, "except for the extremely wealthy, most women don't amble along peering into shop windows as if they haven't a brain in their head. Most are trying to figure out how to feed their children or put a roof over their—"

She broke off as they stared ahead of them at the throng of people, predominantly women, doing exactly as Jasper had predicted.

He grinned at her surprised expression.

"They can't all be the extremely wealthy, can they?" he teased, just as a member of the middle class, or so he guessed by her style of dress, pushed past them carrying packages. She was accompanied by two young girls, who looked to be her daughters by their resemblance.

"Normal families," he pushed his argument, "enjoying the fine weather and the shops. Surely, once in a while, you can do so as well without it harming London's poor in any way. Or do you still insist on staying to the parklands? Perhaps you should attempt to swing from tree to tree to reach Hanover Square."

As he knew she would, Miss Sudbury started to laugh. It bubbled out of her until she had to cover her mouth with her white-gloved hand, and after a deliriously refreshing chuckle that made him join in, she caught her breath.

"I love the way you laugh," he confessed, surprising himself.

Her eyes widened. Then she made a confession of her own. "I seem to do so around you more than at other times."

"I am pleased to be of service." And he was damnably pleased with himself.

They started a companionable walk along Old Bond Street to New Bond Street toward her home. Not only did she let him point out curiosities he noticed, she relaxed enough to exclaim over the odd bric-a-brac that caught her eye.

And on nearly every corner, she bought three-penny posies. Finally, after the third stop for such a purchase, he had to ask her.

"You have quite a love of flowers."

She nodded. "I do, yes, but even more a desire to get my pennies into the hands of as many flower girls as possible."

Finally, he had an explanation for the many posies he'd seen upon his two visits inside old Worthington's house. She was a good soul, even if he thought it a naïve effort.

When he bid her good day on her doorstep with the promise of seeing her at the upcoming Wendelsons' ball, Jasper couldn't help thinking how easy it had been to keep her in good humor and how much he'd enjoyed doing so.

Flagging down a hackney, he knew if he could get her into his bed as adeptly, his own enjoyment would be complete.

"WHY ARE YOU COMING to *this* ball?" Julia all but whined when she discovered Sarah was attending instead of the negligent Mrs. Zebodar. She didn't learn this fact until she came out of her room, ready to go, dressed in a diaphanous cream gown with a Pomona green bodice.

And there was her sister wearing violet satin.

Sarah stared at her. "Whyever not?"

Julia snapped her mouth closed as there was no good reason why her sister shouldn't go out into the world. Her mourning was long past.

"Are you hoping to see Viscount Denbigh?"

"No," her sister proclaimed, and instead of her cheeks blushing pink with happiness, her mouth became a thin, firm line. "I am no longer interested in him, but you and I shall have a splendid evening."

It would make it more difficult, but not impossible to go about her usual endeavors. Although, she supposed she could take a break and simply enjoy one event without worry.

Particularly since Lord Marshfield would be in attendance. She came to the conclusion she was more excited to see him than she should be. Despite sticking up for him to her sister and despite what a gentleman he'd been at Lord's Cricket Ground, he had earned his reputation over at least the past four years. He wasn't going to shed the skin of a rake in a couple of weeks. Certainly not for her.

A penniless miss from Chislehurst.

Not only that, she was a thief and potentially in scorching hot water. Julia was worried daily about that wretched reticule incident, waiting for something further to occur.

Yet none of that mattered when the Earl of Marshfield boldly crossed the room to greet her and her sister.

With the speed and expediency of a royal officer, he commandeered a table for them. By the time the music began, Sarah had obtained a partner, and they all convened for a quadrille. Simply for the ease of doing so, Lord Marshfield asked Sarah for the next dance, and Julia danced with her sister's partner.

After that, however, when the men went to do their duty securing other partners, Sarah and Julia awaited the onslaught. It happened quickly and soon Julia found herself with a gentleman she knew she'd met previously, but with whom she couldn't quite recall ever dancing.

"Your hem is holding up this evening," he remarked.

She started slightly, realizing he was one of those she'd left on the floor when going about her stealthy business.

"It is," she agreed amiably. "A better seamstress, to be sure."

For the midnight supper, her sister was quite satisfied to be escorted by the man she was lately partnered, and as Julia had hoped, Lord Marshfield appeared in time for the dance just prior, and thus, offered her his arm to go into the dining room.

"What a surprise?" he quipped drolly when the one and only course arrived. "White soup."

"Easy to make in large quantities and filling, all in one course," she defended the ubiquitous dish she'd encountered during the Season. "I confess I never had it before I came to a private ball, but I've grown very fond of it. And look, there's bread and butter, too."

He glanced at her, seeming amused. "Then for your sake, I'm glad of the pottage, and I shall watch you lick the last drop off your spoon."

His words sent a thrill through her. *What a scoundrel!*

However, not wanting to disappoint, she did in fact turn to him as she licked the last drop, and their eyes met. Her insides went as hot and liquid as the soup, and again, she wanted to experience a particular pleasure for the first time with this specific man.

To that end, after dinner, she accepted his invitation to go for a stroll in the dimly lit garden.

"Your sister would have my tallywags in a sack," he quipped.

She let out a laugh at the term, not entirely sure she knew to what he was referring, but feeling wicked all the same.

"My sister is my sister, and thus, not a true chaperone."

"With that notion in your head," he admonished, "you are apt to get up to all sorts of dangerous trouble."

"Too late," she muttered, but he heard her and shook his head, probably recalling when he'd saved her from the viscount. "Anyway, sir, I thought your idea to take a little air to be a good one, as this room has grown stuffier by the hour." It wasn't as if she were hoping for either an assignation or a dash over the stone wall and a trip to Gretna Green.

Without delay, he led her surreptitiously out one of the back doors into the garden. Whispers and giggles from more than one location met her ears, and Julia realized another world of intrigue was happening all around her.

Recalling how she'd arranged for them to be alone in Sarah's home, and yet he'd left as swiftly as Odysseus's arrow, she wondered if tonight—

Julia found herself yanked out of the torchlight and into the shadows before she could finish her thought. In the blink of an eye, they were on the other side of an arbor, shielded by a topiary shaped like a pineapple. His arms encircled her immediately.

Maybe the earl was now more like Eros's arrow, its tip dipped in desire.

Her heart beating at double speed, she raised her face to his and welcomed the crush of his mouth upon hers. In fact, she sighed through the beginning of it, enjoying pure welcome relief. Then his tongue tickled her lips, and she parted them.

While his tongue slid along hers, his hands skimmed down her thighs to draw up the sheer outer layer of her gown, as well as the chemise beneath. She began to tremble, but when the cool night air whispered across her skin, Julia went motionless. *If someone should stumble upon them* . . .

"This is what most of us come to these infernal gatherings for," the earl said, having kissed his way from her lips along her chin to her neck, speaking softly against her skin. "The rest of it, the dancing and such, is for the simpering innocents and upstanding hum-drum fellows."

His words sank in as his palms touched the soft cotton of her unfashionable drawers, inching toward the apex where they opened.

Wasn't she one of those innocents? she wondered.

His fingers slid between the space where the fabric crossed, and he touched her, a mere gentle brush across her curls. She shuddered.

"You're damp for me," he said softly.

Rather than feeling embarrassed, his knowledge of her body heightened her excitement. However, when one of his fingers flicked across her most sensitive spot, fearing her legs would collapse, Julia grabbed ahold of his lapels.

"Easy," he whispered. "I only want to please you."

And she let him. While keeping herself upright by hanging onto him, she let him stroke her shamelessly, and when she felt his finger enter her, she bit her lip and moaned.

"That's it," he said, claiming her mouth again. "Let me satisfy you."

And Julia realized she was moving up and down upon his hand, unable to stop as the pressure of exquisite sensation built.

Suddenly, his other hand slipped into the bodice of her gown—an easy passage between the fabric and her heated skin. His palm stroked her breast and then he took her hardened nipple between his thumb and forefinger. At the same time, he flicked the throbbing bud between her legs with his thumb while one of his fingers was still inside her.

He was a sorcerer!

Reaching the pinnacle of sensation, pleasure released through her like hot water poured across her skin, unleashing a dam of desire that made her want to sink to the garden floor. Yet still impaled on one of his hands and her breast palmed in his other, she could do naught but rest against him.

Finally, her breathing began to calm, and the tingling between her legs disappeared along with his hand, before her gown fell into place. He'd already withdrawn his other hand from her bodice, but he took a moment before releasing her entirely.

When she opened her eyes, she was looking directly into his unfathomable gaze. His words echoed in her head.

"What most of us come for."

And just like that, quick as a whip, her exultation vanished. He had probably done the same with many women, countless times. And he'd probably done quite a bit more. For while she'd been taken to the heights of ecstasy, he'd remained with his feet firmly planted on the grass.

Her cheeks flamed. *Was she supposed to have done something for him, either at the same time or in return?*

Feeling awkward, Julia took a step back

The smug grin on his handsome face only made it worse.

"I had best go back inside and find—"

Too late!

Julia spied Sarah on the veranda, looking hither and yon, and a wave of guilt washed over her. She had probably caused her sister no end of worry. What's more, despite having escaped with her so-called virtue intact, she didn't feel particularly virtuous at that moment. She could hardly understand what she did feel.

If Marshfield had tried to spend himself inside her, seeking his own pleasure, she would just as easily have gone along with that plan, too.

Her fascination for this rake was all-consuming.

"Don't follow me," she begged and ran out of the cover of darkness and into the light from a nearby torch. "Sarah, I'm so glad you're here. Come see what I've found."

She hoped there was something interesting on the other side of the yard or she was going to look an utter dunce. And a prevaricating one, at that.

CHAPTER TWELVE

"At Lady Daphne Rancur's dinner party, Lord M__ was
seen again going upstairs with a certain blonde country
miss who has been much in his company lately!"

—The Times

Jasper watched her expertly lead her sister away on a wild
goose chase. One minute, she was a blushing innocent,
wondrously finding release at his touch. The next, she was
quite expertly using her cunning to trick her sister.

He sighed. At twenty-eight, perhaps he was becoming
too old for this indulgent licentiousness. No one was who
they seemed. When the ladies had moved a goodly distance,
he dashed from his cover to the steps and then to the
veranda before slipping indoors.

Then he paused. *Should he go back out there and ensure their
safety?*

He thought better of it. Miss Sudbury would probably
be furious. Besides, it was unlikely Lady Worthington would
believe he'd happened upon them accidentally. Moreover,
he hadn't escorted either one to the ball, so it wasn't his
place to watch over them.

So why was he feeling so protective? A libertine such as himself didn't care for the well-being of others, especially not women who didn't belong to him. Yet he'd already saved Miss Sudbury once.

Yes, that must be the reason for wanting to keep her safe.

The only reason!

Regardless, he kept his eye upon the door and waited. If the sisters weren't back by the time the current dance ended, he would go out there and find them, come hell or high water. Meanwhile, he withdrew a silver flask from his pocket and took a sip of brandy.

With his hand close to his face, he caught the essential scent of Miss Sudbury. He took a long sniff and his groin ached as it had when he'd watched her climax, wishing they were some place where he could have drawn the process out far longer and joined her in the act.

Still, he recalled vividly the way she'd tilted her head back, closed her eyes, parted her lips and panted. He groaned. Everyone at the ball would see his arousal if he didn't get a handle on his thoughts.

But she was superb. The way her nipple had pearled, he'd longed to take it between his lips. And the way her passage dripped its honeyed desire on his fingers . . .

He took another sniff and then sipped the brandy, blending the two. He wanted her neck arched back and her lips parted while he stroked the inside of her with his cock.

Then he would be finished with this obsession!

God, he hoped so, for not another woman in the room held a candle to her. The music ended, and he started to walk toward the veranda door when it opened. The sisters entered holding hands and laughing.

Julia must have found the fountain with the four silly nymphs, each holding a different animal. Once, he'd had a bold tryst with a woman on the other side of the fountain, seated on a stone bench. It had been a bad idea and most uncomfortable, not to mention cold. Worse than that, he couldn't remember the female's name or face.

Shaking his head, he sipped again. Maybe it was time to give up his rakish ways for good.

And then the ladies were upon him.

"Where did you disappear to?" he asked, smooth as cream, keeping his gaze on the countess so as not to make Miss Sudbury's cheeks flare with guilt. It was a delightful trait, blushing so profusely, but not handy in polite company.

It was the countess who answered first while, he noticed with amusement, Miss Sudbury kept her eyes averted.

"We found the silliest fountain." Then she glanced at her sister. "We also found a couple—"

Miss Sudbury coughed delightfully to stop her, but the countess shook her head.

"I'm sure the earl has seen the same before," Lady Worthington said. "I fail to understand the lure of a chilly garden with gnats and scratchy plants and the very real fear of discovery. How do they even enjoy themselves out there?"

Miss Sudbury coughed again, sounding as if she were choking. He longed to pat her shapely shoulder.

"Are you all right, dear sister?" the countess asked.

"Perhaps one of those gnats got into her throat," Jasper suggested helpfully.

His blonde minx shot him a quelling look.

"It hardly seems an appropriate topic, that's all," she said.

The countess stared hard at her sister. Then she frowned, maybe thinking Miss Sudbury had become an utter stick in the mud.

Jasper knew better. However, given her sister's sudden reticence to light banter about backyard lovers in his company, he feared Lady Worthington might guess something had passed between them.

"The countess is correct," he began, causing both sisters' gazes to land upon him, one wary, one interested. "While I have strolled the garden a time or two, I have seen my fair share of amorous couples."

And been one of them on numerous occasions, he made sure not to add.

"As Lady Worthington says, it seems an uncomfortable business."

But often so exhilarating, he added to himself.

"On the other hand, sometimes desperate lovers grasp at any opportunity to be alone, knowing how difficult it is to get to know a member of the opposite sex in private. Nevertheless, a drawing room sofa, even stiff and hard-backed, is preferable to a stone bench or a patch of damp grass."

Both women were staring at him, mouths agape. Apparently, he'd offered *too* much opinion on the matter. Giving a little laugh, Jasper shrugged. All he could think about now was how Julia Sudbury had offered herself to him in the dining room of her sister's house, and how uncharacteristically he'd walked away.

After their garden encounter, he wouldn't make the same mistake twice. She was ripe for the plucking. If not him, it would be some other undeserving rascal who might not know how to treat her gently and respectfully while ravishing her at the same time. *He* would be that rascal!

"Would you like to go riding in the park?" he asked Julia. "With a chaperone, naturally."

Watching her carefully, he noticed interest spark in her eyes. She turned to the countess as if to ask permission before catching herself.

"Yes, my lord. That would be a welcome treat."

"Do you have a suitable mount, not a carriage horse?" he asked, wondering if a vicar's daughter could ride—at least something beside his hand, which she'd done admirably.

"Alas, no," Lady Worthington said, not looking pleased at his pursuit of her sister. "And I'm not even certain Mrs. Zebodar can ride."

Good. He hoped she couldn't, for he could not pay off that woman to leave them alone. Of that, he was certain.

Thinking quickly, he offered, "I have a gentle mare in my stable. And I can bring along a chaperone."

The countess arched her eyebrow.

"Come now," Jasper said. "Your sister is not a child, and I am talking about a public ride." Which, with any luck, he would turn into a private ride at his home for at least an hour—if Julia was willing. He had a feeling she would be. Her eyes were certainly alight at the notion.

Without awaiting her sister's response, she nodded. "I thank you for the invitation and for loaning me one of your mounts. I accept."

"On the first sunny day, then," he offered. "Now, shall we dance?"

And he took her to the floor for one of the long country dances, leaving the countess staring after them. Lady Worthington's power over her sister was no match for his, not when he could offer her kisses along with the rest of what would make Julia Sudbury cry out in delight.

To his dismay, he awakened the following morning to a steady downpour. Today at least, they would not ride.

JULIA WATCHED THE SKIES anxiously, wanting nothing more than to spend time with Lord Marshfield. She had relived his touch in her memory each night when trying to fall asleep, and every time, she'd ended up touching herself, thinking of him.

While a ride in Hyde Park wasn't exactly on the same level of excitement as what had occurred in that wicked garden, any time they spent together might provide the opportunity for some sort of close interaction, although she couldn't imagine how.

She wished she could simply invite him to her home again. However, Sarah no longer went to Lord Denbigh's, nor spoke of him, and only went out in the evenings when it was to accompany her if Mrs. Zebodar was unavailable.

Regardless of the weather, Julia needed to focus her efforts once more upon her goal of giving money charitably at least once a week. If she could attend balls and go riding, she could make herself useful and manage to feed the hungry.

She simply needed to attend some dinner or dance without her sister and, just as importantly, without Lord Marshfield being there. His eyes were too watchful and his presence was too distracting.

To that end, on her sister's behalf, Julia accepted an invitation from Lady Daphne Rancur to an intimate gathering of twenty, didn't tell Sarah, and went in her place.

"My sister is suffering from a megrim this evening, but she didn't want to leave you with an odd number. I hope I will be a suitable spare."

It worked. And Julia didn't even need a chaperone since she would be partnered with a guest while there but had arrived and would leave alone.

Everything went smoothly, until, directly before they went into the dining room, the last guest appeared—the Earl of Marshfield.

Blast!

Since he was a friend of the hostess's, he was seated near the head of the table to Lady Daphne's left. Since Julia was a nobody, she was pleased to be seated at the other end with her partner for the evening, the youngest son of a viscount, so in some regards, also a nobody.

Jasper didn't appear surprised to see her, and she couldn't help wondering if he'd known she would be there. When she excused herself toward the end of the meal to use the facilities, a trick that had worked well before as no one would question her, when she came out of the water closet, the earl was standing in the hallway.

"What are you doing?" she asked bluntly, having intended to dash upstairs to the hostess's chamber and snag something glittering.

"I thought to escort you back to the dining room."

She couldn't help frowning at him. If he was hoping to get her alone, this was not the time nor place.

"That was unnecessary. Besides if any man should escort me, my dining partner should. Didn't our hostess think it rude of you to leave the table after me?"

Jasper offered a shrug she was becoming used to. It told her nothing and was beyond infuriating.

"Shall we?" he asked, offering her his arm.

Feeling annoyed as a wet hen, Julia took it and let him take her back to the dining room. Somehow, he was on to her, or he thought he knew something. She would have to become a little smarter.

After dinner, there would be dancing, rather in the reverse of usual things, but their hostess said she found it easier to dance on a full stomach than a rumbling one, and no one had gainsaid her.

In the meanwhile, Julia had only to bide her time. When Jasper was about to begin a waltz, when it would be utterly beyond the pale for him to beg off, she did exactly that to her own partner.

"I'm so terribly sorry. My hem has come down. I shall return as quickly as possible."

While across the floor Jasper's back was turned, she dashed from the small ballroom.

JASPER TURNED IN TIME to watch Miss Sudbury disappear from the room. Claiming a sudden cramp in his leg, he escorted his partner to the side of the room and swiftly followed the brazen baggage.

He was in time to see the skirt of her gown disappear up the staircase. *Odd!*

While he was always up for a lark where a female was concerned, he couldn't fathom her strange actions at balls and parties, so at odds with her normal behavior. Moving fast, his footstep was on the first stair when she reached the top. For a few steps, Jasper had a view of her shapely bottom outlined by the silken fall of her gown and a glimpse of her slender ankle as she stepped onto the landing above him.

Normally, he would assume her to be headed for an assignation, except all the guests were downstairs. Then he had a thought. She'd glanced over in his direction more than once that night. *Had she intended for him to follow her and be the recipient of her pent-up passion?*

Continuing to the second floor, he took a left, trailing in the direction she had gone. Along the hallway, all the doors were closed. Listening intently, he could hear nothing.

He nearly laughed, feeling like a child at play. A quick tupping in any one of the rooms wouldn't necessarily be noisy. He could capture Miss Sudbury's desire-filled mewling in his mouth, and gladly. But he needed a clue as to—

The door farther along opened, luckily not the one he stood beside. Jasper flattened himself against the striped wallpaper. In the dim light, she didn't see him. Instead, she went in the opposite direction and slipped into the next room.

Even odder!

He followed, and after the hesitation of a heartbeat, he opened the door and entered.

CHAPTER THIRTEEN

"A certain popular hostess, Lady R__ was stunned to learn
the Earl of M__ might be running through his family's
fortune at an alarming rate."

—The Gazette

In a short time, Julia was in Lady Daphne's private
chamber. Luckily, despite nothing but moonlight, she
had no need to rummage through a jewelry box as a number
of exquisite baubles lay on the dresser. Perhaps the lady had
picked through them before the party and chosen what to
wear.

For a brief instant, she felt a slice of remorse. After all,
there might be something that was special to her hostess,
something she treasured as Julia did her mother's small ruby
ring.

On the other hand, there was enough wealth scattered
carelessly on the lace doily to feed and clothe an entire
orphanage.

These disturbing thoughts delayed her as she tried to
choose something that didn't seem incredibly unique. After
a few moments, she settled on a bracelet of gemstones.

She'd seen similar before and doubted it was a family heirloom like the unusually shaped brooch she left behind.

"Miss Sudbury?" came a voice at her back.

Egad!

She yelped, spun around, her heart racing.

"Who's there?" she asked unable to make out anything but a silhouette as dim light from the hall backlit the figure.

When Jasper stepped into the moonlight streaming in the casement window, she sagged with relief.

"Lord Marshfield," she greeted, keeping her tone light and even welcoming, as if nothing were amiss.

FOR THE BRIEFEST INSTANT, he imagined they were about to have a flyer against the wall with her skirts bunched at her waist and his shaft keeping her upright.

Yet she was holding something glittery in her hand.

"What are you doing?" It seemed a reasonable question for which he hoped she had a perfectly reasonable answer. However, it appeared as if she were stealing something from their hostess.

"And don't give me any more poppycock about seeking a token or looking at artwork when you have a bracelet draped between your fingers. You are snaffling jewels like a common thief!"

Jasper's fury was growing not receding as he spoke. *Why would she risk her freedom, possibly even her life?* Especially when she had a sister who must have a comfortable income.

Julia stared back at him, her pretty eyes wide. He thought he heard her sigh with exasperation. She had no possible defense to her actions, so he reached out and snatched the bracelet from her hand.

He still hoped she would say something which would alter what he'd seen with his own eyes. Instead, she pursed her lips and glared at him, unremorseful.

"Why are you here?" she demanded.

"I followed you, of course."

"You shouldn't have," she said adamantly.

Pushing past, she skirted him but was unable to escape before he snatched hold of her arm with his free hand.

"And why not?" Jasper demanded. If he hadn't, she would have put the bracelet in her reticule and escaped back downstairs to the dinner with no one the wiser.

Her damned reticule! He recalled dancing with her and being hit by a bag that seemed filled with rocks. Undoubtedly, he'd been assaulted with her stash of pilfered precious stones!

"How dare you!" came the outraged voice of Lady Daphne Rancur.

"*That's* why not," Julia muttered.

Slowly, Jasper released Julia's arm, and they both faced their apoplectic hostess.

"Marshfield, if this were merely your taking liberties with my home and having a dalliance with one of my guests in *my* bedroom, that would be outrageous in the extreme. However, worse than that, I catch you stealing from me."

Jasper felt the full weight of the situation, as he looked from Lady Daphne to the bracelet between his fingers, then to Julia's pale face. He could take the blame, which made him appear to be the worst slithery blackguard, or blame Julia, which could end with her going to trial. Or he could try to talk his way out of it.

"This is not what it looks like, Lady Daphne." Those were the words he'd hoped Julia would say to him. And they sounded ridiculous.

Their hostess's anger didn't diminish one whit.

"No? Then why don't you explain why you and Miss Sudbury are loitering in my chamber, with you holding my bracelet." With those words, Lady Daphne held out her hand, palm up.

Quickly, Jasper deposited the jewelry onto her palm. He'd been acquainted with Lady Daphne for years, although they'd never had a romantic liaison. Their parents knew each other, and her brother had been at All Souls College with him. Because of this, she knew he had an eye—and more—for the ladies, and he decided to rely upon that.

"It's true I'd hoped to have a moment alone with Miss Sudbury. You know me," he added.

"I'm not sure I do know you," she countered.

He smiled. "I simply wanted to kiss the lady. We breached your private floor and were about to enjoy a moment in the hallway."

He had Lady Daphne's interest, but Julia was listening to his tale with an expression of horror upon her face.

"A servant came near so I opened the first door and drew my lovely quarry in here. Can you blame me wanting a single kiss?"

Julia groaned with humiliation.

"I heartily doubt you would have stopped at a kiss," Lady Daphne said. "You rakes never do. I would have come in here later to find my bedlinens rumpled."

She sounded a little less peeved, however.

"Gentleman's honor," he said, offering her a grin. "Nothing but a kiss."

"The bracelet?" Lady Daphne asked, jangling it in front of him.

"It was on the floor, right there," he said, gesturing behind him toward the dresser. "I had only just picked it up to replace it. Miss Sudbury, whose reputation is spotless, was about to leave, so I grabbed her arm, and then you came upon us. The blame is all mine, but the crime was passion, not theft."

"*Hm.*" Lady Daphne passed him by to examine her dresser. Apparently seeing nothing else amiss, she dropped her bracelet atop the rest of the jewels. "I suppose it's possible I swept it off by mistake," she allowed.

"After all," Jasper reminded her, "I am the Earl of Marshfield, and have no need to steal your baubles, no matter how pretty."

"Normally, I would say that was undeniably the truth. However, I had heard whispers of your being unable to afford a horse at Tattersall's."

His jaw dropped. *Such rubbish belonged in the dust-bin!* Someone had started a vicious rumor and slandered his good name. He would rip them limb from limb.

"From whom did you hear such a thing?" he demanded, feeling as if his cravat were suddenly tied too tightly.

Lady Daphne was known to gossip. If she thought this to be a juicy tidbit—true or not—the rumor would be everywhere. It was probably already too late.

The lady merely pursed her lips. "The *who* is unimportant, and I shall say nothing more. But my bracelet would have fetched a pretty penny."

"I promise you," Jasper ground out, trying to unclench his teeth, "I didn't need a pretty penny, nor a bloody pretty pound!"

Although Lady Daphne nodded, he wasn't certain she'd accepted his vehement assertion. Then she spared Miss Sudbury a withering glance.

"You are a foolish girl to come up here with him."

Jasper waited. He'd never seen Julia Sudbury behave submissively to anyone. To his amazement, his blonde bandit looked sheepish and compliant.

"Yes, my lady," she said quietly.

"I think it best if you both leave my home," Lady Daphne added.

Jasper had never been thrown out of anywhere in his life.

"Come now, don't be like that. No harm was done."

"Her ladyship is correct," Miss Sudbury began. "We should go."

"No," Jasper said, more forcefully than he meant to. "I know how rumors begin. If someone noticed our absence from the ballroom, and then also sees us both leave at the same time, your name will be dragged through the mud before morning."

He offered Lady Daphne a beseeching look.

"You both should have thought of that," she snapped.

"My lady," he began, stepping closer to her, until he could practically peer down her décolletage. Gazing into her eyes, he implored her. "Would you punish us for a mere kiss? One that never actually happened?"

They engaged in a silent battle. He wondered if she would take a night with him as payment to be silent and let this go as if it never happened. To hint at that, he dropped his glance to the exposed tops of her breasts, then back to her eyes, seeing her pupils dilate.

"Just a kiss," he added on a whisper, as if they were the ones who would share it.

After a moment in which she raised a delicate eyebrow at him and then a confounded glance toward Miss Sudbury, Lady Daphne did the unexpected. She laughed at him.

"Please, Marshfield. Don't try to turn your charms upon me. I think of you like a brother." She guffawed with hilarity and, to his consternation, clutched her stomach.

While relieved at her levity, Jasper was also insulted. He was most definitely *not* her brother. Moreover, he thought he had a chance with every woman, and a good one at that. It was galling to realize such wasn't the case, despite having no real interest in her.

Eventually, their hostess gathered herself.

"For the gift of that delightfully uplifting hilarity, I'll let you both stay for the remainder of the evening. Marshfield, you go downstairs first. I'll escort Miss Sudbury back into the ballroom *after* I give her a stern talking to about staying away from the likes of you."

"But—" he began.

"But me no buts," Lady Daphne insisted. "Or you'll be tossed out."

He closed his mouth. The damage had, at least, been mitigated, and Miss Sudbury wouldn't end up in Newgate, not that evening at any rate.

With a nod to the ladies, he departed.

The notion that people were talking about him didn't bother him in the least. As a libertine, he was used to his name in the paper as *Lord M__* or the *E__ of M__*, usually with the words "behaved dreadfully" somewhere close by. However, to his knowledge, no one had ever besmirched his family's fortune. He wasn't prone to profligacy, nor to wasteful extravagance or uncontrollable gambling. His finances were as sound as ever.

Perhaps Lady Daphne had simply got the wrong end of the walking stick and misheard the gossip. But the idea that one of his Jockey Club fellows was saying such a thing pricked his ire, and it must certainly be one of those who'd stood beside him at Tattersalls.

Also, he dearly hoped Lady Daphne wouldn't actually have any sway over Julia about keeping company with him. For he still intended . . .

What did he intend?

To enjoy her, at least, because she wanted that as well. That much was obvious. He wasn't trying to coerce an unwilling female, but satisfy a willing one. However, there was something more brewing besides desire, or he wouldn't be so furious over her ridiculous compulsion to thievery.

If she were an earl's wife, she would have to curb any such—

An earl's wife?

He yanked his brandy flask from his pocket and drank heartily before reentering the ballroom.

CHAPTER FOURTEEN

"Lord M__ was seen riding in the Park today with Miss S__. We cannot tell if he has taken a liking to Lady W__ or her country sister. Perhaps both, dear reader?"

—The Sun

As soon as Lord Marshfield left, Lady Daphne turned on Julia.

"I don't know you, nor your sister except for her good fortune in marrying an old man."

Julia opened her mouth to defend Sarah for, as usual, the lady made it sound as though her sister had done something premeditated to secure a fortune and a title.

"No," Lady Daphne said, "don't speak. I am not judging, nor condemning. Not her, at any rate. But you are going down a dangerous route, Miss Sudbury. I have been in London all my life, and I've seen Marshfield and his ilk destroy, albeit sometimes unintentionally, too many hopeful young women. Rakehells to a man, they are driven by their desire to the detriment of all else, including common decency."

Julia swallowed. "I understand." It pinched her pride to think how much she wanted to toss her decency to the far winds where Jasper was concerned.

"Do you truly?" Lady Daphne demanded. "It's not only *your* future that would be squashed during a moment of passion, no matter how pleasurable. Your sister would be dragged down with you. Her position is already slightly precarious as among the *bon ton*, her quick marriage and widowhood begs the question as to whether they even consummated. She has an air of illegitimacy to her title. The Crown could and probably would send your sister back to obscurity in a heartbeat if someone at the palace wanted the Worthington earldom."

Julia couldn't help her eyes widening at this heretofore unknown information.

"What has that to do with myself and Lord Marshfield?" She cringed. Even linking their names sounded as though they were up to something sordid.

Lady Daphne pursed her lips for a moment.

"You truly are not one of us." She sighed. "It works like this. If you are disgraced by Marshfield, you must throw yourself into the Thames or flee to the Continent even with the continued unrest against the English. Or you may go into hiding in the country and never return to London. And your sister would then be looked upon as less than desirable company. You will taint her tenuous hold upon fine society. When they see her, they will think of you and Marshfield, who will escape unscathed as usual because men will be men. The *quality set* will believe you might not have been innocent to begin with. They'll think you were trying to entrap him and set your trap unwisely since no one who knows Marshfield believes he will marry one of the many foolish females he plays with."

The lady rolled her eyes in silence with a shake of her head, and Julia's heart fell. The rebuke sounded worse when coming from someone who was not her sister.

"Make no mistake, though," Lady Daphne continued. "The earl is one of us and will be forgiven because it is easier to blame an outsider. Including your sister. Obviously, people will say you weren't raised properly, and she must not have been, either. The whispers that only recently died down about her being a fortune-hunter, a scab who prays with her knees up, will begin anew."

Slightly shocked, Julia soaked in all the complexities of the small world of Mayfair. She certainly didn't want to harm Sarah in any way. *A scab, indeed!*

"I do understand," she said, more emphatically. At the same time, she resented the notion of giving up her flirtation with Marshfield because of disapproving tongue-waggers.

Something must have shown in her eyes, for Lady Daphne shook her head.

"Oh dear! Never say you have feelings for the man." For the second time, the woman broke down in laughter.

"For Marshfield? Don't be a silly goose! He will have to marry someday, of course, but it will be to a titled lady at the very least, and more probably to a titled lady with a splendid fortune. And most certainly, to a newly minted debutante in her first Season, with the purest of reputations. She will have to be strong enough to hold her place in society even while everyone knows how he continues with his rakish ways. Most of the noblemen of my acquaintance have a mistress, just like the Prince Regent, and many bring these courtesans to balls and dinners *instead* of their wives."

Then Lady Daphne frowned. "It can become a bit tricky as a hostess, especially if the wife also shows up and has a lover with her, although that is much rarer." Then she shook her head. "This is all making me weary. Don't fall for a rake, Miss Sudbury. Men like Marshfield do not change their feathers for fur. Either do as your sister did and get yourself a nice old man who is nearly ready to slip the wind, or get yourself a man firmly in your own class, who will be more than happy to come home to a lovely wife like you. It will save you a great deal of heartache."

Julia could do nothing but nod.

"Come now," Lady Daphne said, "don't look glum. It doesn't mean you can't dance with Marshfield tonight and a few other handsome gentlemen."

With that, they returned to the party. Julia's partner had long since given up waiting for her and was on the floor with another. Lord Marshfield was leaning against the far wall, looking like thunder, and Julia knew why. He'd caught her red-handed, a fact she'd nearly forgotten among all the words of wisdom and caution from Lady Daphne.

It might be best if she didn't dance with the earl or, indeed, even go near him again that night. Alas, she wasn't given the choice.

When she was escorted from the floor following the next dance, Jasper awaited her. He didn't ask permission, but highhandedly took her away from her partner and toward a quiet corner.

"I assume your next dance is free, and I insist it be with me. That is unless you have some reason to leave the ballroom again."

"No," she said, hating the meek tone to her voice. "I was planning on staying right here. I'm not sure it's a good idea for us to dance, however," Julia added.

That seemed to annoy Jasper even more.

"Being seen with me in public is the least of your problems, if you ask me."

"I didn't," she muttered.

"You must never again traipse around your host or hostess's home. That's twice now you've been caught."

"Two times out of—" Julia snapped her mouth closed, realizing the confession she nearly made.

Too late!

"Are you mad, woman?"

She sighed.

"No," he insisted. "I am quite serious. Do you have an affliction that causes you to behave so recklessly, a lack in your intellectual capacity, perhaps? At least, that would be some small explanation as well as a possible defense when you inevitably go to trial."

She ignored his words, although again, they sounded worse than when Sarah said the same thing.

The next dance was about to begin. Without asking, he placed her hand on his arm, clamped his own over hers, and strode toward the room's center, making it difficult for her to keep up without trotting. They took up their positions, facing one another.

"Lady Daphne said I may dance with you here, but I should be very careful of any further association with you."

"Did she? And yet she associates with me and with a few other blackguards."

"Are you calling yourself a blackguard," Julia asked, "or saying the others are?"

He didn't respond but began the first steps of the cotillion, hands high, their palms touching as they circled. As soon at their gloved hands met, she could focus on nothing but the warmth flowing through her.

And then they moved on through the line, dipping and twirling, always ending up reconnected as a couple until the dance ended.

"Are you thinking after this evening never to see me again?" he asked, his tone mocking.

Julia thought first about Sarah. Then she recalled the frisson of pleasure she received even with his simple touch while dancing, the likes of which she'd never experienced, not with any of the men she'd met and danced with in London, nor even with those she'd kissed.

The sensation of wanting and something more—akin to affection—seemed to be growing every time she was near the earl. And of course, there was the garden tryst when he . . .

"Yes," she blurted, finally answering his question. "It would be for the best if we never were alone again." Because she would give in to him, shamelessly, wantonly, willingly.

"What about our ride in Hyde Park?" Jasper reminded her.

"We shouldn't." The notion of *not* riding with him put an immediate damper on the evening. Yet the earl wasn't giving up.

"I didn't take you for a coward. What do you think can possibly happen if we ride three feet apart?" His sardonic smile gave her pause.

When he put it that way, it seemed foolish to call off their plans.

"Very well. If the weather ever turns fine again." And she left it at that.

JASPER WAS DELIGHTED LADY Daphne's attempt to deter Julia Sudbury from seeing him hadn't worked. It nearly had. But when the evening came to a close, their plan to ride was still as intact as a virgin's virtue.

In two days' time, with the best watery London sun shining on the cool early-Autumn day, he showed up at Lady Worthington's home at two o'clock in the afternoon having sent word that morning.

When Miss Sudbury came outside, a vision in her bright green riding habit with its black military ornaments running down the front and at the cuffs, she clapped her black gloves at seeing the attractive mare he'd brought for her. He nearly clapped his own hands upon witnessing her joy, as well as his own delight at the ease with which his plan was working.

After introducing her to the chaperone he'd brought, Mrs. Crowley, a matron in his employ for a decade who could well sit a horse, Miss Sudbury let him assist her onto the sidesaddle. The chivalrous act offered him a paltry, brief thrill compared to what he hoped awaited them shortly if she was willing. First, however, he wanted to discuss her nasty habit of going into other people's chambers. She would be a more desirable bed partner if he knew she wasn't going to knock him over the head and ransack his armoire.

He thought again of his sapphire cravat pin. With his groom making up the group, they set out for the park, entering through Grosvenor Gate, not far from his home, walking their horses in companionable silence until they were nearly at the southeast entrance of the King's Road when he turned to her.

"Do you still have my pin?" he asked, deliberately hoping to catch her off-guard.

Miss Sudbury jumped, then turned slowly to face him.

"I have no idea what you're talking about." Her cheeks flamed with her lie.

Jasper sighed. "I think we're beyond such prevarication, aren't we? I found you in my room, which actually makes three times I've caught you, not two. And then my father's cravat pin went missing."

"Your father's?" she repeated.

"Yes. It meant a great deal to me. I would like my pin back."

She looked down at the pommel, silent for a moment.

"I do not have it," she said to her gloves.

His heart sank. *Had she given it away to some other man?*

"I see."

"It's not exactly what you think," she began, echoing the words he'd said to Lady Daphne, except in this case, it *was* exactly what he thought.

"But you did take it." He didn't even turn it into a question.

She didn't respond, obviously still unwilling to confess or to trust him. It didn't matter. He knew the truth, and it was shocking. She seemed like a perfectly normal and nice young woman, other than her penchant for stealing.

"You might see if Mr. Bridge has it," she added quietly.

"Of Rundell and Bridge?" Jasper clarified, realizing without her saying it directly, she'd pawned his pin.

"Rundell, Bridge, *and* Rundell," she amended.

Her correction irked him.

"That seems incredibly unimportant," he snapped.

"I'm sure it is important if you are the second Mr. Rundell."

He stared at her—a hard penetrating stare—until she shrugged daintily.

"Are you and your sister in desperate need?" he asked, unable to fathom any other reason she would take something of his and sell it.

"No," she bit out the single word.

Apparently, Miss Sudbury had a terrible compulsion or even some sort of mania. Also, quite clearly, she felt no to need explain herself.

"Will you steal from me again?"

She raised her head, looking at him with a frown.

"How could I?" she asked, still not confirming, nor denying.

He cocked his head. "What intent to your words?"

"We are riding," she quipped. "How could I take anything from you?"

Blasted woman! She was being purposefully evasive.

"In the future," he asked, annunciating his words clearly, "if given the opportunity?" Because Jasper still saw a future, at least for a short while, in which they could keep company and hopefully put out the fire of longing, which hadn't diminished one whit.

"I don't imagine you are having another party anytime soon, are you?" she asked.

He sighed. She was still dodging, and he was ready to give up.

"Besides, sir, you are bewattled," Julia said, looking forward out over Rotten Row, past the breath of the horses, visible in the chilly air. "You do not have the right of things, I assure you."

Bewattled? Yes, he was most certainly confounded by her.

"Will you promise to stop?" he implored.

"I will not speak of this any further," she said.

Jasper swore under his breath. "We're not speaking of simply picking a gentleman's pocket of a silk handkerchief, although even that can result in being flogged or spending time in jail. This is larceny that can end with your death."

She swallowed. He hoped he'd frightened some sense into her. Instead without looking at him, she gave a rather glib comment.

"I believe the courts are sentencing thieves less and less to hang and more often simply transporting them."

He wanted to scream.

"To die in the airless belly of a vessel en route to a penal colony thirteen thousand miles away? That doesn't sound much better than a quick dance on the end of a rope."

He wiped a hand over his eyes. "I cannot believe we are discussing this almost as matter-of-factly as bantering over the cost of a pound of coffee beans."

"Then let's stop. I already told you I do not wish to speak any longer about it."

He decided to let the matter drop. Maybe he could bring it up again at a more favorable moment. Perhaps when she was more open and vulnerable. He knew the perfect time.

"Let's speed up a little, shall we?" At this slow walk, they would run out of their precious time before he could get her alone.

Going no farther, he turned them expertly, so they could trot back along the quicker diagonal path toward the same gate they'd entered.

"Back home already?" she asked, seemingly unalarmed, but glancing back to make sure the two other riders followed. "It was a shorter ride than I'd anticipated."

"We don't have to end our visit yet. We could share some coffee or a glass of wine?"

"That would be most agreeable," she said. "My sister has very good claret."

"*Mm*, yes, I know she does. I recall tasting it that night over dinner."

Miss Sudbury fell silent, thinking, if he guessed rightly, of what they might have done. Hopefully, her body would start to hum with anticipation of what they could, in fact, still do.

To that end, he steered them toward his own home, a few streets from the park. Miss Sudbury said nothing to deter him. Soon, the party of four, appearing innocent to any onlookers drew up outside his house. Still without speaking, he assisted her down, knowing she would be unknown to any prying eyes peering from neighboring windows.

While his footman led the horses away, Mrs. Crowley walked up the three front steps and through the door behind them. It all looked perfectly benign. Once inside, however, as soon as his butler had closed the door, Mrs. Crowley disappeared to the rear of the house. And after Mr. Greer had taken Jasper's hat and riding coat, he, too, vanished without a word.

"Come into my drawing room," he invited Julia, who looked neither entirely willing, nor frightened. A measure of curiosity stole over her fine features before she preceded him.

The fire was lit in the hearth, a tray with a carafe of wine and two glasses was laid out on the low table before the sofa, and the curtains were drawn. It could be evening as easily as a sunny afternoon.

"A setting of wine. How contrived of you," she said with a hint of humor.

He smiled. She had spotted his premeditation.

"I like to be prepared. Also, as you chastised me for lack of smooth deceit the last time I invited you over, I thought I would handle it more gracefully this time. Your sister is none the wiser, correct?"

"True. However—"

"Don't say you've changed your mind."

"I didn't realize I'd made a decision in the first place," she said, but to his delight, she took a seat on his pale-gray divan.

"I detected an invitation when I had dinner with you," Jasper told her. "Moreover, you seemed to enjoy yourself in the garden to the point I believe you would like to repeat the experience."

It had been bold of him to say any such thing, to make mention of his pleasuring her. Yet that was his nature—to be bold where females were concerned. It usually served him better than skirting his intent with vague intimations.

Luckily, the blush to her cheeks and the way her lips parted expectantly proved he was on the right path.

Not to mention how her gaze dropped to the front fall of his breeches.

He had guessed correctly, and her subtle response enflamed his desire.

She reached for the wine with a noticeably shaking hand, and he rushed to her side to take the carafe from her and finish pouring for them both.

"Here, in my home, we will be undisturbed to enjoy one another as men and women are meant to do."

Her eyebrows arched at his words. She sipped, pondered, and sipped again. Then she set her glass down.

"Kiss me," she demanded.

CHAPTER FIFTEEN

Jasper's glass was raised to his lips, but he set it down with
a clunk upon the table and wrapped his arms around her,
drawing her close. Without hesitation, he claimed her
upturned mouth, taking in her citrus and floral scent. A soft
lick across her lips, and they parted for him to plunder.

With their tongues dancing, he reached down, lifting the
heavy fabric of her riding skirt with its train for modesty
upon the saddle. This he bunched upon her lap before going
down for another handful. It would take more work than
with a light, gauzy ballgown to expose her soft skin, but he
was up for the task.

Yes, his body was quite up for this woman.

She let him continue until his fingers trailed across her
silken stockings, and then she drew away from him.

"No," she whispered.

"No? Not here, you mean. Shall we go up to my bedroom?"

"No," Miss Sudbury repeated and ended with a little sigh. "I simply wanted a kiss. They are so delightful, but that is all. We can finish our wine, but then I must be heading home."

Thunderstruck, Jasper stared at her, his heart still racing and his shaft throbbing with need.

"Can you mean what you say? We are finally alone. We have a bed, more than one," he jabbed his hand upward to indicate the many rooms on the next floor, "any of which we can press into service. Come now, you haven't been coy up until now. Are you hoping for flowery talk first—about the beauty of your eyes or your superb breasts—or mayhap vague promises you know I won't keep?"

She shook her head. "No, it's not that. I do desire you, as you can tell. And I was previously willing to allow the most decadent of liberties because I am fair weary of waiting to experience the grand mystery of love-making. However," she paused.

"Yes?" he asked, realizing his tone was a little harsh.

"It's my sister and Lady Daphne," she finished with a shake of her head.

Jasper couldn't help frowning. Then he grabbed his glass of wine, sat back, and drank the whole thing down. Finally, while knowing the invocation of Daphne's name didn't bode well for an afternoon's assignation, he still had to ask.

"Please explain what you mean by your sister and Lady Daphne. They have not formed an attachment, have they?"

That made Julia smile for the first time since they'd entered the drawing room, changing the mood.

"No, but Lady Daphne explained the ramifications of my becoming involved with you, and particularly of my being caught in precisely this type of situation." She gestured around her with a wave of her dainty hand. He wanted to grab it and press it against his aching arousal.

"For me, I think the consequences would not be so grave," she continued. "No one knows who I am nor cares what I do, but for my sister, a countess, still scrabbling to gain a foothold in the world to which her husband thrust her, it would be ruinous. She would be tarred by the same bucket of shame as myself."

Jasper knew Lady Daphne was correct in this advice, but it galled him how easily she'd turned Julia from him.

"That is all true, I suppose, but only if we're caught," he reminded her. "If I take you home now *without* our having enjoyed ourselves, there is no difference than if we had rolled around on the floor, rutting like beasts."

Her lovely blue eyes opened wide while she considered his words.

"My apologies," he said quickly, "for the vulgar image. I assure you our joining would not be like rutting farm animals."

Although, if Jasper's lust grew any greater, it was quite possible he would take her like a randy dog. At least the first time. And then the second time would be accomplished with his usual skill.

"What you say is correct," she agreed, "but the sooner I go home and with my virtue intact, the easier it will be to look my sister in the eye should she ask anything."

Her sister could take a long walk off the end of a short dock as far as he was concerned.

And the strangest thing was this refreshing woman seated beside him, not even asking Jasper to declare himself, to propose marriage, nor even hint at a future for them. She'd honestly disclosed her own desire for him, and then was willing to sacrifice it to keep her sister's reputation safe.

She was the most intriguing female he'd ever encountered. And for that reason, he was persistent.

Setting his glass down again, he said, "I am unwilling to give up on what I know will be a stupendous coupling."

With that, he leaned toward her until she had to lie back against the arm of the sofa.

"Why don't we spend a little time and see where we end up?" he suggested.

She giggled beneath him. "I am quite certain where we'll end up."

But she let him kiss her again anyway, and since he was atop her, he could grind his rock-hard staff into the soft cradle of her skirts, directly between her thighs.

It was beyond vexing for both of them, as she arched and writhed, finally thrusting her breasts against him until he broke free of the kiss to nuzzle the dark valley she offered. She was a bewitching siren—and also a trusting innocent!

He jumped off her.

"*Gah!*" Jasper exclaimed, his hands going toward his hair before he realized he truly was going to tug at it in abject frustration. His valet, Blumsey, would be most dissatisfied. Fisting them at his sides instead, he stared at her, rumpled and pink-cheeked and panting.

"I had best take you home."

Her expression saddened.

"I suppose after this, I will never see you again," she said, sitting up and beginning to straighten her clothing.

"Nonsense. You shall see me again. However, I tell you plainly that my fervent wish remains to strip you bare. Thus, each time we are in one another's company, I cannot pretend I will not try to entice and coerce you."

"Might we still kiss occasionally?" she asked, sipping her wine again, not looking the least daunted by his proclamation.

Looking heavenward, he saw only his white-painted ceiling high above.

"Miss Sudbury, if I kiss you and we are discovered, then you will be in exactly the position Lady Daphne warned you about. You cannot pretend to believe a kiss will leave you any less in ruins than if we were discovered tupping. Well, maybe a little, but not much. The incident would be exaggerated beyond all measure."

"You are correct," she said, rising to her feet. "I had best be getting home. I'm not such a horsewoman that my sister will believe I could enjoy riding this long."

"I could ride you forever," he muttered, and her gaze flew to his.

Jasper hadn't realized he'd spoken out loud. Shrugging, he offered her what he knew was a charmingly wicked grin, raising an eyebrow and making light of his words. He must stop saying things to lead her on, even if they felt true when he said them.

Miss Julia Sudbury—*his, forever!*

"Perhaps I should sneak out with only your Mrs. Crowley and a footman. And since it wouldn't do to be driven home in your carriage, I would prefer to walk. It's not far."

"A fifteen-minute stroll," he agreed, still feeling off-kilter by the attraction and, dare he think it, the tender affection he felt for this woman. "A very convenient distance between our two homes."

And yet, whether fifteen minutes or a handspan between them, until he had her in his arms again, she would be too far away!

Thus, Jasper couldn't resist drawing her to him, taking one of her nether cheeks firmly in each of his hands, squeezing them in spite of the thick riding fabric, and drawing her hips close against his.

When her mouth touched his, he sunk his teeth gently into her lower lip and ground himself against her.

"Mm," she moaned, the sound going right through him and making his loins hitch.

This was intolerable. Her tongue touched his lips, and he was the one to open his mouth and accept her sweet assault.

Continuing to rub against her, he felt like a raw youth. *Was he going to spend in his breeches?* The thought of doing so, at his age, made him stop completely.

Julia, however, continued to suckle on his tongue and press close. She would drive him straight to Bedlam.

Firmly, with hands on her upper arms, he set her back before walking, a little gingerly, to the bell-pull.

"Let's get you safely home, shall we?" He tried to sound casual, not as if he intended to go straight upstairs and bring himself to swift release in the privacy of his bedchamber. All the short while, he would recall how it felt to slip his fingers between her damp petals in the dark garden, and how hard the peak of her nipple had become with his ministrations.

"Thank you for understanding, my lord."

She was *thanking* him. He shook his head. Luckily, Mr. Greer arrived, ready to summon Rigley and Mrs. Crowley.

In a very few moments, the blonde gilflirt had departed, looking perfectly respectable, and Jasper took his stairs two at a time to offer himself relief.

THE FOLLOWING MORNING, JASPER went to number 32 Ludgate Street, entering the shop of the royally appointed jewelers, Mr. Philip Rundell and Mr. John Bridge. It was known among those who gambled how Mr. Bridge in particular helped out many a young, foolish nobleman, giving plenty of good coin for their aigrettes, signet rings, and pins and even for their wives' brooches and necklaces in order to bail them out of debt.

Although Jasper had a few careless friends who'd gambled and gotten into trouble, he had never imagined something of his would have ended up being pawned.

As it turned out, it was neither the older Mr. Rundell nor Mr. Bridge who assisted him, but the other Mr. Rundell, the nephew, whom Julia had mentioned having added his name to the old establishment.

"May I be of assistance?" the man asked.

"I'm looking to retrieve an item of mine that was sold to your shop. Hopefully, it still resides here."

"We can but hope," the man said.

Jasper narrowed his eyes. *Was Rundell mocking him or being genuine?* He nearly mentioned Julia, thinking to advise the jeweler not to let her sell anything more. Yet deciding upon discretion, he held his tongue.

"It's a sapphire cravat pin."

"If you'll step this way, my lord, out of the showroom and into the back, I'll see if I can find it. How long ago did you pawn it?" he asked over his shoulder as he went deeper into the recesses of the store.

"*I* didn't pawn it," Jasper practically spluttered, passing the elegant display cases as well as two gentlemen he knew, nodding to each in turn.

When Rundell faced him over a counter at the back of the store, Jasper couldn't tell if the man believed him or not. Then he decided he didn't care.

"How long ago did you say we acquired it?" Rundell asked, pulling out a ledger and placing it on the counter. Next, he drew spectacles from his pocket and affixed the wires around his ears until they were firmly in place.

"A few weeks," Jasper said vaguely. It felt as if he'd known and been entangled with Miss Sudbury for quite a bit longer. "But my name won't be in there."

The man eyed him. "No, of course not, sir, yet a description is made of each piece that is *pawned*."

Rundell said the last word so the *P* made an explosive sound. Jasper took a step back, feeling a little soiled.

"*Ah-ha,*" the jeweler said after a minute. "Here it is. You were correct, sir. There is no name as to the seller." He looked up at Jasper again over his spectacles as if he suspected him of something nefarious.

He shrugged. This was beyond tedious, watching Rundell shuffle through small boxes lined with felt. One labeled "Gentleman's Jewelry" and then another labeled "Sapphires." Then the man reached up onto the next shelf and drew down another labeled simply "Pins."

"I'm terribly sorry, but I don't see your pin here."

Jasper's disappointment must have shown upon his face, for the man made a clucking sound more apt for an older woman soothing a young child.

"Come now, sir, all isn't lost." He glanced again at the ledger. "It doesn't say it was sold. It may have been so handsome a piece that we cleaned it and set it out already for sale. I'll show you where they are kept in the store."

"Very good." Jasper let his hopes rise again. He even managed to tamp down the retort that the man had insulted his valet. His pin would have needed no cleaning. Blumsey made sure every jewel the earl owned sparkled and every white cravat was snowy as a swan.

He followed the man back onto the main floor.

"Perhaps your cravat pin is over here," Rundell said, as they passed the same two gentlemen. Again, Jasper nodded to each.

Approaching the display case of pins, Jasper spied it at once.

"That one," he said, more loudly than he ought, so relieved to lay eyes upon it again.

"Ah, yes. That is a fine pin." Rundell set it on a piece of black velvet atop the counter.

Jasper picked it up, immediately slipping it into his pocket.

"If you'll put that on my account," he began, but the man frowned, his gaze going toward the pocket.

"I'm sorry, sir. We don't sell pawned items on credit. They must be paid for as we have already laid out the money for the piece." Rundell held his hand out flat, awaiting the return of the pin. "I'm sure you understand," he added. "If you were unable to pay, we would be out the money *and* the pin."

Jasper blinked, his mouth agape.

"Unable to pay," he echoed, surprised at this turn of events. "That pin belonged to my father. It's a family keepsake. And not just any family—*my* family. I am the Earl of Marshfield!"

"Yes, I am aware you *say* you are, but—"

"Say I am!" Jasper's surprise became outrage. Turning around, his gaze landed upon the two men from his club. He didn't know them well, but one was a baron named Thomas, and the other . . . ? He searched his memory, but he couldn't recall. Regardless, he assumed one of them would know his identity.

Stalking toward them, he said, "Do either of you know who I am?"

The men glanced at one another before the baron said, "Yes, my lord."

"Then come over here please and tell this *store clerk* precisely with whom he is dealing."

Another glance passed between them before they followed him.

"Tell him," he said, pointing to Rundell. "Tell him who I am."

"Certainly," said the other of the two. "He is Lord Marshfield."

"Ha!" Jasper exclaimed, feeling vindicated.

Mr. Rundell sighed, looking unimpressed. "That is all very well, but we still have a policy at our store, one we've had since first accepting goods as pawn in the mid-eighteenth century."

"Pawn?" exclaimed the baron, and Jasper's stomach clenched. He'd made a tactical error.

"Yes," Mr. Rundell said. "If his lordship wishes to buy back his pin, which he is more than welcome to do, he must produce ready money or a London bank note."

"I see," Jasper said, realizing it made perfect sense and avidly wishing he hadn't let his pride get the better of him. "Thank you, gentlemen. That will be all."

"I can lend you some money," the baron offered. "After all, it's not like I can't find you at the club to collect it should you try to hide on me." He finished with a laugh.

Jasper felt his face grow warm. "That won't be necessary. Just hold the damned pin," he barked at Mr. Rundell, wrenching it from his pocket and slapping it back upon the velvet. "Do. Not. Sell. It. I'll go to the bank and return with the funds directly. How much for it?"

The sum made clear to him he was being swindled, but he would pay anything to get his goods out of the store.

And he would compare the price later with Julia to find out how much profit Rundell, Bridge, and bloody Rundell had made! At which time, he might wring her pretty neck.

"I'll hold it for the rest of the day, sir," the man called out after him as he strode across the store. The implication was clear—if you don't come back because you don't have the cash, then I'll sell it.

For the first time in recent memory, Jasper knew what it felt like to be on the high ropes of anger. *Glimflashy*, his mother used to say when she was particularly nettled by some injustice or annoyance.

At least he'd found his property and had the means to retrieve it. Why she'd done it, he couldn't fathom. But at all costs, he hoped to convince her never to do it again.

THE WORTHINGTON BUTLER BROUGHT in the mail as he did every morning and afternoon. Julia had become in the habit of looking through it after she'd moved in with Sarah to be her companion during the long mourning period. Even though her sister had not actually been grieving for a man she barely knew, handling the onslaught of mail from the earl's peers—and from those looking for a smidgen of the inheritance—had given Julia something to do. She'd answered most of the condolence notes and then let her sister sign them.

Recently, she'd hoped every day to receive some missive from Lord Marshfield, despite having thwarted his advances. *His very welcome advances.*

"Forbidden fruit," she muttered to herself, pouring her chocolate and examining the bowl of pears on the table before her, a luxury her sister had indulged in as soon as they'd appeared in Covent Garden's fruit stalls that month.

Drat the man for being a rake! Any other man who showed such interest, and who seemed to like her as he did—enough to save her from the varlet viscount and to keep her from being accused of stealing and even to take her riding on such a sweet mare—any other man might possibly offer for her. But not him, not a libertine!

A libertine who sorely missed his father's cravat pin.

Today, her heart skipped a beat when instead of the coveted black seal of the Earl of Marshfield, she saw a piece of grossly expensive lavender stationery addressed to Sarah with a *C* stamped into the blue wax. Either Lord or Lady Chandron, Julia surmised. Of course, it could be from someone else entirely, but she simply knew in her heart she was right.

Folding the letter, she tucked it into the small seam pocket of her day gown just as Sarah entered. She spent the next half hour eating eggs and toast while chatting with her sister as they opened the rest of the mail, sorted through the invitations, and read aloud a short letter from their father.

Feeling as if the lavender notepaper was burning a hole in her dress, Julia finally excused herself and dashed back to her room.

Lady Worthington,
I thought to have heard from you by now after I returned your reticule. I would hate to have to disclose your nefarious ways to our fine Metropolitan Police Force, but do not doubt I shall. That is unless you appear at my home on Friday at 9 p.m.
Lady Chandron

It was blackmail. What's more, the viscountess wanted to extract her retribution from Sarah!

CHAPTER SIXTEEN

"Lord M__'s house on Grosvenor Square was a hive of activity yesterday afternoon with not one but two females coming and going. Our favorite rake does not disappoint."

—The Morning Post

Julia could easily explain how she'd borrowed her sister's reticule, but what could the woman possibly want in order to remain silent about finding her jewelry inside the bag? Perhaps Lady Chandron would extort such a large sum of money Julia would have to ask Sarah for help, for she could hardly steal to pay off the wealthy!

What a dilemma!

The Earl of Marshfield came to mind. He was undoubtedly in a position to help. He could tell the viscountess how her husband had attacked Julia.

Pacing her room, she knew in all likelihood, he would help her, but at what cost? She had an inkling of the bargain he would strike and the payment he would demand. It would put her right back in the precarious position of which Lady Daphne had soundly warned.

It was times like these when a young woman was glad there was strong milky tea at hand. Nevertheless, when she was no closer to a solution by the end of the day and had drunk enough tea to float the Royal Navy, Julia began to think asking Jasper for help was her only choice.

Waving an invitation under Sarah's nose to attend an all-female gathering in the early evening, knowing her sister despised the particular hostess, Julia left without a chaperone.

Approaching Lord Marshfield's home on Grosvenor Square, she hoped he was at home. Half past seven was, after all, too early for rakes to be out gallivanting. Undoubtedly, he would think her mad with all her coming and going, but to protect Sarah from the consequences of Julia's rash behavior, she would do just about anything.

Lord Marshfield's butler allowed her entrance and said his lordship was at home.

Waiting in the drawing room, she glanced at the sofa, thinking it looked more wicked than any ordinary sofa ought. She hastily averted her eyes.

To her surprise, she heard Jasper's footfalls thumping down the stairs, as if he were running to reach her.

Stepping into the room, he grinned and her insides melted. She came to a decision, and smiled back. In the next instant, she was swept into his arms.

"You have returned," he murmured against her lips.

"Apparently," she said.

"Were you wanting more of my delicious claret?" he asked, already nibbling his way along her chin and down the column of her neck, making goosebumps break out across her arms. She shivered.

"This room is cold," he said. "I apologize. No fire tonight as I wasn't expecting to be in here. Let me—" He turned away toward the bell-pull, and she grabbed his arm.

"Is it warmer *upstairs*?" she asked, amazed at the husky tone to her voice. Yet as soon as she saw him, she'd known what she wanted to happen.

His eyes widened for a brief moment. Then he nodded. "Let's go to my study and wait while the maid lights the fire in my . . . bedroom?" the earl finished with a questioning note.

"All right," she agreed despite her knees feeling shaky.

And as easily as that, Julia found herself going upstairs with a scandalous rake. Her heart was beating fast as a bird's, and she wondered if he could hear it, for it seemed extraordinarily loud in her ears.

They crested the first landing, and he drew her along the hall to his study, all paneled wood, large oaken desk, and a roaring fire. There was a small sofa and two chairs and even a chessboard, with a game halfway played.

She wondered momentarily with whom he'd been playing. That question would wait, along with asking for assistance regarding the Lady Chandron. *Until after . . .*

Jasper pulled the bell. When there was a tap at the door a minute later, he went to it rather than having the servant enter. Except for the butler, no one had seen her. Feeling reassured, Julia could still flee if she changed her mind with hardly anyone the wiser.

When he closed the door once again, he came to stand beside her before the hearth.

"My bedroom should be warm soon. Meanwhile, I suggest a glass of brandy."

"Will I need it?" she asked, thinking of the pain she'd heard accompanied a proper deflowering.

He coughed, then lifted the crystal stopper from a decanter. "I certainly hope not. I will endeavor to make this nothing but pleasurable." He handed her a glass of amber liquid. "I confess I am surprised you came back, given that nothing has changed."

Nothing *had* changed—she still wanted him with a mad, almost inexplicable passion. The way she felt when he looked at her, how his sultry cologne made her heart race, and the constant longing for him to touch her again—none of that would change. Except perhaps, afterward, when she had been thoroughly and truly tupped, then maybe she would lose some of the craving for him.

"We seem to have a spark, sir."

"Call me Jasper, and yes, we do. Quite a remarkable one at that."

"Is it?" she asked. For she had no way of knowing if this was regular or something special.

"I promise you that it is."

She nodded, taking his word. He could easily be lying and say the same to every woman he bedded. But for her, there was a spark . . . and more. There was no denying she had grown a *tendre* for him.

Tonight, she might rid herself of these fond feelings by seeing his baser side, the one that drove him to such lusty behavior.

"Do you normally bring women here?" she asked. "I don't mean to your study of course, but to your home. It seems risky for the female concerned, especially if she is a wife."

She watched the earl sip his drink, his eyes flashing with secrets, perhaps memories of other women.

"In truth, no, my home is my sanctuary." And he said no more.

"Then why am I allowed?" she asked.

"You came here," he reminded her.

"You invited me, not once but twice."

"True," he said, setting his glass down. "Because you are not like other women."

Involuntarily, Julia took a step back, unsure if he was insulting her.

"Don't misunderstand me." He closed up the space with a single step across the plush gold-and-red carpet in her direction and put a hand on either side of her waist.

"Miss Sudbury, you are unfettered by any parents, at least in London. You are of an age when most women are married or engaged. You are innocent yet the most independent, bold woman I've ever met. And you are enticing beyond belief. In a word, you were meant for a tryst. And I can think of no better place than in my own bed, in the heart of my home."

The heart of his home. What an odd thing for a man to claim. Nevertheless, he had made her feel special. And his fingers kneading her lower back made her feel other things. She tingled at his touch and the sensation spread, maybe helped by the brandy she finished in two gulps.

"Do you think the room is ready?" she asked, then hiccupped. She wanted to get started, sure once they undressed and he began to stroke her, all her anxiousness would dissipate.

He smiled again, a wicked, sensual smile, causing her stomach to flip.

"Even if the air hasn't warmed yet, we will manage to heat up the chamber nicely." Taking her empty glass from her, he set it down. Then he paused.

"Is something wrong?" she asked.

He sent her a brief enigmatic look. "I thought to discuss an important matter, but suddenly, it seems less important."

"I, too, have something to speak with you about," she confessed. Julia wondered if maybe they shouldn't simply pour another glass of brandy, stay in his study, and chat like magpies.

Then he brushed his thumb across her lower lip, and she trembled. It was too late to turn back.

"It seems odd to take your arm as if we are entering a ballroom," he said. "I could pick you up and carry you."

She grimaced. It sounded most uncomfortable.

"Why don't you take my hand?" She peeled off her gloves and tucked them inside her bag. When her eyes found his again, she was astonished by his glittering gaze.

"I like the way you strip off your gloves. Most alluring."

How sweet! How absurd!

She nearly giggled with nervousness, but then Jasper threaded his fingers through hers, and it felt perfectly natural. He led her across the hall to the familiar door beyond which he'd first caught her, knee-deep in trouble.

There would be far more agreeable trouble that evening.

His was a magnificent bedroom, befitting an earl, she supposed. Before, she hadn't seen it with welcoming lamps lit. The fire was barely visible behind an elegant fire screen and had hardly begun to remove the chill. She recalled the thick Persian rug under foot, but a small table set with claret, fruit, cheese, and bread rolls was now laid before the fire. She supposed that was for afterward, if they needed sustenance due to their . . . exertions.

Shivering at the thought, Julia wondered what would happen next and how quickly.

As Jasper shut the door and twisted the key in the lock behind her, she turned her gaze toward the bed. A large mahogany four-poster was prominently centered on the wall to her right. It looked indulgent, luxurious, downright sensual, and almost medieval with a brocade canopy and matching hangings.

The satin cover had been turned down.

Dragging her gaze from it, her attention was snagged by a large wooden globe with no map painted upon it. Crossing the room to where it perched high on four gold-tipped feet, she inspected it.

Jasper was suddenly at her back, his warm body pressed against hers. Reaching around her, he swiveled one half of the top of the globe open to reveal a clever writing desk. Julia opened the other side. It was tidy inside and out with little drawers and cubbies. A few items were strewn on its surface, a couple gold coins, a medal of some sort with a royal ribbon attached, a pocket watch, and some pearl buttons.

"How curious," she said. "I've never seen anything quite like it."

"I don't use it. It's too small, and I prefer to work in my study, but I like the look of it."

Then he turned her slowly in the circle of his arms. "Are you stalling? Or would you like to examine my armoire as well for its quality craftmanship?"

Not wanting to let her fears get the better of her, she blurted, "No, I think we should get started."

"You think we should . . . *Oh!*" he exclaimed, taken aback.

"Only to quell the anticipation, you understand," she added.

"I do. In that case, your wish is my command." Starting with her black beaver hat with its tassels and feathers, Jasper deftly withdrew the hatpins before placing them alongside it on the now open desk.

Julia let him shed her layers of clothing starting with her blue gown trimmed in black and her petticoat, and then he released her stays. Soon, she stood in only a knee-skimming, soft cotton chemise and stockings. Hugging herself, she blinked at him.

"Your turn," she said softly.

JASPER HAD NEVER UNDERTAKEN such a calm seduction before. He couldn't truly even call it such, since she'd presented herself for the taking. As he'd told her, he wasn't usually in his own bedroom with a conquest, but in some rented room or a widow's chamber or a courtesan's apartment.

Moreover, it was odd not to be kissing hurriedly and throwing clothing along with caution to the far corners of the room, ending up as two heated bodies tangled in the bed linens.

Instead, he'd draped her gown and petticoat over the nearest chair as if he were her maid.

Shrugging out of his jacket and removing his cravat, braces, and shirt, he felt a little awkward under her unwavering scrutiny. Even Blumsey didn't survey him so closely when preparing him for a ball.

"You have a fine-looking chest," she offered, still hugging her arms around herself. "The perfect breadth, I think. And your arms are most appealing in their bulk."

"Thank you." He couldn't recall a woman appraising him in such an open way before. He was half afraid next she would measure the length of his cock.

After kicking off the slippers he wore at home, he removed his stockings before facing her in his trousers, having eschewed his breeches for the less dressy ankle-length inexpressibles while at home.

Surprising him, Julia reached out and gently stroked the smattering of hair on his chest, tracing its path downward. With his gaze, he followed the movement of her fingertips until she stopped at his waist. He sucked in a breath at her bold touch, his member, which was already hard, stiffened further, jutting against the heavy twilled cotton.

And there it was. Within the space of a heartbeat, she had enflamed him beyond all reason.

As most men of his class, he wore no drawers, using the long tail of his shirt to protect his manhood. Thus, in short order, after unfastening the fall front, he tugged down his trousers and stood entirely bare before her, hoping he wasn't frightening to look at. A certain part of him felt as fierce as an infantryman's pike.

Pulse racing, he swept an arm behind her knees and lifted her off her feet, cradling her for the three paces to the bed, where he gently lay her down.

"Mm," she said. "Very comfortable."

He didn't feel like talking. Instead, he undid the simple bow at the top of her chemise, widening the neckline until her breasts were exposed.

At last!

She was as beautiful and perfect as he'd imagined. Immediately, he bent low to kiss the valley between her full mounds, his hands cupping each before he took one of her pert nipples into his mouth.

She gasped, making him smile against her soft skin even as he licked and sucked her rosy peak. When she arched off his bed, he slipped an arm beneath her, holding her up so he could easily give similar treatment to her other nipple. And all the while, he breathed in the alluring scent of her, a heady blend of citrus and jasmine.

Her hands sank into his hair and tugged, then pushed, and then tugged again as if she couldn't decide what she wanted yet mindlessly wanted more.

Happy to oblige, he moved down her body, settling between her thighs before lifting the hem of her chemise, rendering her motionless.

"Jasper," she said on a panting breath, which shot bolts of desire straight through him.

"Julia," he returned. Without hesitating, he kissed her most intimate spot, burying his face against her soft curls.

Again, she gasped. Her hand shot down to cover herself and ward him off.

"It's all right," he told her.

"It's . . . I don't know. I didn't think . . . ," and she trailed off, but removed her hand.

Carefully, slowly, he drew apart the petals of her female flesh, hearing her intake of breath when he exposed her little nub.

He could wait no longer, touching it with the tip of his tongue.

"Oh!" she cried out. *"Ohhhh!"*

He took that as a good sign. She wasn't a prude but a passionate woman, ready to experience everything he had to offer.

To that end, he continued a tongue-lashing assault that had her writhing beneath him. He could coax her to a climax so easily, but there was much more to experience. Kissing her inner thigh, feeling the goosebumps raise under his fingers, he nibbled her softly.

When she moaned, when her dampness was obvious, he reached for the finest French protection in his bedside drawer and slid it on. The very act itself, seeing her curious eyes watching him intently, nearly made him spend.

"May I?" he asked, never having voiced the question at this late moment before, yet wanting her permission all the same.

"Yes, please," she said. "I am all a-tingle. Hot and . . ." She fisted her hands on his silk counterpane. "If you don't quench the fire within me, I shall have to do it myself."

"I promise, I will take care of you."

"I think I would reach the pinnacle," she said, her eyes firmly closed now, "if you merely blew your breath upon me."

He was going to do a damned bit more than that. Seating the head of his cock to her ready opening, he stroked it up and down, coating the thin sheath he wore with her sweet juice.

"Despite your demands, we'll go slowly so as to cause you the least discomfort. I want—"

The sudden knocking at his bedroom door seemed impossible. He was master of his house, lord of his domain, and the only other occupants were his servants, trusted staff who knew better than to interrupt him in the middle of an assignation.

Jasper hoped he'd imagined it, that it was simply the sound of his heart—or hers.

The knock came again. He knew it was real when Julia sat up, eyes wide, and grabbed for the counterpane to cover herself.

Someone was going to lose his or her place of service in about ten seconds. Pushing himself off the bed, Jasper stalked to the door and, bare naked, yanked it open.

Mr. Greer stood there. How unfortunate. Jasper quite liked his butler, but the man would have to go. Even if he'd been holding a bottle of the finest champagne, he would be relieved of it without a nod of gratitude and then given the boot.

"Your employment is terminated."

The man didn't bat an eyelid. "Yes, my lord. Lady Worthington is downstairs," Mr. Greer said, keeping his gaze trained on Jasper's face, never wavering, nor looking down even an inch, his face a permanent mask of placidity.

"Well, damn!" Jasper said, hearing Julia shriek something behind him. Obviously, she had heard.

"Can you not send the countess away?" he asked Mr. Greer, whom he'd quickly decided not to sack.

"No, sir. She will not go. I could only barely manage to keep her from coming upstairs."

The man had actually earned himself a raise.

"What does she want?" he asked, feeling himself lowering to half-mast. As if he didn't know.

"She wants her sister, sir."

"Don't we all," Jasper muttered, hearing the female in question scurrying around behind him, probably in full view of the butler while she retrieved her clothing. Not that Mr. Greer would dare even the tiniest peek.

"Very well. Tell Lady Worthington Miss Sudbury and I shall be down upon the instant. If she tries to come up here again, you have my permission to lay hands upon her and restrain her. In fact, since I've re-hired you, it's an order."

"Yes, my lord." With the slightest inclination of his head, Mr. Greer retreated.

Shutting the door, Jasper turned around.

CHAPTER SEVENTEEN

"What type of party was it, dear reader? Lord M__ and Miss S__ showed up at Lady Ch__'s home at a late hour. Separately. Neither stayed long enough for a civilized dining experience."

—The Sun

J ulia was tying the neckline of her chemise with trembling fingers. Not an excited, anticipatory, please-Jasper-touch-me-again trembling either. This was the true trembling of fear. Her older sister had come to the earl's house. Worse, she was downstairs and knew Julia was upstairs.

Upstairs, about to be ruined!

And how she had wanted to be ruined, too. Even then, she couldn't keep her gaze off of Jasper's magnificent figure as he stalked around the room, snatching up his clothes. The muscles of his rear end particularly fascinated her, slowing her attempt to do up her stays. She finished with them a little loose but hurriedly stepped into her petticoat, thankful he hadn't removed her stockings.

Far more swiftly than her, Jasper was dressed, albeit not as neatly as when his valet assisted him. He stood beside her holding her gown. Raising her arms, Julia allowed him to slip it over her head before she donned her short bustier.

"My spencer," she urged, and he jumped to grab it from the chair. She shrugged into her favorite blue and gray coat. "Ready."

"Your hair," he said. "I'm afraid it is hopeless to think I can recreate the style in which it was done before I caused you to writhe upon my bed."

Had she been writhing?

She ran to his long mirror. Plainly, she looked a fright. With quick fingers, she smoothed through the locks of her hair before snatching up his comb and using it. Even more quickly, she made one thick braid.

"Do you have a ribbon?"

Surprisingly, he nodded. "I believe so." From the drawer of his side table, the same one from which he'd extracted the strange covering for his lengthy organ, the sheath that had long since been discarded, he withdrew a gray ribbon.

She didn't even ask whose it was or why he had it, but used it to secure the end of her thick plait.

Another knock at the door, and Jasper went to open it.

From what she could overhear, her sister was about to storm the stairs, and Julia's temper started to simmer.

"My hat," she hissed and smacked it upon her head, before sticking in a pin so hard she grazed her skull. *"Ow!"*

"Are you ready?" he asked.

"Yes. What's more, I've gone from mortified to blistering angry at her interference."

With those fighting words, Julia marched past him and the silent butler, who waited just outside the door. She headed downstairs, stomping as she did.

As expected, Sarah wasn't waiting politely in the drawing room, but was pacing at the foot of the staircase.

"How dare you!" Julia said, preempting anything her sister was about to say.

"How dare *I*? How dare *you*?" Sarah retorted. "And *why* would you?"

"You shouldn't have come here," Julia countered.

"Nor should you. You are supposed to be at Lady Rendon's gathering for women."

"I changed my mind. Let me remind you, I am a single woman, unattached, beholden to no one."

Sarah's mouth opened, then closed, before she looked past Julia to the man coming down the stairs. Her expression became a mask of anger.

Julia didn't turn, thinking it better not to make eye contact with the earl.

"Countess," came Jasper's smooth tone.

Julia had assumed he would be contrite or, at the very least, embarrassed. Instead, he passed her before coming to a stop directly in front of Sarah as if to welcome her. He didn't take her hand, though, since he was as likely to be punched if he tried.

"To what do I owe the pleasure of your unexpected visit?"

There was a hard edge to his voice, and Julia realized he was as upset at the interruption as she was.

"Lord Marshfield, can you truly be asking me that question," Sarah spat out each word, "when my sister was here. Alone. With you!"

When Jasper said nothing, she added, "*Without* a chaperone."

He gestured behind him, in Julia's general direction.

"As you can see, you had no call to rush to her aid. Miss Sudbury is unharmed."

"Is she?" Sarah snapped. "What about her reputation?"

Julia swallowed, watching the battle unfold.

"Her reputation," Jasper repeated. "Why, it is as solid and unblemished as ever it was."

Julia tried to make out if he was insulting her, saying she'd never had a perfect reputation to begin with, or was defending her.

"What's more," he continued, "she will have no cause to worry about her respectability unless *you* choose to tarnish her name."

"Me?" Sarah took an indignant step back. "I will always protect my sister."

Julia recalled how she'd intended to follow Lady Daphne's advice and protect Sarah, but her good sense had gone out the window when Lady Chandron's strange and threatening missive had arrived.

Turning to Jasper had seemed a good, albeit wanton and self-indulgent, idea. Moreover, she'd never got around to asking him for assistance.

"It is *you* who is tarnishing her," Sarah continued. "You were entertaining her in your private rooms. Even if alone, you both would seem less guilty if I'd discovered you in the drawing room. My sister showed terrible judgment going upstairs with you."

"I think she made a particularly fine choice in doing so," Jasper shot back.

Julia was about to berate them for discussing her as if she wasn't there when her dear sister turned her gaze upon her and said words that broke her heart.

"I have failed you."

Julia rushed forward and clasped Sarah's hands, hearing Jasper mutter something under his breath that sounded like "calculating crone."

"No, you haven't," Julia insisted, feeling tears well. "There is no calamity." She knew Sarah would say nothing to anyone, and thus her reputation was as intact as her frustrating virginity.

"Why are you trying to throw your life away on this worthless rogue?"

"I say," Jasper began. "That's rather harsh."

"You don't even know him," Julia said, although she didn't know him too well herself—except that he kissed divinely, smelled like a God, had muscles as if sculpted by

Michelangelo, and had the ability to make her purr. "He isn't worthless."

She couldn't quite get herself to declare him *not a rogue.* In fact, she feared he was.

"I know his type," Sarah continued. "More to the point, *you* know his type. Again, I ask, why are you being reckless?"

Julia could do nothing but sigh. She could hardly say she wanted to experience passion. Nor could she confess she was growing a ridiculous affection for this particular rogue. That way lay madness. She knew it, but there was no denying her heart had become entangled.

"Let's go home and leave his lordship in peace," Julia said.

"Miss Sudbury," Jasper started behind her, sounding as if he were going to protest her imminent departure.

Finally, she looked him squarely in his coffee-brown eyes. She could clearly recall how he'd watched for her reaction while sliding down her body to kiss her most private area. She curled her hands at her sides, thinking of his gaze holding hers, then lowering at the last second, as his mouth touched her—

"Surely you must understand," Julia said, "I need to leave with my sister." Sarah would probably wash her hands of her altogether if she did aught else. And what an unfathomable insult it would be to send her away and return to Jasper's warm, inviting bed.

Still, she couldn't help wishing her sister had never come and interrupted them.

"Will I see you again?" he asked, rather outrageously given the circumstances.

"No," Sarah's voice exclaimed.

Julia sighed and offered him a smile, thinking it best not to give him an answer until she sorted out her emotions.

"Good evening, my lord." With that, she turned, took her sister's arm under hers, and departed.

Sarah had come after Julia in a hackney, and so they drove home together in the Worthington carriage she'd borrowed. Resting against the late-earl's leather squabs, Julia saw no reason to speak, but simply let Sarah lecture her endlessly.

Something had shifted irrevocably inside her that night. She'd meant what she'd said in Jasper's foyer. She was beholden to no one. As outrageous as it was to even think it, Julia was determined to make Sarah understand she would no longer allow herself or her actions to be curtailed. She was not of the Mayfair set, and she would stop pretending as though she had to be ruled by their strict code.

"If discovered, you wouldn't be allowed to attend the meanest of social gatherings, never mind a ball at Lady Stilton's."

Those few words penetrated her brain. The only thing Julia would continue to do was take Mrs. Zebodar as chaperone when necessary in order to gain proximity to the *bon ton*'s wealthiest members—and their jewelry—for as long as she could. *How else could she help the poor?*

If her father or sister ever saw the types of places she'd been going to, carrying large amounts of coinage and bank notes, they would be livid. But the workhouses in Shoreditch, Whitechapel, and Wapping, the better of the worst districts east of London, had received her donations gratefully.

Occasionally, she caught families of women and children at the poorhouse gates prior to admitting themselves. Then Julia gave them enough money to turn away from the institution. At least for a month, sometimes longer. Now, as the winter months approached, the biting misery on the streets of London would get worse.

Sometimes, Julia felt as if she were the only one throwing money at the problem.

"I could send you back to Father," Sarah continued.

That got Julia's full attention. But it wasn't the threat her sister supposed. After all, life was peaceful and easy in Chislehurst. If Julia could forget the squalor she'd seen and the hollowed cheekbones and sunken eyes of the Rookery children, perhaps she could relax in the country and find herself a solid gentleman farmer—*a Johnny-raw*, as Jasper had once called such a fellow. She might become a contented wife.

The earl's wicked grin came to mind, along with his sparkling eyes. Even then, her stomach did a delightful twinge, imagining him touching her again.

She sighed loudly.

"Don't worry," Sarah said, mistaking Julia's emotions. "I won't do it. I would miss your company too much. And I would worry you'd never find a husband. But you must behave yourself."

Julia opened her mouth to argue, then closed it. She would tell Sarah of her burgeoning notion of independence another day. Tomorrow, she had to meet Lady Chandron and discover her fate.

JASPER WAS SHOWN INTO Lady Chandron's sitting room without delay. The missive requesting his presence had been short and mysterious, saying only it would be to his benefit to come. No matter. He'd been sent enigmatic notes from women before, and even though he had no further romantic interest in this particular one, his curiosity was piqued.

As long as she wasn't going to beg him to rekindle their association, he didn't mind a brief detour in his day. Also, if some good brandy was offered or at least some tawny port.

"A drink, my good man," he asked the Chandrons' butler before the man could disappear and leave Jasper alone to wait. "Brandy, if you have some decent stuff. Nothing homemade, mind you."

"Yes, my lord." And the butler disappeared. His answer told Jasper nothing about whether he would receive something potable and if so, when.

The door opened again two minutes later, and the butler entered with a silver tray containing a glass of amber liquid. All expectation of a soothing drink was instantly shoved from Jasper's mind when Miss Julia Sudbury followed the man into the room.

The mystery had deepened tremendously.

She stopped and stared, her mouth forming a beautiful O. Clearly, she was as surprised by his presence as he was by hers.

He bowed to her, then took the brandy from the tray.

"Perhaps you wish to order a beverage." He sipped the drink. "The Chandrons' brandy is good."

"No," she said. "Thank you." Then she looked to the butler. "Are more . . . guests expected tonight?"

"I wouldn't know, miss." And then he left them alone.

"We meet again," Jasper said, then offered Julia the glass, which she accepted without looking at it, keeping her gaze on his. Her cheeks had already developed a healthy rosy color. Not surprising as his own thoughts of her were decidedly blush-worthy.

Taking a small sip, she coughed, took another, then returned the glass to him.

"Brandy is as helpful as tea for such situations," she remarked.

He nodded. "What *is* the situation, as you see it?"

She blinked. "I received a strongly worded invitation. I assume you received one as well, and I also assume it has to do with our entanglement here the night of the ball."

He supposed she had the right of it, and the mystery was starting to make sense.

"I was summoned because she found my reticule in her chamber." Julia hesitated, and Jasper had a sickening feeling the reticule contained something belonging to the viscountess.

Julia looked as nervous as a fox at a hunt. "I must have lost it when her husband attacked me. Why were you brought here?"

"I have no idea." Downing the last sip, he set the glass on a round table inlaid with heavily polished leather. Unable to fight the impulse to get nearer to Julia again, he closed the distance until he could detect her pleasant fragrance of flowers and orange oil.

Could he take her in his arms? He glanced behind her, but the door was ajar. Too risky!

Still, he could at least steal a kiss. Leaning forward, while her eyes widened in surprise, he claimed her lips with a quick but firm kiss, tugging on her lower lip as he drew away.

Looking a little dazed, she put a gloved hand to her mouth.

He couldn't help tracing a finger along her jawline, wishing he could do so with his tongue and then lick the rest of her.

"I was told something of particular interest to me would be taking place. I came from sheer curiosity," he confessed. "I didn't really think I'd been *summoned*."

Yet Jasper considered the tone of the note. "Now that you put it that way, I almost feel like leaving."

"I hope you don't, Marshfield," the viscountess said, having entered the room without his noticing. Then the infernal woman looked at Julia and smirked.

"The wrong sister has come, I see!"

CHAPTER EIGHTEEN

Julia was pleased to have the opportunity to set Lady Chandron straight.

"I believe you're laboring under the misunderstanding my sister attended your ball the night you discovered the reticule. Yet it was I who enjoyed your hospitality."

Although *hospitality* wasn't the word that sprang to mind when she thought of the odious Lord Chandron. She glanced at Jasper, who remained silently watching her explanation.

"Her calling cards were in it, but I assure you, Lady Worthington was not carrying the reticule," Julia continued, "nor did she set foot here that night. My sister merely loaned me her bag."

"I see," the viscountess said, moving around the room with a swishing of satin. "Then your sister is *not* a jewel thief."

Julia felt her stomach drop as Jasper startled beside her. *Drat and double drat!*

"Certainly not," she said, trying to sound as if the notion was too incredible even to suggest, and by inference that nor could she be one, either. "The very idea," she added, hazarding a glance at Jasper, whose mouth had compressed into a tight line of disapproval.

"*Tsk, tsk,*" Lady Chandron said. "The idea of it! So distasteful. Only imagine my surprise to find my bed in disarray and a strange reticule with two pieces of my jewelry in it."

"*Hm,*" was all Julia could think to say until she learned which way the wind was blowing. Thus far, the viscountess didn't seem too threatening. But her gaze darted again to the earl. If he hadn't already guessed, now he knew for certain his pin had not been the sole instance of her snabbling the belongings of others.

Jasper didn't raise an eyebrow, but his jaw tightened almost imperceptibly.

"Why am I here?" he asked, sounding bored. "This lady and I have no understanding between us, nor do I with the Lady Worthington."

That stung. But after the kiss and caress he'd just bestowed, Julia believed he had an ulterior motive to proclaiming his disinterest in her.

"Not true, Marshfield," the viscountess refuted. "I saw you escort them both to the cricket match. I know you. You don't do that unless you're enjoying the favors of one or both."

Julia felt her cheeks heat up, but determinedly didn't look again at the earl.

"Besides my husband said you defended the owner of that reticule the night of my ball."

Julia had to interrupt. "Did your husband also tell you he assaulted my person?"

Instead of appearing in the least upset, Lady Chandron lifted a shoulder with a shrug of utter disregard.

"Lord Chandron can be a bit feisty," she allowed.

Feisty! At that softening of the event, Julia did glance at Jasper, who appeared to be seething.

"Besides, that changes nothing," Lady Chandron insisted. "To put it plainly, you were in my bedroom stealing my jewels. My husband, luckily, retrieved them for me. And now, you owe me a boon, or I shall tell everyone what I know."

Julia frowned. Lady Chandron dismissed her husband's brutish behavior at the same time as threatening her. She simply did not understand Jasper's peers.

"No one cares about my doings," Julia said softly, wishing that were true.

"In case you hadn't noticed," Lady Chandron said, narrowing her eyes, "you've already been honored by our gossip rags. But I wasn't talking about you. I have your sister's cards. It will be the countess's name I shall drag through the mud. She shall be under suspicion wherever she goes."

Stunned, Julia fell silent. With one thing and another, she was starting to wish Sarah had never married an earl and moved to London.

"And then there is Marshfield," Lady Chandron continued. She offered him a smug smile.

He barked out a laugh. "You cannot muddy my name," Jasper pointed out. "My reputation has already been well tarnished under the heels and wheels of my fellow noblemen. At least until it's their turn in the gossip rags, and then the position, like the wheel of fortune, is reversed. Sometimes I'm in favor, and sometimes I'm out of it."

"A pretty speech, but I wasn't going to say you were having an affair with the Lady Worthington, or even with this one," she added, making Julia feel like a bit of carpet fluff. "That's too easy, too expected, too obvious. Even telling everyone you're with both sisters at once will hardly raise an eyebrow where you're concerned. I seem to recall your name was linked with twin sisters before. From Coventry, weren't they?"

Again, Julia swung her gaze to the earl. *Was that true?*

He didn't look at her, keeping his attention trained firmly on their adversary and ignoring the baiting remarks.

"What's this about, then?" he demanded.

The viscountess smiled. Julia thought she looked positively devilish.

"You and I were a good match, weren't we?" Lady Chandron asked.

Julia stifled a gasp. She hoped the viscountess didn't mean—

"In bed and out of it," the woman added.

Julia felt her stomach drop. Jasper had gone to bed with Lady Chandron! *Why hadn't he mentioned that before?*

"Yet I've dangled an invitation more than once lately, and you haven't taken me up on it. Why?"

Julia watched, fascinated by this exchange. The married viscountess was truly asking the rake why he didn't wish to compromise her further. *And in front of a stranger, no less!*

Why, the woman had no morals at all. What's more, Julia wanted to hear his answer nearly as much as Lady Chandron. After all, the viscountess was wealthy, attractive, and apparently available for the taking.

Jasper didn't speak immediately. He was clearly weighing his words. Finally, he came up with a line that Julia thought rather smart, designed not to offend.

"I didn't want to endanger your marriage," he said.

The viscountess appeared momentarily taken aback, then her face broke out in a smile, and finally, she laughed.

"I thought for a moment you were serious. Now I realize, you're just playing with me. You know I would have left him for you years ago."

Gracious! Julia wondered if the woman were in love with the earl. She actually started to feel sorry for Lady Chandron, trapped in a marriage she so obviously didn't want.

"You're treading carefully, Marshfield. You don't want to say anything that might hurt my feelings. I suppose I should appreciate that, but I think you're foolish not to take the offer to save yourself and this girl's sister. After all," she put her hands upon her shapely hips, "everyone is the same in the horizontal position with one's eyes closed."

Jasper had a mulish expression, and Julia was certain he wasn't going to be pushed by the viscountess into doing anything.

Lady Chandron recognized the same and sighed.

"Anyway," she turned her attention to Julia again, whom she'd all but dismissed. "I like new experiences and new people, too."

"No," Jasper said firmly. "Do not even think it."

Julia's gaze swiveled between him and the viscountess, puzzled as to what was happening.

Having got his dander raised, Lady Chandron looked pleased with herself.

"I'll let you both off my fisherman's hook for the price of one of you. I prefer Marshfield, but I don't particularly mind which one I take."

"I beg your pardon," Julia said, having lost the thread of their discussion. "Take one of us where?"

For the second time, the viscountess dissolved into riotous laughter.

"Exactly what hook do you think I'm on?" Jasper asked, looking decidedly unamused.

"Why the loss of your fortune, of course. A desperate secret you want none of our set to discover. Why else would you be helping this girl steal jewelry and selling your own at Rundell and Bridge?"

Jasper's gaze darted to her, and Julia flinched from the flash of anger she registered in their tawny depths. This was her fault. And she'd learned when they were at Lady Daphne's, the earl did not like his fortune to be called into question.

"I assure you, madam, the Marshfield estate is as healthy as ever it was," he said. "Your information is wrong, and I am not on your hook in any manner whatsoever."

"Really? So, you can afford to buy a pair of horses?" The viscountess pursed her mouth into a petulant moue. "Too bad." She turned her attention back to Julia, licking her lips as she carefully scrutinized her from head to toe. "I guess I'll take you, then."

A shudder raced through Julia as she finally grasped the woman's meaning.

"But I . . . that is . . ." *Good lord!*

"No," Jasper said again.

"Then you'll give me what I want," Lady Chandron concluded, taking a step toward him. "We'll take up where we left off."

His clenched his jaw again, no longer even glancing at Julia. Then he nodded.

"My word!" the viscountess exclaimed. "Chivalry has reared its head in the form of a rake saving a woman's virtue. How rich!"

Quick as a whip, she pulled something from her side seam pocket and handed it to Julia.

"A token that I shall keep my word and not bother your sister, or you, any further."

Staring at her sister's calling card in her palm, Julia ought to feel relief, but her thoughts were swirling. Jasper was going to "take up" with this woman again. *For her sake!*

"I won't let you do this," she told him, wishing he would look at her.

But it was the viscountess who spoke. "This has nothing more to do with you. Consider yourself lucky. If Marshfield hadn't agreed, I would have given my distraught statement to *The Times* about two sisters who work together. One uses her title to garner the invitations, the other enters in her place and nabs the baubles. I suppose after the outcry, I would have had to go to the magistrate's office as well."

At that moment, with Lady Chandron's face twisted into petulance and threat, she looked like a monster.

"You can go," Jasper said evenly, and Julia realized he was dismissing her from harm's way.

"Unless you want to watch," the woman quipped. "In which case, I will offer you a comfortable chair in my bedchamber. In fact, let's all have a glass of wine and go upstairs. I'm already feeling quite damp at the thought of our fun tonight." And she whisked out a fan from her sleeve, popping it open before waving it over her face and neck.

"Miss Sudbury will leave at once," Jasper said, this time forcefully.

There was nothing she could do. With tears in her eyes, not knowing why she wanted to cry over a libertine getting to tup a beautiful woman, Julia fled.

JASPER WATCHED JULIA LEAVE. The tightness in his chest eased, knowing she was safe, and then he turned to the conniving female who had an expression of a cat licking cream.

"I'm leaving, too," he said.

"Don't be foolish, Marshfield. Just because I gave her the calling cards doesn't mean I won't go to the authorities."

"I know. But tonight is inconvenient. I am expected elsewhere. I only stopped by briefly out of curiosity. Now that I know this will be a longer visit, I will have to postpone to another time."

She paused. "I suppose I've waited this long. You will make it worth my while, I'm sure." Then she shook her head. "So, you really care for this country girl?"

He wasn't about to discuss Julia Sudbury with her or anyone. He was still digesting the knowledge she was a habitual thief. He'd guessed as much since discovering her in Lady Daphne's room holding the bracelet, but he hadn't believed it.

Without further delay and with no niceties of gracious departure, Jasper strode from the room. Not waiting for the Chandrons' butler, he threw open the front door and, feeling dangerously tweaguey, left it wide open to the elements.

His carriage was waiting out front, but as he put his foot on the bar to alight, he looked down the street. There was Miss Sudbury, ambling along.

Annoyed at the very sight of her, he had his driver pull up beside the brat nevertheless.

"What the devil?" he asked.

"I came by hired carriage. I didn't want to use my sister's again, nor tell her where I was going. But my hackney seems to have vanished."

"You should never pay them until the end of your journey," he snapped irritably. No one from Town would ever make such a mistake. "We might as well travel together in my carriage."

"My reputation," she reminded him.

"I don't think a carriage ride can make anything worse, and we must speak privately."

She let him help her into the two-seater carriage, and as she leaned back against the squabs, he realized she was shaking.

Sitting beside her, Jasper draped an arm around her shoulders.

"She's as mad as a march hare!" Julia exclaimed after they set off.

"Nonsense. She's quite sane."

"But she said she didn't care whether it was you or me."

"Pleasure is pleasure," he said, feeling weary. At least, he'd always thought that to be true. Now however, when faced with performing a service for the viscountess, one that ought to be pleasurable, he felt not a twinge of desire, nor even anticipation. What he felt was revulsion.

"Perhaps you're correct," he amended. "That woman has to be a little touched in the head not to care whether I want to participate."

Silence met his words, then she said, "We could try blackmailing Lady Chandron in return."

This caused Jasper to turn his head, bringing their faces close.

"I would say 'continue with your plan,' except I don't think she has any shame, nor would she care about her reputation since everyone already knows about her many infidelities. She's like a female rakehell," he concluded. "Thus, she cannot be blackmailed. Even her husband already knows and cares not a whit."

"We could toss her in the Thames," Julia suggested with a bitter laugh.

"I'm not eager to dance on the end of a rope," Jasper retorted.

"I suppose you could go to her and be absolutely offensive, unclean, disheveled, with bad breath and knotted hair, and try to put her off."

"I could try," Jasper said.

Julia sighed. "I would find it difficult to imagine you not being entirely desirable," she said softly.

When he heard those words, he forgave her getting him under the hatches of trouble. Cradling the back of her head, holding her steady, he claimed her warm lips.

When she parted them, he swept his tongue into her mouth, stroking her, hearing her moan.

Her blossoming desire was evident, and he placed her hand upon his lap so she could feel his own. The rest of the ride passed with their mouths fused as one, and his only thought being when he could attempt to seduce her out of her clothing again.

Having the viscountess confirm his blonde baggage was *on the game*, spicing jewels from his peers, hadn't dampened his passion after all.

Realizing they'd stopped moving and were probably conspicuously parked in front of the Countess of Worthington's house, he drew back.

He'd hoped they would come up with a plan to get him out of tupping Lady Chandron but feared it was inevitable. And while holding Julia in his arms, he was dreading riding St. George all the more, when St. George would be the viscountess.

Would he even be able to put in a good showing, or would it be a dry bob?

"I shall get it over with," Jasper said, half to himself, hoping Lady Chandron would be satisfied with a single ride.

Julia stared at him. Then she blinked and her gaze hardened.

He shouldn't have mentioned it, not directly after kissing her. *Where were his manners?*

"YOU'RE THE TRUE RAKEHELL," she bit out, reaching for the carriage's handle. "Why don't you go back there immediately and give her what she most wants. I'm sure you'll manage to derive some enjoyment, about as much as any paid courtesan in London!"

When Jasper said nothing, Julia glanced up at him. His expression was stony.

"You know something, you're perfectly correct. I should do exactly that. It is nothing to me whom I bed. I shall do it and set us both free from her threats."

Julia bit her tongue and wished she hadn't spoken out of jealousy. She didn't believe for an instant he wasn't discerning about whom he took to bed, although to learn he'd already had an affair with Lady Chandron had been a blow.

Besides, she must recall with whom she was dealing. That very night Jasper might be visiting a mistress whom she knew nothing about. Moreover, it was none of her business. Unfortunately, her heart was becoming ridiculously possessive.

How terrible! It was utter idiocy to feel that way over this man. She would have to give herself a stern talking-to later. Right then, however, she wanted to make him say he wouldn't go through with it, or at least that he wouldn't enjoy it.

"How do we know if you do what she wants, she'll stop her extortion?" Julia wondered.

"More importantly, how do we know you'll stop your infernal behavior so no one else can threaten you with a trip to the Bow Street magistrate's court."

Julia opened her mouth, but nothing came out. He wouldn't understand how much good the money from pawning was doing across London. As an earl, he would value property rights above the far-reaching social good.

Still, she could try. "I put the money from their sale to good use," she began.

"There is no excuse," he interrupted. "And I might not be of interest to the next blackmailer," he continued, his tone scathing. "We're fortunate she wants me. Otherwise, she would be on her way to the authorities tomorrow."

Julia knew he was shaming her and trying to make her feel guilty. As to the latter, it was working. He shouldn't be involved with the problem she'd created.

"Next week, Lady Chandron might make fresh demands," she pointed out. "And as you said, you're not in danger of losing your reputation. You have no stake in this. You should bow out. It is all my fault."

"True," he agreed, pinning her with a harsh look. "Clearly, you are to blame for the predicament, but she thinks she knows something about me that is patently false. If she further spreads the rumor my fortune has dwindled or my coffers are low, the ramifications will be unpleasant. Silly as you may find it, I have my pride about such things. Plus, my mother will become distraught, and shopkeepers will demand I pay the balance on all my accounts. What's more, the members of my club will whisper and start offering to pay for my drinks and my dinner."

She frowned. *Pay for his drinks and his dinner?* In comparison to Sarah being cast out from the upper echelon of British society, Jasper's worries seemed trite.

"How awful for you," she said, trying to sound sincere and failing.

"You don't understand, but that's to be expected."

How could he say such a belittling thing? "Because I'm a woman and too stupid to comprehend?"

"Of course not," he snapped. "Because you were not born of the nobility, nor do you have to remain in the good graces of powerful people who can make your life difficult. Even my seat in Parliament can be called into question if they think I cannot manage my own estate."

Digesting his real concern, shame truly was starting to rest upon her shoulders.

"I had best go inside and hope Sarah didn't miss me. Perhaps you'll think of another solution."

"Do not worry yourself," he said. "As you said, I'm a rakehell. I'll bed her so hard she won't be able to walk for a week."

His words rattled her as he helped her down onto the street. She most certainly didn't want him doing any such thing to anyone—except her!

"I'll watch and make sure you safely reach your front door," he offered, his tone softening.

A gallant rake! One would almost say a caring rake, she mused.

"One more thing, Miss Sudbury. When last you were in my bedchamber, did you steal from me?"

How dare he! Narrowing her eyes into slits, she told him, "You had nothing I wanted."

"Are you saying if I had, then you would have stolen from me?"

"Of course not. I don't do such things." She glanced around to make sure no one was listening, then added, "And if I did, I wouldn't want your silly mother-of-pearl buttons or ugly king's medal, nor your gold pocket watch, and certainly not the pittance you left lying around. Like a trap." She tilted her chin.

He laughed. "I noticed every damn thing was exactly where I left it on the globe desk you were examining, although it seems you took careful inventory."

"I'm no petty thief," she insisted.

"No, you prefer the grand larceny of jewels, don't you?"

Turning away, Julia waved her hand in his direction, before hurrying up the steps to her sister's home, in better standing than when she left. The threat over her head was gone, but the threat to her heart had increased ten-fold.

CHAPTER NINETEEN

"Although London's citizens have a massive thirst for ale,
the terrible accident at Meux's Brewery this evening was
not a welcome one, despite the suds flowing in the streets
for anyone to enjoy."

—The Times

Awakening two mornings later from a nightmare in which both Lord *and* Lady Chandron were chasing her, Julia threw back the covers and set her feet on the floor.

Brr. Even the rug beneath her feet exhibited the autumn chill. She spied her slippers across the room and dashed to retrieve them as well as her wool dressing gown she'd draped over a chair the night before. Parliament was starting on the eighth of November, less than a month away. The rest of the month would fly by during another whirl of balls with anyone who remained in Town before the mad rush toward the end-of-the-year parties, especially the house parties outside of London.

She and Sarah would go visit their father sometime around Christmas or just after.

Meanwhile, despite recent events, Julia was determined to continue to do what she could for the poor, particularly since they would need warm clothes and more blankets as the temperatures continued to drop. The Thames might freeze over again for a Frost Fair as it had in February. Even London's poorest children from Dark Entry, Cat's Hole, and Pillory Lane went to it in droves. Although dressed scarcely more warmly than for the rest of the year, they'd hoped to sell any little thing they'd found or made, including twig-and-acorn dolls, or something their parents had managed to buy in bulk, such as apples.

It had broken Julia's heart to see the rags they wore in the below-freezing temperatures, while those well-off around them drank hot cider wearing fur from head to toe. Before the bitter cold set in again, she must do her part to help them.

That night, with Mrs. Zebodar, she stepped into yet another splendidly furnished home for a well-attended ball. Julia was determined to make up for the failures of the last few disasters.

"Six dances," Mrs. Zebodar said, eyeing the crowded room. "That seems like one too many."

Julia only smiled, secured a partner for the first dance, a Scotch reel, and then prepared to make her disappearance. And for the first time in far too long, everything went smoothly. She had a necklace and earrings in her reticule before the third dance. The rest of the evening passed by slowly, however, with her missing the earl's distracting presence.

The following day, she returned to Rundell, Bridge, and Rundell to sell her ill-gotten gains and attempt to retrieve Jasper's cravat pin. Instead of receiving a goodly sum for the sparklers, however, she was told her custom was no longer welcome as there was some doubt as to the ownership of the pieces.

"Our store is a reputable one," Mr. Bridge said. "You seem like an honest young woman, but the scope and number of items you're bringing us is raising eyebrows with my partner and his nephew. We sold a piece the other day to one who claimed to be the original owner."

Julia swallowed back her fear, glad Mr. Bridge hadn't secured a constable to take her in for questioning.

Deciding not to inquire about the earl's cravat pin, she hurried home with the baubles weighing heavily on her heart. No matter how beautiful, jewelry was useless to her until she found a new place to pawn them. She would have to go somewhere with a less respectable address.

It occurred to her it would be better to amass more and get rid of it all at once. She could deal with the pawnbroker less often and give the poor a large influx of funds before the year's end.

With that in mind, she hid the jewelry in her armoire's bottom drawer, less thrilled with what had once seemed a perfectly easy and sensible scheme. Now Jasper was involved, and Julia could only wish without any real hope that he might come up with a way to put off Lady Chandron without resorting to bedding her.

WHEN JULIA ENTERED THE foyer of another strange home for a dinner party the following evening, she spied Jasper through the open door to the drawing room. Her heartbeat sped up at the same time as her hope for an opportunity to secure anything more for the poor was dashed.

Since the married hostess would provide Julia with a dinner partner, she had brought no chaperone. Immediately, she considered that an egregious error considering how her reason flew out the window when encountering the earl.

Unsure whether she wanted him to behave or not, she entered the drawing room, glowing with candlelight and abuzz with happy voices. To her dismay, she realized he was escorting a young lady, and instantly the shine went off the evening.

Lady Arabella Doulton, a dark-haired earl's daughter, had been linked with at least two other noblemen that Season. Both of them reportedly were overcome with disappointment when she'd moved on, at least according to the *Morning Post*. Even Julia, who was on the outside of the quality set, recognized the woman's popularity, for her looks and her fortune.

As everyone was circling the room meeting the other guests, it was inevitable the earl and his lady would reach her soon. Their hostess had not yet told her with whom she would be partnered, leaving Julia feeling every bit the shabby-nab, standing by herself.

As expected, Jasper and Lady Arabella came over.

"Do you two know one another?" he asked before making introductions.

Also as expected, the earl's daughter had no interest in speaking with a scrub, and she soon rumped Julia, giving her a good view of her backside as she wandered off.

"What a pleasant companion," Julia remarked.

"I'm not with the lady for her kindness," Jasper returned evenly, raising an eyebrow, leaving her in no doubt why he was with the beauty.

With Lady Chandron to be taken care of and now Lady Arabella in his sights, her favorite rake was going to be quite busy. She should give him the cut infernal and examine her shoes until he gave up taunting her and walked away.

However, the smirk upon his handsome face was a warning he wasn't finished with her yet. In fact, he was staring at her, waiting for something. When he was close enough to touch, Julia saw it—his sapphire cravat pin, nestled in the folds of his elegant neckcloth. Her gaze flew to his.

"Is something wrong, Miss Sudbury?" he asked, knowing full well the reason for her look of surprise.

"No," she said. "It seems everything is quite right."

He was plainly the reason she'd lost her pawning privileges at Rundell, Bridge, and Rundell. Yet knowing he'd retrieved his father's pin, she was glad of it. She only wished she could have returned it to him, redeeming herself a little in his eyes while putting a smile on his face.

"Who is your dining partner this evening?" he asked. "Some eager, artless young man?"

"Such as Mr. Furley from your dinner party?" she asked, keeping her tone light. Truthfully, Julia couldn't imagine being interested in anyone so simple after having dallied with the complex Earl of Marshfield.

"Furley would have been an awful match for you," Jasper declared. "And with his mother being part of the package, a large part, I cannot imagine any woman—"

"Then you didn't see the papers?" she interrupted. "For I read recently, he has in fact made an engagement."

"Is that so?" Jasper appeared surprised. "My sympathies go out to the unfortunate young lady."

She might have chuckled if she wasn't preoccupied by one sobering thought.

"Have you done it yet?"

"It?" he asked, genuinely perplexed.

"With the viscountess. Bedded her, I mean?"

Both his eyebrows rose that time, probably at the boldness of her question.

"No," he said quietly.

"Why?" she fired back, hoping he would say he couldn't go through with it regardless of how that would thrust her and Sarah back into the threat of blackmail.

He shrugged. "Luckily, she was out when next I went to her house. Her husband was there. I wanted to punch him for not being able to satisfy his own wife. But, of course, I've already done that."

So, he was truly ready to perform the service.

"It's really all Lord Chandron's fault," Julia muttered, causing Jasper to send her a withering stare.

"I know it's mine," she corrected. "I am aware of that. But I don't suppose you've come up with a plan to discourage her."

"No, I don't suppose I have," he said and sipped his wine.

"I cannot let her threaten Sarah."

"As I told you," he reminded her, his expression hardening, "I will not let that happen. I can pride myself I am still the coveted prize she seeks, and she'll leave you and your sister alone."

That brought a wry smile to her lips. "A dubious honor, but yes, I believe you are."

Ultimately, he would go through with the deed. And she would try not to even feel sorry for him.

At that moment, their hostess, brought over a perfectly bland young man to be her dining partner. With a bow, and a quick touch of his cravat pin as a salute, the earl retreated, taking all the evening's excitement with him as he returned to Lady Arabella's side.

When the three-hour dinner concluded with a gorgeous display of pastillage flowers strewn along the length of the table and poached pears with custard in crystal bowls for their dessert, Julia was more than ready to go home. She'd been unable to disappear for even a second under Jasper's watchful gaze.

Worse than that, he'd managed to unnerve her throughout the many courses, even from the far end of the table with his direct stares and slightly inappropriate smile. The man could heat her body at twenty paces. She left before he did, not caring a whit for his dinner partner, since by his inattentiveness to Lady Arabella, he didn't care a whit for her either.

Jasper had a woman on his arm whom in all likelihood he intended to tup for mere sport, or on a whim change his mind. It was by all accounts perfectly normal for him. Julia didn't like it, but she liked even less how she couldn't stop torturing herself with thoughts of Jasper undressing and lying with Lady Chandron.

Her Jasper. *With that horrid woman!* He would touch her, perhaps kiss her. *Good God! Would he kiss Lady Chandron?*

She was still thinking of him while futilely struggling with sleep. At some point, he would settle between the viscountess's thighs and take her to the height of pleasure.

Julia wanted that for herself. *Who wouldn't?*

The following evening, Sarah's butler entered the drawing room without his usual calm demeanor. He was fairly fizzing when he handed them a single newsprint sheet from the *Times*, part of their special evening edition with news that was already blanketing Mayfair and beyond:

A dreadful accident has occurred at Meux's Brewery, about 6 o'clock this evening. Due to a compromise, one of the vats in Banbury Street, St. Giles, said to hold over thirty-five hundred barrels of beer, burst without warning. A wave of liquid flowed down St. Georges Street. Loss of life is still being determined, but amounts so far to six.

Thus, it was with wondering glances, she and Sarah went into the dining room and talked of nothing but the bizarre notion of being at home and suddenly drowning in a veritable river of strong beer.

It certainly stole their appetites. Julia watched her sister move the roast chicken and vegetable croquettes around her plate just as she was doing, while hardly taking a bite. Indeed, it seemed like a long and somber evening, causing them both to retire by eleven.

After dousing the lamp on her bedside table, Julia snuggled beneath the bed linens, feeling unsettled by the strange news. As she closed her eyes, something struck the side of the house close to her window. If she didn't know better, she would say it was a pebble.

When another one hit, she sat upright. She'd read about this in more than one fanciful, improbable novel, involving simpering females, strapping men, and secret trysts brought about by stone-throwing at some mansion window. Yet right then, it seemed perfectly real. She swiftly re-lit the oil lamp.

Slowly, giving time for another stone to be tossed, she went to the window, drew back the curtain, and pushed up on the sash to raise the lower panes. When she was sure the weight and balance was holding and she wouldn't be beheaded, she leaned out, surveying the darkness.

Standing in the small yard that buffeted the Worthington home from the mews behind, was none other than the Earl of Marshfield, his visage lit by a lantern.

"Come down here," he ordered.

Was he a madman or merely in his cups?

"Decidedly no," she called down, although sorely tempted because the man had become her weakness.

"I have important news," he said, "and I was passing by on my way home."

"Indeed!" She was sure now he was spoony drunk. "Can it wait, my lord, until tomorrow?"

"Are you 'my lording' me after what we've done together?"

His voice had grown louder. If Sarah was listening, Julia was going to be in trouble. If her neighbors were listening, she could be ruined after all.

"Hush, please, *Jasper*," she said his name to appease him. "Go home and go to sleep."

"You cannot order me. I'm an earl. And I'm not impoverished, no matter what those men think of me at Rundell, Rundell, Bridge, and Bridge, and Rundell."

Then he laughed.

Oh dear! Who would tuck him into bed and give him some quinine for his aching head come the dawn?

"Lady Chandron passed away earlier tonight," he told her out of the blue, sounding cheerful.

Julia gasped, grasping the windowsill to stop herself tumbling out in shock. She was a vicar's daughter and had prayed for a way out of that woman's clutches, but she hadn't wanted her to die.

"Are you sure?" she asked.

He nodded, barely visible in the darkness except he was doing it so enthusiastically.

"She was at the Tavistock Arms pub in St. Giles."

He paused and let the words of a lady being in a common pub sink into Julia's brain. She was about to ask why when he spoke again.

"The pub offered *special services* greatly enjoyed by the viscountess in one of the basement rooms. I shan't describe them. The services I mean, not the rooms."

Julia nodded. She didn't particularly want to know.

"Did her heart give out?" For Julia had imagined hers could explode it beat so hard and fast when Jasper put his mouth upon her—

"She drowned."

"In a pub?" He was talking nonsense again. For all she knew, Lady Chandron was perfectly healthy and at home thinking about whom next she would blackmail. Then Julia recalled the news and gasped again.

"Are you saying she drowned in beer?"

"Yes!" he exclaimed. "You did hear!" And then he started to laugh. His loud guffaw would wake every member of the Worthington household.

"Please hush, Jasper. And don't laugh. It's not civilized considering what happened."

After a moment, he managed to curtail his ill-timed humor.

"The entire tavern was flooded," he declared.

"How do you know all this?" she asked.

"I was close by when it happened. I heard a roar as if an entire building was falling down, and then there were beery fumes floating in the air all about me, although the flood was not in the exact street where I was walking."

"You didn't drink any of it, did you?"

"No, I went to my club, and that's when I heard about the countess."

"The viscountess," she reminded him.

"Just so. We all drank a toast to Lady Chandron's memory, and then we drank to Lord Chandron's health."

"And then you simply drank," she muttered, realizing the lantern was moving. "Is someone with you?"

"Of course. My footman is with me. Aren't you, Rigley? Yes. He says yes, he is. I brought him to throw the stones at your window and to hold the lantern. I'm an earl, you know."

"Yes, I know." Julia wondered how long he'd been at his club, bending his elbow.

"I'm teasing you. I threw my own stones. And I hit the mark, too."

"You did." She was glad he hadn't broken a pane. "Thank you for telling me. I am greatly relieved, although I feel badly for Lady Chandron. Drowning in beer seems a terrible death."

"I can think of worse," he said. "Such as—"

"Please, don't. I can well imagine them for myself. I'm going back to bed, and I suggest you go home and get to your own."

"I could join you in yours," he offered.

Her cheeks warmed, knowing the footman was listening to all this.

"No, you couldn't. We're not married," she said firmly, mostly for Rigley's sake.

Jasper started to laugh, and then he laughed harder. Shutting the window, she sighed. At least she could amuse him.

Lady Chandron! Dead!

Shaking her head, Julia slipped under the covers again. In truth, a weight had been lifted unless, in his inebriated state, Jasper had got it all wrong. But if he was right, she no longer need worry about Sarah's good name nor the man she'd come to care for bedding someone else due to her own carelessness.

CHAPTER TWENTY

"You seem quite chipper this morning," Sarah said. "Sleep well?"

Julia had in fact slept soundly after the earl and his footman's strange visit. She reached for the morning's stack of papers.

"It's true," she said after a moment's inspection of the *Times*.

"What's true?" Her sister poured them both a cup of tea.

"Lady Chandron was killed in the St. Giles beer flood."

Sarah gasped. "How awful! Wasn't she the strange woman from the cricket match?"

"Yes," she murmured. "The strange woman."

"But how did you know?" her sister questioned.

"How did I know what?" Julia asked, still reading the article for more details on those who'd perished in such an unlikely manner.

"You said, 'it's true,' as though you already suspected it and were verifying the lady's death."

"Did I?" She was terrible at lying but would have to give it a whirl. "I meant the whole beer flood is true and not simply something I dreamt of last night. It's hard to believe there's so much beer in a single vat as to flood a street and basements, too."

Sarah stirred sugar into her tea.

"What on earth was Lady Chandron doing in St. Giles at sixish?" she wondered aloud. "Or at any time for that matter? Hardly seems the place a member of the *ton* would be strolling or dining."

"*Mm*, hardly," Julia agreed before setting down the paper and deciding it best to change the subject. "There are a number of balls coming up before everyone departs London. Some holiday-themed parties and whatnot. Are we attending? And what of father? When are we going to Chislehurst?"

Sarah sighed, and Julia knew at once her sister was thinking of Denbigh. For it was the sigh of a woman mooning over a man.

"I don't know."

"You don't?" Julia nearly laughed at her sister's vagueness, which wasn't like her at all. She hoped Sarah found a new man to take her interest and lift her spirits. "Well, do you want to go to some holiday parties? The morning mail should be here shortly with invitations. We'll go through them together."

Although, as usual it would be easier not to have her sister at any parties while Julia *appropriated*—a nice word, she'd decided, for obtaining more jewelry.

"We'll see," Sarah agreed. "I'm sure I'll go to some. Perhaps we should stay with Father for a few months. I am sick of the soot and smoke of London, not to mention its inhabitants."

Julia blinked. Her first thought was how she would miss Lord Marshfield. Her second thought was how she needed to stop thinking the first one. Besides, there would be no question of her being able to stay in London without Sarah. The house would be closed up until the countess wished to return. In that, Julia definitely had no say.

And then Mr. Dawson entered with the silver tray of missives.

There were invitations, some on blue and rose and even lavender paper, but Julia no longer had to worry about something coming from the viscountess, and she felt guilty in her relief

And then she spied thick cream paper perfectly folded with the bold black seal stamped with the letter *M*.

"Marshfield," Sarah said, noticing it at the same time.

"I suppose it is," Julia tried to sound nonchalant but her fingers snatched it off the tray. Trembling slightly, she opened it.

"What does it say?" Sarah asked.

"I haven't even read it yet." And she proceeded to do so, hoping her sister would start on the other invitations.

Dear Miss Sudbury,

Now that we have one situation taken care of, I would very much like to handle the other one. To that end, another ride is in order, don't you agree? Please send me your response as to when.

Yours truly,

Marshfield

Just like that, his words made her pulse quicken and her breasts feel heavy, not to mention a terribly distracting tingling between her legs. Lust, to be sure, except her emotions were also now thoroughly engaged. She no longer feared a *tendre* had blossomed in her heart. She knew it!

"Now you've read it," her sister pointed out.

Julia refolded the note and put it on her lap. He must have written it early and given it to a footman to deliver. She would go upstairs and respond in a timely fashion.

"Yes, the earl has asked me to go riding again. I enjoyed it very much last time and might go again." On purpose, she didn't give even the hint of asking permission. It wasn't her sister's to grant, in any case.

"I suppose nothing I say will stop you, not even the fact that he's now escorting Lady Arabella Doulton around Town."

"If I decide to go, then no," Julia said. "As long as Lord Marshfield and I are in public with a chaperone, riding with him cannot harm me, nor reflect badly upon you."

"Upon *me*? Of course not. What have I to do with your poor choice in men?"

Julia sipped her tea before rising to her feet to help herself to a plate of eggs and bacon from the sideboard. If her sister knew the threats from the dead viscountess and how Julia's actions could impact her, Sarah would be far less cavalier.

Nevertheless, having just got out of Lady Chandron's frying pan, she oughtn't to jump immediately into another possible fire. Sarah was correct how unseemly it would be to go riding with him while he had a known association with Lady Arabella. There was no sense in causing tongues to wag merely to please herself. None at all.

She would see Jasper again at the next ball, should he attend. And if not, all the better.

THE QUADRILLE, USUALLY AN endless dance was over far too quickly since Julia was partnered with Jasper, who'd claimed her the moment she'd entered the ballroom. Foolishly, his eagerness had wrapped her in a blanket of happiness.

When they left the parquet dance floor, he steered her toward the refreshment table that ran the length of a wall in the adjoining parlor. She couldn't help asking the question that had been on her mind.

"Where is Lady Arabella this evening?" Julia hoped he would say he'd tired of her already and had broken it off.

He shrugged. "I am not certain she's coming. Besides, I came to dance with you."

The earl was smooth, and Julia reminded herself precisely *how* smooth and why. Because he'd been perfecting his pursuit of women for the past few years.

"I keep hoping you'll put me out of my misery," he continued, "and agree to a ride in the park."

Unless she was gravely mistaken, his invitation to ride in the park meant stopping at his home to finish what Sarah had interrupted. And Julia no longer intended to gift him her innocence.

"I know the Thames hasn't frozen, but it's cold enough out there to freeze my blood," Julia said. "I don't wish to ride in anything except a closed carriage with a warming brick at my feet."

"We can do that," he agreed. "A carriage can have a certain rocking motion, perfect for—"

"I understand the concept." But she'd decided not to ever indulge herself—and that's what it plainly was, *an indulgence*—with him again. Moreover, it made her look a fool. The *Gazette* had mentioned him coming in from the garden of Lord and Lady Woodling's house with a flustered Lady Arabella, despite bitter temperatures a mere two nights' earlier.

"What possible reason could Lord M have for going outside with Lady A in such chilly weather? Not to smell the flowers, surely!"

The silly little statement had made Sarah roll her eyes at breakfast. And rightly so. Julia, on the other hand, had felt a rush of envy and jealousy, two unpleasant emotions she desperately wanted to be rid of. Now, here he was trying to turn his rakish charms upon her again.

"I have no doubt one such as yourself can find a myriad of women who would love to enjoy a carriage ride with you."

"Naturally," he said, not seeming the least bothered by her dig at his fickle plurality of females.

Why would he? Unlike her, he knew exactly who he was, not conflicted by heart and mind and body.

"Then I suggest you find one of them and stick her on the hot brick in your cozy carriage." She walked swiftly away, glad she hadn't mentioned Lady Arabella twice. Then he would know of her unreasonable possessiveness, and he would probably grin with vanity.

After all, he had never belonged to her.

JASPER HAD HOPED IT would all happen as before. He would take Julia riding and divert their horses to his home—except this time, he wanted to carry their intoxicating attraction through to its inevitable completion. By now, she must have got over Lady Daphne's bothersome warning, and as they didn't have Lady Chandron's threat hanging over them any longer, he was assured Julia would give in to the powerful pull between them.

So why was she walking away?

He reached for a glass of lemonade on the table. He thought he was the experienced one, but Miss Sudbury seemed to have him wrapped around her finger. And each time she blew hot or cold, he was on tenterhooks.

Where *was* Lady Arabella? She was beautiful and easy to control, and he never felt off-kilter in her company. That made her the perfect female. Yet all he could think of was his blonde minx.

What to do? Julia was ruining all his fun. It made no sense to be London's most notorious rake if he couldn't even participate in his usual licentious activities.

Draining the last drops of the lemonade, he wondered why he'd bothered instead of drinking from his flask. Although, he had to admit, it was refreshing.

Like Julia Sudbury.

In frustration, he ran a hand through his hair, knowing Blumsey would be annoyed to see him looking less than spectacular as it reflected badly on one's valet. Yet Jasper knew what he had to do. He had to claim the infernal woman as his own. He would spell it out for her this very evening. Nothing permanent, not at this juncture, but he could inform her of his desire to have an exclusive arrangement—more than a mistress but less than a wife.

A chit from Chislehurst ought to be satisfied with such.

So what was he waiting for? Why hadn't he pressed his case more quickly, especially after her willingness in his own home? Indeed, what could possibly have caused him to hesitate from the first time her sparkling spirit had reached inside him and taken hold of his . . . his soul?

Fear, plain and simple, that's what stopped him. Liking a woman, admiring her, wanting to be in her company— and all without tupping her regularly—was a new and terrifying experience. A weakness that left him vulnerable.

Dammit! He was no coward. He'd been to war in France and faced the enemy with more grit than he felt squaring off with Julia. Tugging upon his waistcoat, he straightened and decided to engage with the enemy that very evening.

What better place than a ballroom?

JULIA HOPED SARAH WOULDN'T want to stay late. Having danced with Jasper and desperately wanting to give in to his invitation to ride straight to blissful purgatory, she needed to leave. She ought to go home, remove the fancy gown and undress her hair so it was back in the plain braids of youth, and remember who she was.

However, Sarah wasn't waiting for her by the tall windows. Her sister was actually dancing, which was a lovely sight, warming Julia's heart. She wandered the edges of the dance floor until she reached the far end by the musicians, and then she strolled back again, just in time to see Jasper heading directly for her.

At the look in his eyes, she caught her breath. Clearly, he had something important on his mind.

About ten feet from her, Lady Arabella Doulton stepped into his path, her back to Julia, her mass of dark curls flowing down her back.

Faltering, she couldn't continue her own forward movement or risk running straight into the couple. But at hearing the young woman immediately raise her voice, sounding in high dudgeon, Julia paused.

"I have never been treated so shabbily," Lady Arabella proclaimed.

Around Julia, the murmur of voices died down, as the evening's real entertainment began.

"I am sorry you feel that way," Jasper said, his head darting sideways so he could look past the peeved woman and catch Julia's gaze.

Taking a step back, Julia couldn't imagine why he was drawing her into the unhappy tableau. She shook her head ever so slightly, warding him off.

"Are you listening to me?" Lady Arabella screeched.

"Everyone is," he told her, keeping his voice calm. "Thus, I suggest you lower your voice." Then he did the unthinkable. He placed his hand upon her arm. "Let's go somewhere private where you can tell me what has you up in the boughs."

Lady Arabella wrenched her arm free. "I am most definitely not going anywhere *private* with you. Not ever again! Unless you are making me an offer of marriage, sir."

Silence and the collective holding of breath by everyone around them. While the musicians played on, even some of the dancers had stopped to listen, ruining the perfect formation of the quadrille. The rest had to grind to a halt as well including Sarah, who came to stand beside Julia.

Lady Arabella had thrown down the gauntlet in front of Mayfair's elite. If Julia had ever thought she'd done anything embarrassing or improper at a party, it paled in comparison. She had never witnessed such a scene, and surely, most of the other guests hadn't either. It was simply not done.

For Lady Arabella to imply she'd *already* been alone with him.

For her to demand a public proposal.

Sweet Mother!

Yet Jasper raised an eyebrow, looking decidedly unperturbed. And Julia wondered if she were greatly mistaken. Perhaps some of the guests had witnessed the like, and maybe this was a common occurrence in the life of a rake. He might be used to dealing with wronged women confronting him in front of others, but it made her want to cringe as fans opened and heads leaned together. Then the whispers started.

CHAPTER TWENTY-ONE

"Grosvenor Square was a bustle at Lord M's home last night. A certain Miss S__ was there, as was an angry Lord N__. From the look of Lord M__'s face today, fisticuffs ensued, but over which woman?"

—The Sun

"And that is why you should stay far away from men like Marshfield," Sarah said from the safety of their carriage's interior on the short jaunt home to Hanover Square. "Dear God! That woman must have been out of her mind to have lost all sense of decency and behave in such a manner. I cannot think but she will never recover her place in society. What man will ever offer for her after that?"

"Maybe Lord Marshfield will," Julia put forth from the darkness of her side of the carriage, clasping her mantle around her for warmth. Jasper had always treated her with kindness and even behaved as her champion. She could imagine him offering Lady Arabella his name and his protection after what she'd just witnessed.

The poor woman had finally burst into tears and fled the ballroom, leaving stunned guests to glance awkwardly at one another. The musicians hadn't stopped, which was a blessing as it gave people a way to quickly return to normalcy. While some were positively gleeful at the juicy disaster that had befallen Lady Arabella, most were simply shocked or saddened. Each and every one wanted to avoid Jasper's gaze as they ducked to the side or turned away when he followed her from the room.

Julia was only glad he hadn't looked at her again, for she most certainly didn't want to be associated with Lady Arabella's humiliation.

"Marshfield," Sarah spat out. "He will never offer for her. Hasn't it been made plain to you? He uses women for his pleasure. We are a sport to him, like his horses. I would feel sorry for Lady Arabella except she knew as well as any of us, including you, what he is like."

When had her sister become so harsh and jaded?

Julia said nothing more despite having seen a better side of the earl. He could have taken her in Sarah's own home, and he hadn't. Moreover, he'd saved her from Lord *and* Lady Chandron. And he'd let her walk away from him after a kiss.

There was more to Lord Marshfield than merely being a libertine. Of that, she was sure. If he married Lady Arabella, it would prove him to be a good sort after all, and Julia should almost wish he would do it.

Yet if he married the lady, it would break Julia's heart. She could deny it no longer. She loved him.

DEAR MISS SUDBURY,

You were correct, it is too cold to let you sit upon horseback. I would fear you'd catch a chill. Instead, will you come to my home for dinner tomorrow night? To be clear, there are no other guests. I hope we can speak plainly.

Regards,

Marshfield

If Sarah ever saw this, she would fly into a temper and probably lock Julia in her room if possible. The man was ignoring their last encounter and even pretending he hadn't been the central figure in a ballroom drama.

Go to dinner? Alone? Was he a lunatic?

She paced her room, holding the letter against her chest, alternately sniffing it to catch the scent of his fragrance.

It had been only a few days since last she'd seen him, but it felt like an eternity.

Would she accept his insane invitation?

Of course she would!

The following evening, at seven o'clock, she alighted from a hackney, deciding not to ask if Sarah's carriage was available, nor have to explain her destination. She hadn't even pretended to ask permission.

When the earl's butler admitted her, Jasper was standing in the front hall waiting. It was sweet of him, lacking all pretention. Moreover, he looked as if he'd spent extra care with his toilet and dressing. Every hair was in place, his cravat perfectly tied, his waistcoat smooth, and his jacket pressed to perfection.

She couldn't help smiling when he immediately stepped forward and took her hand. He grinned in return, and her insides melted.

"How can you possibly look lovelier than usual, when your usual loveliness is beyond compare?"

Julia let herself blush. There was nothing she could do about her obvious emotions. Besides, she had dressed with him in mind, wearing her favorite blue gown.

The butler coughed.

"We shall go into the salon, Mr. Greer," Jasper told him, "before the dining room."

Thus, Julia found herself in a room more intimate than the drawing room, and yet, perfectly respectable, except for the fact she shouldn't be there at all.

"I'm grateful you came," he said, leading her to sit on the sofa before taking the chair opposite.

Distracted by his distance, by how he hadn't drawn her into his arms already and kissed her, she nearly patted the sofa cushion beside her before stopping herself. If he could behave, she could, too.

"I wasn't certain you would accept my invitation," Jasper said, leaning forward to pour her a glass of wine from the carafe. "In fact, I would have wagered you would not."

"I will be leaving soon. I suppose that convinced me to come, albeit against my better judgement."

"Leaving?" Jasper echoed. "I thought you liked living in London."

"I do. Parts of it, at any rate. The city has much to recommend it," Julia agreed. "However, I am only here due to my sister's kindness. When she leaves, I shall, too. We'll be going to our family home in Chislehurst, and Sarah said she thinks we might stay with my father for a while."

"I see." He didn't sound happy at all, matching the way she felt about not seeing him possibly for months.

"Chislehurst will be strangely quiet after the excitement of living in Town," she added.

"I'm sure it's a far cry from what goes on here," he agreed. "Especially recently."

She nodded. *Would he say more about the scene with Lady Arabella?*

"You've been busy," she prompted, imagining what must have ensued to warrant the young lady's outrageous public display. She'd guessed they'd been making the two-backed beast, and Lady Arabella, someone befitting Jasper's station, someone who had wanted to be his countess, had made assumptions.

"Less busy than you might think," he said.

She might as well be direct. "I take it you didn't pick up the gauntlet and offer to marry the lady?"

Jasper halted mid sip of claret.

"Christ, no!" he said. "Married to that one? I think not."

Julia knew she was being petty to feel such a flush of pleasure over his words. Poor Lady Arabella, led on and then disparaged. She ought to defend her. She tried.

"*That one*, as you put it, was good enough for you to escort for nearly two weeks and even to take into a garden."

His eyes rounded. "Did the papers say all that? I suppose it's true, but the garden was her idea, and did not result in an experience such as you and I shared."

Julia knew her cheeks had reddened, but there was no helping it.

"Because the lady said no," she guessed. "As any modest, upstanding female ought to." *So why had she felt helpless to give in?*

Jasper laughed, and Julia had the uncomfortable feeling no lady had ever said no to him.

"Because Lady Arabella is waspish and peevish, which erases nearly all of her appeal. Yet in the garden, she hoped to entice me to into basket-making to seal my fate."

Julia frowned. "I don't follow."

"*Hm,*" he stalled. "Well, as opposed to being careful when," he coughed, "when swiving, if one behaves rashly, it can result in a babe, which would need—"

"A basket to sleep in. I understand," she said quickly to stop him further discussing the different types of love-making. She supposed rakes knew a hundred methods and as many silly words for each.

"Despite knowing it was against the pluck, I went outside with her," he added, "freezing though it was, merely because it was discourteous not to."

"Discourteous?" Julia prompted. "To dissuade a young woman from trying to get herself ruined?"

He had the grace to look sheepish. "I mean, it would be discourteous of me to rudely turn her down, especially given my reputation. It might have dented her confidence forever!"

She thought he was serious until he started laughing. He was arrogant, to be sure, but not to that extent.

"Naturally, I tried to warm us both with a kiss."

Julia grimaced before she could stop herself.

This made him smile. "It was nothing, I tell you, like our kisses."

"Stop," she begged. "Please don't compare and don't speak of us in the same breath."

His expression grew serious. "You're quite correct, but I promise you there's no comparison. And I did nothing more than kiss her so she could save face. When she understood I wouldn't step into her trap, she stormed back into the ballroom."

Julia nodded, emotions warring in her as to why he would do more with her than with Arabella. *Should she be flattered or offended?*

"But that's ancient history," he reminded her, "compared to what happened the other night."

"It was ugly," Julia agreed.

"It was humiliating for all involved." He sighed. "I offered to escort her again so she could give me a public redress and repair her dignity, but she turned me down flat."

"You would do that?" Julia was shocked to learn he cared how Lady Arabella had appeared unhinged.

"I would," he agreed. "Poor girl doesn't know I have the impenetrable shield of a gentleman's wager at White's, one I have no intention of losing."

"Do tell," Julia couldn't contain her curiosity. It wasn't often one got to hear about the happenings inside a gentleman's club.

"I shall not marry until after the thirty-first of December of next year. If I do, I would forfeit five hundred pounds, and I have no intention of looking into the smug faces of my fellow members as they take my money."

Five hundred pounds on such a matter! Julia couldn't help being upset by the frivolity and waste of money better used elsewhere. Not to mention the twinge of disappointment over Jasper being so set on not marrying he'd bet against it.

Then she had an idea.

"If you win your wager at White's—"

"*When* I win," he interrupted.

"When you win, will you donate your winnings to the poor?"

He narrowed his eyes. "What have the poor got to do with my marital state?

"Nothing at all. But you will take in quite a bit from the other men when you win. From your boasting over the soundness of the Marshfield accounts, you don't need the money."

"Need is not the point," he said.

She sighed. "Nevertheless, will you donate the money?"

"Why?" he asked.

"Because I ask it of you," she said, and tried an unfamiliar tactic of batting her eyelashes.

Laughing slightly, he nodded. "As long as we can stop this tedious conversation and speak about us, instead." Then he used his own tactic of persuasion, cocking his head and grinning at her, looking so devastatingly charming, she thought she might melt onto the sofa cushion.

Julia shook her head. "You are incorrigible."

"I used to think so," he said.

The way he looked at her as if she might somehow hold the key to his rehabilitation caused a warm flutter low in her stomach.

"Why did you invite me here tonight?" she asked.

"That's a pertinent question, deserving an answer. I invited you because I'm a soldier. I've fought Napoleon's army, and I refuse to be cowed by a blue-eyed country miss."

She tried to makes sense of his words as he rose to his feet. When he reached down a hand to her, unthinkingly she took it, letting him draw her to her feet. Without preamble, Jasper kissed her, stealing her breath and starting a concert of sensations throughout her body, ending in a shiver running down her spine as he sunk his teeth into her lower lip, gently but firmly nibbling on her.

There was a tap at the door. Slowly, he withdrew, leaving her weak-kneed, and went to open the door himself.

"Dinner, my lord," was all she heard.

Julia was relieved there really was going to be a meal. For a moment, she'd feared *she* was the feast, and it would have been impossible to deny him partaking of her. Instead, in the same dining room in which she'd sat next to Mr. Furley months earlier, she now let Jasper pull out her chair. They sat close, with him at the table's head and her at his right side. And the footman began to serve the procession of courses.

If anyone asked, Julia might be unable to discuss the food, as she wavered between enjoyment of the earl's ability to tell stories and her anxiousness as to what would happen after the dessert.

Was his plan to take her upstairs?

She knew she ate, for the footman cleared away her plate at regular intervals, replacing it with a new one, and her stomach was full by the dinner's end. Yet she could hardly recall anything until the splendid barberry ice served in crystal *tasses à glaces* and with it, biscuits accompanying the sweetest wine Julia had ever tasted.

"Dip it," Jasper offered, picking up a round cookie and dunking it gracefully into the wide-rimmed glass. This he popped into his attractive mouth while she stared.

Following suit, Julia did the same, reveling in the myriad tastes bursting on her tongue before jumping slightly when he suddenly touched his thumb to her chin.

"Just a drop of wine," he told her, then brought his thumb to his own mouth and licked it. "Delicious!" he proclaimed, while she could barely catch her breath.

His tongue, his fingers, his mouth—gracious, what a wicked man!

She would go upstairs with him and finish what Sarah had interrupted. Her intimate parts were throbbing at the notion.

JASPER COULD TELL HE was winning her over. He had no doubt after witnessing the mêlée with Arabella, Miss Sudbury had her reservations. That she'd come at all to his home had been a wonder, but when she'd agreed, he knew the curiously strong and sizzling bond between them would ensure she went upstairs with him before the night was over.

Before deflowering her, he would assure her of his . . . *devotion*. Moreover, she would no longer need to steal and pawn to pay her expenses. He intended to keep her under his protection. *Like a wife.*

He frowned at his own discomfiting thoughts.

"Even when you frown, sir, you are the most handsome man I've ever met."

The woman had no idea she was supposed to hold something in reserve, to at least *not* let him know how greatly she admired him. That was for him to do, to woo her out of her clothes and into his bed. But her honesty was entirely disarming.

"Julia," he said her name because it gave him a surge of pleasure whenever he took such a liberty, "you are the most—"

A pounding on his front door made them both startle.

Bloody hell! And just when he was about to suggest they go upstairs, where the fire was already lit in his hearth and his bed linens were even then heating with an iron bed-warmer. He was so close to holding her in his arms, naked and willing.

In an instant, Mr. Greer appeared in the dining room doorway to learn Jasper's wishes.

Given the hour, he would be within his rights to ignore the intruder altogether. Rising to his feet, he gestured for Julia to remain where she was while the knocking only grew more fervent and, if possible, louder.

"Your sister?" he wondered.

"I don't believe so. Not unless she's brought a cudgel with her."

"To beat me senseless," Jasper surmised.

"I can't dismiss the notion entirely," she said. "But doubtful."

If it wasn't the Countess of Worthington, then he couldn't let Miss Sudbury be discovered by anyone else.

"Stay here," he ordered, before nodding to Mr. Greer that he should investigate Then he left her, following his butler to the front of the house.

If it was his mother, they were in a bit of a pickle. The dowager countess would barge right into the parlor for a glass of sherry without a by-your-leave. After all, this home had once upon a time, before his father's death, been hers. She would have a hundred questions and possibly take a dim view of both himself and Miss Sudbury, whom he couldn't leave stranded in the dining room forever.

However, it wasn't his mother who stepped into the foyer, pushing rudely past Mr. Greer, but a red-faced man Jasper thought vaguely familiar.

"What's the meaning of this?" he demanded as his butler grabbed at the intruder's arm, trying to drag him back, a futile action since the stranger was built like a dock-worker and clenched his hands into fists the size of hams.

"Don't you know who I am? You know my wife, Lady Neville, well enough," the stranger announced, and Mr. Greer instantly dropped his gloved hands. "I would tell you to call off your butler, but apparently he has heard of me and has good sense."

Indeed, Mr. Greer took a healthy step back—*the cowardly shake-bag!*

Unfortunately, Jasper had heard of Neville, too. Quite a skilled bruiser, as he'd seen for himself at Jackson's Academy. What's more, Jasper knew the man's wife—in every sense of the word. But that was old news, by at least two months, maybe three.

Surely Neville couldn't be there because of—

"My wife said you laid hands upon her, like a rabid dog."

Jasper considered this for a moment. Telling Neville that a dog, rabid or otherwise, had no hands did not seem like a prudent course of action. He'd behaved more like a *randy* dog, and Lady Neville had enjoyed herself with much more than merely Jasper's hands.

Why on earth would she have brought up his name at this belated juncture?

Hoping to get the right end of the walking stick before he confirmed or denied, Jasper considered inviting Neville into his drawing room to appease him *and* his large fists with some expensive brandy. But he wasn't going to leave Julia waiting.

"It's inconvenient tonight, but would you care to return tomorrow to further discuss this?"

The man stood, legs slightly apart as if on a ship, and gawked.

"My arse on a bandbox!" he exclaimed. "Are you mad? I've just accused you of tupping my wife, and you want me to go away and return when it better suits you?" He sneered and shook his head. "Shall we toast her many fine features together, too?"

No, probably not! Jasper thought.

"I think there has been some misunderstanding," he began.

"Lady Neville is enceinte!" the man declared.

CHAPTER TWENTY-TWO

*T*here was no misunderstanding that!

"Congratulations?" Jasper managed, with a question in his tone. *Why the devil was the man involving him?*

"Why, you satyr!" And with that, Neville launched himself at Jasper, tackling him to his prized Italian tile floor in one go.

"Oof." That bloody well hurt.

At once, Neville began an assault. Jasper might be less meaty than this brute, but he knew his way around a good fight. As Neville first tried to sock him in the jaw and then strangle him, Jasper twisted and turned before managing to get his knee into his attacker's stomach to create a little distance between them.

When the man arched in pain, Jasper had room to get his other leg between them and shove him off. And then, once standing again, they fell to blows in earnest.

"This is poppycock!" Jasper declared, realizing the last punch to his eye was going to darken his daylight, which he disrelished greatly. Blumsey would have to apply some magical potion to disguise it.

Nevertheless, there was simply no possibility Lady Neville's babe was his. He was careful with the women he bedded, always using a protective sheath or pulling out and spending on the sheets, usually both.

"There. Has. Been. A. Mistake," he added between dodging facers and throwing wisty castors in return. A hamfist connected with his ribs, and Jasper was sure he'd heard one crack. In retaliation, he ducked low and came up swinging with a muzzler, catching Neville in the chin and sending him reeling.

Suddenly, from the hallway, Julia appeared. Neville was surprised enough to pause in his assault and take a step back. Jasper nearly clocked him a stinger to the head but decided that would be poor sportsmanship and lowered his hands.

Without hesitation, she strode to the center of the foyer and halted between the men, her back to Jasper.

"This must cease at once. You're behaving like children with big sticks."

Oh, he had a big stick all right, Jasper thought smugly. But he hadn't used it to get Lady Neville pregnant. In fact, if he recalled rightly, he hadn't even penetrated her. She'd said they must do *other* things only. For all he knew, she had been having an affair with another man. *But why blame the babe on him?*

"My wife *knew* I would leave her," Neville vowed, "if she was ever unfaithful."

And there it was, Jasper had his reason. Perhaps she'd fallen in love with someone else, a man who would stay in the shadows. She could get rid of her husband on her own terms, put the blame on Jasper, and end up with her lover who would seem innocent as snow.

At Jasper's silence, Neville seemed to get wound up again, perhaps imagining a scene of passion. He took a step toward Julia, who unflinchingly stood her ground.

"Look, miss, I don't know who you are," Neville declared, "another one of this lech's doxies or someone's misguided trollop of a wife, but you'd best stand aside because I aim to take Marshfield's head off."

Jasper didn't like the sound of that. Neither did Julia. She stomped a slippered foot before fisting her hands on her hips.

"I assure you, you're making an error," she told him. "Your wife may have pulled the name of the most convenient rake out of her hatbox, but the Earl of Marshfield could not have caused your wife's condition."

"Why the hell not?" Neville demanded.

"Don't swear in front of her," Jasper ordered the man. Then he realized what she'd said.

"Yes," he chimed in. "Why not?"

"The earl is utterly impotent," Julia declared.

"What?" Jasper realized Neville had said the word at the same time.

"Naturally, he doesn't want anyone to know he has a *lobcock*, if I have the correct term. Thus, he cultivates the reputation of a reprobate wastrel."

"That's harsh," Jasper began, but she interrupted him, still addressing Neville.

"In truth, Lord Marshfield's private life is quite the opposite. Would I, a fine, upstanding woman be here in his home if I weren't perfectly safe around him?"

Neville frowned, darted a questioning glance at Jasper, and then nodded as if it made sense.

Julia nodded back at him while Jasper digested the harsh annihilation of his virile character.

"Either the babe in question is actually yours," Julia said to the man, "or it belongs to another, but *not* to the Earl of Marshfield. I'm sorry to say Lady Neville must be lying, perhaps to protect someone else. Or perhaps simply to test your love for her."

Silence met her words. Jasper knew he'd best keep his mouth shut while Neville pondered. No point in defending his manliness or his skilled abilities to the cuckolded husband. But it grated on his pride all the same.

After a moment, Neville looked past Julia, catching Jasper's gaze.

"Man-to-man, is my wife carrying your child?"

Jasper was pleased to answer, "I promise you, with the honor of my forefathers, my earldom, king and country, she is not."

Lord Neville nodded again and looked very sad, even sparing a pitying look at Jasper, which he didn't appreciate. In fact, he couldn't help returning with a pitying glance of his own.

Watching the man leave wordlessly, he hoped never to find himself in a similar situation, in love with someone who so cold-heartedly betrayed him. On the other hand, Jasper fervently wished he had never touched Lady Neville or any other man's wife.

JULIA HAD REPAID HER debt to the earl, and she'd done so by a furlong.

At the same time, she had felt the slap of reality when listening by the open dining room door. Jasper had casually and carelessly slept with another man's wife. All her pleasant thoughts of him as chivalrous and kind had vanished in an instant.

"Thank you for that," he said, smoothing his jacket and tugging at his coat sleeves, probably not realizing how his mussed hair and battered face ruined his perfect appearance. "A clever defense, if a little embarrassing."

Julia lifted a shoulder in dismissal, but a question came springing to her lips.

"Are you the babe's father?"

"No," he insisted.

"Seriously," she said. "Please do not give me all that king and country nonsense."

"I meant every word," he said evenly.

"Then you didn't make love to his wife?" She held her breath, hoping he said no just as assuredly.

"Yes, in a manner, but not so she could become with child. I promise you it's the truth."

In a manner! Julia didn't need to hear the details.

"Thank you for dinner. I had best be returning home before my sister starts to worry."

He gave her a long look as if he would say more, but really, what else could he say? She knew what he was, and still, she'd willingly taken every step along the path to where she now stood. Yet at that moment, she realized her obsession had to end. What if she were to become *enceinte* despite his practiced methods?

After a moment, he turned to his butler, who had remained in the foyer, practically melded into the wall plaster during the entire *imbroglio.*

"Miss Sudbury's mantle, Mr. Greer, and please make sure a hackney is out front."

"Yes, sir."

After a last glance at him before she left, Julia added, "You ought to apply a poultice to your eye."

"A poultice of what, Doctor Sudbury?" He gave her a crooked smile, as if this were no more serious than playing ducks and drakes or a game of bagatelle.

Jasper's problems were his own, mostly self-inflicted ones at that, and he would have to deal with them by himself.

"Having never been around such behavior before, sir, I haven't a clue." She let him drape her mantle around her shoulders before stepping out into the cold night.

HUMMING TO HERSELF, JULIA let her sister's maid dress her hair for an upcoming dinner party. She could hardly recall to whose home she was going. Sarah was coming, and they each would be assigned partners. Regardless, she was determined to get another bauble tonight because soon the nobility would vacate Town, taking many of their extraneous sparklers with them. When the wealthy attended country parties over the Twelvetide, they would be as festooned as they were in London.

It had been a week since "the incident," as she thought of the dinner at Jasper's home on Grosvenor Square. Having been prepared for whatever might follow their meal—except for what actually happened—she'd expected to be walking around as an experienced woman at last.

Instead, she couldn't dismiss the notion of him blithely having an *affaire de coeur* with Lady Neville, even if his *coeur* hadn't played much part compared to other parts of his body. If Lord Neville hadn't shown up, she might not still be an innocent, yet in many ways, the angry cuckold had been the final straw in removing the shadow of innocence from her eyes. Jasper's irresponsibility and true nature had been thrust in her face, as surely as Lord Neville's fist into Jasper's eye.

That was just as well, she supposed, tapping on Sarah's door to indicate she was ready. What life would it be for a woman who became the consort of a rakehell?

A disastrous one!

Nor had she heard a single solitary word from him since he'd put her in a carriage and kissed her hand. True, his gaze had lingered on hers, until she could feel the pulse beating in her throat, but he hadn't pressed a last kiss upon her lips.

"Come in," Sarah called.

"You look beautiful," Julia said. It took a moment to realize Sarah was standing in the middle of her room, wearing only her undergarments.

"Let me get my mantle, then," Sarah quipped, "and we'll be on our way."

"Sorry. That was stupid of me," Julia needed to stop musing upon the earl. "But your hair does look pretty." It had been put up by her maid with a feather-and-pearls aigrette on one side, looking rather jaunty and confident.

Why hadn't he at least sent her a note? She'd looked every day for a missive with his black seal. Every day, she'd been disappointed and tried to quell the unwanted sadness. Expecting something uncharacteristic from a rogue like Lord Marshfield and then being disillusioned when he didn't play the part was unfair. What's more, it was a sentiment bound to cause her heartache.

She ought to simply enjoy the strange and sometimes thrilling friendship they shared, without expectation.

"Silver and plum or jade and cream?" Sarah asked.

"Jade and cream," Julia said.

"But you're wearing jade and cream."

Julia looked down. "Yes, I am. Then why did you ask me? You must wear the plum and silver. You look dazzling in that gown."

Sarah sighed greatly, and then the maid, whom Julia hadn't even noticed standing by the armoire, withdrew a silver gown with pale purple ribbon woven under the bustline and through the caps of the sleeves.

"Why are you sighing like that?" Julia asked.

"Because you've been twitter-pated for nearly a week."

Julia shook her head, glancing at the maid who ignored them both while draping the gown over Sarah's head, taking care not to make a mess of her coiffure.

"I haven't." Then Julia paused. "Have I?"

"See, that's what I mean. There you go again, acting like a pudding-head. Do you want to tell me why?"

No, she most definitely didn't. "You're imagining it. Do *you* want to tell me why you foolishly let Becky do your hair *before* you chose your gown? I think your aigrette has moved."

Reaching up to adjust it, she stared at the nakedness of her right hand and gasped.

"What is it?" Sarah asked. "My hair can't be that bad."

"Mother's ring," Julia whispered. "It's gone."

They stared at one another. With her heart instantly racing as if Lord Marshfield were touching her, Julia dashed back to her own room. She scanned the polished surface of her chest of drawers, then she opened her glove box perched atop and rifled through all her recently worn gloves.

She had the awful notion she hadn't seen the ring on her hand all day but had been too buffle-headed lately to be certain.

Sarah entered behind her. "I'll help."

Julia nodded, looking under the bed, then going to her bedside table while her sister went to the armoire. Too late, Julia recalled her hidden treasures.

"Oh my God!" Sarah's words sliced through the silence of the room as Julia faced her, her stomach clenching with sickening apprehension.

Her sister rose to her feet, holding a handful of jewels.

"How could you? That first earring fell at your feet, but when you told me your idea, I thought it merely a fantasy, a silly whim." Sarah shook her head. "But you've done it. You've taken someone else's jewelry."

"Yes," Julia agreed. There was no question of denying it.

"All this time, I wondered why you were going to these dances and parties without caring about securing any man's favor. You weren't interested in finding a husband."

"I told you I wasn't," Julia tried to defend herself.

"This," Sarah said, shaking her clenched hand from which the jewelry dangled precariously, "this cannot be all of it. Where is the rest?"

"Sold," Julia snapped, stepping forward and holding her palms open. "Give it to me, please."

Sarah hesitated. Ignoring Julia's request, she went over to the bed, sat heavily upon it, and dropped the jewelry in her own lap.

"And the money?" Her voice had lowered to a whisper.

"Already given to the poor." Julia confessed.

"You will cease this madness at once." Her older sister's tone had an edge Julia had never heard before.

She remained quiet, not wanting to argue, nor lie to her. Yet Julia saw no other way to help, and she'd seen the evidence of how much good the large donations could do.

"Tell me to whom each of these belongs," Sarah added.

"Why?" Julia felt a quiver of fear.

"Because I intend to return them to their rightful owners. And you will go back to buying posies to help the less fortunate!"

JULIA HAD BEEN UNABLE to talk Sarah out of the idea of reuniting the stolen jewelry with its owner, and that had effectively put a stop to her own adventures since she feared Sarah would search out every piece she brought home and then put herself in danger to return it. She and her sister were at a stalemate.

After Sarah stormed out, Julia proceeded to tear apart her room and, while searching, had shed a few tears at the loss of her one and only connection to her deceased mother.

All thoughts of going out that night fled, and she doubted Sarah would let her out of the house in any case. Instead, stepping over the petticoats and gowns and shoes she heaped into piles while searching, she sank onto her bed.

All was lost. Her ring was well and truly gone, she had no more jewels to sell for the poor, and Jasper was a dissolute rake. Julia didn't care if she ever left her room again.

CHAPTER TWENTY-THREE

"At Lord and Lady Stridewell's dinner party last night, Miss S__ reappeared in public, only to become involved in a case of misplaced jewelry. Shouting ensued with some unwise gentlemen calling Lord M__'s solvency into question before the party ended abruptly."

—The Times

Ignoring her sister's disapproving looks, Julia remained in seclusion, awaiting the time when they would head to their father's. Jasper had written, more than once, but she'd barely glanced at his invitations, given them a surreptitious sniff, and put them aside. That hadn't stopped her from reading the papers, nor hunting for news about Jasper to torture herself.

Perhaps to punish her further, Sarah left a paper open on the breakfast table.

"Lord M__ has a new lady love. Could Lady V__ be the one to finally trap and tame London's worst rake?"

Knowing about his wager at White's, Julia heartily doubted it. But that was the mysterious Lady V's problem.

All she could do was be as good as gold and hope Sarah stopped treating her like a pariah. For in truth, she'd made no other friends in London, except Jasper.

Thus, she was delighted when Sarah came rushing in, cheeks red, calling her name. Had she been forgiven?

"I saw your ring," her sister declared.

"What do you mean? Where is it?" Julia demanded.

"I went to tea at Lady Bromley's with all those peahens. The conversation went quickly from the tedious, regarding latest sleeve styles, to the vulgar, with whose husband was being cuckolded."

Julia nodded. That was the way of it. "Yes, but my ring," she prompted.

"I ended up beside Lady Stridewell. You know, the baroness."

Julia shrugged having a vague idea of a portly woman who spoke more than she listened.

"Lady Stridewell drank her tea with the most unbecoming affectation, holding her little finger up while she sipped. And that's when I saw it. Your ring. In fact, I believe she was trying to show it off."

"What did you do?" Julia asked. "Did you tell her it was mine?"

"Off course not. I couldn't just proclaim the lady had your ring. I asked her where she got it, and she said from her husband."

"Did you press the issue?" Julia hoped for more.

Sarah shook her head. "What could I do?"

Julia's mind was racing. Her sister might not be able to do anything, but Julia certainly could. All she needed was to get invited to their home for dinner.

WHEN JULIA WALKED INTO the Stridewells' house later in the week, she had a singular purpose—she would leave with her ring, if she had to take the baroness's finger with her!

She barely flinched when she noticed Jasper, all his bruises and his black eye healed, standing beside Lady Violet Rearing. A nice enough young woman with two particularly plump features that any man would admire, Julia almost felt sorry for her and refused to let seeing them together disrupt her goal.

Jasper spied her the minute she entered the drawing room, but Julia did her best to give him the cold shoulder while still greeting her hostess, whom she barely knew. By the grace of a countess for a sister, Julia had finagled a last-minute invitation and was warmly welcomed.

"Miss Sudbury," Lady Stridewell met her with a gracious smile, "let me introduce you to my husband."

Julia had no interest in the baron except to wonder how the man had obtained her mother's ring. She also noticed at once the baroness wasn't wearing it. Instead, she dripped with emeralds, from her eardrops to her necklace to her bracelet, and sported a large emerald-studded band on her left hand.

Julia sighed. *Surely the woman didn't need her little ruby ring.*

"Don't be nervous," Lady Stridewell said, misinterpreting Julia's emotions. "The baron won't bite." And then the baroness laughed at her own words. Julia tried to join in, glancing past her to see Jasper watching intently.

Then her view was blocked by the portly baroness who grabbed Julia's hand as they crossed the room to where Lord Stridewell stood beside the fireplace, chatting with three others.

"Dear husband," the baroness said, interrupting him mid-sentence, "this is Miss Sudbury. I believe I mentioned her sister, Lady Worthington, complimented me on my new ring. My husband is exceedingly generous," she added, sweeping the group to make sure they all heard her.

The smallest flash of something appeared in the baron's eyes—perhaps alarm, yet perhaps not.

Julia dropped into a curtsy, then asked, "May I know, my lord, where you obtained it?"

"It was one of a kind," he insisted, pursing his lips against any further words.

"Naturally," she said, her tone pleasant despite wanting to scream. "Still, I thought to surprise my sister with something similar since she was so taken with it, if you will but tell me where you . . . bought it."

After a brief hesitation, he said quietly, "I would rather not say."

The baroness made a perfect *O* of her mouth, then looked sideways at Julia before turning back to her husband.

"Whatever can you mean, sir? Why won't you tell Miss Sudbury? I thought you said it was from Neate's shop."

The others in the small group were also staring at the baron, whose face reddened. Finally, he made an exasperated sound.

"Honoria," he snapped, making those around him flinch at the use of her first name in public, "I do not wish to discuss it further."

Julia hoped the floor would open up and swallow her for causing such an embarrassing scene. The baroness, however, instead of backing down, took a step closer to her husband.

"Herbert Poulet, Baron Stridewell," she said, annunciating each syllable loudly so the entire drawing room hushed. "If there is a secret regarding my new ring, I shall smoke it out of you."

"You shall not," he insisted. "Not here, not now."

"Why won't you tell me where the ring came from?" She waggled her hand in front of his face, even though she wasn't wearing the item in question.

Lord Stridewell glared at Julia as if this were all her fault. Suddenly, Jasper was beside her, taking her smoothly by the arm and leading her away from the tiff.

"Why are you causing trouble?" were the first words out of his attractive mouth, while in the background, she could hear the Stridewells still arguing.

Julia carefully disengaged her arm from his.

"You should be attending to Lady Violet." She glanced at his latest quarry, who was staring with obvious curiosity.

"She is none of your concern," he said coolly, his words slicing her heart.

"No," she agreed. "You are quite correct. Nor am I any of yours."

"Only because you won't allow it. You've ignored my missives and shunned my visit."

He'd come to her home? She tried not to let on that this was news to her. Sarah undoubtedly had thwarted him, and for once, Julia was grateful.

"You must cease this hovering over me and interfering," she said, knowing his being there was going to make her retrieval of her ring that much harder. And of all the times she'd hoped for success, this was the most important. "It is insulting and draws unwanted attention. I would hate for anyone to think you and I have any sort of connection at all, given your sordid reputation."

He looked stunned, perhaps thinking how he'd rescued her once or twice and deserved to be treated better. She supposed she ought to forgive him for being who he was and never lying about it, except he wasn't asking for her forgiveness.

The best she could do was show a kindness to the other woman whose heart might be lost to him already.

"Why, look at how you are causing Lady Violet undue concern," she added.

As soon as he glanced toward the young woman, Julia slipped away. She could only go as far as the other side of the drawing room in hopes their hosts would stop the loud disagreement and recall they had a duty to make their guests comfortable.

And then, with any luck at all, she would recover her ring before they were sent out into their carriages at the end of the evening.

By the pudding course, however, Julia still wondered how she would get upstairs. While the hosts had recovered themselves enough to sit at opposite ends of their dining table, each carrying on separate conversations, Lord Stridewell hadn't disclosed anything, and Lady Stridewell made sure to send him a scathing glare every few minutes. The tension during the meal was palpable.

Moreover, with Jasper sending her warning looks every few minutes, Julia hadn't tried to use the facilities, knowing he would follow her as he had at Lady Rancur's home.

And then an opportunity presented itself. After dinner when the women left the dining room while the men remained for brandy and cigars, Julia managed to be last through the door, trailing behind the bevy of silk-clad ladies. When the last of them disappeared into the salon for madeira and poetry, she lifted her hem and dashed up the stairs.

It was easy to find the baroness's bedroom, all overdone with lace and more lace. A smattering of jewelry lay on a mirrored tray upon the chest of drawers, and there, right before her, was her ring. She snatched it up, knowing she couldn't put it on her finger. Instead, she tucked it into the small, elegant reticule dangling from her wrist, feeling her first sense of peace since it had disappeared.

Not risking detection by pausing—indeed, no longer interested in taking anything after feeling the terrible loss of her own single piece of jewelry—Julia hurried along the hallway to the stairs. She was halfway down when Jasper came into view, making her falter. He stood, looking up, arms crossed and wearing a face of severe judgment.

"I greatly disrelish your behavior," he said quietly.

She barely hesitated before continuing her descent. *After all, what could he do?*

"Hand it over," he ordered, his tone still soft, when they were nose to nose with her one step above him.

Julia made a face and tried to skirt around him. He effectively blocked her.

"The ladies are awaiting me," she said, but he snagged her arm.

"They are awaiting a guest, not a thief."

She looked from his hand holding her arm and back to his disapproving face. They were too close should someone discover them.

"If you must know, I had to reclaim something that belongs to me."

One of his eyebrows rose. "Really? Something of *yours* was in the private rooms of Lord and Lady Stridewell?"

"It's true." She didn't particularly care whether he believed her.

"I bet it sparkles."

"It does."

"Let me see it," he insisted.

"No. Release me before we're discovered. Don't you have a glass of brandy to drink?"

He ignored her question. "I cannot allow you to do this."

"It is not your place to allow or disallow. Just as I cannot make you behave better. I don't *allow* you to trifle with women and then discard them. You simply do it."

She bit her tongue, having started along the path of a vitriolic diatribe which she didn't truly wish to traverse. It showed him far too much of her vulnerability.

"You have always known how people view me and how I conduct myself."

"Yes," she agreed, feeling defeated. He wasn't denying his awful behavior, nor had he any intention of reform. That much was certain.

"Release me," she repeated.

Instead, he snatched her reticule off the arm he was holding. Gasping, she tried to take it back, but before she could stop him, he undid the drawstring and upended the contents onto his palm.

"*Ah-ha!*" he said when the ruby ring fell out.

"It's mine," she hissed.

Julia saw the moment he realized the truth, for he frowned, realizing he'd seen it before upon her hand. Without waiting, she grabbed it from his palm.

"What is going on here?" Lady Stridewell's outraged voice came from behind Jasper, and Julia flinched, peering around his shoulder to see their hostess standing outside the drawing room. Seconds later, the other ladies streamed out to witness the evening's latest entertainment.

Thinking quickly, while he still shielded her, she tucked the ring between her breasts, hoping her stays would hold it against her skin. And then Jasper turned to greet their audience.

At the same moment, Lord Stridewell came from the other direction, having apparently just vacated the dining room with the other male guests following behind him.

Julia swallowed. It dawned on her that instead of being her savior, perhaps Jasper was the most infernal bad luck she'd ever had. For when he wasn't around, she never got caught and definitely never ended up surrounded by onlookers.

Even Lady Violet's eyes had grown large, staring at the man who was supposed to be *her* escort for the night.

"Miss Sudbury has just come from using the facilities," Jasper intoned. "And I was waiting to escort her to the drawing room."

Lady Stridewell stared pointedly toward her husband and the hallway behind him, from which Julia would have had to come if the Earl of Marshfield spoke the truth.

"Is that so?" the baroness asked, her tone dripping disapproval, obviously believing she'd caught them in a moment's inappropriate behavior, sullying her stairwell and staining the honor of her dinner party.

Julia wrenched her reticule from his grasp and took the last step off the stairs, thinking if they weren't practically touching, they would look slightly less guilty.

Then she felt it. The ring slipped past the satin cord that cinched the high-waist of her gown, down through the space between the front of her bodice and her stays. With nothing to catch the ring, it slid between her petticoat and her gown before hitting the tiled floor at her feet.

In the absolute silence that followed, her ring rolled in a slow arc toward Lady Stridewell's kid-leather slippers.

CHAPTER TWENTY-FOUR

"Lord M__ returned to Lord S__'s home the following day. Perhaps he was looking for Lady V__ whom he left at the party the night before. A singular occurrence, as our favorite rake is known for attracting females, not for losing them."

—The Sun

"Gracious me!" the baroness exclaimed, putting the back of her hand to her forehead in dramatic fashion usually reserved for the stage. "My ring!"

Julia nearly dove for it, but Lady Violet reached the ring first, bending to retrieve it. Holding the ruby ring between her thumb and forefinger, her gaze swung from Julia, who'd taken a single step forward, to the baroness who held out her pudgy hand.

"A thief!" Lord Stridewell exclaimed.

"I am not," Julia said. "The ring is mine!"

"Then why were you asking where my husband bought it?" Lady Stridewell demanded. "You said you wanted one exactly like it for your sister."

With those words, the baroness snatched it from Lady Violet and shoved it onto her own smallest finger.

Julia closed her eyes a moment. She was back where she started, only worse!

With nothing to lose, she turned to the baron. "Won't you please explain where you got it? It was not from a jewelry shop. I promise I won't press charges."

He laughed as did the men around him. "You? Press charges? It is I who shall prosecute you to the full extent of His Majesty's law. I knew better than to have someone like you to dinner."

Julia felt her cheeks flame, but she would not be intimidated by the likes of him.

"My sister, the Countess of Worthington, will show you the ring's match. She wears the necklace that was paired with it. They have the same workmanship, made by the same jeweler."

At last, Jasper spoke up. "I have seen the ruby ring on Miss Sudbury's hand before."

While she appreciated it, all eyes again turned to him standing so close to her, making them both look guilty of one thing or the other.

"You would say such," the baron sneered. "For all we know, you've got a pocket of my wife's jewels."

"Whatever can you mean?" Jasper demanded, sounding indignant.

"Word at the club is you're in a bit of financial trouble. You were seen pawning jewelry at Rundell and Bridge. Then we find you assisting this woman to steal from us."

Another man, Lord Jeggins if Julia recalled correctly, piped up, "Some overheard him say that he cannot afford a rum horse at present."

Lady Stridewell clucked her tongue. "I've heard from a few people how their jewels have gone missing after they've held balls or dinners in their homes, which was why my staff was instructed not to allow anyone onto the upper floors." She pierced Julia with a hard stare. "I would bet this woman attended those parties as well."

"Perhaps both of them were," said Lord Jeggins from the safety of the back row.

"You ought to be more careful," Jasper warned, his tone calm but firm, "than to throw such accusations around."

"You're lucky Parliament is in session," another man called out.

The insult was clear, as even Julia knew a seated member couldn't be put in debtor's prison while Parliament was open.

"Fine words from tag-rag scum!" Jasper returned.

It was all unraveling. Julia took a deep breath, trying to come up with a diversion because they were guessing a little too close to the truth. And then she recalled her mother's ring.

"Why won't you say how you really procured my ruby ring?" she demanded of Lord Stridewell.

The baron reddened, as all the fascinated gazes turned his way.

"I don't have to tell you. All we have to do is speak with the authorities and get you sent to Newgate before morning."

"Then *you* shall join me," Julia said, "for I believe you stole my ring to give to your wife."

This time, Lord Stridewell went white as a sheet.

"I . . . ," he trailed off, looking at the baroness, who was exceedingly interested. "This party is over," he said, turning on his heel and storming up the stairs.

Julia had one last chance. She turned to the baroness.

"Will you not return my ring to me? My mother had two pieces of jewelry and gave one to me and one to my sister. I will be happy to pay you for it."

Lady Stridewell hesitated, giving Julia a glimmer of hope.

"I will think on it," she said finally.

With that, the baroness turned to her other guests. "I apologize for this evening's disastrous turn. Reginald will get your coats and hats."

Then, Julia was forced to stand with the others, blanketed in the humiliation of being caught trying to take her ring when she ought to have simply asked the baroness for it and offered to pay her at the start.

Eventually, the butler sorted out everyone's accessories, although every titled lord and lady received theirs before her, including Jasper. He left without another word, not even to Lady Violet, which was the only bright spot in the evening.

JASPER DIDN'T KNOW WHAT to do with his fury, at least not that night. In the morning, he went to Jackson's pugilist's club and worked up a pleasant sweat, imagining his hapless sparring partner was first Stridewell and then that other toad, Jeggins. He could also picture the faces of the men at the jewelry store when he'd retrieved his pin. They must have gone flapping their gums at White's, getting the story all wrong, making it seem as if he were pawning the family jewels for ready coin.

Even the men at Tattersalls had heard his lighthearted remark and fell all over themselves to assume the worst. He threw another fister into his opponent's gut.

And it was all because of Julia Sudbury. *So why wasn't he terribly angry with her?* Perhaps because he was seeing his peers in a new light. The women were spoiled and the men were odious. Not that it excused her from stealing, but he didn't feel sorry for her victims in the least.

Moreover, she who had very little had somehow lost her ring, and that seemed to be his fault.

Belatedly, he recalled abandoning Lady Violet without a backward glance or a single thought, and couldn't work up any guilt or shame. His concerns had been only that Julia wasn't charged with theft.

In fact, she seemed to be his only guiding star and motivation. He felt it in more than his cock, for that matter. All the more disturbing to realize he wanted to see her, talk with her, laugh with her, pleasure her until she was senseless, and then do it all over again. Add to that was a certain tenderness and wish to protect her—dare he say, even a possessive feeling he'd never had before.

It was enough to make him lose his breakfast!

Because of all that nonsense, he had decided to confront Stridewell, resolved to get the truth out of the man. Then when next he saw Julia . . .

He stopped abruptly as he entered his study. *When would he see her again?*

As word spread of the goings-on the previous evening at the Stridewells', it was quite likely she would be effectively removed from society. Of course, no one could do such to him, but Julia Sudbury might never be seen again in a ballroom or drawing room of Mayfair unless it was in her sister's own home.

At the polite hour of three o'clock, Jasper went uninvited to the Stridewells' house, determined to help Julia in some way.

The baron was at home, although he was not seeing visitors after discovering the name of his guest. Jasper folded his arms and glared at the butler until the man returned to his master's study with the message that the Earl of Marshfield would speak to him there privately, or would call him out on the floor of Parliament if need be, or even worse, at their club.

In short order, he was shown into the study.

"What do you want, Marshfield?" the baron asked, not bothering to stand when Jasper entered, nor did he offer him a seat. Jasper took one anyway and gave the man a once-over.

It had occurred to Jasper during the night that a woman must be involved. A woman was nearly always at the heart of any trouble. There was no other reason a man would be so reticent over a silly ring.

"Is she a powerful man's wife?" he asked boldly. "Or some three-penny upright whose got under your skin?"

Stridewell's nostrils flared. "I don't know what you're talking about."

Clearly, Jasper was on the right path.

"The ring was either meant for your mistress and given to your wife by mistake or you obtained it as a guilty penance to appease the baroness, somehow procured in an illicit fashion. Those are the only options that make any sense as to why you would have Miss Sudbury's ring."

"If it *is* hers," Stridewell said, shuffling the papers in front of him on his desk while keeping his gaze upon Jasper.

"The Countess of Worthington will testify it is. I suggest your wife be prepared to part with it."

"She already has," the baron said in clipped tones. "Once she found out it hadn't been purchased new from William Neate's in Sweetings Alley, as I'd led her to believe, she was quite done with it."

Jasper sat forward. "Where is the ring?"

Unexpectedly, the man opened the top drawer of his desk, reached in and pulled it out from where it had been sitting amongst pen nibs and stationery. Placing it in front of him on the desk, he laced his fingers and peered over them.

"Why is this important to you, Marshfield?"

Jasper hadn't expected the question. "Miss Sudbury is a friend." It sounded implausible to his own ears. Sure enough, the baron grinned.

"I doubt a man such as you has a female for a *friend*." He paused. When Jasper said nothing more to enlighten him, the baron shrugged.

"How much can you afford?"

"I beg your pardon?" *Was Stridewell really going for extortion?*

"The ring is in my possession. It seems your latest lover wants it. How much will you pay me?"

Jasper sighed. "Why don't you tell me what you paid for it? Unless you cannot. Did you steal it?"

The baron laughed. "That's rich, when half of London is starting to think you're an accomplice to a jewel thief. Do you know some people are cutting you from their party list, Marshfield? You may find yourself alone at Christmas if these nasty rumors continue."

"I could tell the baroness I've discovered who your lover is," Jasper threatened in return.

"You wouldn't," the man said, foolishly confirming there was one.

"Or I could tell my mother," Jasper continued. "The Dowager Countess of Marshfield pours just about the largest cup of gossip-water in all of Britain. She would be interested to learn how you stole a ruby ring from a poor untitled nobody because you were too cheap to go to a jewelry store."

The baron began to look a tad unsettled.

Tossing barbs was growing tedious. "I suppose we can take the ring to a jeweler and have it appraised in order to settle on a fair amount."

"That won't be necessary," Stridewell said. "I can tell you what it's worth to me, and I won't take a penny less."

"I'll double it if you tell me from whom you acquired it."

"That wouldn't be very gentlemanly of me," Stridewell began, but he didn't look closed to the idea of making a profit. "I take it you aren't on the books at some gaming hell, unable to afford a horse."

Jasper shook his head but refused to divert from his purpose. "Tell me how you got the ring. Perhaps this person is London's latest jewel thief."

Stridewell barked out a short laugh. "Doubtful." He seemed to consider. "I know it's early, but would you care for brandy?"

"It is never too early for brandy," Jasper said and decided he was going to get somewhere after all. And Julia was going to owe him a debt of gratitude.

CHAPTER TWENTY-FIVE

"The premiere event of the winter months was held at Apsley House when the Marquess of Wellesley hosted a ball. The marchioness was notably absent, but the host didn't lack for female company. And shockingly, Lord M__ is now openly escorting the untitled Miss S__. As expected, many noblemen's daughters gave her the rump."

—The Morning Post

Dear Miss Sudbury,

May I escort you to the last ball of the year at Apsley House? Lord Wellesley will be hosting. I assume Mrs. Zebodar can accompany us.

Yours truly,

Marshfield

"An invitation?" Sarah remarked. "From the Earl of Marshfield? Does that man have no shame?"

Only then did Julia realize her sister was looking over her shoulder as she read the afternoon mail. Snapping the piece of fine stationery upon her lap, she turned to Sarah who was poised behind the sofa, a book in her hand, making her way past to the better lighting of the wing-back chair by the fire.

"A coveted invitation to an exclusive ball is not shameful," Julia said, "especially when I've all but made myself an outcast."

Sarah pursed her lips. "I thought he was linked with Lady Violet Rearing at present, and yet he invites you. What do you make of that?" Sarah continued.

Julia's heart had already sped up accordingly with excitement. "I make of it that you are walking too quietly and snooping dreadfully."

Sarah frowned and took her seat by the fire. "I had no intention of snooping. I let you open all the mail. It could as easily have been a missive meant for me."

"From whom? Are you seeing Lord Denbigh again?"

"No," Sarah insisted. "And all I meant was that your last invitation from the earl was ages ago and suddenly out of the blue, he is sniffing around your skirts once more."

"That's a very unpleasant picture you're painting. Anyway, if you recall I saw him at the Stridewells' dinner party a few nights ago."

She'd already told Sarah about the ring fiasco and been duly reprimanded for her terrible handling of it, although she'd skipped over the worst bits of the tale.

"Alone?" Sarah asked.

"Of course not alone," Julia snapped. "There were other guests at the dinner."

"I know *you* weren't alone with him, you ninny," Sarah gave it right back to her. "I meant was *he* alone or escorting his latest prize?"

"The latter." Julia tried to sound unbothered. "Lady Violet was there. Insipid thing."

"Is she?" Sarah blinked.

"No, I suppose she's not. No more so than Lady Arabella."

"You don't like seeing him with anyone else," Sarah guessed, "but you'd best get over that. After all he's a—"

"A rake, I know! You don't have to keep reminding me," Julia said wearily. "Anyway, he left the party without her."

"And suddenly, he wants to spend time with you again." Sarah's tone was mocking.

Julia shrugged, trying to tamp down any enthusiasm already building for another encounter with Jasper. She'd been doing well to avoid him before the Stridewells' party, having tried desperately to eradicate him from her heart by thinking of him as a licentious monster.

Reminding herself of poor Lord Neville and of Jasper's flagrant disregard for marital vows, she again successfully cooled her ardor. Calming her heartbeat, she considered. Just because she chose not to give in to his immense draw, it didn't mean she had to skip the final ball of the year—as long as she kept her emotions under control in his company.

"What impertinence!" Sarah insisted. "I cannot wait to hear how you shall set him down in your response."

"Oh," Julia said quietly.

"Oh, indeed!" Sarah said. "Please don't tell me you're considering lowering yourself and letting Marshfield into your good graces once more."

Julia shrugged. "I could lower myself just a little, only to find out what he wants. After all, it's Apsley House! After the debacle at the Stridewells, I would be lucky to get invited to a public concert at Vauxhall."

"Apsley House or not, what Marshfield wants is to have his way with you. He didn't get it before, thanks to me, and that grates on a man like him, so he's trying for another go round."

Thank God her sister didn't know she'd already been alone with the earl since then. Besides, until the fisticuffs in Jasper's foyer, Julia had been prepared and willing to let him have his wonderful way with her.

"Did you just sigh?" Sarah asked.

"No."

"I am sure you did. I believe you sighed over the wretched Earl of Marshfield."

"Maybe. After all, he is amusing, good company, and as attractive as Adonis." She might as well be truthful.

"But what good is all that when he's amusing some other woman two minutes before and two minutes after you?"

Sarah was right. Instead of wondering what to wear to the ball, Julia ought to tell him to go to the devil.

But his kisses were so delicious, and his hands and his . . . other parts were so—

"You just sighed again."

"I did, didn't I? I suppose the problem is I haven't seen a spark in any other man this Season. Marshfield is the only one with dash-fire."

"That's because you have spent all your time in the bedrooms and dressing rooms of London's finest lords and ladies, rifling through their jewels. Luckily, I have managed to get myself invited to Lady Macroun's house party over the Twelvetide. I intend to return some of what you took."

Julia sat up straighter. "That's impossibly dangerous for you."

"I know. It's rather exciting." Sarah had a little pink in her cheeks as if the danger pleased her. "In any case, having days to reunite the pieces with their owners shall certainly be easier than what happened last time. I didn't tell you I was nearly caught and had to scuttle under the Marquess of Fairway's bed with his ring in my mouth. And I quickly discovered his chambermaid is not nearly as good as ours." She scrunched her pretty face as if reliving the dusty experience.

Julia's mouth dropped open. "What if you'd been caught?"

Sarah raised an eyebrow. "I hope I am as careful as you."

Julia ought to tell her sister how many times she had, in fact, been discovered, but she hated to receive another lecture.

"Besides," Sarah continued, "you'll never guess our good fortune. Four of your hapless victims will be in the same place. I'll simply drop each one's bauble in a shoe or pocket and they'll think it was there all along. Even that poor old Lord Devonshire will be there, the one who made such a fuss in the papers about his ring going missing."

"Don't go marrying him," Julia said, trying to lighten the discussion. "However, I should be the one to do it," she protested, thinking how relieved she would be to get her own ring back. "Let me go to the party with you."

"Would you promise not to take anything else?" Sarah asked.

"I would never put you at risk."

"Then I'll see if I can secure another invitation. I had to play the lonely widow who desperately wants to get out of London for a bit. Perhaps you can come along as my companion with whom I can't bear to be parted."

"Dear God, we sound like a couple of maiden aunts—a lonely widow and her companion! But what about Father?"

Sarah gave a little shrug. "We shall see him in the new year instead."

"CAN YOU ACTUALLY BE angry at me?" Jasper looked bewildered by her expression, as they stood by the tall windows of Apsley House, overlooking Hyde Park.

Looking as ridiculously handsome as ever, he'd come to collect her along with Mrs. Zebodar. Behaving perfectly, he was in a good mood, smiling and charming, as they rode the short distance to the Marquess of Wellesley's gracious home, and it had grated on Julia's every last nerve.

The grand home was situated in a prominent place beside the main southeast gate to Hyde Park. That night, the red brick house was lit from the many oil lamps around its exterior. Inside, shuffling slowly with the other guests through a grand entrance hall into a smaller chamber, Julia and Mrs. Zebodar changed into their dancing slippers while Jasper dropped off their coats. Then Julia placed her hand on Jasper's arm, and they ascended the U-shaped staircase, her chaperone trailing behind them.

Upstairs, the main reception room had been transformed into a glittering ballroom for the event. Julia tried to enjoy her surroundings, but felt increasingly in a snit, as Jasper smiled at one lady, nodded to another, bowed to a duke, and shared a quick word with Lord Wellesley, their host. His wife, the former French actress Hyacinth-Gabrielle was not evident. Instead, the marquess's young mistress Elizabeth Johnston played hostess, offering Jasper a warm welcome and her hand to kiss.

All this before they'd even made it across to the ceiling high windows on the other side of the grand room. So much for Lord Stridewell's threat over Jasper being cut from society! The man could get away with anything, it seemed.

Julia considered her emotions. After being shocked by the distressed state of Lord Neville, she had been angry with Jasper at first, but then she'd realized her true anger was at herself. She'd known better than to invest even the smallest part of her heart in a rake.

Known better and done it anyway!

After the Stridewells' dinner party, her anger had doubled—after all, he'd cost her the ring, which she'd heard no more about from Lady Stridewell. Moreover, Julia couldn't deny feeling miffed at the ease with which he'd moved on to Lady Violet. But that was the very essence of the man.

Now, seeing him in his element, her pettish expression had prompted his charming tilt of his head and his silly question.

"Can you actually be angry at me?"

What a waste of a dashing man! He was like a woebegone dog who stole a chicken from pure instinct yet meant no harm, nor even knew what he'd done wrong. She might as well be angry at the sea for being wet.

"No. I'm not angry," she lied, at once leaving Mrs. Zebodar, who was busy lining up potential dance partners, and striding away through the next drawing room into a third at the back of the house. Julia knew Jasper would follow.

When he did, she said over her shoulder, "I know I have behaved badly where you are concerned, and you did nothing I didn't let you do, and freely, too. However, I am still sane enough to feel ashamed of my behavior and yours, for that matter! And I don't wish to be treated like I do not matter. Like a courtesan."

"A courtesan?" he echoed.

She stopped in front of a window overlooking the garden. He came to a halt beside her, regarding her with his dark-brown gaze with the slightest of frowns upon his forehead.

He still looked infernally dashing. *Devil take the man!*

"We've had a waggish good time, have we not? Whenever we're together, be it riding or for dinner or whatever else we've managed."

"Yes," she agreed. *How many more good times had he experienced with other women in the past few weeks?*

"Ah, I see." His frown disappeared. "You've missed me, and it's put you into a case of the blue devils." His face broke out in a sensual grin that made her stomach twinge with yearning.

She *had* missed him, but she wouldn't tell him such. Besides, it seemed terribly hypocritical of her to be annoyed that he'd take up with other women and done the honorable thing by leaving her alone.

A rake's honor, to be sure, one that suited his fickle way of life!

Jasper leaned close, causing her to take a step back, eventually pressing herself flat against the gold-and-green wallpaper. He put a hand up beside her head, standing most inappropriately, holding her captive in the corner of the room.

Bending down, he nuzzled against the side of her face and then lower, placing a searing kiss just above her collarbone.

"I've been wanting to do that since I helped you into my carriage with your ridiculous excuse for a chaperone."

She'd been wanting him to do that and more, not that she would tell him so.

"I hope I can bring you out of your melancholy," Jasper added and took her mouth under his.

They were being terribly risky. In his company mere minutes, she was already letting herself be compromised in a deserted drawing room. And willingly.

As he deepened the kiss, she moaned, hearing him growl in response. With her pulse beating at the apex of her thighs, she was floating, light-headed, tethered only by his arms around her. When he finally drew back and looked into her eyes, his own were dark, his pupils dilated. He looked almost surprised by the passion flowing between them.

"God, I have missed you," he confessed.

Again, she had to bite her tongue from saying the same. It was all right for a confirmed rogue to speak such words to a woman for whom he'd not declared himself or made any promises. But it would not be wise to give him any more power over her.

"Mrs. Zebodar will be concerned. I had best return to the ballroom."

"True, you should. She looked positively thunderstruck when you walked away. I told her not to worry, that I would find you."

"Did you?" Julia couldn't see how Jasper, with his reputation, telling her chaperone he was going to find her would put Mrs. Zebodar's fears at rest.

"In that case, I shall run. Poor lady, she—"

Her words were cut off by his mouth claiming hers again, causing her stomach to flip delightfully. Her hands grabbed him, practically of their own accord, clutching his lapel and holding him close.

He slanted his mouth atop hers, and then his wicked tongue stole between her lips.

"Mm," she murmured, her knees weakening as his tongue stroked hers.

Suddenly, his large palms clutched her bottom, bringing her up against him.

Gracious! That kiss moved quickly enough to steal her breath and fuel her desire to the boiling point.

"Do you think she would notice if we were gone another ten minutes?" Jasper asked.

With her heart thumping like a trapped rabbit, Julia pushed at him, and he released her.

"No, th-thank you," she stammered, then wished she hadn't said anything so silly. *Pudding-head, indeed! Thanking the man for suggesting a tryst!*

Before she'd taken more than a step, he said, "Promise me you won't snavel anything tonight."

She froze. "I am here only to dance."

With that, she smoothed her gown and started back the way she'd come. Hearing his footsteps, Julia held up her hand, and he halted.

"I think you should let me return to the ballroom on my own. Or have you forgotten who and what you are?" She turned away just as she saw the tightening of his mouth, evidence of his displeasure.

Continuing along the hall, she was surprised by Jasper's irritation. If he didn't want to be called out as a rake, then he should behave better.

CHAPTER TWENTY-SIX

"Not only do the ladies catch the Earl of M__'s eye, but so
do their baubles. Lord M__ pocketed a brooch belonging
to Lady R__, who was most upset by the incident. The
guests at Apsley House bore witness as Lord M__'s
finances were again brought into question."

—The Times

The evening was nearing its end with one dance left, *La
Boulangere.* Julia had managed to regain her good sense
and avoided being alone with Jasper the rest of the evening
in an attempt not to make a moonstruck fool of herself.
She'd even left her reticule with Mrs. Zebodar, hoping he
saw it as her promise to behave.

Turning to leave the ladies' retiring room, with a
disobedient lock of hair secured, and Mrs. Zebodar in front
of her, Julia stood upon something sharp. Looking down to
see what had pained her through the sole of her slipper, she
caught her breath and moved slightly forward so her gown
covered the dazzler.

Without hesitation, she bent and retrieved an exquisite
brooch from the polished parquet floor.

Ostensibly, her prayers to continue helping the poor had been answered.

A hundred blankets, a hundred wool coats, a hundred loaves of warm bread and bowls of hearty stew—she wasn't sure what the piece of jewelry would turn into but something exceedingly wonderful. Something far superior to diamonds and emeralds.

In an instant, she pressed the large jeweled brooch into her palm and followed Mrs. Zebodar back into the ballroom. In a few steps, she would reclaim her reticule and secure the jewel in its satin depths.

Before she reached their table, Jasper appeared at her side.

"I should have asked earlier, but you've been a difficult woman to catch tonight. Do you have a partner for the next dance? It's the last one."

"No," she blurted, still thinking of hiding the brooch.

"Perfect." Without waiting, he took her hand, luckily the free one, and placed it on his arm.

Julia found herself being led to where the other dancers were lining up. This was untenable. She couldn't possibly press palms, hold hands, or get through an interminable quadrille with the brooch still clutched in her grasp.

Heart pounding, she reached across her body and under his arm, fearing she would drop the brooch, but managed to slip it into Jasper's pocket, despite it being angled back fashionably toward his buttocks.

He must have felt something, for he started to look down just as she yanked her hand back.

The music began. Julia would have been glad to partner with him and enjoy the final dance, except she couldn't think how she would retrieve the brooch.

"My apologies," he said, snagging her attention. "That was not well done of me, earlier tonight."

She couldn't believe her ears. *Was he apologizing for his usual behavior?* "I believe I led you to think it would be acceptable, even welcome. The fault is not all yours."

She felt somehow purer for speaking the truth. It certainly wasn't fair to put all the blame on him when she'd been such a willing culprit.

"Be that as it may," Jasper said, "I do know better and promise you I can behave in a manner befitting a gentleman, although you are the most tempting female I've ever encountered." He finished by offering her his most charming smile, and she nearly forgot about the brooch.

And then the quadrille ended, and Jasper returned her to her chaperone.

"All in all, a splendid evening, over too soon," he declared. "Shall we go?"

Unless she were in his bedroom sometime soon, Julia could think of no other reason for him to remove his coat in her presence or for her to have access to his pocket. Letting him make love to her would certainly be no hardship, but seemed a rather drastic manner of recovering the jewelry.

Inspired, Julia gave him a little shove back toward the chair while taking the one beside him.

"Let's avoid the crush downstairs," she said amiably. "Why wait in such a crowd for your carriage when we can stay here and chat." Somehow, she would get her hand into his pocket.

Jasper beamed, obviously flattered by her invitation and by being entirely forgiven for his earlier improper behavior. Lowering himself onto the cane chair beside her, his smile slowly died and a strange look came over his face. Then he wriggled.

To her dismay, he yelped and sprang back to his feet.

Most bewilderingly, at the exact same time, a woman cried out a few yards away.

Splitting her gaze between Jasper and the lady in distress, trying to determine if they were somehow connected, she nearly missed him digging into his pocket.

His pocket!

"No, no, no!" wailed the woman, coming closer, clearing a path as she did by wildly gesticulating with her arms, her head swiveling from side to side. "Help!" she added, regaining Julia's attention even though she knew Jasper was at that very moment discovering—

"My brooch!" shrieked the lady.

"A brooch!" exclaimed Jasper.

Hearing him, the woman made a line as straight as the crow flies. Not even pausing for courtesy, she snatched it from his hand.

"Where did you get that?" the woman demanded,

"From my pocket," he said, sounding mystified.

"Your pocket! *Oh!*" she howled. "The clasp is bent." She began to moan again.

"There, there, dear," said a bespectacled man coming up behind her. "No need to fuss." Apparently, he couldn't stand his wife's caterwauling any more than Julia could. What's more, she'd just lost the means to make a final large donation of the year.

"Lord Marshfield had it all along," the man continued in a soothing voice.

"And why is that?" the woman demanded, her apoplectic visage pushing close to Jasper's chest and glaring up at him. "Why did you have *my* brooch in *your* pocket?"

"I haven't the foggiest notion, madam. All I know is I just sat down, and your brooch nearly did me in. It's got quite a wicked pin attached."

"Your backside crushed it," she accused.

"Lady Rampley, I appreciate your grave concern over my backside," he said wryly, but Julia could hear the irritation growing in his voice despite how he tried to keep the situation light. "I suppose there is no harm done now that you have it back."

"No harm!" the lady repeated, sounding unconvinced.

"Perhaps he needed to pawn it," came a loud male voice from somewhere in the throng.

Julia and a few others nearby gasped. Whoever had said the offensive remark, she couldn't tell. Luckily, nor could the earl, for in the blink of an eye he appeared livid.

Before he could pursue the matter, perhaps call the man out, Lord Rampley spoke again.

"Come now, my dear, let us thank your good luck to discover the brooch almost as soon as you'd lost it."

"Did I *lose* it?" Lady Rampley persisted, not taking a step back, nor taking her gaze from Jasper.

Julia wondered at the impertinence of the lady, staring directly up Jasper's nostrils. At the same time, she hoped he kept his temper and his patience.

"Or did this man steal it?" the lady wondered loudly.

Julia nearly smacked her own forehead at the turn of events.

Lady Rampley had all Jasper's attention now. In the silence that followed her accusatory remark, he slowly looked down at her. While Julia couldn't see his expression, it must have been quite something to behold for even in high dander, the lady took a self-preserving step backward.

Her husband grabbed her arm protectively.

"My lady, I think you owe the earl an apology. Perhaps he found it on the floor and put it in his pocket."

Jasper still said nothing. And then, to Julia's horror, he turned toward her. She tried not to flinch, to give no indication at all, even when he narrowed his glittering gaze. Now she knew precisely how terrible his expression was, and she had to press her fingers into her palms to keep from flinching.

He knew. Somehow, he knew she was the cause of this. The blood left her head, leaving her woozy. *Would he say something in front of his peers?*

He turned back to Lady Rampley.

"As your husband said, I found it over by the door earlier. Then we started dancing, and I simply forgot. I fully intended to give it to the footman downstairs handling the coats."

"Hm!" The woman made a sour face. Without so much as thanking him, she turned on her heel and walked away, with the other guests parting for her.

Everyone watched her go, then as if all of one mind, their heads turned to look at Jasper once again, and Julia knew his story was doubted. After all, unless he were feeble-minded, he would have recalled how the brooch ended up in his pocket and said so immediately.

She ought to speak up, to protect him. She could confess to finding it and putting it in his pocket. *Was it too late? Did it matter?*

Taking a step toward him, she opened her mouth, "It was—"

"All a misunderstanding," Jasper interrupted, cutting her off. When he looked down at her again, his message was clear. *Say nothing.*

She swallowed, glad when Mrs. Zebodar took her arm.

"Come along. That's quite enough excitement. I'm sure his lordship's carriage has been brought to the front by now."

The few stragglers in the crowd wandered away, and once again, Jasper looked at her. Although his face was placid, fury danced behind his eyes. Julia had to say something.

"It isn't what it looks like," she said softly.

When she saw his jaw clench, she fell silent, and Jasper turned to walk stiffly in front of them.

"What isn't, dear?" Mrs. Zebodar asked.

Julia nearly laughed, except she wanted to cry. She had the only chaperone in London, she was sure, who missed every nuance, every situation, every clue. *And thank goodness for that!*

JASPER DIDN'T SAY A word to either female for the interminable jaunt back to the Worthington home. If that made him ungentlemanly or boorish, so be it. It didn't matter, for Mrs. Zebodar kept up her usual steady stream of chatter, signifying nothing.

Crossing his legs and his arms, he tilted his head back and closed his eyes rather than look at Julia's lovely face with its worried expression.

He'd had enough of her ridiculous compulsion. Moreover, it pained him to think she couldn't be trusted. She'd actually lied to his face, and for the third time, if he counted being caught in Lady Daphne's bedroom, he'd been drawn into Julia's perfidious world.

When the carriage stopped, he opened his eyes, staring straight into her blue gaze.

He sighed. They waited for Rigley to jump down and open the door. In the interim, Julia gave an almost imperceptible shake of her head.

What was she trying to tell him? That she was innocent? When he'd had the evidence in his hand and even felt it in his rear end?

When the door opened, he got out and held his hand for hers, assisting her down, and then did the same for her chaperone. He was prepared to leave them on the pavement, nodding to Rigley to escort them the few steps to the door.

"Good evening, my lord," Mrs. Zebodar said, turning away.

But Julia hesitated. "I'll be along in a minute," she said. "I need a word with his lordship."

"Oh no," Mrs. Zebodar said. "That won't do. Whatever you wish to say, you can say in front of me."

If Julia were a normal female, that might be true, Jasper thought, but she was an incorrigible jewel thief.

He watched as Julia straightened, growing an inch. With her delicate shoulders set, she rounded upon her chaperone.

"Mrs. Zebodar, I am on a public street with a driver and a footman close by. I am in front of my sister's home. And

I am a grown woman. Either you will go inside and leave the earl and I to have a private word, or I shall get into his carriage with him for a private ride."

Jasper nearly clapped at her gumption. The chaperone's eyes had grown exceedingly wider and her mouth had dropped open. She closed it with a clack of her teeth. Looking from him to her charge, her nostrils flared.

"I will wash my hands of you, Miss Sudbury. If you wish to be alone with a libertine, so be it, but I shall no longer be held responsible."

Thus, instead of going inside, Mrs. Zebodar marched off down one side of Hanover Square.

"Will she be all right?" Jasper asked, thinking to send Rigley to accompany her.

"She'll be fine," Julia said. "She lives in the next street and knows everyone in every house between here and there. Regardless, I cannot let you think the worst. I *found* that brooch upon the floor."

He considered this. "You should have tried to discover its owner or, at the least, turned it into our host. It doesn't really matter how you acquired it. It seems you intended to keep it."

She hung her head and looked adorable. Moreover, some of his anger flitted away, knowing she hadn't gone prowling around Wellesley or his wife's or even his mistress's bedchambers.

"I won't always be there to protect you," he said finally, thinking about what was really bothering him.

"No," she countered with her usual spirit, "sometimes you're there to make a chop into a stew and get in my way."

In a flash, Jasper wanted to roar and tear his hair out.

"May I suggest you hurry inside before I thrash some sense into you," he all but growled, "and I'll start with my palm across your pert backside."

She paled in the light of a Hanover Square oil lamp. But she seemed to get the message, for she nodded and turned to go. Then he remembered something. Much as it pained him to think of not seeing her around Town, the notion of her being tucked away safely in Chislehurst appealed to him.

"If I do not encounter you again before you leave, I wish you a pleasant Twelvetide in Chislehurst."

"Our plans have changed," Julia said, "my sister and I are going to Lady Macroun's house party. It's in Great Oakley."

"I know where it is," he said. "And I forbid you to go!"

CHAPTER TWENTY-SEVEN

"Lord M__'s Grosvenor Square home had two visitors
from opposite ends of the social stratum. One can only
imagine what trouble he is in with both."

—The Morning Sun

"I beg your pardon." Julia mustn't have heard the earl
correctly. "Did you just say you *forbid* me?"

"Indeed. It would be too tempting for your affliction.
Very little supervision. People dripping in extravagant
holiday jewels, too many libations causing exceeding
merriment and very little caution. In short, a disaster. You
would never make it back to London except in chains for a
trial."

Rendered almost speechless, she finally spluttered, "You
are in no position to lecture or attempt to control me, sir."

He shrugged. "Perhaps not. I am curious, Julia," he said,
his use of her name making shivers run up and down her
spine, and not from the chilly December evening. "How
badly do you want your ring back?"

She gasped. "Why?"

"Because I have it, and I'll tell you the entire sordid story
of where it went and how it came to be in my possession."

"Why didn't you say anything earlier?" she asked, hardly able to believe his words.

Withdrawing his flask of brandy from his pocket, he offered it to her. Only because of the chill, she accepted and took a drink before handing it back, watching him take a healthy swallow.

"The right time didn't come up," Jasper said at last, and she had a feeling he'd been waiting to tell her when he could make the most use of it. "Will you come back with me to my home?" he asked. "Your sister probably thinks you're still in Mrs. Zebodar's company."

Julia's pulse quickened, imagining how easily she could give in and what would await her if she did. Even then, he stroked the side of her face, and it was as if he were stroking her elsewhere. In truth, she wanted to go with him and let him touch her body, and this time, enter her. Already feeling damp between her legs, it would take almost more fortitude than she had to deny them both.

"Do you mean to say, sir, I must go to your bed in order to receive my ring?"

She watched the play of expressions cross his face. Awareness, perhaps shame, then determination as his visage slipped into the well-known mask of a devilish libertine.

"It wouldn't be the worst bargain ever made. For either of us."

Sarah would want her to put him in his place.

"It would make me feel used," Julia said, still watching carefully to see if it caused him the tiniest pang.

Apparently, it did.

He grimaced, then he swore in a most ungentlemanly way.

"Very well. We shan't *enjoy* ourselves if you're going to couch a delightful encounter in such terms. I don't *use* women. I relish them and offer them pleasure."

She hated how it sounded as if he were ready to be of service to the entire female sex in Britain and probably beyond, too.

"Why don't you tell me exactly what I need to do to recover my ring?" The tenor of her voice sharpened. Jasper knew how important her mother's ring was to her, and he was playing games.

"Will you stay away from that Twelvetide party at Lady Macroun's country manor?" he asked.

Julia was caught off guard by the sudden change of topic. Then she realized his intent.

"Yes," she declared at once.

He grinned. "Liar! Maybe I should send word to Lady Macroun that you are not to be allowed under the roof of Forde Hall, no matter how you beg."

"You wouldn't!" she exclaimed, thinking of the humiliation were he to get involved, not only for her sake but for Sarah's.

"Stay in London," he said, "where I can see you and keep an eye on you."

"For how long?" Julia asked.

"Meaning?" he asked, tipping back his flask again.

"How long before I get my ring back?" She was seething now at his high-handed maneuvering, making her warmer than any brandy ever could.

"If you do as I say, it will be your Christmas gift from me."

"My own ring is your gift to me," she scoffed. "How generous! I shall make sure to give you one of your own stockings in return."

The earl laughed hard. Despite her acute annoyance at his manipulation, knowing her ring was safe and that she would soon have it back eased her mind.

"So," he prompted once again, "would you like to come back to my house? I can make you forget all about the ring."

She almost groaned aloud. The man was infuriating and cock-sure of himself with good reason. Luckily, his own actions had persuaded her not to succumb to his tempting offer. Then there was the other obvious reason.

"What of Lady Violet?"

He raised a dark eyebrow. "She will not be in my house. I promise you that."

Julia huffed. It was about the only promise he would make concerning another woman.

"But will she be on your arm tomorrow?" Julia pressed.

He paused, and she considered how proprietary and jealous she sounded and bit her lip.

"You know who I am," he reminded her.

"Yes," she said quietly. "I know."

"Still, the answer to your question is no. Lady Violet and I have parted ways, I believe."

Feeling a little jolt of happiness, Julia asked, "Have you? What do you mean 'you believe'?"

There was that attractive, rakish shrug again. "I suppose since I left her behind the other night at the Stridewells— quite by accident, I assure you—and since I haven't had a moment to contact her, we are probably finished."

He didn't sound the least bit unhappy. Moreover, he'd found the time to get her ring back and escort her to a ball. He certainly could have found a moment to communicate with Lady Violet if he'd wanted.

"Don't let it go to your head," Jasper added, possibly reading her thoughts.

But since he said nothing more to dissuade her, she let it go to her heart instead.

"Your cheeks are growing all sweet and pink, like juicy cherries I want desperately to taste. What are you thinking, as if I didn't know?"

"My cheeks are red due to the cold. Nothing more. I must go inside before I lose my nose to frostbite."

His chuckle indicated he didn't believe her. "Come now, don't be peevish," he said. "I retrieved your ring for you, and you'll have it soon. I won't even make you pay what I paid for it."

Another surprising disclosure. "You paid the baron for it?"

"I did." He looked supremely pleased with himself.

"Will you tell me how much you paid?"

"It's no matter. I don't want your money," Jasper reminded her.

She had the feeling it was going to cost her far more than a few coins to retrieve it, even after she paid the price of staying home from the house party at Great Oakley.

JASPER WAS IN A good humor the following day. He had ensured he would have Julia Sudbury all to himself. He was going to show her how much pleasure two people could enjoy, and he was going to do most of it while she wore nothing but that damned ruby ring!

He would kiss the nape of her neck, capture her enticing scent, and lick the soft skin beside her navel. He wished to discover if and where she was ticklish, and then hear her laugh.

Jasper liked how she spoke to him as if she were his equal, despite her not being born of anyone who was anybody. So very unexpected and delightful. Thus, he treated her more forthrightly than any other woman he'd ever met.

Even stranger was the warmth that infused him whenever he thought of her, quite apart from his proximity to the hearth in his own study. No, he was decidedly sure his thoughts about her were what was making him so content, and always filled with eager anticipation of seeing her again.

Musing on her person instead of working on the bill he would present to Parliament in the new year, he considered sending her a note that very moment, inviting her to a winter concert. However, a pounding on his front door, echoing all the way to his study, brought him out of his chair. *What the devil!*

Surely not Lord Neville again. Without Julia there to protect him, he might be in for a bellyful beating.

"Mr. Greer," he called as he made his way to the foyer, despite the fact his able butler was already at the front door drawing it open.

Jasper waited, arms folded, tapping his foot while the intruder spoke in loud tones with Mr. Greer. This went on for a full minute before his butler firmly closed the door.

"Do tell," Jasper said at once.

"A gullgroper, sir," Mr. Greer said.

"I beg your pardon!"

"To be precise, my lord, a man who wishes to lend you money because he—"

"I know what he is, but why does he believe I've lost my money at gaming? And what cheek, this *gullgroper*, as you call such a shark, making a ruckus on my doorstep."

"He thought you would be pleased to speak with him, sir. I told him he was mistaken. He said you would change your mind when the creditors come ferreting you out. 'Better to deal with him,' he said, 'than shove the moon.'"

"Shove the moon?" Jasper repeated. "I actually don't know what that means, Greer."

"That's understandable, sir. Why would you? You would not have had cause to flee during a moonlit night to prevent your belongings beings seized by your creditors, sir."

His butler's no-nonsense delivery of such information would be laughable if the matter weren't so serious.

"Hell's bells!" Jasper swore. "If Mother gets wind of this silly rumor, she'll be mad as a wet hen. Then I will need to shove the moon, as you say."

"Not me, sir, the gullgroper."

Jasper sighed. "I don't suppose he mentioned how he got this notion into his head."

"Yes, sir, he did. All his sort, the moneylenders, get wind of any nobleman in danger of whitewashing—that is, declaring insolvency, sir, to avoid creditors. I believe the shopkeepers keep them apprised in order to be paid before there's nothing left."

"Nothing left!" Jasper shook his head. "In case you're wondering, Mr. Greer, I have not spent the family fortune, nor have I lost it at the gaming tables. The Marshfield estate is sound, and you along with all the staff will be paid as usual."

"Very good, sir." Mr. Greer made a point to sound bored.

Regardless, Jasper knew his personal assurances would be passed along to the other servants who might be getting nervous. *Nervous enough to start pawning his belongings!*

Before he could turn away, there was another rap at the door, and then the sound of someone actually attempting to push it open. His butler turned to investigate the latest insolent visitor.

"I'll deal with this," Jasper said, marching to the door, turning the lock, and yanking it open. His mother collapsed into his arms.

"Jasper! You dragged me off my feet." Then she gasped. "It's true, isn't it? All true! Elsewise why would you be opening your own door? You had to sack all your staff."

She moaned loudly, pushed herself away from him, and staggered past into the drawing room from whence she called out, "Mr. Greer, sherry if you would be so good."

Jasper sighed. She'd just blithely given an order to one of the "sacked" staff.

"Would you care for something to drink with her ladyship, sir?" his butler asked, looking characteristically unbothered by anything that happened in the foyer.

"Need you ask." And he followed the dowager countess into the drawing room. She was sprawled upon the sofa, fanning herself, eyes closed.

"We are ruined."

"We are not ruined, Mother. Pull yourself together. And if we were, you ought to be angry, not wilting like a week-old rose."

Opening her eyes, she glared at him. "Did you call me old?"

"No, Mother."

"Well, I *am* angry. Your father should have appointed an executor before he so thoughtlessly passed away. Clearly, you don't have a head for anything other than females, and certainly not for finances."

Where was his drink? He yanked the bell-pull despite knowing it wouldn't bring Mr. Greer or the parlor maid any quicker.

"You say you expected me to be angry?" she demanded. "When was that, when you were gambling away our last farthing?"

"Yes, precisely at that moment, as I turned over the losing hand and saw my future going into the rubbish bin, I thought to myself, Mother will be angry."

"You are mocking me," she declared, as the maid came in carrying a tray with two crystal glasses. Wisely, she went to the dowager countess first, curtsying low so his mother could take the glass without sitting up.

Upon taking a hurried sip, a little dribble of sherry went down her chin.

"*Oh!*" she said, sounding furious as she sat up and drew a handkerchief from her sleeve, causing her to nearly spill her drink onto her lap.

Jasper took his own glass, nodded to the parlor maid to retreat with all due haste, and added, "Close the door after you."

When they were alone again, and he'd had a steadying swallow of brandy, Jasper took a seat at the other end of the sofa.

"I don't like to see you so overcome. I assure you whatever you've heard is an outright lie. Our accounts are as solid as ever they were. We made a substantial amount investing in the Gas Light and Coke Company, and our accountant will tell you the same. In short, it is all rumor and innuendo, a misunderstanding over my cravat pin being pawned."

"What?" the dowager countess roared. "Why would you pawn your pin?"

Her words made him grin, which only infuriated her further. She drank the rest of her sherry in a single long gulp.

"It was an error," he said to calm her, "and I have it back now."

This was met with silence. Then she narrowed her eyes.

"This is about a woman."

He flinched. *Wasn't that precisely what he'd thought when dealing with Stridewell?* Women and trouble seemed to go hand-in-hand.

"I can see upon your face I've hit the mark with my first arrow. You must leave Town at once."

"Whyever for?" He crossed his legs and leaned back, wondering why he hadn't asked for the entire cask of brandy. His mother was simply being hysterical, and he wouldn't feed her hysteria by telling her about Julia Sudbury.

"Everyone who is anyone leaves Town for the winter," she continued. "That is *if* they can afford to open their frigid, drafty country manors. Can we?"

"Yes, I told you that, but—"

"Then we shall go. I'll leave tomorrow, and you shall join me before there is a line of merchants outside your door and mine, too, with their hands out. Your tailor and my dressmaker, even Berry Brothers will be on the step soon demanding coin for their wine. Good Lord!" she exclaimed. "Every last cheesemonger will expect to be paid."

He smiled at her again.

"I don't owe every last cheesemonger. I don't believe I owe any, for that matter, but I will have to take that up with Mr. Greer. He would know if there are any outstanding household accounts, particularly for cheese."

"You're mocking me again." His mother's voice had turned to brittle ice.

"Because you're being a ninny. We are not compromised, and we don't need to run away and flee London. Besides, it's nearly Christmas."

"Nevertheless, you shall do as I say."

"I won't," Jasper said, knowing full well he sounded like a quarrelsome brat.

She snagged his gaze and held it. It was a long, hard, cold stare—the type she'd only ever used when he'd been particularly naughty. When he'd slid down the banister and crashed into their old butler or when he'd performed vigorous somersaults along the wide upstairs hallway of their country manor and destroyed a porcelain vase and a marble bust of some dusty old philosopher.

At present, it seemed as if she could also suck all the air out of the room.

Jasper swallowed and tried to loosen his perfectly tied cravat, for he suddenly seemed to be choking. Holding her gaze, he realized they were locked in the eternal battle of mother and son.

How could she go so long without blinking? His eyes were starting to burn, and he knew he was holding his eyelids extraordinarily wide while trying to appear entirely dispassionate.

"Gah!" he exclaimed as he blinked and had to rub his sore orbs.

His mother, to her credit, merely turned her mouth into a moue of displeasure and continued to observe him.

"Won't it look as though we are running away from something?" he pointed out.

"No, because we will pay off every single account that is currently on credit at once, first thing tomorrow morning."

He opened his mouth to retort. After all, just as anyone, they lived on a budget, and sudden expenses, such as paying off entire balances to their long-term creditors, could dwindle their bank account somewhat. Better that, he supposed than having everyone in London consider them on the way to being whitewashed.

"All right. We'll open up the manor for the remainder of the Twelvetide."

"Yes, and we shall host a Twelfth Night celebration, with lots of food and drink and whatever musicians we can scrounge up in Marshfield. We'll invite all the local gentry and a few of the close-by nobility."

He didn't want to do any of that. Moreover, he would have to cancel any parties he'd been invited to in Town. And then there was his intention to spend time with Julia Sudbury.

All his plans—ruined by wretched rumor!

"Will all that suffice to make us appear sufficiently plump in the pocket and set your fears at rest?" Jasper demanded.

"Yes." His mother sniffed. "I believe it will."

Rising to her feet, the dowager countess looked far calmer than when she'd arrived. He stood and walked her to the door.

"I'm going home to get the packing underway," she said. Jasper raised an eyebrow.

"Oh, you know what I mean," his mother said, leaning in to kiss his cheek, and smelling familiarly of lavender water. "I'll get Mr. Jeffers to organize everything and Emily will start the packing. Also, I'll make sure my housekeeper produces a list of accounts that need to be paid off and send it to you immediately. You'll see to that before you leave, of course. Also, send word to the staff at the manor of our imminent arrival. I wouldn't want to show up and find there's not a crumb in the place."

"Or a bottle of brandy," he muttered. *Dammit all!* She was turning him into her private secretary.

"What's that you say, Jasper? I hate it when you mumble."

"Only that we must make sure a bottle of sherry awaits you, as well."

"Hm," she said, departing through his doorway as swiftly as she'd arrived. He watched her climb into her carriage and head down the street.

Sighing, he turned around and nearly bumped into Mr. Greer.

"I'm going back to my study. Bring another glass of brandy, will you? And tell Blumsey to start packing my things for a fortnight in the country."

TWO DAYS LATER, ON the morning of Christmas Eve, about to leave London, Jasper was more worried about Julia than about the weather for his trip or the care of his precious horses or even his now thinner bank account. Without him there to keep her out of trouble, he imagined returning in the new year to find her deep in the suds.

After twice trying to see the infernal wench the day before, he'd finally sent her a regretful note that morning, hoping it was too late for her to accompany her sister to Lady Macroun's house party. He'd decided it best if she stayed in London where, given recent events, she wouldn't find herself invited to anything with the quality folk and their jewelry.

Thus, instead of preparing for a night of passion, he would be speeding to his unwarranted punishment in the country. Setting out in his packed travelling coach, barely thirty feet from his own front door, he heard his name.

"Lord Marshfield," came a cry. "Lord Marshfield, please stop."

Her voice! He would know it anywhere.

CHAPTER TWENTY-EIGHT

"The households of both the Earl of M__ and the
Dowager Countess of M__ have left London unexpectedly
for their country estate. No one was invited for the
Twelvetide, but shopkeepers breathed a sigh of relief when
all outstanding accounts reportedly were paid prior to their
departure."

—The Times

Tapping on the roof of his coach with the top of his
walking stick to alert his driver, Jasper lowered the
window as the horses drew to a halt.

There she was, both the bane and the blessing of his
existence, looking flustered and distressed, yet still perfectly
tuppable.

Before he could greet her or even ask her how she fared,
Julia looked wildly around, peered over her shoulder, and
then wrenched open his coach door.

"I say," he began. "My footman would have done that,
that is, if I'd invited you to enter."

In any case, with the step not down and no one to assist
her, she could do little more than lean in and stare up at him
beseechingly.

"Please, Jasper, let me into your carriage."

He'd nearly escaped the pull of her, or at least the constant reminder of his near-obsession by seeing her at every ball and party. Each time, he hoped for more of her and very much wanted to give her more of himself.

Now, here she was in need of his assistance, her large blue eyes blinking up at him.

He sighed. "Very well. Rigley," he called to his footman, who had already jumped down from the back perch and whose sandy-haired head popped into view behind Julia.

"You must back up, Miss Sudbury, so my footman can draw down the step."

"Hurry," she said, again glancing along the street the way she'd come. "There is little time."

He heard a commotion and craned his head out the opening. It did appear that two men were trotting along the street in their direction, waving their arms and shouting.

"Bow Street Runners," he muttered aloud, recognizing them instantly for what they were. Seeing her pale face and desperate situation, he reached down and grabbed hold of her arms, just in front of her shoulders, yanking her onto the floorboards.

"Barnes," he yelled to his driver, "off at once!"

With the door still flapping and Miss Sudbury's feet hanging out, they jolted forward. He heard Rigley jump on the back—*thank goodness!*—*as* Jasper would hate to be short a good footman. And then they were off.

"Lord Marshfield," someone yelled.

Blast it! They knew him by his family crest, emblazoned on the coach doors.

"Ow," she exclaimed as every bump in the road was undoubtedly bruising her ribcage.

As expediently as possible, Jasper pulled her farther inside, leaned out and managed to grab the door handle, although a jarring of the coach made him whack his head on the side of the opening.

He swore loudly, but in a tick, he had the door closed and secured.

Julia Sudbury was getting to her knees, a fetching image, but he thrust away his improper thoughts and assisted her onto the rear-facing seat before resuming his own.

"What trouble have you brought me today?" he asked, rubbing the side of his bruised noggin.

She said nothing while adjusting her bonnet and attempting to brush down her coat, which was smeared with dirt. After a moment, she gave up and folded her gloved hands, also grimy, upon her lap.

"Whatever can you mean by trouble?" she asked.

He couldn't help himself. He laughed. When she said nothing else, he folded his arms.

"Come now, not every citizen of London is lucky enough to be chased by the famed Bow Street patrolmen, a cut above the ordinary thief-taker."

"Is that who they were?" She blinked at him again, trying to appear innocent. "I noticed men following me, and thought they might be pickpockets or worse."

"When did you first notice them?"

She shrugged. "I have seen someone trailing me before when all I did was go on the most tedious of errands."

"What happened today?"

Julia released a large sigh as if she were the most put-upon person in existence.

"I went to the milliner for gloves," she began, "and then to Sarah's favorite perfumery. When she returns from Great Oakley, I thought it would be a nice little gift to give her a new bottle."

"Yes, I can see why they were pursuing you so enthusiastically," he told her, his tone laced with sarcasm. "Gloves and perfume would certainly set off the runners."

"Then I may have stopped in at the pawnbrokers to sell something."

He uncrossed his arms, gripped the edges of the leather squabs, and tried to keep his head from exploding like a cannon blast.

"It was something that had come into my possession weeks ago," she added, as if that excused her.

Jasper closed his eyes and leaned back. There was a silver flask of brandy in his pocket. It was the only thing that kept him from throwing himself out of the moving carriage, or maybe throwing Miss Sudbury. However, he would save the soothing drink for later in the journey, when he grew desperate.

Hell! Even though they were barely passing Shepherd's Bush, this *was* later! Drawing it from his pocket, he took a swig, keeping his eyes closed. He didn't offer her any. She didn't deserve it.

"Say something," she said after a minute, not sounding as sorry as he wanted her to.

"Do you know who I am?" he muttered.

"Of course," she said after a brief hesitation.

Finally, he opened his eyes to see her staring at him as if he were a dunderhead.

"You're the Earl of Marshfield," she added.

"I *know* you know that," he growled.

"Then why did you ask?" Julia tapped her foot impatiently, which both irritated him and made him want to take off her boot and draw her leg onto his lap, run his hands up her calf, and . . .

"It was more of a question I was asking myself, or the world at large."

She cocked her head, looking charming but infuriating, as if *he* were the one with all the problems.

"Are you well, sir? Perhaps you hit your head a little harder than I thought."

Gah! He took another sip of brandy and returned the flask to his pocket.

"I am, as you pointed out, the Earl of Marshfield. The *sixth* earl to be precise. How is it possible I am running from pursuers, hearing Bow Street men yelling my name for all to hear in Grosvenor Square?" He looked skyward before resting his gaze directly on *her*, the object of all his woes. "Because of you, Miss Sudbury, that's why."

She started to open her mouth, but he shook his head.

"Don't say anything."

"I just—" she began.

"For a moment, don't speak," he ordered. "Let me look at you and recall how much I desire you and forget that you're a thief and have convinced half of London I'm going into bankruptcy and am most probably your willing accomplice."

Her eyes widened at his words, and then she nodded. However, she remained silent for barely a minute.

"I simply want to know where we are going."

"To Marshfield Manor. I am fleeing London for the country." He smiled. It was his turn to discomfit her. "And you are going with me."

Her mouth dropped open.

"That's impossible. You must take me back home. I can't possibly go anywhere, certainly not all the way to Gloucestershire. I don't even have any clothing."

Jasper couldn't help grinning. He liked the idea of her without a stitch to wear.

"We can't possibly go back to Hanover Square," he told her. "You are on the run, and like it or not, so am I. Besides, Bow Street's finest will be waiting on your doorstep if they know who you are. Do they?"

She looked unsure. "I don't really know."

"If they've followed you more than once, then they must have identified you, or how would they have found you a second time? And then you led them to my door. To my coach, in fact."

She bit her lower lip, drawing every tiny speck of his attention, and then she turned and looked out the window.

"I have brought this upon myself," she said miserably.

"Undoubtedly, you have. And now you've brought it upon me, and I am paying the price with you. They will be watching my house for the notorious blonde jewel thief. No matter, we won't be there, will we?"

"How long?" she asked, still looking out the window.

"The journey takes all day if we ride straight through. And since there are so many feed merchants and farriers along the way, no reason to think we won't be there by one in the morning."

"Travel in the dark?" She looked at him as if he'd suggested a trip to the moon.

"We have four large lanterns and good wheels. If there are any hold-ups on the road to delay us, and I don't mean highwaymen but disagreeable ruts the size of caverns or accidents or even toll-takers asleep in their little houses, then we may have to stay the night at an inn."

This brought her gaze around to his.

"Don't sound so pleased about the prospect," Julia said, regaining her usual gumption. "But that's not what I meant anyway. How long will we be away from London?"

"Until the Epiphany, at least, if Mother has her way."

"Mother?" she echoed.

"Yes, the dowager countess is there already. She expects me anytime."

Poor Julia Sudbury paled, and he had a dreadful thought.

"You haven't taken any of my mother's jewelry, have you?"

"Certainly not."

"Then why have you transformed into a bloodless, porcelain doll."

She sniffed. "Your mother will hate me for getting you involved. Moreover, she'll think I am chasing after your fortune and title."

He considered her statements.

"If I were you, I wouldn't tell her you were the one who pawned my cravat pin, as that has led to some nasty rumors, distressing my mother out of all proportion. However, if you were chasing me, she would be most excited. She wants me married and producing an heir forthwith."

"But I am a common mopsey," she whispered.

"What the devil!" He leaned forward. "Why would you say such a thing? There is nothing common about you—well, yes, your birth, but apart from that, nothing. As for being a mopsey, only someone in need of spectacles would ever say such."

"Lord Chandron said—"

"He's an ass, and it's a pity he wasn't swept away in the flood with his charming wife."

"That's a wicked thing to say," she said without much forcefulness.

"They were wicked people," he retorted, then sat back. "Anyway, you're as lovely a female as any I've ever known." Her cheeks pinkened again in a manner he liked. "Most women I know don't truly blush," he added. "They put on rouge powder to have permanent red cheeks that fool no one. Not like you, with your rosy hue coming and going for various reasons."

He waited and watched.

"There now, it's deepened. I suppose I've embarrassed you with compliments."

"I suppose you have," she agreed.

"Anyway, I suggest you settle in for the journey."

Nodding, she leaned her head back and even closed her eyes. After a minute, however, she opened them. "I cannot believe you were leaving London without telling me, especially after ordering me to remain in Town. Most thoughtless of you."

"On the contrary, I sent you a note about my involuntary departure this very morning," Jasper said. "If you hadn't been out pawning things, you would have received it."

"I would have found out too late to go with Sarah, who left early for Great Oakley."

"Naturally," Jasper confessed. "That was my hope. Since I had to run due to your troublesome behavior, I didn't want you creating more problems at Lady Macroun's party."

She made a face at him.

"Do you want me to believe you are slipping out of London to avoid being questioned about a pawned pin? I doubt it. I saw for myself the jealous husband having caught wind of your indiscretion. You don't think the hounds chasing you from your home have anything to do with your being an infamous rake?"

He crossed his arms. "Absolutely not. This is because of you. Anyway, I don't dally with married women."

She pursed her lips and blinked.

"Hardly ever," he amended, "and not recently. Lady Neville was months ago. There is really no need for me to fish in that pond when there are so many willing widows around."

"Miss Tufton was not a widow, nor Lady Arabella, nor Lady Violet."

"No." He rubbed his chin as the carriage approached the Hanwell toll and all points west. "More's the pity, too. What a mess that is. She eviscerated me in the papers."

"Which one?" Julia snapped.

"All of them," Jasper returned, feeling sorry for himself. "I fail to see how my breaking it off so neatly could get me into as much trouble as if I'd ruined each and left them with their skirts up and their hopes down. I tupped not a one of them."

An arched and doubting eyebrow from Miss Sudbury caused him to disclose the reality. "I didn't. I swear it. After you and I were almost intimate," he said the words carefully, hoping she deemed them polite.

But she frowned. "Almost?"

"I only mean that your sister stopped the finality of the act. Anyway, after that day, Lady Arabella no longer held any interest for me, neither did Lady Violet despite them both being diamonds of the first water. All I can think of are your soft, full breasts, and the way you opened your thighs to me, and the sweet sounds you made when I touched you and nibbled upon you."

"I see," Julia said quietly, and he was glad he'd told her the truth. However, by her scarlet cheeks he ought not to have been so blunt.

"If only you hadn't turned out to be a thief," he added, breaking the sudden tension in the carriage. "I wouldn't be in this mess."

"You're not in any mess," she insisted blithely.

"All of London thinks I was helping myself to Lady Rampley's bloody brooch!"

She lifted a shoulder in an unimpressed shrug. "You are an earl, as you keep reminding me, and you have no reason to steal. Just remind anyone of that exact fact should they come knocking at your door, unless they are angry husbands. Besides, why would the *bon ton* think you capable of stealing anything?"

"I pulled it from my own damned pocket!" he reminded her. *Like a fool.* Then he came to a terrible conclusion. "You placed it in my possession so I would take the blame!"

"Of course not!" she fumed. "How can you think such a thing?" She folded her arms, pushing her lovely breasts up for his notice now that she'd unbuttoned her coat in the stuffiness of the coach.

How could he think that? Because she was, indeed, nothing but a suds-maker. He crossed his own arms and waited for her to say more.

"I admit I dropped it into your pocket."

"*Ah-ha!*" he exclaimed, although it gave him no satisfaction to think she could be so ruthless.

"But only because you forced me to dance when I had no intention of doing so. Naturally, I assumed you wouldn't be so ninny-pated as to draw the brooch out in full view of everyone." Her eyes were flashing.

"Can you possibly be blaming me?" He was stunned. "It stuck me in the arse," he reminded her.

"That brooch would have done a lot of good in the world."

He shook his head at her brazenness. "It's doing a lot of good where it is, in its *owner's* possession."

"Pish!" she said.

"And then there was the matter of my own cravat pin at the pawnbroker's. You heard that white-livered cur at the ball, hiding somewhere behind the ladies' gowns. He shouted out about my pawning things. My peers assume I am all but penniless, selling off my bits and bobs for pittance."

"Not pittance, I promise you. I got quite a—" she clamped her mouth closed.

He couldn't believe it. She'd nearly confessed that time.

"Ah-ha!" he said again, this time a little too loudly for the confines of the carriage.

She kept her face entirely placid, neither confirming nor denying, as usual. *Exasperating woman!*

"You don't want to know any more," she said quietly. "It might put an end to our friendship."

"Is that what you call my trying to keep you out of jail while keeping myself from being gutted in the society pages."

"As to the former, I am quite capable of handling my own affairs, thank you."

Strangely, she didn't look the least bit grateful, nor did she see the irony of saying such a ridiculous statement while riding in his carriage which she all but threw herself into.

"As to the latter," she continued, "you are 'gutted' weekly for your own dreadful behavior. You can blame no one but yourself. You should have taken a more honorable path in life."

He felt his eyes grow larger. She, a light-fingered Lucy, was lecturing him on his moral behavior.

"I'll have you know for the most part every single woman I ever had relations with knew exactly what I was about and what we were going to do."

"For the most part?" she repeated, prompting clarification.

"A few thought the bedding would lead to a wedding, but that was hardly my fault. Why would I marry them *after* I'd already enjoyed the best they had to give?"

Her face reddened, and Jasper considered he might have spoken rashly that time. After all, she was a vicar's daughter *and* he'd nearly bedded her.

"Not that I think the same way about you," he hurried to add. After all, they were about to be alone together for many hours. He didn't want to anger her and ruin all chance for jollification.

Too late! Her expression turned, if possible, more outraged.

"Come now," Jasper soothed. "Your best was better than anyone else's, and we didn't even finish." He spoke the truth.

Leaning forward, he hoped to make amends with one of the kisses she enjoyed so much.

She pressed herself back against the squabs.

"We have no chaperone," she reminded him.

He needed no reminding of that delightful fact. There was no better way to be with a woman than unchaperoned, as far as he was concerned. Deciding to test the boundaries of what might happen, he reached out to touch her knee.

CHAPTER TWENTY-NINE

"In Lord M__'s absence, all of London is wondering what
has happened to Miss S__ who vanished at the same
time."

–*The Gazette*

Quick as a driver's whip, Julia smacked Jasper's hand. She
might be at the earl's mercy, but she would not become
his "bit of stuff" during the trip to his country home. When
she got out of the coach to meet the Dowager Countess of
Marshfield, she didn't intend to be disheveled like a cockish
wench.

"I shall scream," she promised.

Adorably, Jasper tilted his head and narrowed his eyes.
"Whyever for?"

"You cannot have your way with me on a whim. I shall
scream and your driver will stop the coach," she said,
frowning at the bemused look upon his face.

"If I had *my* way, you have led me to believe it would be
your way, as well. You're blushing again. Besides, if you
screamed, I'm not sure my driver would stop. Shall we try
it?"

"No, that's quite all right. Please keep your hands to yourself."

"How about if I sit next to you?" He had a gleam in his eye.

"Definitely not." She sighed, feeling weak at how much she wanted him to kiss her and do more. Daily—sometimes hourly—she yearned for his hands upon her bare skin.

"Lord Marshfield, while my mind and morals insist I resist you, we both know the closer your proximity, the more I want you to kiss me."

His eyes widened. "I'm honored you would be so candid with me. It gives me hope this forced banishment to the country won't be entirely wasted time."

Yet he didn't press the issue. She viewed the outskirts of London through the carriage window, passing a herd of cattle heading for Smithfield market, and then fewer and fewer people, and soon, the countryside. The conversation turned to a parliamentary bill he was going to put forth in the new year, designed to prohibit unlicensed medical practitioners.

"Quacks!" Jasper proclaimed, "endangering our citizens," and Julia agreed.

After another long while, he drew out a basket from under his seat and offered her some ale, which they shared, slaking their thirst before he also withdrew rolls stuffed with cheese and spiced beef.

She hadn't expected to be fed, especially not in such a rustic way, by an earl.

"I don't like to waste traveling time sitting in a public house being fleeced of my money for inferior food," he explained while she stripped off her gloves.

Julia couldn't discount his reasoning. Moreover, the roll was delicious.

"Surely, we'll have to stop somewhere for . . . ," she trailed off and raised an eyebrow.

"I can easily stop anywhere for that," he reminded her. "Yet I suppose you need privacy."

She felt her cheeks heat again and wished she and her sister didn't share the trait of every emotion being played out upon their faces.

"Let me know when, and we'll stop," he offered. "I brought more food and drink, and both my driver and footman also have such. I try never to stay the night at a tollhouse inn."

"But we must stop to change horses."

"Yes, of course, although not as often as if we drove them at a quicker pace. My driver keeps them steady and lets them rest twice, and they shall make it through to my preferred coach house where they'll be stabled until our return journey. We'll pick up four more Cleveland Bays or at the worst, Norfolk Trotters. If your pursuers had been Robin Redbreasts," he added, mentioning the branch of Bow Street that rode out into the countryside to pursue highwaymen, "and we were racing ahead of their fast horses, then we would be in bad bread, to be sure."

The notion of being chased by either the authorities or highwaymen was a grim one. Julia was glad she'd caught up to Jasper when she had, imagining otherwise she might be seated at the Bow Street magistrates' court being questioned.

Into her continued silence, he began to stare at her, his gaze resting first on her lips and then lower.

Julia cleared her throat to bring his attention back to her eyes.

"Will you do me a favor?"

His face split into an impish grin. "Just ask." His tone would melt ice.

"When we stop at the coach house, will you dispatch a message to Hanover Square so my sister's servants don't start to worry and send a frantic missive to Sarah?"

"That's all?" He looked disappointed. "Yes, of course."

Then Jasper sighed, perhaps realizing she wasn't going to let him push up her skirts and petticoat, nor lay her back against the comfortable squabs and move between her thighs. Just the thought was enough to make her damp, however, and she had to try to think of something else besides wanting him.

"Will you tell me about my ring, which I don't suppose you have with you?"

"Sadly, no," he said. "It's a sordid tale. Are you ready?"

She nodded.

"Very well. Lord Stridewell was a naughty boy, something I can get away with but a married man cannot. At least not some, not those married to a formidable shrew such as the baroness."

"He is having an affair," Julia surmised.

"Too simple," he said, "although that was what I first thought, too. Have you heard of Rudley's?"

She shook her head.

"Nor should you have," he agreed. "It's a private club for gamblers who like interesting stakes."

"Interesting?" she queried.

He tilted his head, considering her. "Sometimes exorbitant amounts of money, but more often property such as real estate and jewelry."

"I see." Her ring had been part of a wager.

"And women," Jasper added, his voice so soft she almost missed it.

A tremor of shock rocked her. "You mean women can be offered as a wager in a game of cards?"

"Yes." He wore the smallest of smiles, giving her pause.

"And do you go to Rudley's?"

"I have in the past, not for a couple years. I don't need to *win* a woman," he pointed out.

Grateful for his honesty, she couldn't help wishing he weren't quite so mesmerizing, to her or to other females.

"My ring was part of the stakes at Rudley's, and the baron is not supposed to be gambling. The baroness doesn't approve. Is that it?"

"Precisely. And his luck held well that night. He boasted to me after a glass of brandy. Not only was your ring tossed in when his opponent was out of all else, but he received a night with a particularly talented Cyprian. Naturally, he doesn't want Lady Stridewell to know any of that."

"Naturally," Julia echoed quietly. Then her curiosity got the better of her. "During the card game, does the woman stand there, knowing she is part of the stakes?"

"Yes. If one has such a high-flier at one's disposal for the night, she's been paid in advance and up for the excitement. She usually stands nearby, in all her finery, showing her wares. Sometimes, things get quite heated if her value goes up while they're in the middle of a game."

Julia tried to imagine the scene.

"But who had my ring?" she asked, recalling what was important.

"Lord Evingdon. Were you at his home recently?"

"Yes, I went to a dinner party."

"Did you steal from him?" he asked immediately.

Julia made a face. "Did he steal from me? That's the question."

"Doubtful," Jasper said. "Most of my set do not go around spicing their guests."

Julia thought about the Evingdon party. "There was a dance first and then a meal. My sister's maid will have a record of what I wore, but I seem to recall I had on a coral-colored gown and fussy gloves with pearls." It came to her in a flash. "The gloves were a tad too tight. I bet my ring came off when I removed them for dinner and put them in my lap. If my ring ended up in my lap, when I stood up, it might have dropped under the table without my noticing. I suppose it's possible there was nothing nefarious about the loss after all."

And she'd spent weeks thinking it had somehow been stolen.

"A servant must have found your ring while cleaning, and being *honest*," he pointedly emphasized the word, "he or she turned it in to Lord Evingdon rather than pocketing it."

"Then Lord Evingdon used it as part of his wager. Along with his mistress," Julia concluded.

"Precisely. Baron Stridewell said he felt a little guilty over accepting the Cyprian's services so he gave the ring to his wife."

"How philanthropic of him," Julia remarked. "I thank you for retrieving it, although it was mean of you not simply to give it back to me."

Jasper shrugged. If he'd hoped for a quick tupping in exchange for his good deed, then he hadn't got his part of the bargain either. Yet. Almost instantly, she could see his thoughts going in such a direction once more.

When he began to undress her again with his eyes, she asked, "Did you bring cards perchance?"

"Naturally not," he said. "I believed I would be alone."

"What would you have done through the entire journey?" If she'd had the chance to plan, she would have brought a good book and maybe some needlepoint.

"Believe it or not, when I leave the hurly-burly of London and am ensconced in my coach, I welcome the quiet and solitude. I wouldn't 'do' anything, nor would I feel compelled to converse."

She hesitated. "Am I a dreadful intrusion?"

Jasper put his head back and laughed before asking, "Do I strike you as such a rash idiot as to answer that question in the affirmative?"

Glad for his laughter, she said, "I suppose not."

"You are a welcome intrusion," he said. "Moreover, I have a satchel filled with newspapers and Parliamentary bills."

Better than nothing, she supposed. "Shall we read, then? Or continue to stare at one another?"

He flashed her his winsome smile. "I am happy to stare at you for hours, but since it inflames my passions and makes you uncomfortable, I'll concede that reading the newspapers would be a good idea, at least until we lose the light."

Bending down, he drew a rubbed leather satchel out from under his seat, opened it, handed her the first papers he took out and then put the rest on his own lap.

"If you read anything interesting, let me know," he said, already opening the first.

His remark made her smile. It was so very domestic of him, this rakehell, to read the news with her and want to know what she considered interesting.

"And you do the same," she replied. "We'll soon discover if our interests are at all similar."

"All right, but if you reach the page that nearly always states 'the E of M was doing this and that,' ignore it. You know more about me than any half-witted gossipmonger, I dare say."

Her smile grew, until she wondered if her own name would be in the papers as the suspected jewel thief of Mayfair. And then she sobered quickly. The officers of Bow Street were renowned for writing up accurate descriptions in the papers so people could more easily identify the criminals.

Pushing that unpleasant thought from her head, she began to read the *Gazette*.

"WE'VE ARRIVED," CAME A soft male voice near her ear.

Julia was roused from a pleasant dream of riding in Hyde Park. As she opened her eyes and yawned, she realized she was on the same side of the coach as Jasper, sharing the seat. What's more, she was pressed up against his side with her head upon his shoulder.

As she straightened, she couldn't help groaning.

"What's the matter?" he asked, stretching now that he was free to move.

"My neck is stiff," she couldn't help complaining, raising a hand to rub it, but he stopped her.

After their last snack, she'd put her gloves back on for warmth, but when his hand suddenly slipped between her coat collar and her skin, she realized he was ungloved. As his warm fingers began to knead and caress her neck, finding exactly the right spot, she shivered.

"Are you cold?" he asked, still very close.

"No."

"You shivered," he said.

"You're touching me," she pointed out.

"I would very much like to do more," he said. With that brisk warning, he swooped low and claimed her mouth.

Turning to make access easier, she reached out to hold his lapels with both hands as her insides became molten.

They shared a hurried plunder of a kiss, one that left her quite breathless. And then, after he tugged on her lower lip with his teeth, sending a delicious jolt of pleasure to her female parts, it was too quickly over.

"I've wanted to kiss you since you entered my coach, and couldn't let an entire journey go to waste."

Julia nearly told him how she'd been wanting him to do that, at least since they'd given up reading when the sun had set hours ago. But he ought to have started such a kiss earlier. Now with her body tingling, she feared she would go to bed frustrated.

However, to keep his pride in check, she said, "That was nice."

"Nice?" he snapped. "That was a hell of a lot better than nice."

She ignored his outburst. "I didn't realize I'd fallen asleep, nor do I recall changing seats."

He shrugged. "When you started to doze, I helped you onto my side and easy as a cat, you curled up and fell asleep. However, we only have a couple minutes," he continued. "We have just turned up the drive to my family's estate. Hopefully, Mother has already gone to bed. She didn't know when to expect me, so I see no reason why she would wait up, but if she has, we should agree upon what you wish me to tell her."

"Jasper, we've had many hours. Why didn't you bring this up before?"

"I hated to wake you, and I didn't think about it until you were leaning on me, snoring like an old dog."

"What!" She tried to push away from him, preferring the notion of being a sleek cat to an old dog.

"Calm yourself. I didn't mind. The noise was almost musical, a low rumble followed by a short whistle. Actually, I drifted off to sleep because of it."

Jasper released her and opened the short velvet curtain. Julia couldn't see much except for moonlit trees, but soon, a grand house came into view. Lamps were in many of the ground-floor windows and a few in the upper chambers, as well.

"It's magnificent," she offered as they rocked to a halt.

"If my mother is awake, I shall tell her your sister was invited away for the winter season, and you were unfortunately left alone in London for the Twelvetide and needed a place to go."

"Without my maid or a trunk of clothing?" His mother would think them both fibbers. "She'll wonder if I'm a lunatic."

"*Hm.* Perhaps you're right. Quite on a whim, you came to say goodbye and discovered you were being pursued by an angry man. Naturally, I offered to help. That's the truth. Mother will think your pursuer to be some rascal from the middle-class, no doubt, an unwanted admirer you're trying to be rid of."

"Why not a nobleman?" Julia asked, scooting to the edge of the squab so she could better peer out into the darkness.

"Because you're a common mopsey."

Without thinking, she turned and punched him in the shoulder, making him chuckle. He'd succeeded, however, in alleviating some of her apprehension over arriving at his country estate. Regardless, she hoped his mother was soundly asleep and would save her questions for the morning.

A WEARY RIGLEY OPENED the coach door, unlatched the step and set it down, then offered a hand to Julia. Although Jasper couldn't see her well in the dim light, she glanced back at him, looking a little uncertain.

Something in the vicinity of his heart clenched. There was that sentimentality striking him again—he wanted to keep her safe, even if it meant hiding her there in Gloucestershire for the rest of her life.

Nodding with encouragement, Jasper grabbed his satchel and his discarded overcoat, before heading out after her.

When they entered the front hall, their long-time butler who traveled with his mother's household, was there to greet them with a bow.

"It's good to see you, my lord," Mr. Jeffers said.

The dowager countess must be asleep after all. Elsewise, she would have pounced on them like a cat upon a mouse.

"Sorry to keep you up so late," he said to the butler. "You shouldn't have waited for us. I know my way around."

The man's impassive face hardly registered the apology, nor did his gaze flick even once to the unexpected guest.

"Her ladyship instructed me to await you, sir. She was certain you wouldn't stay at a coach house, if at all possible. As usual, madam was correct."

"Then you must take the day off tomorrow, and anyone else who is up past their bedtime." Jasper included a yawning maid, waiting patiently for her next order. He thought the butler might argue, but looking dead on his feet, the man nodded.

"Thank you, sir." Then Mr. Jeffers, with his sharp gray eyes never leaving Jasper's, asked, "Would you like your guest put in the gold and green room or the blue and silver room, sir?"

Jasper was amazed at the butler's astute enquiry. Considering he'd never brought a female to Marshfield Manor before, he was impressed by Jeffers choice of rooms.

"The blue and silver has a nicer view," he said, choosing the room closest to his. As lord of the manor, he ought to defend her virtue. However, he couldn't imagine Julia staying under his roof for the remainder of the Twelvetide without their ending up in a sensual dance upon the counterpane. There was no point in her being in another wing entirely.

"I believe my good friend, Miss Sudbury, will be most comfortable in that one."

"Very good, sir." Now that he had an idea of her status, Mr. Jeffers turned to her. "Welcome to Marshfield Manor, Miss Sudbury. Jenny will take you to your room."

"Thank you," she said, but she hesitated, looking forlorn.

"Lord Marshfield's footman will bring your luggage to your room directly," Mr. Jeffers assured her.

"Oh," she said, and gave Jasper a hard stare.

"She lost her luggage," he explained to the butler, unsure why he was doing so. Mr. Jeffers would have had no concern. Indeed, he made no remark, nor changed his expression. It would now be the problem of the chambermaid, and by morning, the housekeeper, Mrs. Bowman.

"You may ask Jenny to bring you anything you need for tonight to be comfortable. Be it nightdress or tooth powders." He couldn't conceive of what else she would need and, if the temperature were warmer, would expect her to sleep bare. He coughed thinking of her in bed only yards away.

"And if you're feeling peckish, I'm sure something can be scrounged from the kitchen pantry. Isn't that right, Mr. Jeffers?"

"Indubitably, sir," the butler agreed with little enthusiasm. Mr. Jeffers would awaken the cook at his peril and thus knew better. If Julia wanted something, he would be forced to make the food himself, even if it were a humble plate of cheese and bread.

"No, thank you," she said at once. "I don't want anyone to go to any trouble. I need nothing but a place to lay my head, I assure you."

"Then I bid you good night," Jasper said, trying not to sound like a man ready to creep along the hallway and sneak into her bedroom.

Sending him another inscrutable look, she followed the maid up the main staircase.

Watching her go, waiting to follow at a respectable distance, Jasper tried to persuade himself the spirit of Christmas was causing his happiness and *not* because Julia was under his roof.

CHAPTER THIRTY

"Lady W__ has gone to Lady Macroun's much celebrated
yearly Twelvetide country party. No one in Town seems to
know whether her sister, who has lately been on the arm
of Lord M__, accompanied her."

—*The Sun*

Julia had more nerves in her stomach upon awakening near
noon on Christmas Day at the Earl of Marshfield's estate
than she'd had when sneaking into his bedroom to steal his
cravat pin months earlier.

And if she spent a moment discerning why, she would
have to ascribe her anxiety to meeting his mother. That and
having no clothing except the dress and coat in which she'd
traveled.

She could do nothing about the former until she went
downstairs and encountered the dowager countess. But the
latter problem, she had to consider immediately. First, she
needed some hot water and soap, and a comb at the very
least.

Upon tugging the bell-pull beside her bed, in a very few
minutes, a maid came in, although not the same weary one
who'd assisted her the night before.

"Good morning, miss. Merry Christmas. I've brought you chocolate, unless you prefer tea."

"That's wonderful," Julia exclaimed. "Chocolate is so much more filling when you awaken hungry."

"Oh dear, miss." The girl said, hurrying to set the tray down beside the bed, but only so she could free her hands to wring them. "I should have brought you some porridge or toast. Her ladyship will be in a right state if she thinks we've let you go hungry."

Julia blinked at the maid's distress.

"Don't be silly. How could you know I was hungry?" Then she had a worrisome thought. "Is the dowager countess fierce?" If the maid was afraid of her, it didn't bode well.

The girl took a step back before lowering her gaze to her shoes, saying nothing.

Julia realized at once her *faux pas*. The maid couldn't talk with a guest about her employer, or she would find herself very soon without employment.

"That's all right," Julia said into the awkward silence. "I'm sorry I asked, only I don't know anything about Lady Marshfield, and I didn't want to step in the wrong puddle. It's bad enough I came uninvited."

"I understand, miss," the maid said, taking the cup off the tray and handing it to Julia. "I'm happy to say her ladyship is usually in good spirits. We all like to keep her happy, though, and that's the truth. So, if you need anything, please just let me know. My name's Emily, miss."

"Thank you, Emily. I'm afraid I do need a few things because I came here unexpectedly. I don't have even another dress to wear save what I came in."

The girl looked over to the wardrobe.

"You can look if you like," Julia said, happy to be sipping chocolate in a warm bed.

Emily crossed the room and opened the right-hand side of a large armoire. Looking rather sad, her cream-colored wool dress hung there beside her gray coat.

Yet when the maid turned, she had a thoughtful expression. "I know we have dresses in the house that are a donkey's age old. They were here when I came to work two years ago. Trunks full of them, miss."

"I cannot simply help myself to someone else's gowns."

"No, miss, but I'll ask Mrs. Bowman. She's the housekeeper. Meanwhile, shall I help you dress?"

Julia wrinkled her nose. "Could I have a quick wash first?"

"Yes, miss. If you'll come with me, just through here," she trailed off as Julia got out of bed in her chemise, wishing she had slippers when her feet hit the cold floor, even with its carpet. Dutifully, she followed Emily through a doorway into the next room.

There was a porcelain tub standing cold and empty, and Julia longed to see it filled with steaming water. However, it seemed an extravagance to ask on the morning of her first day.

"There's clean water for washing, miss." Emily gestured to the washstand where a pitcher and bowl stood with a towel hanging beside it.

Julia went over to examine it, dipping her finger in. *Frigid.* She'd always heard of the drafty, cold, and uncomfortable conditions of the nobility's large country homes. But at least there was a bar of Pears' soap.

"I can bring up some hot water, miss."

"No, it's fine," Julia assured her. The experience would build character and prove how dreadfully spoiled she'd become since living in Sarah's comfortable home where the maid brought in hot water every morning, and they had a bath thrice a week.

"Do you need assistance?" Emily asked, standing in the doorway, clearly ready to go.

Julia supposed the girl had to ask, but since it was going to be a quick flick of cold water on her face and around her neck, she doubted there was much Emily could help her with.

Yet she had one more concern. Her mouth felt like she'd tried to chew wool.

"Any mouth fresheners?" she asked, hoping at least for a comfit.

"In the cabinet will be a toothbrush, miss, and some cleaning powders, and the freshening *eau de bouche* her ladyship raves about."

Julia looked to where the maid indicated. A small cupboard stood directly beside the washstand. She'd never heard of the latter, but freshening mouth-water sounded like something worth trying.

"And a comb?" she asked.

"In the bedroom, miss, on the dresser."

"Thank you, Emily. Where shall I go when I'm ready?"

"Where would you like to go, miss?" the girl asked, looking mystified, as if Julia might want to ride a camel to Egypt.

"Never mind, thank you." She would make her way downstairs and find her hosts.

"Yes, miss. And I'll find out about those gowns by the time Christmas dinner is served."

JULIA COULDN'T RECALL THE last time she went downstairs in a grand country manor house to meet the mother of an earl with whom she'd had inappropriate relations.

Of course, that was because it was as implausible a situation as any she'd ever known. This did not happen to a vicar's daughter who only went to balls at the grace of her sister's good fortune.

The Marshfields' country house was probably similar to where Sarah currently resided in Great Oakley. Massive ceilings yawned overhead, a thick polished oak banister ran smoothly under Julia's hand, old portraits of even older people stared down at her, and chilly air gave her goosebumps in the stairwell despite the wool she wore.

Reaching a two-story front hall which she'd been too exhausted to take note of upon arrival, she crossed its checkerboard black-and-white marble floor. Dust motes floated on the sunbeams streaming through the many windows facing the front drive.

Everywhere was luxury, albeit a little faded, including large mirrors, even larger paintings, oak and mahogany furniture, and gilded whatnots whose sparkle of gold caught her eye.

There was an open doorway on either side of the entrance hall, which she would swear was forty feet long yet hadn't seemed so very large in the wee hours. Passing through the entry at the far end, she traversed a small anteroom before ending up in a spacious billiard room. Julia continued on through more doorways and rooms as it appeared the house was built upon a square of connected chambers.

Finally, she heard voices and entered a salon with a small dining table for six. All conversation stopped and two similar pairs of eyes turned to regard her.

The earl rose to his feet, welcoming her with a smile.

"There you are. I was beginning to wonder if you were hopelessly lost." Jasper turned to a handsome woman in mauve-colored silk with dark brown hair and the very mirror of his mischievous gaze.

"This is my mother, the Dowager Countess of Marshfield. Mother, this is Miss Sudbury, our guest."

"You are most welcome, my dear," said his mother. "Merry Christmas."

The knot of nerves inside Julia loosened at the woman's warm tone.

"Thank you, my lady. Merry Christmas." She curtsied, feeling the moment demanded such formality.

"Heavens," Lady Marshfield exclaimed. "Do sit down. You are rail thin and clearly in need of sustenance. Jasper, fill her plate at once."

Instead of a sideboard, the tureens and platters of food were in the center of the round table. It seemed odd to have the earl serve her when she could perfectly well reach the food herself, but she had no intention of gainsaying a single thing the dowager countess ordained.

Taking a seat, she watched as Jasper took the clean plate from her setting and leaned forward.

"Eggs? Of course," he answered, not waiting for a response. "Sausages and bacon, creamed potatoes, some of Cook's best rolls and jam or she'll have my hide."

His mother agreed with a quick, "She would."

And then Julia found a mountain of food placed in front of her before Jasper murmured "Merry Christmas" in her ear and regained his seat.

The dowager countess stared at her boldly for a moment. But her question was nothing more than a benign, "Tea or coffee? I assume you've already had chocolate."

"Yes, my lady, I have. It was perfectly prepared and not the least bit grainy." Julia ordered herself to stop her babbling. "I would like tea, please."

Wondering with terror if the dowager countess herself was going to pour, suddenly, a footman whom Julia hadn't noticed pressed against the wall like a statue leaped forward, lifted the correct pot from the table and poured her a cup.

"It should still be hot," Lady Marshfield said. "If not, we'll get a fresh one."

"It's fine," Julia said.

"How would you know, dear? You haven't tried it yet," her ladyship said, eyeing her with a sharp, piercing glance.

"I . . . I . . . ," Julia hadn't meant to be impertinent.

"Mother," Jasper said, "stop browbeating Miss Sudbury." He looked at Julia. "Sugar." He pointed to a porcelain bowl. "And milk." He pointed again. "For goodness' sake, taste it quickly. Mother is proud of the quality of our tea."

In response, the dowager countess lifted her hand from her lap, jangling keys.

"The tea caddy has a lock," she said, "as does the cupboard I store it in."

Julia nodded, added sugar and milk, and tasted it.

"You are correct," she said to Lady Marshfield. "Due to my tardiness, it has grown tepid, but it's so delicious, I would not waste it for a new pot."

"Good girl," her ladyship said. "You don't have to agree with me or tell me what I want to hear in order to gain my high regard. Honesty will do you in good standing with me, Miss Sudbury."

Jasper laughed. "There's honesty and then there's honesty."

The dowager countess frowned at her son. "Whatever can you mean?"

Julia hoped he wasn't going to mention anything shady to do with her and held her breath.

"Recall the guest who gave you her opinion on your gown at the infamous Ledley ball or the more recent unfortunate gentleman who didn't like your choice of pottage at—"

"Bad taste is not honesty, Jasper!"

Julia released her pent-up breath, remaining quiet as the two sparred good-naturedly, but she took the hint all the same. Do not placate her ladyship with false praise, whether it be tepid tea or, as Julia had just discovered, stone-cold toast. Instead, she should keep her opinion to herself over matters of style unless asked. And eat her pottage without comment at dinner that night regardless of what flavor it was.

"My son tells me your sister is with Lady Macroun at Forde Hall. Such a pity the Lady Worthington couldn't have accompanied you. The more the merrier."

Julia darted a glance toward the earl. *What about the absurdity of her having no chaperone or trunk?*

"My sister's invitation to Great Oakley came long before Lord Marshfield issued one to me. Sa—Lady Worthington couldn't possibly change her plans without insulting Lady Macroun."

"True, I suppose." Lady Marshfield nodded and sighed. Then she seemed to perk up at a new topic. "What is this about your being pursued by a soulless blackguard?"

Gasping with surprise, Julia choked on the bit of sausage she was swallowing and made a face, causing Jasper to rise to his feet again. Before she could lift her napkin to her lips, she coughed hard, and the offending meat shot onto the lily-white tablecloth.

"Gracious!" exclaimed the dowager countess.

"Are you all right?" Jasper asked while Julia stared mortified at the brown gristle.

"Yes, thank you." To her horror, the footman, who apparently was watching everything like a falcon, rushed forward and covered the sausage with a napkin before whisking it away.

"My apologies," Julia began as Jasper took his seat again. She wanted to rebuke him for whatever tale he'd told his mother. "I was simply not expecting the earl to have told you anything about my circumstances. In truth, I was pursued by a very determined man, although I doubt he was either soulless or a blackguard."

The lady pursed her lips. "Do you have feelings for this violent man?"

"Mother!" Jasper warned.

"No, my lady," Julia assured her, thinking of the Bow Street Runners with their angry faces. "No feeling except for aversion and trepidation."

"As you should," the lady agreed. "You never know, especially with all these chicken nabobs, half-nibs, and mushrooms abounding in London. They get a bit of money and think they can take any woman they want."

Julia realized her mouth had dropped open. Surely, the arrogant noblemen were just as likely if not more so to take what they wanted, be it an unwilling woman of their own class or a terrified chambermaid, than those new to wealth. She glanced at Jasper, who expectedly shrugged.

"I hope my sudden decision to accept his lordship's invitation has not inconvenienced you," Julia said.

"No, not at all. As I said, the more the merrier." Lady Marshfield turned to her son. "Why don't you take this charming young lady on a tour next and then we'll see what entertainment we can scrounge up for the rest of the day as well as this evening. And later, we shall discuss the Twelfth Night party."

"A party of three?" Jasper asked. He'd hoped his mother had given up on the notion of having a hodge-podge celebration, tossed together at the last minute.

"Nonsense," his mother said, standing and causing Jasper to rise to his feet. "We shall invite the local gentry."

"You despise the local gentry. The Woodwynns and the McCauliffs are the bane of your existence."

Her ladyship sighed. "I will see past my disrelish of them for a party. Besides, we shall also invite Lord and Lady Turner from Wildwood Hall, and she is a delight. Perhaps even some guests from London."

He winced. "It seems a little eleventh hour of us, don't you think? Surely everyone has their plans in place, particularly the Turners. What's more, trying to procure enough food and drink on short notice really could tax our coffers."

"Jasper!" she admonished, glancing with embarrassment at Julia, who pretended she hadn't been listening. "I'm sure we could manage a festive party. Although, we must be sure to save enough pennies and pounds for a wedding."

Leaving that suggestion hanging in the air, the dowager countess excused herself and left the room.

Julia almost felt sorry for the earl with a mother who would try to bind her son to an unknown female. Why, Julia didn't even have a dowry beyond a few lacey linens.

Jasper was staring at her oddly, and she couldn't imagine what he was thinking, except perhaps regret at hauling her into his coach instead of booting her back to the London street.

"Are you ready for the tour?" he asked.

CHAPTER THIRTY-ONE

"All of Mayfair feels the lack of Lord M__ at year's end.
Without him, there seems to be a total eclipse of the fun."

–The Times

Julia's soft pink lips beckoned Jasper to kiss her. Or at least, that was what he imagined nearly every moment they toured his family home. From the smallest salon they used for intimate dining to the gray drawing room and then into the larger room, the burgundy salon, where they held receptions and small concerts, he led her, pointing out anything remotely interesting.

From there to a sitting room and then their formal dining room. At this she gasped.

"That is one of the longest tables I've ever seen."

"It's impressive," he agreed, "but nothing compared to Prinny's at Carlton House."

She laughed, a delightful sound. He nearly took her into his arms, but refrained. It was the first day and their first few minutes alone. He didn't want to scare her off.

"My mother likes you," he remarked instead, after they passed through to the garden parlor, pausing to look out the large side exit, before completing the circuit through the library and then into the front hall.

"She looked at me as if I were a mangy cat hacking up a furball," Julia said.

This time Jasper laughed. "I've never seen anyone cough out sausage before, but well done! The alternative was to choke to death. Mother dislikes people dying at her dining table."

"I will remember that." They crossed toward the stairs.

"I like the tree." Julia nodded toward the yew in a prominent position, greeting all who entered the black and white hall. "I noticed it when we first arrived. My father never brought one indoors. He said it was some pagan symbol."

"Don't tell my mother that. She thinks it is simply a royal tradition and perfectly pink of the mode, as she likes to be. Ever since our king's German queen brought a tree into Windsor Castle, Mother has always had some poor defenseless tree hacked at the base and brought in over the Christmastide. She makes the footmen look for one that still has some red berries on it."

"The candles make it especially lovely," Julia said, and he looked at the silly thing again.

In truth, this woman beside him made everything lovely, but such a soppy sentiment luckily didn't reach his lips.

"I agree. But if everyone starts doing it, England will be rendered treeless in a decade, I'll wager. Shall we continue upstairs?" he offered, slipping his hands into his pockets to keep from reaching for her.

"There are two more levels with some rooms of interest. We can skip the attic as it is probably a dusty mess, full of wretched old furniture and my childhood toys. And all my ancestors' toys, too, if they had any. But I think the wine and ale cellars are interesting. They look like dungeons, rather gothic, despite being filled with the best vintages."

"Were they ever truly dungeons?" Julia asked.

"No. The house was built when our family received a baronetcy early in the seventeenth century, and as far as I know, it was never used for any punitive measures warranting cells or torture devices. No ghosts screaming from behind bars, I promise you."

They ascended the main staircase.

"Let's skip all the ordinary rooms. You're sleeping in one of them," he added, thinking of her bedchamber near his.

"That's a lie," she said. "I haven't seen an *ordinary* room in the whole place. I bet even the servant's hall is finer than my family's entire vicarage house."

He couldn't help taking her hand now and leading her into the largest room in the house, perfect for balls or perhaps even a wedding reception.

"I call it the Versailles room, as a jest," he explained, looking around the expansive space with its rose-pink wallpaper and white crown molding. "But everyone else calls it the Belleview room, not only for the craftsmanship inside, but the splendid view of the acreage outside."

Julia wasn't looking toward the two-story windows offering the view, however. She stood in the center of the polished wooden floor looking up at the magnificent vaulted ceiling. She even squeezed his hand.

"It's like icing sugar, truly, as if it has been sculpted from pastillage."

"I suppose it does at that." Then Jasper couldn't help himself a moment longer and wrapped his arms around her, drawing her hips against his. "May I kiss you? Here, in the sunlight?"

The familiar blush stained her cheeks, but she rested her hands on his arms instead of wrapping them around him as he'd hoped.

"A rake asking permission?" she observed. "Not very rakish, I must say."

She was taunting him. That wouldn't stand.

Without any further warning, Jasper lowered his mouth to hers. As soon as their lips met, a rightness settled over him—her taste and fresh floral scent already familiar and adored. This was followed swiftly by the flickering of desire, always ready to leap into flames when he was near her.

Plundering her sweetness, he felt the moment she relaxed against him, when she sighed upon his lips and he could feel her heart beating like a bird's wings.

"I want you," he murmured against her mouth. And it was a fierce wanting he was unable to squelch. Fortunately, he didn't have to.

At first, she said nothing, but when he slipped his tongue between her lips, she moaned.

"Yes," she agreed softly before stroking his tongue in return.

He nearly swept her off her feet to head for the nearest sofa, except there wasn't one in the cavernous, well-lit room with only gild-encrusted chairs lined up like soldiers against the four walls.

"Tonight?" he asked, knowing he was about to set them up for hours of torturous anticipation, unless they both claimed a headache and retired early. *Very early.* In all likelihood, his mother would catch on at once and probably hire a professional chaperone, if she didn't send Julia packing immediately.

As much as his mother was lenient with him, she wouldn't take kindly to his using their family seat as a bawdy house for ruining a young woman.

Regardless of how willing the woman was to be ruined.

They would be discreet and wait until the household was fast asleep.

"At one o'clock, I'll come to your door and knock twice."

Julia giggled. "Why?"

"How else will you know it's me?" he asked.

"How many other men might knock that you need to do so twice? Do you think I might let the wrong one in?"

"Saucebox!" he scolded. "Come along, there's much more to see."

In the library, he kissed her again and was about to knock the ink blotter and dictionary off the writing desk in an effort to spread her before him when Mr. Jeffers sought them out at his mother's behest.

"Do you wish horses to be saddled for a survey of the property, my lord?" the man asked, looking at his feet since he'd surprised them in an embrace. "Her ladyship thought some fresh air might be welcome after spending all day yesterday cooped up in your coach."

Jasper looked at Julia, who was staring out the window to keep from having to look the butler in the eyes after being caught kissing.

Almost imperceptibly, she nodded her agreement.

"Yes," Jasper told the man. "We shall go for a ride, and please invite my mother."

After he left, Julia rounded on him. "Now your butler thinks I'm no better than a Drury Lane vestal."

"Nonsense," Jasper soothed her. "I'm sure Jeffers thinks you an absolute angel and that I'm a worthless thatch-gallows, the very worst of bad characters!" He took her hand and led her out of the library.

"I hope you don't mind my inviting my mother. I fear if she isn't with us, I might find a place just past the terraced gardens and lay you upon the chilly ground."

"That doesn't sound particularly inviting," Julia confessed.

Raising her hand to his lips, he kissed her knuckles, feeling like a randy lad, unable to get enough.

"I vow I would warm you from the inside out."

When her step faltered as she undoubtedly imagined him thrusting inside her—*for that was all he could think of*—he added, "It will have to wait until tonight."

AS PROMISED, AFTER THE long ride and a walk around the outside of the house, Julia found Emily in her room with gowns!

"There's a bath already drawn for you, miss," the maid said, and Julia could easily have hugged her.

Chilled to the bone, sore from both the horse-riding and the walk, a bath was precisely what she needed to get through the rest of the evening.

Moreover, she would be ready for what came later.

"Shall I help you in the bath, miss? I've brought a hair cleanser, too."

"Do we have time?" Julia asked, already beginning to strip off the same clothing she'd worn all the previous day.

"Oh yes, miss. I've got extra towels to dry your hair, and the bellows trick my mum taught me. If we start with your hair and let you sit a bit, then the egg froth can dry enough to rinse it out with the rum and rose-water."

"Very well, Emily. I shall put myself in your capable hands."

Two hours later, with her hair nearly dry and still hanging around her shoulders in need of styling, the maid showed her what gowns she'd scavenged.

"I found a trunk, miss, with some lovely gowns, but I need more time to clean them. They had a musty odor I didn't think you'd care for."

"Thank you." Julia was happy to avoid spending the next few hours smelling like a damp cellar.

"But there were more gowns in a wardrobe on the next floor up. Mrs. Bowman said they'd be all right for you to use. I'm thinking the blue, what with your eyes and fair hair."

"Perfect," Julia agreed, until Emily opened the now-full armoire and drew out the first dress.

Dear God! The size wasn't bad and the length would suit so she wouldn't trip, but . . .

"I know they're a wee bit out of fashion, miss."

Wee bit? Emily had a flair for understatement. Julia nearly laughed except she feared she would look absurd. It was like dressing for a masked ball except instead of a costume, she was choosing something from a time when King George was still young and perfectly sane, or his father before him.

"Are they all . . . of a similar look?"

"Yes, miss."

"Very well. Let's get on with it. The longer we wait, the more outdated the gowns will become."

Apparently, this struck Emily as hilarious, for she dissolved into laughter before going about her duty and helping Julia into first a clean but well-worn and thus extraordinarily soft shift, and then her own stays—*thank goodness!*—before holding up a—

"What the devil!" Julia exclaimed before she could tame her tongue.

"Pocket hoops, miss. Mrs. Bowman recalled her mother wearing them and said you'll need these for the sides of the gown. We're just lucky they were kept in the trunk."

Lucky wasn't exactly the word Julia was thinking.

After letting Emily tie the infernal contraption around her waist, Julia had a three-tiered cage of striped fabric attached to each hip. Then she held up her arms and Emily draped the blue gown over her head and shoulders before tugging it into place.

"Come have a look, miss," the maid invited cheerfully, indicating the four-foot tall cheval looking-glass in the corner. Emily tilted it accordingly and waited.

"I'm afraid to do so," Julia said.

The maid giggled. "You look a vision, miss."

Julia believed she did—a nightmarish vision of lace and pouffiness.

She glanced at herself and winced.

The first thing that took her attention was the low-cut bodice, fringed in sheer silk lace, then the ample floppy sleeves which somehow poofed once, twice, three times before ending just past her elbows in another fit of lace. The bodice was the last-century style coming to a point below her waist and then the skirt billowed out on either side.

Julia swallowed. "Perhaps if we took off the pocket hoops, it would hang a little more naturally."

"Oh no," Emily protested, suddenly a fashion expert, as if a modiste from the heart of London or Paris. "There would be far too much fabric, all shapeless hanging down on your hips."

"You mean like our usual gowns," she said wryly.

The maid, now having fun at Julia's expense, seemed to be the most good-natured giddy girl. "No, miss. Not at all. You know what I mean."

"It could be worse, I suppose," Julia conceded, taking another look as she turned slowly before the long mirror. "A decade or so earlier, and the skirt would be as wide as a sofa. Why, I would have to turn sideways to get through the door. At least, I shall fit into the dining room with this one. But just barely."

"Of course, you will fit, miss. Shall we dress your hair?"

"Will my hair get its own cage, too?" Julia asked rudely. She'd seen some incredible creations in fashion plates from the seventeen-hundreds with stuffed birds, little buildings, or even miniature horse and carriages built in, and the entire monstrosity held together with pomade so it wouldn't come down in a typhoon.

Emily actually appeared to be thinking about it, and Julia feared if she didn't quell any such thoughts, she would also end up with a fake beauty mark on her cheek and a white-powdered face.

"I was speaking in jest," she assured the maid. "A regular tidy plait pinned up with a few curls will suffice, if you please."

"Yes, miss."

Still, somehow, Julia felt as if Emily had given the thick chignon extra height and had overdone the number of curls.

"Will I be late for dinner?" she asked, hoping to stop the maid from any further fussing.

"No, miss. You're the guest. They won't start without you. In fact, I've been instructed to take you down to the gray salon when you're ready."

"I'm ready, Emily. This has taken two hours longer than I normally spend at my toilette."

"Yes, miss. I'm terribly sorry."

Drat her tongue! Now Emily was going to mope.

"I'm not complaining," Julia explained, then outright lied. "I've never been dressed so well or made to look so attractive. You are a wonder."

The girl regained her smile and her cheeks pinkened. Then she led Julia downstairs to the correct room, which she never would have found by herself.

Unfortunately, a moment later, Jasper's raucous laughter rang in her ears.

CHAPTER THIRTY-TWO

"It has come to this paper's attention that Bow Street Runners were seen on Grosvenor Square two days ago calling out for scandalous Lord M__ who eluded them."

—The Morning Post

J asper burst out laughing but managed to stop himself almost instantly, even as he rose slowly to his feet, his gaze fixed on Julia's bewildering appearance. His mother on the other hand got right to the heart of the matter.

"Where under God's heaven did you get that gown, dear girl?"

Julia halted in her tracks.

"I . . . ," she began and turned to where the maid had been standing a moment earlier but she'd already scurried away. Faced with emptiness, Julia glanced back at him and then answered his mother.

"Your staff found this in your attic, I believe, my lady. I came without any clothing, you see."

"Whyever did you do such a thing?" His mother looked at him, then back at Miss Sudbury, clearly puzzled. He wished he'd come up with some sort of explanation, but he hadn't been able to, and thus, he'd said nothing.

"I . . . well . . . there was a bungle," Julia began. "My sister left nearly at the same time, and her footman put both trunks on her traveling carriage. When the earl picked me up, I thought my . . . um . . . my footman had loaded my trunk onto his coach."

"I see," his mother said and sipped her claret. "That makes sense."

Did it? Jasper was impressed by Julia's quick story.

"An egregious error by your servants," the dowager countess concluded. "I suggest you terminate the footman's employ as soon as you return to London. Or you could send a missive tomorrow and sack him by post."

"Thank you, my lady. I shall let my sister handle it as he is in her employ."

"I am only sorry I left my horsehair calf pads in London," Jasper quipped to lighten the mood, thinking of the funny old-fashioned practice of men sculpting their legs with padding.

"Calf pads?" his mother repeated. "Your calves are beautifully shaped, just like your father's. Why would you need pads?"

"Merely a jest, Mother," he said, winking at Julia, who looked a little less self-conscious.

Meanwhile, he got to look at her prinked up like a Bartholomew doll, and a damned salty one at that. Instead of a loose fall of fabric from just under her breasts in the fashion of the day, her upper body was accentuated with a form-fitting bustier. Her gorgeous breasts were pushed upward and placed on daring display.

"Jasper!" his mother admonished, catching his interested gaze. "Offer Miss Sudbury a drink and stop gaping like a dog at a bone. Your tongue is practically hanging out."

"Yes, madam." He tried to sound repentant, but he wasn't. Julia was a tastier treat than any bone. She was luscious and full, and he intended to feast on her later. "Come sit here by the fire and tell me if claret is to your liking or would you prefer sherry."

"Claret is fine, sir."

Directing her to the sofa upon which the dowager countess was seated, he realized Julia was going along with whatever his mother was doing, and it was a good plan.

She lowered herself to the sofa cushion.

"My hand!" his mother exclaimed.

Springing up again, Julia started to apologize. "I'm so very sorry, my lady. It was my pocket hoop which sat upon you, not my bot . . . not me."

"*Hm,*" his mother made a sound of disapproval. Then she sighed. "Sit down, my dear. You know, many ladies would have an absolute fit if they arrived somewhere without their trunk. You might not be pink of the fashion, but you're a tulip nonetheless. I admire your dauntless perseverance."

Jasper rolled his eyes. It wasn't as if Julia was heading off to war unarmed and wearing men's inexpressibles. After all, he'd come away without Blumsey, deciding he didn't need a valet in the country when he'd thought to see no one but his mother.

Still, he was pleased at how well the women were getting along. He couldn't imagine anything worse than his mother not liking his . . . friend.

Especially if Julia became more than that.

He listened while the dowager countess told their guest about the history of the house, his father's contributions, and how she came there as a young bride. But when his mother started in on the stories of how he'd trampled her flower gardens or climbed the apple trees in the orchard, he cleared his throat.

"I'm sure Miss Sudbury doesn't want to hear about all that," Jasper said.

Yet Julia nodded enthusiastically. "I do, sir. I can almost picture you."

She had an enthralled—but almost cheeky—look that made him smile back at her.

"Besides," she added, "if we were in Chislehurst, my father would tell stories of my sister and I that would raise your hair."

"Gracious!" exclaimed the dowager countess.

"Indeed," Jasper agreed. "Why don't you tell us one of your stories from childhood."

"Oh no," Julia said with a shake of her head, sending him a warning look and clearly deciding it wasn't the best course of action to disclose any such tales.

"I know your father is a vicar," his mother said. "A very solid sort of person, I imagine. What of your mother? She has passed away?"

"Yes, when I was three. I'm afraid I can tell you nothing about her except her cheek was soft as was her voice, and her hair was blonde. My sister is two years older and remembers a little more."

Jasper watched with surprise as his mother put her hand over Julia's.

"I'm sorry, my dear. Children, especially girls, benefit from the love and guidance of a mother." He had never seen Lady Marshfield express such a soft sentiment to anyone, let alone a practical stranger. Yet he knew why she had done it, for a lump had arisen in his own throat at the thought of Julia and her sister as motherless tykes.

"I have always felt lucky to have my sister, with whom I'm very close," Julia told them, although he saw a sheen of tears in her eyes, "and to have my father's love, too. Please do not trouble yourself," she addressed his mother. "Besides, given the festive season, we should be merry." She finished with a warm smile and sipped her wine.

Julia Sudbury was a remarkable woman, cheering up both him and his mother when they were sad for her. He was determined to help lift the mood.

"If Cook has her way, we shall be merry *and* fat by the new year," he said. "May I escort you two beautiful ladies to dinner?"

Soon, they were all laughing when, with a female on either arm, Jasper couldn't make it through the doorway.

"It's no good," he said to Julia. "Your gown shall have to be your escort, and you may precede us." He gestured for her to enter ahead of them.

As a benefit, while ignoring the ridiculous girth of her hips, he got to look at the lovely curve of her waist from behind and the slender length of her neck. The form-fitting bodice was an improvement over the current shapeless fashion as far as he was concerned.

Christmas dinner was a decidedly tedious nuisance from the soup to the roast goose to the pudding course. The discussion was lively, the company enchanting, and his mother's overt attempts to discern whether any romantic feelings were afoot was actually rather charming.

Nevertheless, the meal seemed three times as long as usual, and Jasper desperately wanted it to end. They still had to get through cards, charades, or whatever entertainment his mother deemed suitable before it was time to retire, yet all he could think about was Julia stretched out naked on a bed, any bed.

"Jasper, did you hear me?"

"No, Mother. My thoughts were elsewhere." He let his glance caress Julia's face, and her cheeks went nearly scarlet. He'd best be careful, or his mother would send one of the maids up to the attic to rummage for an antique chastity belt.

"I asked if you had any more thoughts about a Twelfth Night party?"

He sighed. She was not going to stop gnawing at that particular bone.

"Simply because we *can* throw a party doesn't mean we should," he said. "Miss Sudbury would have to come dressed like your grandmother, for one thing. And I've been thinking—" although he hadn't "—how the best of the meats and cheeses and wines are too far away to reach us in any substantial amount, so the guest list would have to be small, or we'd have to serve inferior food. Either way, it might give fuel to the rumors of our paucity."

"Heavens!" the dowager countess declared. "Better *not* to have a party than to throw a miserable one."

"Exactly," Jasper agreed, glad Julia was nodding in agreement. She was undoubtedly even less eager to invite England's nobility and gentry than he was, probably fearing they'd point to her as a jewel thief. "We'll enjoy ourselves much more without having to worry about the opinion of outsiders."

"As long as you promise me we are not," his mother glanced nervously at Julia, then at the footman standing against the wall, before lowering her voice to a loud whisper, "in any danger of bankruptcy."

He grimaced. "I assure you we shall not be angling for farthings out the prison window."

"Very well." The dowager countess sat back and raised her wine glass. "Then I shall toast to a very happy Twelvetide with only the two of you, and be quite glad of it."

"I'm honored, my lady," Julia said.

Having put that notion to rest, they retired to the salon for cards until finally, his mother started to yawn.

"The ride today was longer than I'm accustomed to," she said. "The land of nod calls to me. Tomorrow, even though Christmas has passed, we shall gather some holly and evergreens and decorate for our own Twelfth Night celebration, at least all the ground floor rooms and Belleview, of course."

"By which you mean you'll send out the footmen and maids to do the gathering and then trust only Mr. Jeffers and perhaps Mrs. Bowman to direct the decorating."

"Naturally," his mother said.

Julia laughed, and he imagined she was used to being more hands-on at the vicarage.

"We'll keep the yew and add a few more candles to it," the dowager countess insisted.

"Let's try not to set it on fire this year," Jasper quipped.

His mother shot him a smile. "I believe some of the staff have already made a few kissing boughs," she added, heading for the door.

She was incorrigible and wanted a grandchild the way some ladies wanted new bonnets. She'd made no secret of her desire the past year for him to settle down. If only the word *settle* wasn't so unsettling. Moreover, he had his wager to win. Marriage would lose him five hundred sovereigns at White's, not exactly pin money. Also, he feared, it would take him down a peg in the eyes of his peers. Instead of virile and independent, he would be viewed as vanquished and domesticated, like a wolf tamed to a lapdog.

"I, too, am ready to retire," Julia added, surprising him as she followed his mother.

In a flash, he decided it was simply her clever ploy to get to bed as soon as possible so the best part of their evening could commence.

Yet his mother looked surprised. "I assumed you two young people would stay here and enjoy each other's company. Play another round of cards," she suggested. "Or perhaps chess."

"Perhaps another time," Julia said. "I shall accompany you up the stairs, if that's all right, my lady. I wouldn't want to get lost."

The lovely gilflirt's only message to him was a backward glance and a curt, "Merry Christmas, my lord."

"Merry Christmas, ladies," he called after them. Even though it was only eleven thirty, he would not wait until the appointed time of one in the morning. He didn't think he could stand the delay. *And why bother?*

Within the half hour, he had changed into his banyan and slippers and was creeping from his room to hers. Tapping softly on her door, he waited. But no sweet invitation reached his ears, only silence.

He tapped again a little more loudly, but there was still no answer. Only then did he recall his silly idea of knocking twice. *Was she waiting for his signal?*

Very deliberately, he gave two sharp raps and waited. No response was forthcoming. He couldn't bear it. He'd already displayed the strength of Sisyphus and equal resolve by postponing his raging desire ever since watching Julia sway ahead of him into the dining room hours earlier. And all the while undressing, he'd been picturing her wearing nothing but her saucy smile.

In short, he was beyond ready to take her mouth under his and then take her body under his, as well.

Why wasn't the infernal woman answering?

In desperation, he knocked loudly, and finally, the door opened the smallest crack. His hopes surged, his arousal throbbed to life again, and the relief at seeing her—or at least her one blue eye and half her face—washed over him.

He was ready to enjoy himself!

"Are you mad?" Julia demanded. "Your mother will hear you."

Jasper took a step back. That wasn't the greeting he'd expected. Recovering, he put a hand to the door to push it open.

"No," she whispered.

"No?" he echoed. "Whatever can you mean?"

"I mean I will not trample upon your mother's trust in our good behavior."

"What has my mother got to do with this? Didn't we have an agreement? Aren't you burning for me?"

Her hesitation told him she wanted him, too.

"That's beside the point. Lady Marshfield was willing to leave us alone in the salon. She trusts us. Doesn't that mean anything to you?"

"Yes," Jasper put his hand to the door again, ready to press his way inside. "It means she's making it incredibly easy for us to swive."

"No," Julia said again, and he was starting to hate the unfamiliar word. "It means your mother believes we won't behave badly and against all decency. I think that's a gift, and I won't betray her or sully her opinion of me."

"She'll never know," he reminded her, thinking himself quite reasonable in the face of this unreasonable opposition. "Thus, her opinion of you won't change."

From what little he could see of her expression through the sliver she was allowing him, Julia didn't like his answer.

"*I* will know, and *you* will know. What will you think of a woman who fornicates under your mother's roof?"

"That she's a bloody good sport!" He was practically yelling, but his giblets were aching and his rod was having a difficult time accepting its best performance was not going to be necessary.

"Good night, Lord Marshfield."

She started to close the door.

"How about a good night kiss, at least?" If he could get his hands on her, stroke her supple skin and kiss her lips so she moaned into his mouth, then she wouldn't be able to send him away.

"No."

Argh! There was that hated word again.

"If you kiss me, I shall acquiesce," she whispered.

"That's my hope," he muttered.

"At least I am honest," she quipped and closed the door in his face.

"At least I am honest," he mimicked in a sing-song tone, feeling childish but unable to help himself.

After a moment, he stopped staring at the smoothly painted door two inches from his nose and turned away, unable to help wishing she'd been a little less honest and a lot more wicked. *Merry Christmas indeed!*

CHAPTER THIRTY-THREE

"Mayfair is mad for any news of the *ton's* various country house parties as nothing is happening in Town. Word has it that Lord M__ is having a small Twelfth Night country party after all. Quality folk are hoping for an invitation."

—The Gazette

Julia felt prickly as a gooseberry, having tossed and turned all night, thinking of the earl and his blessed mouth and capable hands.

"You're sighing," Jasper snapped, having been less than friendly since entering the breakfast room a few minutes after her.

He wore a country outfit of leather breeches and a fuller coat than he wore in Town, as well as an unstarched neckcloth. She liked his comfortable country look yet the relaxed fashion didn't seem to reflect his current disposition.

Moreover, he'd not bothered to remark on her outrageous gown, another fifty-year-old monstrosity with a tight, flat stomacher that seemed more Elizabethan than last century. She didn't think there was room for much food, so she'd only taken two coddled eggs. Regardless, the dress fit her and was warm and a pretty shade of pumpkin with green and gold accents.

"Are we riding again today?" she asked, although she would probably have to change into her own dress so she could take a full breath.

"You didn't want to ride last night," he quipped sourly.

She wanted to stick her tongue out at his poor manners but was glad she hadn't given in to temptation when his mother appeared.

"Good morning, I slept so well," the dowager countess declared. "They say it's the country air, but I think it's the exercise. A good walk today or a ride or both?"

"I was just asking his lordship the same. I suppose if we are to gather greenery, mistletoe and such, we should walk."

"Oh no, my dear. As my son said last night, I don't—" Lady Marshfield stopped herself. Then she gave a small smile that grew.

"Yes, I say. Why not do it ourselves? It might be fun. I've also decided the party is back on, but on a small scale so as not to tax the stores we have in the cellar and pantry. I've already spoken with Cook, and she says we can put on a Twelfth Night feast for eight without embarrassing ourselves."

Jasper stared miserably, looking as if he would rather eat dirt.

"How wonderful," Julia said, since the dowager countess seemed so pleased. "Is that eight in addition to us?"

"Then it must be seven," Jasper reminded his mother.

"True, eleven would be most unseemly. But we could invite nine."

"Let's invite seven," he insisted and speared a piece of bacon.

"Very well. Nine and the three of us," she said overriding him. "Twelve for Twelfth Night." His mother clapped her hands. "Doesn't it make everything feel more festive?"

"Festive," Jasper muttered.

"What has got into you, dear boy?"

"Nothing that gathering boughs of holly won't cure," Julia remarked, earning a withering look from the earl.

⌒

"SO, I AM TO be tempted by you this entire week without relief?" Jasper demanded.

"Honestly, you're behaving badly," Julia said.

"That's what I do," he reminded her, as she snipped another piece of mistletoe and put it into the basket he carried. His mother, a few feet away, was humming to herself, handing sprigs of holly and long evergreen boughs to a footman.

"We've been out here for hours," Jasper complained loud enough for the dowager countess to hear.

His mother stopped humming to laugh at him. "It's only been thirty minutes, I believe."

Julia heard him say something rude under his breath.

A thwarted rake was not a happy man. That was not her concern. It seemed the height of rudeness to abuse his mother's hospitality by tupping her son in the guest room.

"Like I'm a trollop," Julia muttered, viciously cutting another piece of holly and getting pricked by a barbed leaf, right through her glove.

"What did you say?" he asked, his tone interested. "It sounded as though you said you were like a trollop."

His gaze was suddenly attentive, sliding from her eyes to her mouth.

"I said I like to gallop," she responded, "upon a horse, naturally."

"I think you're lying. Tell me," and then he dropped his voice, "why were you thinking about ladies of ill-repute?"

"Because you are a bad influence, and you're only happy apparently when getting your way." She stormed farther from his mother and the woman's excellent hearing.

He stomped after her.

"I'm certainly not getting my way here. I'm throwing a party for people I don't like and spending my days with a woman who teases me mercilessly."

"I do not tease!" she protested. Then considered it from his perspective. "I merely changed my mind after using better judgment," she added, her tone softer.

"Better judgment! *Bah!* No one ever enjoyed themselves using better judgment."

"That's ridiculous!" she fumed. "You're forever acting the croaker and warning me about getting into disagreeable scrapes."

"To do with purloining," he clarified. "Better judgment in that case is a necessity."

Julia shoved more greenery toward him, which he caught in the basket before it could fall to the ground. "Am I unwelcome to stay if I refuse to bend to your will?"

Jasper took a step backward, his backside hitting the dried, pointy branch of a shrub.

"*Ow!*" he exclaimed. "Of course not. I didn't invite you with the expectation of swiving. Secondly, I think you shall end up bending quite willingly."

She nearly smiled, all annoyance vanishing. He was charming, especially when wicked.

Moreover, she sensed he was right. His draw was overwhelming. She wanted nothing more than to strip him bare and run her hands over the impressive figure she knew lay hidden beneath his respectable clothing.

"Do we have enough?" came Lady Marshfield's pleasant voice as she approached them, her footman trailing with a fully laden basket.

"Not for the entire house," Jasper pointed out, "but then I am not so obtuse that I didn't see you sending footmen out in the other direction to gather the larger boughs and garlands."

Lady Marshfield showed her attractive dimples. Then she shrugged, the mirror image of the earl's familiar movement. Looking from mother to son, Julia's heart gave a squeeze of affection.

"Well, I have done enough," the dowager countess insisted. "My toes are cold, and I fear my nose has frozen off my face."

"It is still there, Mother," Jasper said, making Julia laugh.

"Are you two ready to go indoors? I intend to ask Cook to make some mulled wine directly."

Jasper looked at Julia, and she saw the question in his eyes.

"I don't mind remaining out a while longer," she said. "Perhaps I'll find some bigger holly with berries. However, I should very much enjoy mulled wine when I do go in."

"Then I shall stay out and help our guest," Jasper said.

"Very well. Suit yourselves," her ladyship said, unbothered. "Take her to see the gazebo, but do not step onto the lake. I forbid it."

"Yes, Mother," Jasper quipped.

His mother glanced to Julia. "He acts as if he never fell in, and yet he has."

"I won't let him get into any trouble," Julia promised.

A FEW MINUTES LATER, after a brief stroll, they set down the basket and clippers, and Jasper took Julia's gloved hand in his. Climbing the three steps to the summer pavilion, as he'd always called it, they stood looking out over a small lake.

"It does appear to be frozen over," he mused. "Probably perfectly safe for walking on or even skating, if I can scrounge up some ice-skates."

"Do not even think about it," Julia said.

He chuckled. There was only one thing he was seriously thinking about since they were alone. Turning her to face the frozen view, he wrapped his arms around her from behind and pulled her body flush with his. To his delight, she melted against him, giving him easy access to the column of her neck. If only he could kiss her skin through the layers of wool and silk of her coat and scarf.

Regardless, he could nuzzle her earlobe, which he did.

She giggled, the sound sending a spark of lust to his loins. Unthinkingly, he let one of his hands explore the front of her, over the soft mounds of her breasts and farther, until he pressed the heel of his hand at the apex of her thighs.

When Julia didn't protest but instead lifted her hips slightly and leaned her head back on his shoulder, fire flowed in his veins.

"I wonder if it's too cold to disrobe," he couldn't help saying aloud.

"It is," she assured him. "Besides, I promised your mother—no trouble."

"What about if you simply lift your skirts and I lower the fall of my trousers?"

She sighed, turned in his arms, and kissed him fully on the lips.

He took full advantage of the offering, sweeping his tongue into her willing mouth and grabbing hold of her shapely bottom, although with his gloves on, he was hardly able to discern the soft rounds of it through her layers. His body ached with frustration.

Finally, he lifted his head. "I thought you said you didn't tease."

"Maybe you're the one teasing," she countered, bringing me out here when there is no possible manner in which we can do more than kiss without risk of chilblains."

"I'm more than happy to share the warmth of a bedchamber instead," he reminded her. Yet she'd turned him down. "But I won't come begging at your door again tonight." He had more pride than to do so.

At least he hoped he had.

Julia Sudbury appeared thoughtful.

"At the moment, I would settle for some mulled wine. Shall we go back?"

"May I return the kiss first?" *So much for his pride.*

Again, a thoughtful moment in which she stared deeply into his eyes until Jasper felt like declaring his devotion to her that very instant. *Would she believe how much he admired her or would she think it merely a ploy to get beneath her skirts?*

She nodded. It was all he needed to draw her against him once more.

Claiming her satiny lips under his, he tried to ignore the bulk of clothing between them and make love to her mouth as best he could. Their tongues danced, their lips moved tenderly across one another, and then she sniffed.

"Sorry," she said, drawing a handkerchief from her coat pocket. "My nose is running. I'm sure it's most alluring."

Strangely enough, it was, even when she blew it so hard she sounded like a goose calling its mate. He supposed if he didn't truly care for her, far beyond desiring her so much he hurt, then he might not have wanted to see her wipe her red nose and tuck her handkerchief back into her coat. However, he simply wished to get her indoors by a fire and make sure she hadn't caught a cold.

"Let's hurry back," he said, forgoing any further intimacy in favor of her health. "We'll get a glass of mulled wine inside us both."

WITH THE HOUSE DECORATED under his mother's watchful eye and the efficient direction of Mr. Jeffers, they closed out another day. Jasper was enjoying himself more than he'd expected he would, and it was quite obviously because Julia Sudbury was in residence.

And despite it being after Christmas, he could truly feel the spirit of the season. Marshfield Manor was all the merrier for the holly and mistletoe garlands. Surely, their Twelfth Night guests wouldn't be able to find fault.

After dinner, the three of them took turns playing chess, although Jasper boasted he could take on both the women at once if they had another chessboard at hand. Luckily for him, they hadn't since he wasn't at all sure he could outwit two such clever females.

He even began to look forward to the Twelfth Night party now they'd decided upon it. He had an unusual urge to show off Miss Sudbury as his special houseguest, although they must hide the knowledge of her being without a chaperone.

When he went to bed that night, he felt rather pleased with himself for having no expectations of tupping her. Her company during the day, while not a substitution for a good docking, had been delightful. They'd discussed, debated, and chatted like the friends they'd become. Even better, they'd laughed hard, his mother included. He was starting to understand what companionship with a female would be like—with the right female.

Moreover, the difference between Julia Sudbury and every other lady he'd ever kept company with was stark. He *wanted* to spend more time with her. With the others, he hadn't been able to run away quickly enough.

Feeling at sixes and sevens with desperately desiring her but wanting to show a modicum of restraint by leaving her virtuously alone, he'd brought a book from the library and now found himself doing the utterly unfamiliar activity of sitting up in bed—like a spinster aunt—reading a book, his glass of brandy on his bedside table.

He examined the frontispiece. *The History of Tom Jones. A Foundling.* Seemingly a good choice at the time, a diverting and rousing adventure, but now, knowing the tale, it was assured to get him hot and salty.

After thumbing quickly through Fielding's tediously long, almost groveling dedication, Jasper began to read: "Book I. Containing as much of the birth of the—"

A tap at the door had him laying the book down. *Thank God!* He was bored already. Perhaps he should have jumped to the scene with Molly or better yet, with Mrs. Waters.

"Enter," he called out.

Nothing happened.

What the devil!

"Enter," he said more loudly, and the door whipped open and closed again just as quickly, leaving Julia Sudbury standing in his room.

Jasper rose slowly from the bed, although his heart was instantly racing. She had come. It could only mean . . .

Untying her robe, she dropped it to the floor at her feet, standing before him utterly bare.

CHAPTER THIRTY-FOUR

"This paper is considering sending reporters to the far corners of Britain next year during the winter months, so our society column will not become the place of Grub Street scraps as it currently is. We apologize and hope you will not cancel your subscription."

—The Times

S he was even more beautiful than Jasper recalled, all hills and shadowed valleys in the flickering light of his hearth and the Argand lamp on his bedside table with its twin flames.

His mouth went dry as Brighton sand. For the first time in his adult life, he, an earl, didn't feel worthy.

On the other hand, like Samuel Butler's famed Hudibras, Jasper wouldn't look a gift-horse in the mouth.

In the blink of an eye, he held her in his arms, and he had to wonder if he was dreaming. Precisely as he'd wanted to in the summer pavilion, he could touch her bare skin freely, letting his hands roam up and down her soft arms and then, with a groan, he pulled her against him, clasping her soft bottom.

Julia still hadn't said a word. Her blue eyes gazed into his as her hands crept up his chest before she laced her fingers behind his neck.

His silk banyan wouldn't scratch her creamy flesh, and he was glad he'd already undressed with nothing on underneath it.

"Did I surprise you?" she asked.

"Yes," he croaked, looking down at her open, trusting face. He cleared his throat. "I had given up thinking we would swive. I certainly didn't think you'd present yourself to me like a belated Christmas gift. I thought those were only for children."

She smiled slightly. "Each time we've been alone, you've been very generous."

"And you thought you would repay my generosity by giving me yourself, the rum doxy of my dreams," he teased.

When her cheeks flamed, he realized he'd talked too much and embarrassed her—so unlike his usual polished love-making. Sweeping an arm behind her knees, he lifted her.

"*Oh,*" she startled delightfully.

Holding her naked in his arms, he was thoroughly aroused, and in two steps he was back at his warm bed, glad his amusement for the night had taken a decidedly better turn than *Tom Jones*. After laying her gently on the sheets, he chucked Fielding's work to the floor and undid the tie of his dressing gown.

"You are a fine figure of a man," she declared.

He nearly laughed. "If you tell me you've seen a few with which to compare me, I shall be most disillusioned but also flattered."

"No," she confessed, "only you, but I cannot imagine what you could be lacking or how your shape could be any better."

That time he did laugh. "No, don't blush further. I am not laughing at you. I'm just . . . happy. Thrilled actually, that you're here and that you find me appealing. For I find you to be the absolute loveliest creature I've ever had the honor to see bare."

"And unlike me, you've seen quite a few," she said.

"I suppose I've seen my share."

At her raised eyebrow, he added, "And a few other men's shares, too."

"I should be annoyed by that, but your amorous adventures have caused you to be most skilled. You are, aren't you?"

Jasper couldn't help frowning. "I've satisfied you, haven't I, in our previous encounters?"

"Yes, of course. Exceedingly so, and we haven't even quite done the deed yet. But since you are the only one I know, I must ask you, are all men so . . . that is . . . when men and women make love, is it always . . . do the women always...? Oh, for pity's sake."

She closed her mouth and her eyes, and her cheeks flamed.

"In my experience, sometimes even great skill doesn't mean the greatest of pleasure. Yet with us, we give and receive enjoyment very easily with one another. Don't you agree?"

Julia opened her eyes, and her blue gaze reminded him of a late-September sky.

"We do," she agreed.

An unusual rush of exhilaration shot through him, heightened by her watching him earnestly when he climbed onto the bed and settled between her thighs. Her expression was rapt even before he did anything. It made him want to please her more.

He eagerly kissed a trail across each breast, pausing briefly to lave one nipple then the next—until he heard her moan—before continuing on his way down to her sweet core. He licked a path down the flat of her stomach, breathing in the scent of her skin—not her usual perfume but fresh Pears' soap—until he reached her apex.

Pausing, he blew gently onto her curls, and she dug her fingers into his shoulders. He'd accused her of teasing him the night before. But he could take teasing to a level that would have her practically sobbing with need.

Parting her soft petals, he blew on her again, rewarded with her sharp intake of breath. She lifted her hips toward him, as though offering him a rare jewel.

In a flash he recalled what he'd planned when he'd first found out she was stealing from the *ton*—a little sweet coercion at exactly the right time.

"Promise me," he said, his mouth very close to her nubbin, which he knew was aching for his touch, just as his own cock was straining under him against the sheet.

"Anything," she said foolishly, and he smiled to himself.

With the lightest possible touch, he put his tongue to the very tip of her sex.

She bucked, her fingers grasping him harder, but he drew back an inch, only to blow upon her once more.

"Yes," she hissed.

"Promise me you won't steal another thing."

Her entire body went rigid beneath him, and then she released her hold. She lay with one arm across her face and one hand fisting the sheet, breathing heavily from pent-up desire.

"You don't understand what you're asking," she said, her voice having lost its breathy, relaxed tone.

"I do," he said. "I'm asking you to show an ounce of self-preservation, for my sake. I don't want to think of you losing your pretty head." The way he was losing his erection while they were having this somber chat.

Suddenly, she sat up and scooted away from him and from his touch, grasping the discarded counterpane and pulling it over her body.

He reached for her.

"Don't," she said sullenly. "Hand me my dressing gown."

When he simply stared at her, she added, "Please."

"Do you intend to continue your madness?" he asked, even as he climbed off the bed, stalking across the room to her gown. Picking it up, he threw it at her with mounting fury. *Why wouldn't she see reason?*

Also, he was miffed she would turn down a good docking. He had thought for sure she would give in, especially when she so clearly wanted him.

"You are *not* my husband," she seethed, wrenching the robe around her and shoving her arms in her sleeves with such force, he thought she might rip them. Jumping off the bed as if it were a distasteful place, she marched toward him. "You cannot tell me what to do."

Jasper gritted his teeth, wishing he could, in fact, tell her exactly what to do. When she tried to pass him, he grabbed her arm. They locked gazes, and he could see she, too, was spitting angry.

"If I were your husband, would you obey me?" He hadn't meant to ask such a question, so he quickly amended it. "When you have a husband, you shall have to obey him."

"That is no concern of yours, Lord Marshfield. Let me go."

He wanted to make it his concern, and that frightened him. Julia Sudbury was his house guest, already his friend, the woman he wanted more than any other. Moreover, what he felt for her was blossoming daily into the deepest emotion he had ever imagined. But she was a jewel thief, and she was trouble.

Releasing her arm, he turned away and let her leave.

At his door, she hesitated.

"If I were to have a husband, yes, of course, I would obey him, and thus, I hope I never shall have one."

Sinking onto his bed, Jasper felt defeated. "You would give up the pleasures of a husband and babies so you can take sparklers and . . . ," trailing off, he shook his head. "You don't even seem to care for jewelry. If you stole it for the passion of loving gemstones, that at least would have meaning and sense. But you take them for the money you make selling them."

"Yes," she said. "I do."

She looked so pale and her eyes were so large and blue, he had a sense she was a winter sprite at his door, about to flit away. The fanciful notion made his heart ache.

"The money from the jewelry feeds and clothes and houses a small portion of London's poor," she continued.

"What?" Jasper straightened. She'd spoken so softly, as if the words were pulled from her, that he'd almost missed them.

"It's true. A pair of eardrops can assure an entire orphanage has bread for a month. A bracelet buys warm coats or blankets for those suffering in a workhouse."

Slowly, he rose to his feet. But she took a step back.

"I wouldn't expect you to understand," she said. "But my father raised us to help those less well-off. My sister gives a portion of the Worthington estate, but I couldn't let her do more, as it is not as flush as yours, not by any means, and I wouldn't want her to get into difficulty by giving more. I never set out to steal, it simply fell at my feet one day, and seemed like the perfect answer. Take from those who have more than enough and give to those who have nothing."

"You should have told me." Jasper felt betrayed. She'd made a fool of him intentionally, letting him believe the worst, even though she'd never confirmed her thievery until that moment.

"Would that have made you think better of me?" She sighed. "Actually, what I do doesn't truly make a difference anyway. There are dozens and dozens of workhouses and orphanages in London alone, and I only donate to a few of them. But I can't sit by and do nothing."

He felt gutted. "Don't you think there are other ways to help?" Then he recalled her other habit. "The posies," he said quietly.

"You know how futile that is. Mere pennies for the poor." Her tone was bitter. "I am not a member of the nobility, nor among the wealthiest of our great nation, but those who are turn a blind eye to the suffering."

He wouldn't stand for her condemnation.

"Just because you and your sister have found entrance into the upper class, it doesn't mean you know everything about us, nor should you sit in judgment."

He paced toward her. "Don't you dare roll your eyes. I work with others in Parliament to try to better our nation for everyone, to bring down the price of bread, for instance."

"While you are debating, people are starving."

"We also have charities, and I don't know a member of my class who doesn't give to one or the other during the course of a year." *Well,* he reconsidered, *maybe a few were more miserly than warranted by their affluence.* "Others are the patrons of the poor," he insisted, "sponsoring families or entire orphanages."

"It seems to me, my lord, if you were *all* doing it—every member of the nobility—then we wouldn't see people in rags in every town and village, but the idea that children are starving in London, the richest city on this earth, is an abomination."

He had no argument for that since he agreed wholeheartedly. When he said nothing, she walked out, leaving his bedroom door open. He supposed that was better than slamming it.

CHAPTER THIRTY-FIVE

"A certain Miss S__ appears to be the very likeness of a person of interest in the Bow Street magistrate's latest pamphlet. So far, Lord M__ has not had the dubious honor of being included in that particular listing."

—The London Post

Julia stormed back to her room. *That's what she got for trying to be pleasant!* It had taken her ages to give in to the desire swirling between them, to throw her morals to the wind, to shred the rules of hospitality and go to Jasper for a satisfying swiving. She knew he would be thrilled.

So why did he have to make it complicated?

And then he'd mentioned being her husband. The minute the words were out of his sensual mouth, she saw the outright fear in his eyes.

A rake did not want to think about a wife.

He wanted to save her from the gallows, though. She put a hand to her throat and paced her room. It was a goal they shared, but it was hard not to believe his concern was based on wanting to control her, first by keeping her ruby ring and now by withholding pleasure. And the more he tried to rein her in, the more she struggled against him.

Besides, ever since losing her own ring, she'd lost all stomach for thieving, particularly with Sarah risking her own safety by returning jewelry. Julia had already done precisely what Jasper wanted, but his arrogance in thinking she would obey to have him tup her was intolerable.

But how would she ever sleep that night? Her intimate parts were still tingling. *The beast!* She should go back and demand he finish the job.

Finally, with such a silly notion, she made herself smile and at last lay down on the soft, comfortable bed, snuggling beneath the covers.

"Julia," she could almost hear her sister saying, "you are acting like a pudding-head!"

SURPRISINGLY, THE NEXT MORNING, Jasper didn't look daggers at her. Ostensibly, he had decided to behave like a gentleman instead of a spoiled and thwarted libertine.

And then at the first opportunity to torment her, he jumped.

"Ow!" Julia exclaimed, scalding her tongue on a too-eager sip of chocolate that morning.

"Would you like me to blow on your . . . chocolate?" he asked, his expression beatific, as if butter wouldn't melt in his mouth.

Instantly, heat pooled low at her core, making her squirm in her seat.

Lady Marshfield entered at that moment, forcing him to turn away and stop his wicked gaze.

"Cook said her knee is twinging and there might be rain," said the dowager countess. "We can only hope it comes and goes or doesn't become snow. Gracious! It might be a blizzard and not a soul will come to the party."

"Why don't we get Cook to sit by the fire," Jasper quipped. "She can put her leg up, perhaps wrap some sort of poultice around her knee, and see if she can stave off the storm."

Julia couldn't help smiling.

His mother stared at him, frowning, and then suddenly, she laughed.

"I see. You're making a little joke. But her knee *is* a good indicator, I tell you, and not to be sneezed at. You can fix her knee all you like, but the rain will come if the rain will come."

"Truer words were never spoken, Mother."

Exasperated, Lady Marshfield poured her own tea. "Your humor seems more wry than usual. What have you been up to, dear boy?"

The earl sighed splendidly. "It's what I haven't been up to," he said, sounding woebegone.

Julia knew precisely to what he was referring.

"What do you mean?" his mother persisted.

Julia coughed. *What was he going to say?*

Jasper looked directly at her, and she felt her cheeks warm. Then he turned innocently to his mother.

"I have been missing the company I usually find at my club. That's all it is. Very quiet and dull here in the country. Making my humor a bit caustic."

"I think Miss Sudbury and I should be insulted," his mother said. "In fact, I think that was not well-spoken of you, and you owe our guest an apology."

Julia saw him sit up straighter for being taken to task.

"You're right, Mother." He fixed Julia with his rich brown gaze. "Miss Sudbury, shall we keep close company today? Very close?"

As her eyes widened, he added. "For Lady Marshfield is correct. I must strive to be a better host. I shall teach you to play billiards. Mother, is the table uncovered, I can't recall? And if we get tired of indoor entertainment, then we shall go for a ride? You haven't had a good *ride* in days, have you, Miss Sudbury? I know how much you enjoyed our last one."

Julia sipped her chocolate and tried not to let him get to her. Twelfth Night and the party were nearly upon them. Moreover, his mother didn't seem to detect any undercurrents, nor the ebb and flow of desire and irritation coursing across the table.

She'd shown Jasper a weakness. Now that he knew how much she wanted him—enough to sacrifice her pride and morals and go to his room—he intended to tease her mercilessly, as he'd tried to do the night before between her legs.

All at once she realized what was good for the goose was good for the gander.

"Yes, I should love to try my hand at billiards. First, you must tell me how to set up the balls, and how precisely balls are to be handled. And then, you shall have to show me how to hold a long, hard stick. I'm sure there's a knack to firmly holding the shaft."

She saw him swallow, the so-called Adam's apple in his neck going up and down. Then he tugged at his cravat.

"Yes, I shall certainly demonstrate for you."

And he did. He put her through a hellish hour, insisting on wrapping his arms around her and leaning against her back as he helped her hold the cue and aim at the balls. He took every opportunity to stroke her arm or her back, and even put his cheek to hers on the pretense of making sure she was eyeing the ball correctly.

With tension coiling inside her and feeling heated from top to bottom, she was practically shaking by the time they'd finished. While hardly knowing if she'd managed to get a ball into even one of table's pockets, she could easily recall his hard arousal pressing into her bottom.

For his part, he'd appeared unaffected, but she was determined to get back at him. When they met for drinks before dinner in the gray salon, as soon as Jasper had a drink in hand, she strolled the room to look at the paintings and curios in the Marshfield collection. When she walked past him—and his mother wasn't looking—Julia ran her hand over his firm backside. He dropped his wine glass, and it shattered at his feet.

"Jasper," his mother exclaimed, looking up from the music sheets she was turning over, creating a list for the quartet she'd hired.

"I believe a little too much to drink can cause one's hands to shake," Julia said from the safety of the other side of the room. She was looking at a painting of a man on horseback with a spaniel but turned to send him what she hoped was an innocent smile.

"Have you heard that?" the dowager countess asked. "Miss Sudbury might be correct. Perhaps you should take a break from the wine tonight and especially stop drinking brandy. It's French and probably far stronger than Spanish wine."

"I think it's all poppycock," Jasper declared.

"Then what caused you to drop your glass if not a quaking hand?" his mother questioned. "Perhaps you need a diet of slipslops for a week."

Julia nearly laughed out loud at the earl's expression, plainly finding the idea of having nothing but tea and watery gruel to be beyond distasteful. Especially when they were about to have a festive feast.

"It simply slipped, Mother." He went to the bell-pull and yanked it.

"Easy, dear boy. You nearly pulled the ribbon from the spring, and the whole system is a nuisance to fix."

"Sorry," he muttered.

In a very short time, the maid came and cleaned up the mess. Julia felt terribly sorry for her and resolved to cause less mischief next time.

But she couldn't resist touching the front of his breeches when his mother led them in to dinner.

Jasper was too quick. He clamped his hand over hers, imprisoning it directly over his length.

Gasping, Julia looked over her shoulder. Luckily, Lady Marshfield had already turned the corner.

"What are you doing?" she fumed as quietly as possible.

"What are *you* doing?" he growled under his breath. "If you touch me thusly again, I shall—"

"You shall what?" she demanded. "Treat me to another game of billiards?"

They glared at one another a moment, and then he released her before making an exaggerated gesture for her to precede him.

Julia did so, waggling the massive skirt of her ancient gown, having grown more used to the style with each passing day. Let him stew upon that.

With something of a truce, they got through dinner and cards without incident. As there were only the three of them, by mutual agreement, they didn't engage in any of the lively group games, such as Fox and Geese or Spillikins, and Snap Dragon was too much trouble to set up.

When the evening drew to a close, Julia worried what might happen at bedtime, but Jasper didn't knock upon her door, and she didn't dare tap on his. Still, she lay awake a long while listening—half hoping, half dreading. In the end, she fell into a fitful sleep and dreamed the Earl of Marshfield had his wicked way with her upon the billiards table.

Oversleeping, Julia came downstairs along her usual route through the black-and-white tiled main hall. A commotion at one end caught her attention instantly.

Two men were talking animatedly to Jasper with her ladyship's efficient butler by his side.

Intruders of some sort, and with a menacing air about them, but she approached with curiosity.

The group of four men turned at her approach.

"Speak of the devil," one stranger said.

"And there she is!" said the other. "Our pretty jewel thief."

CHAPTER THIRTY-SIX

"Word from Lady Macroun's Forde Hall is that Lady
W__'s sister is not with her. One can't help wondering if
Miss S__ was invited to Marshfield Manor instead."

—*The Gazette*

Julia gasped. Her heart started to gallop, and at the same
time, the blood drained from her head. She feared she
might faint, but then realized she'd never fainted in her life
and wasn't about to start. Instead, deciding that turning heel
and running would be a better course of action, she took a
step backward about to pivot on her silk slipper.

"Miss Sudbury," Jasper called out to her, and she halted.

He wouldn't keep her there if those men were
attempting to haul her off to the magistrate's court or worse,
directly to Newgate. Not out of spite from a missed tupping!
Would he?

Lifting her chin, she crossed the hall, which seemed to
grow more expansive with every step. Jasper's expression
was wary but not overly concerned.

The men were unfamiliar to her. They were of average
height, physically fit, and wearing decidedly serious

expressions. Very possibly, they were the same ones who'd pursued her down Grosvenor Square's west side.

Perhaps fainting would be a good option after all. Surely they wouldn't take her away in chains if they had to carry her.

"So glad you came along when you did," Jasper said. "These men were of the mistaken impression you were involved in a jewelry theft."

"More than one, my lord," the shorter of the men piped up.

Jasper ignored the interruption. "I was about to explain the implausibility of such a claim."

Wishing she were dressed normally, instead of in a brocade gown with ruffles and bows and wide skirts, feeling almost like the French queen about to be beheaded, Julia simply nodded.

After all, it wasn't implausible at all. Their assertion was patently true in fact. *What could she say?* Better to keep her mouth shut until she had to speak.

"The description," said the other man, drawing out a small pamphlet, matches this woman's." Then he gave her a good once-over, and with utter gravity added, "Although there is nothing in the report about her wearing costumes."

Ignoring the last remark, Jasper insisted, "Many women have blonde hair and blue eyes. I believe you and your associates were after the wrong one, even when chasing Miss Sudbury down my street."

"Then why did she run, sir?" the shorter man demanded.

"Because you were chasing her."

Julia would have laughed at Jasper's response if the situation weren't so deadly serious.

"It was the fact she was on your street and then got into your carriage that made us think we have the right one. Begging your pardon, my lord."

"Nothing to pardon, gentleman. But why do you say such a thing?"

The two men eyed one another. "Because of the recent rumors of your own financial difficulties," said the first. "And of your being linked with the jewel thief to help pull yourself out of them."

Julia wished he hadn't said that. Nothing seemed to put Jasper's back up like false talk of his fiscal ruin. In a blink, the earl's expression turned icy.

"Rumor is all you have, then," he snapped. "You see my home. Do I appear to be having financial difficulties? In two days, we're having a Twelfth Night party. Would we pay for such extravagance if we didn't have the funds? It's ridiculous and insulting!" Jasper folded his arms across his chest.

"But this young woman—" the shorter man began again.

"Rather than hurl degrading accusations which make you look like a couple of gossipmongers instead of sleuths," Jasper said, "I suggest you go back to London and speak with my accountant. I shall give you his name and address."

He turned to his butler. "Mr. Jeffers, please write down Mr. Bartholomew's address for these men."

Julia noted Jasper didn't call them gentlemen, nor invite them farther into his home.

"While that is very accommodating of you," the first man said, "you, sir, are not the one under our scrutiny. It is this woman whose name was upon the list of guests at various parties where the host's jewelry went missing."

"Was I at those parties, too?" Jasper asked.

"Some of them, but not all, sir. Only Miss Sudbury, or her sister, Lady Worthington, was at all of them."

Jasper shrugged. "That is hardly proof. Some peoples' names get left off the guest list, someone may bring a friend who is not noted. And now, it seems, you are implying the Countess of Worthington might also be involved. How absurd! In any case, I can assure you the thief was not Miss Sudbury."

Julia doubted his assurance was going to make these accusations go away.

"What do you say for yourself, miss?" one of the men asked her

His question caught her off-guard as she had, by then, decided the three men were going to work it out between them as if she wasn't there.

"What do I say?" she stalled. "I say there are many people at those parties. And I . . . that is," she trailed off and glanced beseechingly at Jasper, at the same time annoyed with herself for looking to him for help.

He stared directly into her eyes and then turned back to the Bow Street Runners.

"What my fiancée is trying to tell you, in a delicate manner, is that you should go to hell," Jasper ground out.

"Your fiancée?" echoed the second man.

"Yes. What is that to you?" Jasper demanded. "I'll tell you what it is. It is *my* assertion that my future wife is *not* a thief. She may not be legally under my protection this instant, but she will be shortly."

Julia had to clamp her mouth shut upon realizing it had fallen open.

"The House of Marshfield will not look kindly upon your trifling with my wife," the earl added. "As a peer of the realm, I will take this up with the Prince Regent, but you men are finished here."

"We have orders to take Miss Sudbury back to London," said the first man. Then he hurriedly stepped back as Jasper bristled with every muscle in his impressive body.

"By whose orders?"

"The stipendiary magistrate, Mr. Denham."

"You may tell the magistrate that the Earl and Countess of Marshfield will come see him *after* the Epiphany when we have married and returned to London." He paused. "Unless we take our honeymoon first, in which case, we shall be further delayed, perhaps until mid-February. Now, I wish you good day."

Not waiting for a response, Jasper took her hand and placed it upon his arm. Julia had never been so pleased to be in someone else's control. They gave the men their backs and walked toward the open doorway leading to the house's interior.

At that moment, the butler came back with a piece of paper. As they passed him, Jasper snatched it from Mr. Jeffers's hand and crumpled it in his own fist.

"That won't be necessary after all. Show these men out."

Without a backward glance, he led her through the billiards room with the vivid memories of his teasing caresses. They continued walking in silence until they reached the back of the house and the gray salon.

His mother was there, reading. At their entrance, still holding on to one another's arms, she cocked her head questioningly.

Julia had hoped they would have a moment's privacy, but Jasper made his announcement immediately.

"I've asked Miss Sudbury to be my wife, and she has agreed."

The dowager countess gasped, but when she spoke, her tone was one of delight.

"I hoped you two were forming an attachment. I am thrilled for you."

"In point of fact, his lordship didn't ask me," Julia said, although she couldn't find the will to be cross. After all, he had saved her once again.

The rakehell had rescued her and wanted to become her husband!

The dowager countess laughed. "That's just like my Jasper. Not one to really ask but to go after what—or in this case, whom—he wants and make it happen. I couldn't be more pleased. I'm sure he told you how much he values you. I've seen it these past few days."

With Lady Marshfield's face glowing like a noonday sunbeam, Julia couldn't gainsay her, but her son had said nothing of the sort.

A part of her, and not a small part at that, hoped later when they were alone, Jasper would tell her this wasn't merely to save her from jail but because he had feelings for her.

She glanced at him, and he was looking at her mouth.

Feelings beyond the mutual attraction they shared. For strong as that was, she had no way of knowing whether he might feel similar desire with every female he'd ever wanted to tup.

Lady Marshfield rose to her feet. "We must have a celebratory dinner."

Jasper laughed, sounding far more relaxed than Julia felt. He released her as his mother came forward to grasp his hands.

"We *are* having a celebratory dinner," he reminded her, letting his mother kiss both his cheeks. "In just a few days, the Twelfth Night feast."

"Of course," the dowager countess agreed. "We'll announce your engagement then."

Turning, she put her hands out to take hold of Julia's.

"I'm pleased to welcome you to the family, my dear."

"Thank you, my lady."

"Let's go upstairs and sort through the outrageous gowns you're wearing. We'll find something special for the party."

"All right." Julia looked back at Jasper before she was pulled from the room by her future mother-in-law.

He nodded encouragingly, even kindly. Her stomach did an odd little flip of excitement.

Her husband, the Earl of Marshfield.

Then, with amusement in his eyes, he winked saucily at her before he turned and sauntered out the way they'd come.

Her husband, the rake of Marshfield.

⌒〜⌒

JASPER HADN'T EXPECTED JULIA to be able to wait so long, not believing she had the patience. Finally, after they retired and he'd been having another go at reading the naughty bits of *Tom Jones* for a good half hour, he heard her tap at his door.

"Come in," he said, at the same time snapping closed the book.

As expected, Julia entered. But she wasn't wearing a silky, inviting dressing gown he could easily remove. Rather, she was fully dressed in the stiff silver and black dress she'd worn for dinner, with her hair still up, and walking rigidly like she had a stick wedged in her pretty—

"I thought you might come to *my* room," she said, stopping a few feet from the bed.

In truth, he'd considered it but hadn't wanted to scare her off or give her the impression he would expect to have immediate access to her person now they were engaged.

They were engaged! That thought didn't elicit an ounce of fear or trepidation. In fact, he'd felt happy ever since he had the inspiration while speaking to the Bow Street clods and then declared it to be so.

"I didn't want to force myself upon you." Jasper rose from his chair by the fire. Unlike her, he had undressed and wore only his banyan. "I imagined you would want to talk, but I thought we would find a private place to do so in the morning."

He hadn't thought any such thing, but it sounded sensible.

Julia merely nodded. He was dying to know if she was as pleased about the arrangement as he was, even though he knew his own emotions were out of character and somewhat irrational. And he knew it wasn't merely because, after their wedding day, he would have that unfettered access he was trying purposefully to deny.

He and Julia could make the two backed beast any damn time they pleased.

"You're grinning," she said.

"Am I?"

"Yes. Frankly, I'm surprised by all of this. While I appreciate what you're doing, you have gone beyond what anyone else would."

"I am not anyone else," he pointed out, feeling proud of himself.

"I know," she agreed and walked away from him, pacing around his chamber. "You're a notorious libertine of the first order."

True, but did she have to keep bringing that up?

He nearly protested and said he was reformed, but that year, he'd been with a widowed lady at the end of last winter, then Lady Georgiana in the spring, as well as the loose-lipped, conniving Lady Neville, using him against her husband. But he had enjoyed himself with her, too. And then, he'd tested the waters with Miss Louisa Tufton and with Lady Arabella, and more recently with Lady Violet, and sometime during the year, he knew there'd been another baron's daughter and a French countess.

No, *reformed* was too strong a word, but he liked to think he was mature enough to pledge himself to only one woman for the rest of his life. On one condition.

"Are *you* glad about our engagement?" he asked.

"Is it real?" Julia stood in front of the curtains, the candlelight flickering over her, looking ethereal.

"Meaning?" he prompted, rudely lounging against the end of his bed and stretching his feet out in front of him, arms crossed. He supposed this was one thing he could do in the company of his fiancée, almost sit while she stood.

"Did you say we were engaged simply in order to get rid of those men?"

"It was spontaneous genius, don't you think?" He practically patted himself on the back.

"Do you intend to follow through?" she asked.

Is that what worried her? That she would be made a fool of?

"I told my mother we were engaged," he reminded her. "I wouldn't have done so if I didn't intend to marry you."

"That's what I thought."

Jasper waited, while she chewed her bottom lip. She didn't sound thrilled at the notion of becoming the next Countess of Marshfield. *What was wrong with the minx?*

"I vow we shall be married," he said, "at the earliest possible time, right here in the same country church in which I was baptized. We won't wait three weeks for banns, though. For ten shillings, I'll get our good clergyman to issue a common license, although I suspect it will be the only thing common about our marriage."

"Are you willing to part with ten whole shillings for me, my lord?"

"How will I bear such a saucebox for a wife?" he returned, wishing she would match her expression to her jesting words. *What was jabbing at her?* "Naturally, we shall send word to your father. He is welcome to travel here. Your sister, too, I suppose, although that will delay the ceremony."

"You seem to have it all arranged," she said, still not sounding the least joyful.

Perhaps she had other worries. Jasper wanted to allay every last one.

"I will request an audience with the Prince Regent for us both after we return to London. I'll tell him the accusations against you are a silly misunderstanding. He'll fall in love with you at first sight."

Her eyes widened with alarm.

"Don't worry. This isn't the Middle Ages. He can't force one of his subjects into a liaison unless she chooses. And while Prinny is a powerful man, I am confident his appearance won't appeal to you."

She shot him a frosty glare. "My morals would have me refrain from jumping into the royal bed even if I found him to be Adonis himself. I—for one—will hold true to any marriage vows I make."

"I, for two, shall do the same," he insisted and realized he meant it.

Yet the chit laughed out loud at him.

"What?" he demanded, uncrossing his arms and standing up tall. "You don't believe I can be a faithful husband?"

"I would hate to wager upon such an uncertain hand of cards or such an erratic horse."

He frowned. *Uncertain and erratic?* There was one thing she didn't know about him.

"I shall say this only once and hope you understand its import. I have never gone from one woman's bed to another and back again, unless she be a Cyprian."

Silence met his soulful confession. She didn't look impressed as he'd intended.

"I beg your pardon?" Julia said finally.

"I am only ever with one woman until I set her free. I have never dishonored a female by letting her think we were a couple only to go to another's bed in secret."

"Except with a Cyprian," she echoed.

"Naturally. They don't count."

"They do," she said.

"I beg to differ, but they don't."

She took a deep breath, and in the gown she was wearing, her breasts rose almost until her rosy nipples crested the neckline.

"I shall say this only once and hope you, sir, understand its import," she mimicked his words. "Cyprians, indeed, harlots or mistresses of any caliber do count, at least to me. *Any* other woman counts. If you were to leave our marital bed and go to a flashy mollisher or a high-born lady of the *bon ton*, I would consider it the same betrayal. Since I cannot imagine you can assure me of your fidelity to one woman, one wife, one bed, I cannot do else but break off our engagement."

With that declaration, she started toward him, not to embrace him but to pass by and leave. He had to stop her. Suddenly, her believing he could do this meant more to him than anything. He needed to know he could be the upstanding, faithful man his father was after he settled down, and her faith in him and this endeavor was crucial.

"Julia, please don't go." He didn't grab her arm, as that would be too easy. "Please," he repeated when she brushed past and had her fingers on the door handle.

"I intend to honor my vows before God and my mother—and your father, too, of course. I will shed my rakish reputation by becoming a dutiful, faithful husband. "

He waited in the silence. She stared at him, and he hoped at any moment, she would fall all over him with kisses and words of praise.

"Poppycock!" she exclaimed.

With that, she opened the door and strode out.

CHAPTER THIRTY-SEVEN

"At Marshfield Manor, a Twelfth Night party was held
with, aptly, twelve people attending. Apparently, one guest
thought it was a costume party! No one from London was
invited leaving many to wonder—what the fig?"

—The Times
*(This tidbit brought from Wiltshire county exclusively for The Times
by a stableboy seeking better employment in our fair city!)*

The devil take him! Acting so sincere with his soft brown
eyes, Jasper had nearly succeeded in placing the wooly
crown of an utter nincompoop upon her head. Julia refused
to fall for such soppiness. Next thing one knew, she'd be
completely in love with the rogue, married, and crying her
eyes out as he tupped everything in a skirt.

After slamming her own door, she cringed. She must
recall this was not her home, and Lady Marshfield might be
disturbed by the ferocity of her emotions.

When the door was thrust open behind her, Julia whirled
about just as Jasper entered without a by-your-leave and
nearly ran her down since she'd barely taken a step into the
room.

"Oof," she said when he collided with her. But then he caught her up in his arms to stop them both from toppling over.

"If you were a man, I would call you out," he said.

"Over what offense, sir?" she demanded, foolishly happy to be in his arms, smelling his warm sandalwood and juniper scent, and looking into his tawny eyes.

"You called my honor, my vow as a gentleman into question. I have never given you cause to doubt me, have I?"

She considered. He hadn't.

"Your reputation," she began.

"Your reputation," he mimicked in a sing-song voice.

She laughed at his expression of pursed lips and wrinkled nose, like some disapproving old fussock.

"My reputation is that of a lover of females. That won't change, but it doesn't mean I can't keep my hands and the rest of me reserved for you and you alone. I'm ready to do it, I tell you. And you're making it bloody difficult. We will marry, you will cease prowling people's bedrooms and taking their jewels, and we shall be blissfully happy."

"All right." After all, she loved him. She might as well take a chance on him as any man.

"Why must you constantly foil and thwart me?" Jasper raged. "How can you prefer a life with the risk of getting caught, of eventually having to be on the run from the law and the authorities, as we were a mere few days ago, may I remind you? How can you prefer that over being my countess?"

"I said all right," she repeated.

"Did you?"

She nodded.

"That's fine, then," he said and claimed her mouth under his. A long while later, he let her breathe again and turned her in his arms.

"What are you doing?"

"I'm going to get you out of this gown, although I have to admit the fashion of our grandmothers has grown on me. I thought I was going to see your nipples about a dozen times tonight, and it kept me quite on edge."

"The fasteners are a little tricky," she began, yet far more quickly than Emily had managed, Jasper had her out of the bodice and skirt. "You have more experience than your mother's maid at getting a woman out of her clothing."

"I probably do," he agreed cheerfully. In another few moments, he had stripped her bare except for her stockings.

Dropping low, he slid first one, then the other down her thighs, over her knees, and to her ankles. As he did, he dropped a kiss upon her inner thigh, causing her sharp intake of breath each time his lips touched her skin.

"Thank you," she said, as if he'd done her a service.

Standing, he grinned. "You're most welcome." Then he shed the banyan, standing before her in all his proud glory. He was breathtaking.

Trying to maintain her dignity, she climbed into the high bed, hoping he wasn't looking directly at her backside while fearing he was.

"You have the roundest bottom I've ever had the pleasure to view. And now I get to squeeze it." He dove onto the mattress after her, making her shriek with delight.

However, when their mouths met again, they sobered. Her heart was racing as it always did at his touch, and she was thrilled to feel his intense reaction to her. And now they were engaged, she could lie with him without guilt, or at least with less worry over the consequences.

Suddenly, he rolled her on top of him. While she looked down, resting her hands on his bare chest, he tugged clumsily at the pins holding her plait coiled in place at the back of her head. When her blonde braid was free, he ran his fingers through the skeins to unwind them until finally, her hair hung loose.

"Like a golden waterfall," he said. "So silky."

She shivered.

"Cold?" he asked.

"No." Before she could say she was trembling with anticipation, he rolled her under him again.

"Mm," she sighed, relishing the warmth and weight of his body atop her own.

Another slow kiss, and then he picked up where they'd left off before. Leaning on his elbows, he dropped a kiss on her parted lips, making sure her tongue was thoroughly stroked and sucked.

When she couldn't help mewing like a cat, he kissed his way down to her breasts, cupping each, thumbing her nipples, which pebbled instantly, and then bending low to suck one before the other.

Unexpectedly, he offered her his thumb while keeping his mouth on her body.

After the briefest hesitation, she took it into her mouth.

He groaned against her plump breast.

She sucked.

He groaned again, and she felt the sensual sound all the way to her womanly core.

"Do you like that?" she asked.

"Do you have to ask?"

"How odd," she said, and sucked again.

To her surprise, she felt his shaft twitch against her leg.

"Not odd," he said, licking her skin. "Every part of the body is sensitive and can play a part in love-making. You'll see."

He seared a wet trail to her sweet navel, swirling his tongue around it, and her stomach clenched beneath his mouth.

"Some places more than others," she admitted, her tone breathless.

"True," he agreed, and finally quenched her anticipation by settling his mouth upon the soft curls delicately covering her entrance.

With nimble fingers, he parted her, touching the tip of his tongue to her bud, which seemed to swell slightly when he did. Gently, he took it between his lips and sucked.

"*Ohh,*" she moaned, already wet to his touch, already arching against his mouth.

"I'm aching so badly for you, my lady," he vowed, "but I don't want to rush this."

"Jasper," she whispered. "Jasper, please!"

After a few minutes of his teasing and her body turning molten, she needed him inside her.

"Please," she said, breathing hard, urging him with her hands until he covered her body again with his.

Nestled between her open thighs, he gazed down and she looked back, memorizing his expression as he thrust into her, inch by inch.

She bit her lower lip, still watching him, trusting him, feeling curiosity at this new sensation. He caused her no pain, and soon, he was sheathed inside her as far as he could go, with their hips touching.

"I thought it would hurt," she said.

"You were so slippery and ready," Jasper reasoned. "I'm going to move now," he added. "All right?"

She clasped her hands around his bare back, feeling a sheen of sweat dampening him. He was restraining himself, she thought, probably desperate to pull back and plunge again.

She nodded.

Raising upon his hands, straightening his arms so he had leverage, he drew back slowly, and she sighed.

"That feels very good," she confessed as her body tugged at his shaft. When he drove forward again, he filled her. Again, and again. It was an amazing, exhilarating, intimate dance.

For a few delicious minutes, he repeated this movement, his hips rocking gently and hers mirroring his.

"Good?" he asked, his voice rough.

"Yes," she said. "Oh yes!"

"I've wanted you for so long," he confessed, "I'm afraid I cannot prolong our ride." His voice sounded strained. "But if you'll let me stay the night, we can go more slowly the second time."

They could do it a second time in one night? This was an interesting nut of information she hadn't known before.

"Julia, darling, reach between us and hold yourself open so you can feel me better."

She did as he instructed. When he angled his hips, running his hard length across her sensitive nubbin, she could think of nothing at all. The next few minutes were solely the give and take of their bodies as they partook of a wickedly sensual, horizontal waltz.

He lowered onto his forearms and kissed her again. Despite the passion between them, she felt his tenderness. Parting her lips, Julia welcomed his tongue into her mouth, as he mimicked the thrusting of his hips, and she would swear she saw stars. Finding the boldness to suck his tongue in return, she heard him moan.

When her hips left the mattress to meet his, feeling desperate for release, Jasper leaned slightly to one side slipping his hand between their bodies, brushing her fingers out of the way before he stroked her throbbing bud.

As if he'd pushed a magical lever, her body tensed and her inner muscles tightened around him while her hips stilled.

Drawing in air, not realizing she'd been holding her breath, Julia arched her neck. Closing her eyes, she let her pleasure overtake her in waves, her body clenching and unclenching around his hardness.

She was still shuddering when he seated himself to the hilt and spent deep into her womb.

For a long moment after, they were both still, hearts pounding, her hands resting on his back, feeling him drawing large breaths.

When he drew out and lay beside her, he took a moment to cover them both against the winter chill that the fire never quite chased away.

"At least no one interrupted us," she quipped, putting a hand to his cheek and stroking him endearingly.

He made a choking sound. "I cannot believe you are making a jest after what we just experienced."

She laughed, feeling exhaustion slide through her.

Turning his face to her palm, he kissed it.

"If someone *had* knocked," Jasper said, "I couldn't have stopped to answer the door. I don't think I could have stopped if the house was on fire. I was randy as a goat."

"How romantic!" she said.

This time, he laughed. She didn't mind. She had appreciated his impersonation of a goat.

Yawning broadly, her eyelids had grown almost too heavy to hold open, but she tried.

"No covering," she muttered.

After a puzzled moment, Jasper said, "Do you mean the sheath?" Grinning, he leaned over and kissed her.

"Never again will I need it. Such is the freedom afforded by our upcoming marriage. I, for one, enjoyed it better that way."

"I, for two, did as well, although I only experienced it for a second the first time before my sister interrupted us. But I could readily feel your—" she yawned again "—your . . . uh . . . private tackle, both its heat and smoothness."

"You're speaking with your eyes closed."

"*Mm,*" she agreed.

And the last thing she felt was his arm drawing her against him as she drifted off to sleep.

✦

THE TWELFTH NIGHT PARTY was a great success. Jasper couldn't remember ever enjoying a party so much, and it was all because of Julia. She made everything they did fun. All eyes turned, but no one said a word when she entered the Belleview room on his arm in her eighteenth-century gown of stunning blue velvet with gold piping and thread. At least, they didn't dare say an unkind word about her strange fashion sense.

And when he announced their engagement and everyone toasted with egg-and-milk flip laced with rum, he felt the right of it. For the first time in a long while, he was behaving like a responsible man, a nobleman in every sense of the word with all the responsibilities that engendered. He intended to make Miss Julia Sudbury proud to be his wife.

The feast was splendid, and Cook outdid herself in every regard. Moreover, the musicians whom they'd managed to scare up on short notice performed well enough for dancing to go on until the following morning. He didn't even mind that some people had to sojourn in his guest chambers.

"As long as they are all gone by the time we go downstairs mid-day," he said to Julia when they basked in the glow of love-making in the wee hours. He wasn't going to suddenly play host to the entire damn village and county simply because he'd shed the trappings of capricious, mercurial rake.

Since they didn't get out of bed in time to be married on the Epiphany—even Jasper knew there could be no wedding after twelve—they went together in the afternoon to purchase the common license from the parson.

Julia had decided a visit to Chislehurst would be a more desirable way for Jasper to meet his new father-in-law, which suited him fine. As for her sister, his bride was unsure of the response, knowing the countess was of the opinion Jasper was irredeemable. Deciding they wouldn't tell Lady Worthington until they returned to London, they had to wait upon no one's arrival and got married the following morning.

Jasper and Julia, who took Emily as her bride's maid and Rigley as his groom's man, along with nearly the entire staff of Marshfield Manor, joined the Dowager Countess of Marshfield at St. Mary's Church. The ceremony was short, and everything was going smoothly until Julia suddenly squeezed his hands and halted the proceedings.

"Lord Marshfield, what about your wager at White's?"

The parson paled at the mention of gambling under his holy roof, and Jasper thought his bride ought to know better, seeing as she was a vicar's daughter. In any case, he told her the truth before God.

"You are certainly worth the five hundred pounds I shall lose. And if I ever need to sell you, I shall know what price to ask in the marketplace."

The parson gasped, and Jasper thought the man might faint.

CHAPTER THIRTY-EIGHT

"Harken, dear readers. Lord M__ has married Miss S__ in
a stunning turn of events. An utter surprise from this
rakish earl. Many young ladies hoping to be countesses did
not get their wish this Christmas!"

—The Morning Post

When they returned to London a few days later, he
realized his long-time companions at White's treated
him a little differently after he settled up with a smile on his
face. He was no longer a Corinthian, shirking his
responsibilities in society. Amongst those who knew him
best, there was utter disbelief, but it gave way to
encouragement. He was welcomed to the band of brothers
who'd made the step into matrimony.

Knowing he would never again chase a skirt or end up
in a mysterious woman's bed didn't unnerve Jasper in the
least, not when he lay between Julia's thighs. Their second
night back, her face wore an expression of pure desire,
looking up at him as he strove to take her over the edge.

She fairly flew apart, gasping out his name, making his
own lusty climax follow swiftly. Jasper would swear each
time they docked it was better, another new experience for

him. Instead of becoming bored, he would swear she grew more interesting to him by the day. After all, he could never grow tired of the woman who now lived within his heart.

She wore his banyan and he wore nothing at all, as they sat in bed on Grosvenor Square, drinking claret after an hour of passion. It would be absolute decadence if they weren't already happily married.

"We are the talk of London, but in a good way. For me, that's a first," he declared.

She laughed. "I suppose for me as well."

"Congratulations are pouring in. Mother feels like a queen whose heir is finally doing his duty. Speaking of heirs, I sent word to Prinny today, asking for an audience."

Instantly, her face came over anxious.

"Have you been contacted by Bow Street?" she asked him. "There was a letter dated Christmas Eve at my sister's home from the magistrate's office, summoning me for interrogation."

"They know better than to bother you now that you're the Countess of Marshfield." He liked to watch her nose crinkle with a bemused expression whenever he said that. "They understand you are under my protection. And yes, to be honest as I always will be, they have contacted me. They want to talk to you, but we will speak with the Prince Regent first. Have no fear."

He made sure to look into her worried blue eyes. "Truly, do not let this concern you another instant. Do you trust me?"

Trying to be brave, she offered a crooked smile that endeared her to him.

"Yes, in fact I do."

"Good, for I've already spoken to one of Prinny's friends, and our meeting with him is a formality. All will be well."

She breathed a sigh of relief, and he liked the way his robe, too large on her, gaped open, displaying the lush curves of her beautiful breasts.

"Now that's settled, close your eyes."

She hesitated.

"You said you trusted me. Go ahead. Close them and hold out your hand."

When she did, he reached over and opened the drawer beside his bed. Withdrawing a black velvet pouch, he placed it upon her palm and closed her fingers around it.

"I have the perfect wedding gift for my new wife."

She made a funny squealing sound, like a child. "A gift? May I open my eyes now, my Lord Marshfield?"

"I grant you leave to do so, my Lady Marshfield," he teased.

She looked down at the pouch. "If I'd known I would receive a gift, why, I would have got married years ago."

They both laughed, something they did a lot, which he found nearly as enjoyable as tupping her. *Nearly*. Moreover, her happiness had become as important to him as his own. And this gift was sure to make her exceedingly happy.

"Open it. Hurry." As he'd hoped, her expression became joyful when she saw the contents spill out onto her palm.

"It's *my* ring, I would recognize it anywhere, but it's also very altered."

"Do you like it?" He had been worried she would disapprove. "I know you are not one for jewelry."

At his words, they grinned at each other again, and then he picked up the creation he'd directed to start while they were still at Marshfield Manor in Gloucestershire.

After he slipped it upon her finger, she examined it closely.

❦

JULIA WAS DELIGHTED TO have her ring back, but having it returned to her by Jasper was even more special. Somehow, it linked the love she felt for her mother with the love she felt for her husband.

Her mother's ring formed the base of the new creation, with the modest-sized ruby in the center. Cleverly crafted, two new gold rings had been attached, one to either side, and each of these held a semi-circle of perfect circular diamonds. All together, they encircled her ruby and looked to be one piece, creating the illusion of a thick, three-fold band.

"It's perfect," she told him.

"You're perfect," he said unexpectedly, and her gaze found his.

Those chocolate brown eyes were her downfall from start to finish.

"I love you, Lady Marshfield."

It wasn't the first time he'd declared the words, but each time he did, she experienced a tickling thrill of delight. And gratitude. She no longer needed to guard her heart.

"I love you, Jasper Ashton, Earl of Marshfield."

He stroked his gentle finger down her cheek, leaned in close and kissed her. When he drew back, he had a mischievous look in his eye.

"Let me give you my second gift," he said.

Before he could give it to her, she made a clucking sound.

"You see, that's what's wrong with your class. This ring is exquisite, but if you give me anything else, such as a matching necklace or bracelet, you will have been far too extravagant. It will dilute the perfection of the former."

He shook his head. "I know your thoughts on *my* class, which is now yours, too, by the way. However, I think you will like this gift very much."

"Oh," she said, imagining he was speaking of another ardent tupping. Smiling up at him, she put her arms around his neck.

"No, not that either," he said. "Although we certainly shall do that in a minute." He pressed another kiss to her lips. "I can hardly think when you're in my arms."

She released him and settled back onto the mattress. "Please, go on."

"Right now, the next gift is merely words," he explained. "But it will become tangible. You said your sister returned from the Great Oakley Twelvetide party ready to marry that Denbigh fellow and is leaving her house on Hanover Square to you. Since you no longer need it, I think we should turn the Worthington house into a home for the poor." He grinned. "Right in the heart of Mayfair."

"In the heart of Mayfair," she repeated, scarcely able to breathe.

Sarah had, in fact, come home with the extraordinary news of being engaged to Lord Denbigh. Her sister had been shocked when Julia had topped it with the announcement she was already married to Lord Marshfield.

But right then, all she could ponder was Jasper's brilliant idea.

"Perhaps for orphans?" she wondered.

"Maybe not of both sexes in one place," he said. "Children grow up so quickly and I was already thinking of females when I was—"

She gave his chest a slap to stop him, not particularly wanting to know what age his virility started.

"I take your point and can hardly match you since you know exactly when my first experience with men occurred."

He took her hand and raised it to his lips, turning it so he could kiss her palm. Shivers ran down her spine.

"I'm thrilled and honored you waited for me. Let's endeavor to get you caught up in the acts of amorous congress, as long as it is with me and only me."

Slowly, he slipped the banyan off her shoulders.

Julia slid her hands behind his neck and threaded her fingers into his soft brown hair. She was going to like being the Countess of Marshfield very much.

EPILOGUE

"**I** knew the Prince Regent would like her," Jasper said to his new sister-in-law in the Worthington dining room over a dinner for four. "My wife charmed him until he was practically ready to imprison anyone who so much as looked at her crossly. Bow Street will bother her no more."

Sarah smiled but sent a wary glance toward Lord Denbigh. "I'm both relieved and grateful that awful misunderstanding was sorted out."

Jasper supposed that was as good a way to put it as any. Regardless, he gave Denbigh a particularly hard stare, as he knew the man had ties to the bloodhounds working for the Bow Street magistrate's office, as well as to Prinny.

"His Highness wore three rings and had a gold necklace over his cravat, as well as a massive bejeweled cravat pin," Julia commented while idly stirring her pottage with her spoon and staring into the middle distance.

The rest of them fell absolutely silent until she looked up to find three pairs of eyes staring at her.

"Whatever is the matter?" his minx of a wife asked. "I was merely commenting."

Jasper thought of the fun he would have searching her later, every inch of her, to make sure she hadn't snaffled anything belonging to the Prince of Wales.

"And your financial difficulties are all sorted out?" This quip from Denbigh nearly got Jasper's dander up, but he knew it for what it was, a test to determine his sense of humor. Julia had already disclosed the viscount offered to put Jasper's "gingambobs in a twist" if he ever hurt her.

Absurd! He could certainly beat the man in a fair fight, and barring that, he could probably outwit him in an unfair one.

"The house of Marshfield is as secure and solid as that of the house of Denbigh," Jasper retorted.

"Touché," said the viscount.

"I adore the idea of turning this house into a home for waifs," Lady Worthington said. "I bet the new Lady Marshfield will fill it with posies." She winked at her sister.

Jasper watched Julia's eyes light up at the mere mention. He knew she could hardly wait for her sister to get married and move out. They needed only to turn some of the public rooms into extra bedrooms and hire staff.

"It will be perfect," Julia said.

Jasper wished he could reach his wife to give her a kiss at that moment, or at least to squeeze her hand. To do so, however, he would have to lean through the stewed beef-steaks and the salmon pie, as the serving style was *à la française*, with all the courses laid out in the middle of the table.

"Lord Marshfield believes members of the *ton* will donate to our cause," Julia continued.

"Most assuredly, they will," Jasper promised. "If they don't do so willingly, we'll shame them into it by publicly putting out a list of each month's sponsors. If the gossip rags can wield power, so can we. Why, we'll have them vying to be listed weekly as the most generous benefactor of the Sudbury Home for the Poor and Indigent."

"Sudbury Home," Julia repeated, glancing at her sister. "Isn't that a lovely name?"

Even Denbigh, soon to be Jasper's brother-in-law, seemed impressed by their plans.

"I believe Marshfield is correct," the viscount said. "Nothing gets the upper class moving off their arses like the notion of taking credit or being praised for doing nothing."

If anyone else had said it but a fellow peer, Jasper might have had to call him out. Instead, they could all chuckle. Denbigh seemed a decent enough fellow, as it turned out.

In fact, Jasper had a sneaking suspicion Julia needn't have met with Prinny at all, as this man might already have had it all sorted out for the sake of his own fiancée's happiness. Clearly, Denbigh would do anything for Julia's sister.

"Wouldn't it have been nice if we'd had a double wedding?" Lady Worthington mused.

"No," both men said at once.

Jasper looked at the viscount, who stared back at him.

"Never mind," Julia's sister said, "I shall have to put up with a separate expensive wedding, since nothing done in London can be done by halves."

Jasper looked at Julia, who'd fallen silent. After a moment, his new wife smiled.

"You could go to Gretna Green," she suggested, looking between her sister and the viscount. "Only think of all the money you would save, enough for a hundred blankets, a thousand loaves of bread, perhaps a new poorhouse west of the city and—"

"She won't stop now," Jasper said, and he imagined if he hadn't married her in Gloucestershire, he would have ended up saying his vows north of the Scottish border if that's what his bride had wanted.

WHEN JASPER HELPED JULIA down from the carriage in front of their home, she paused.

"It's a miracle," she said.

"That a rake like me won the heart of a lady like you? Agreed."

She smacked his arm. "No silly. That I can see the stars tonight. I don't feel a breeze, but there must be a high wind up there," she pointed above their heads, "blowing the smoke away."

He put his arm around her to keep her warm, and they looked up. The dull grey mantle that normally blanketed the city had been lifted.

"At least from Mayfair," Jasper agreed. "I've decided we should keep the air clear over our heads and thus ordered it so. It cost me a king's ransom, but you know how extravagant we nobby gents can be."

She laughed but then stopped. "Listen."

From one of the nearby houses, music played. Someone was having a ball, right on the earl's own Grosvenor Square. She sent him a querying look.

"It seems the Belmonts are home from the same house party which your sister attended if I'm not mistaken. Before you ask, no, I was not invited to their ball."

Julia was shocked. He was Lord Marshfield, after all. "Nor were my sister and I, come to think of it. I looked through all the mail that had arrived while I was busy getting tupped and married."

Jasper smiled. "If you say that aloud in mixed company, you might want to switch the order of your words." Then he cocked his head toward the music.

"For the time being, I suppose we are not welcome in a ballroom anywhere in London, nor at most dining room tables except your sister's," he surmised. "Simply because we ran away for a fortnight doesn't mean the quality folk have forgotten their doubts about you or about me."

"You mean your woefully low accounts?" she teased.

"That, yes, and many are still wary I'll steal their wives or daughters, even if they have heard of our marriage."

"Oh." She didn't like to think of that aspect of his life.

"And they're afraid you'll steal their necklaces and earrings," he added.

"Oh," she said again.

"Never mind. The music is loud enough. We shall dance together right here." Jasper took a step back and raised his arm, palm toward her, as if they were already mid-dance.

In the carriage, so they could interlace their bare fingers while holding hands, they'd both removed their gloves. They'd carelessly left them on the squabs.

"Dance outside in January?" she asked. "Without gloves on? They'll take us to Bedlam." But Julia raised her arm and pressed her bare right palm against his bare right one.

As usual, sparks not merely of desire, as she now realized, but of richly layered love burned through her.

Feeling as if she were practically unclothed in public, she stared Jasper right in the eyes and willingly let her husband take the lead. They took a few steps in the circle, switched to press left palm to left palm, and circled again.

"I can hear your teeth chattering," he said.

Julia couldn't speak for trying to clamp them shut.

"This was a bloody awful idea," Jasper pronounced, grabbing her frozen hand and dashing for the steps.

"Bloody awful," she echoed, gleefully matching his footfalls as they dashed toward the front door.

Inside were a blazing fire and a lifetime of love well worth running to.

Finis

ABOUT THE AUTHOR

USA Today bestselling author Sydney Jane Baily writes historical romance set in Victorian England, late 19th-century America, the Middle Ages, the Georgian era, and the Regency period. She believes in happily-ever-after stories with engaging characters and attention to period detail.

Born and raised in California, she has traveled the world, spending a lot of exceedingly happy time in the U.K. where her extended family resides, eating fish and chips, drinking shandies, and snacking on Maltesers and Cadbury bars. Sydney currently lives in New England with her family—human, canine, and feline.

You can learn more about her books, read her blog, sign up for her newsletter (and get a free book), and contact her via her website at SydneyJaneBaily.com. She loves to hear from her readers.